F
R72   Rosenbluth, Sally.
            A feast of ashes.

F
R72   Rosenbluth, Sally.
            A feast of ashes.

Temple Israel Library
Minneapolis, Minn.

Please sign your full name on the above
card.

Return books promptly to the Library or
Temple Office.

Fines will be charged for overdue books
or for damage or loss of same.

A FEAST OF ASHES

A FEAST OF ASHES

Sally Rosenbluth

NEW YORK

ATHENEUM

1980

Library of Congress Cataloging in Publication Data

Rosenbluth, Sally.
  A feast of ashes.

  I. Title.
PZ4.R81164Fe 1980   [PS3568.O797]   813'.54   80-13195
ISBN 0-689-11071-5

Published simultaneously in Canada by McClelland and Stewart Ltd.
Composition by American–Stratford Graphic Services, Inc., Brattleboro, Vermont
Printed and bound by Fairfield Graphics, Fairfield, Pennsylvania
Designed by Kathleen Carey
First Edition

For Aaron

He feedeth on ashes: a deceived heart hath turned him aside, that he cannot deliver his soul . . . .

—ISAIAH, 44 :20

A FEAST OF ASHES

1

ON WEEKDAYS, IF GIORGIO WAS THERE, HE'D GET UP EARLY and go down to the *fornaio* for hard little rolls, and to the coffee bar on the corner for a small carton of milk. At least that.

The letter came on a Tuesday. I remember that, and everything else about that day, too. Giorgio went down and came back up, and the letter was clamped between his teeth because his arms were full.

He'd bought an *etto* of freshly ground coffee—I could smell it—because he was always too cheap, or too prudent, to buy more than the ritual hundred grams. And this time, besides the rolls, a small block of butter in silver paper, the milk, and a tin of apricot jam—his favorite. All these he brought into the bedroom, to show me, I suppose, that he too was putting something toward the housekeeping, however infrequently he stayed. He leaned over the bed, opened his mouth, and the letter fluttered downward and came to precarious rest on top of the covers.

It was a business letter. Businesslike. One of those long white envelopes Caroline uses. Her letter. I knew that without moving, just from watching it seesaw there, just above my hipbone. My

3

mouth went dry. I remember closing my eyes, wishing for the slow wash of sleep again. I heard Giorgio retreat to the kitchen and lifted my head from the pillow; otherwise, I did not move.

The envelope bore a smear of Giorgio's saliva, the semicircular imprint of his strong, square, white teeth, and my name and address. He had met the postman in the lobby and introduced himself, no doubt as *il fidanzato della signorina*, which in Rome can mean anything, up to and including regular customer.

I dropped back into the wheeze of soft pillow. It was freezing; the radiators leaked, and the red tile floor sealed in a numbing cold. The body works hard to overcome such cold; the heart beats in fury. I could feel my own heart against my ribs, the pulse behind my knees, in my fingertips, I burrowed deeper into the bedclothes, a mole in the confusion of wrinkled sheets, still faintly warm from our bodies, redolent of what Giorgio and I had done together. Or he had done to me. Or I to him. I brought my knees to my chest, and my palms prayerfully together, and thrust them between sticky thighs. I could still see the letter from where I lay—riding aslant the covers, long, white and cool. My mother's letter, and like her; chaste, even in a way innocent. I didn't need to open it. I knew what it would say. I dozed off again. I opened my eyes, I saw the letter—things remained as they were, where they were.

In the kitchen, Giorgio made noises. He was humming (*"Arrivederci, Roma"?*) and measuring out the coffee, with a hollow metallic click, spooning it into the aluminum pot. There was the scrape of a match, a minor explosion as the gas was lit. *"Cara,"* he called out. *"Dimmi. Che cosa ha scritto la mamma?"*

Trust Giorgio. He knows. Perhaps he's opened it? The envelope looks untouched. No return address. Giorgio must have stopped on the second landing, out of sight of the *portiere* and the mailman, put all his little packages carefully on the first marble step of the next flight, and held the envelope up to the light of the frosted window. The rest, deduction. No blue-green oblong inside, no check: not, therefore, from Rob. Therefore, *la mamma*: Caroline wrote the letters. My ex-husband sent the checks.

Each month, in fact, a little check, a terse note wrapped

4

around it; a check I must endorse, then ship all the way back to New York. I do it, but resentfully; it seems to me there must be a better way. I know I should not complain. The checks, though unrequested, are not returned. They come on time, are deposited, spent. And Caroline esteems me for this, though she would not admit it: down deep, she thinks men ought to pay, and pay, and pay. Obviously, Rob thinks so, too. He is aware of his responsibilities, he will say, unfair though the burden is. He hugs guilt, dreams about how much he has hurt me. A fantasy, but it makes him feel better. Besides, a slightly seedy but romantic aura of social injustice adheres to men paying off unloved, unused ex-wives. He is aware of it, of how much it impresses the girls on the cocktail party circuit, how much it softens them up. Every month, I think this. Every month I think, this is the month—it won't come. But it does. So, in some obscure way, it must satisfy something in him to keep paying for so ludicrous a marriage. Or is it that Rob really is responsible? Not Giorgio. Responsibility sits lightly on Giorgio. He appears in the doorway.

Dressed that day, in his randiest dandiest: a pale blue tie, carefully knotted; a pearl gray suit. That long sleek jacket is double-vented in the back—very fashionable. All the Giorgios in Rome are wearing it. If he should turn quickly, the jacket flares out like a short, flirtatious skirt over this Giorgio's tight little behind. Last night, he spent twenty minutes ironing a knife-crease into those narrow trousers. His prowl clothes.

"Darling," Giorgio says, for the sight of me reminds him: a pity not to practice his English. His mouth is full. He remembers only when it is full. "Darling?" His voice is a muffled bell, the one word blurred with apricot jam.

"*Fa freddo*," I moan.

He looks blank for a moment, as though he cannot understand me. Really, my Italian is not that bad. Then he shrugs, gives it up, tells me—in Italian—that it will be warmer soon. The heat is coming up at last, hissing its approach. "*Faccio colazione*," he says, and raises his coffee cup to show me. As though I cannot see this, or the saucer in his other hand. I know what will come next: his English translation. "Look, I am eat

5

breakfast." I wince. He's waiting, confident that I shall correct him if necessary. I should, but I don't, not this morning.

There is nothing to be done. I whip back the covers, grope on the chair for the old red woollen bathrobe already rubbed pink in spots, and pull it on. I've got to wash the sleep away now, and last night's "ecstasy," as Giorgio calls it. I know he's watching me, his eyes narrowed over the rim of the cup, studying my brief nakedness before it is swallowed up in worn wool. Estimating my age, though I've told him, or my weight, or deciding whether he'll want to return again in the evening. Or perhaps, only wondering if I look—my body looks—satisfied enough this morning to want to lend him five thousand *lire* until payday. Before I shut the bathroom door, I see that he has turned from gazing, bemused, at me to staring at himself, very intently, in the long mirror of the wardrobe door.

An ordinary domestic scene.

I was halfway through breakfast before I remembered the letter. By then I was alone. Giorgio had left for work, vague about the evening, disappointed in his request for a loan, his English endearments almost inaudible.

Not that I wanted to deny him. In fact I liked to please him. Why not? But I could not get to the bank that day and had only five thousand *lire* myself until Friday. When I tried to explain, he was unbelieving, then peevish. He looked at me coldly when I said I was sorry. I remember thinking that he would probably not return in the evening. That, quite soon, he'd disappear.

This did not trouble me so much; it was more in the nature of an inconvenience. A replacement would not be hard to find. Rome is full of young men like Giorgio. They cluster thickly, like ripe fruit, in the streets branching out from the center of the city. They line the bars, three deep, in the Via Veneto. They're very pretty, they glisten: their eyes, teeth, pointed shoes. Most of them are slender—in fact, hungry. Not all, of course, as grossly efficient as Giorgio. Some depend too much on an ersatz tenderness, some on sentiment. But I'd been lucky. On the whole, really lucky. There'd been two other such Giorgios, a Piero, a Vittorio, a Lucio. It was for this Lucio, in fact, that

I'd lingered on in Rome, having nothing better to do elsewhere. Ages ago, it seemed. Only two years.

I sat at the kitchen table for a time and thought about that—about what I would do next, about what I wanted to do. If anything. Then I thought about how tired I was, and bored, and whether it was worth the effort. I don't think I ever considered abstinence. No, what I considered was death. I knew I wouldn't mind that—dying; but as for the logical next step, I didn't have passion enough, nor the will for it. Suicide, after all, means moving in some direction. All I seemed capable of was drift.

I was afraid, I suppose, or something was lacking in me. Well . . . lots of things were lacking. I'd emptied myself, and I felt no anger, no hatred, certainly no love; consequently, no pain. I didn't need the physical pain of death to obliterate the other, for I felt nothing. In a sense, death was redundant. I think it's as simple as that.

Then I remembered the letter. I went to the bedroom to get it. It had fallen off the top of the covers, and a draft had sent it into the long, gray curls of dust under the bed. I got down on my knees to reach it. The floor was icy. When I rose finally, I had a raging headache.

2

I CARRIED THE LETTER BACK TO THE KITCHEN, PROPPED IT
still unopened against the sugar bowl, stared at it as I drank the
last of the coffee—tepid, bitter, gritty—and chewed on the last
morsel of roll. Then I licked the butter and jam from the knife,
and worked the point of the blade under the flap of the envelope;
pressure upward, forward, and it parted with the peculiar rasp
of good paper.

The letter was short, like the others, and typewritten: good,
clean, professional typing, dictated to one of the institute secre-
taries who probably had been sitting foolishly idle as Caroline
hurried past. Caroline in her starched white lab coat, unbut-
toned, disclosing the requisite pastel feminine frill of blouse;
Caroline's voice just audible over the hum of the electric type-
writer; Caroline began with the news. About a new government
grant and the fact that she feels she is very near success in
isolating some microorganism or other (Caroline's field has
narrowed considerably: she does research on a rare form of
cancer), and how livid her male colleagues are. I find myself

8

hoping that there is a new girl in the office and Caroline has dictated this letter to her, for she said much the same thing in the letter before this one, and she doesn't like to repeat herself. Except to me, of course, because repetition may do some good there.

Now there is something new, something about my birthday. She apologizes for not remembering. In fact, she has forgotten not only the last (the month before, when I turned thirty-one) but also the two others before that. You can sympathize: reminders of time passing. She wishes me a happy birthday now but does not say which birthday it is. None of the typist's business.

Happy birthday, Caroline writes; she meant to send me something but has decided to wait until I get home. Until my trip is over. I've lived more than two years in Rome, almost a year and a half in London, and six months in Paris. Caroline regards these four years as extended vacation. This is only form, like those first newsy paragraphs, a polite fiction, more for typist consumption than delusion. Now, though, something uncharacteristic: precise questions. When was I returning? Would I get back before the academic year began? I would have to hurry if I wanted to begin graduate work in September. Which university had I in mind? Which applications should she send on? Could she speak to anyone for me?

At first, I was puzzled. I had no universities in mind, I wanted no applications; we'd never discussed, not even in passing, my going on to graduate school, which she now says she can afford. (But I could not remember when she couldn't afford it; her mother had left Caroline a good deal of money.) Then, for a moment, I felt jolting terror. I thought: she's sick, and she's going to die. There's no one else to turn to—only Sara Elizabeth. Which, I must reassure myself, means no one. This is like her—this sort of information by indirection. I felt rather ill, I wanted to vomit. But that passed.

The last paragraph is almost an afterthought: By the way, your father has telephoned me from Israel to ask where you are living and how he can reach you. He tried to call the last number

9

he had, but it was disconnected. I gave him your address. I hope you don't mind. He wouldn't say exactly, and it was hardly my place to probe, but I gather he's ill. A malignancy, probably, and I would guess the lungs. Statistically speaking, that seems most likely. He's always been such a heavy smoker. Of course, this may be an unwarranted conclusion. In any case, *do* write him. The address, if you've forgotten, is. . . .

Here the typist had indented and single-spaced the name of the institute where Gideon does his research, in physics; his home address (which, it appeared, was now on the grounds) ; and the name of the town in Israel where the institute is and where, presumably, he now lived with his third—or, perhaps, his fourth —wife.

"Well, Sara," Caroline continues, "write to me soon. And, of course, do write your father." She signs off: "Mother." A measure of something or other. She has always been Caroline to me, for as long as I can remember; it was what she'd wanted.

I put down the letter. I can imagine Caroline dictating it. She is in midflight—a white bird. She touches her hair—a nervous habit. It's streaked with gray now, and she wears it in a soft chignon. I know this because I have recently seen a photograph of her in an American news magazine: *Who's Who in American Cancer Research*. What I remember is the shoulder-length campus queen hairdo that she wore for twenty or more years, until she was well into her forties, the hairdo Gideon must know, too. She touches her hair, smooths it. Then she slides her hands —thin, nervous hands—down into the pockets of the white lab coat, reaching for something. Aristocratic was how my grand-mother used to describe those hands—her hands, Caroline's, mine. Three generations, but I felt no connection, nothing.

Well, not precisely nothing. Detachment. That's really the best way to put it.

The Roman sunlight was warm for winter, slanting into the room. The kitchen table was littered with pale crumbs and flakes of darker crust. The butter sat in gaping silver paper, beside a small puddle of bluish-white milk. In the small, now-open tin, the apricot jam absorbed light; it looked like glue. Giorgio's

10

empty coffee cup sat opposite, and between it and me, the aluminum pot, its sides streaked with soot, its handle charred.

Very domestic.

There was a thin line of glistening sweat in the seam of flesh where my arm bent to brace itself against the table.

3

GIORGIO RETURNED THREE NIGHTS LATER, CAREFULLY RE-
hearsed. A series of joyous celebrations had kept him from me
—no time even to telephone. Indeed, there had been many such
family occasions lately: christenings and communions, engage-
ments and weddings, birthdays and name days and saints' days;
also, sadly, funerals. This time, his mother's sister's daughter-in-
law's father's name day. And a christening. Or two. He went on
about these at some length, too lavish with detail. I reflected, as
I watched him, that he must really have a time of it, keeping it
all straight. In the middle of the recitation, he leaned forward,
and ran a roughened fingertip down my cheek.

I smiled at him instantly, but I wasn't listening anymore. I
was thinking about Gideon again; I'd been thinking about him
for three days. His image burned on the inside of my lids: it
wouldn't go away. Now it struck me that talking about him
would help. If I could talk about him to Giorgio, perhaps I
could talk him away. If I could talk about him to anyone—but,
of course, there was only Giorgio. I didn't know how to begin.

Our communication, you see, was confined to this—to empty

smiles and exuberant descriptions of family feasts, to which I
was never invited; to a kind of frantic fumbling at each other's
clothing, and to what we did in bed. Oh, there was conversation
too, of course, but conversation that was worldly yet innocent
in a materialistic fashion. I mean, we talked about cars and
clothes and movies and movie stars and pop songs and popular
singers. (Giorgio was not one of your Italian opera lovers.) We
seriously considered the relative merits of the Fiat and the
Volkswagen, though neither of us owned a car nor could hope
to. We discussed whether Giorgio ought to buy a royal blue
cravat or one in plum and whether it should be silk (more
elegant) or nylon (more durable). Sometimes we debated more
serious matters. Whether Sophia Loren would stay with Ponti
(he was too old for her, Giorgio said). Whether Rita Pavone
was losing her voice. Whether Giorgio was photogenic and
whether it paid for him to frequent certain cafés near Cinecittà
or others in Piazza del Popolo, where the movie people went.
Did it pay to spend all that money for coffee at a table in the
hope that Fellini would wander in while he sat there and discover him? We talked about that a lot. You can see why I didn't
want to spoil things.

But then I didn't have to. Giorgio touched me again, and we
got undressed very quickly and he did things with his body and
his hands which blotted out Gideon. For at least twenty minutes,
I didn't think about my father at all. The trouble was the rest
of the time: after, before. He was always there, his face just
under the surface of my mind, like a troublesome splinter
under the skin—but it was dead skin, and did not hurt.

Then I began to wake up in the morning. I'd wake up too
early, long before dawn, and lay there, wide awake, watching
the sky lighten. The image persisted, my eyes closed or open.
He's not dead yet, I thought, but he's haunting me.

Even Signora Bassanio noticed that something was wrong. I
worked as I usually do, just well enough not to lose my job. I
smiled at the customers, chatted with them; pulled, pushed,
tugged, smoothed tight silky kid gloves down over slim or pudgy
fingers, over creamed wrists. I searched for and found and
showed other sizes, styles, colors; I wrapped each pair of gloves

13

in tissue and took the money and brought it to where the Signora sat at the register, staring as usual out the window at the steet. Then, when the last customer of the day had left—an American woman who had bought half a dozen pairs of our cheapest model and been grossly overcharged for them—when I turned the key in the lock and pulled down the shade on the shop door, Signora Bassanio addressed me. She spoke in a whisper so that the little stock girl, still straightening up in the back, shouldn't hear us. "*Signora?*" Her dark eyes glinted beneath heavy lids. "Have you bad news?"

I didn't know what to answer. I must have looked bewildered. "No," I said, finally. "Not exactly. It's my father."

I could see at once that she was sorry she'd asked. She liked gossip about adulterous love affairs, about who slept with whom and where and whether there was going to be a scandal. Parents were not very interesting. You loved them—you had to. It was expected of you. They sickened; then they died. When the Signora spoke to her mother on the shop phone, her voice was crisp, contemptuous, and wheedling, all at the same time. When she hung up, she brooded.

Now she made a tapping sound with her long red fingernails on the metal rim of the cash drawer. Her husband would be coming any minute with the proceeds from the other glove store, and they would go over the day's take together, in private. I got my coat and put it on. I said, "I must write to him." And when I said it like that, aloud, I realized that yes, that was what I had to do. If only to exorcise the living ghost.

All told, I spent three days browsing among picture postcards, pausing at every newstand, lifting out one postcard after another. A letter was out of the question: I had too little to say, too little even for a postcard, actually. After all, what was the sum total of our shared experience? Six weeks. Six parched weeks of an Israeli summer fourteen years before, the year I was seventeen. Before that, seventeen years of nothing. For I certainly could not remember the beginning. He'd left when I was three months old—left physically that is, though in other ways, I imagine, even before that. Left Caroline, left me. Maybe he could remember the first three months, but I could not. So there was only that summer and, afterward, the phone calls, all his. The last of those a long time ago, too—almost five years before.

I was living alone then. It was almost midnight. When the phone rang, I knew who it would be. He was not calling from halfway across the world that night. He was at the airport, and he'd only just landed, en route to Boston for a conference, but would be back in New York in less than a week, when we could see each other. Could we get together? He wanted to see me.

I didn't answer at once. In the silence, Gideon almost sighed. After another moment he said, "So. How are you, Sara? How are you?"

I said I was fine. "And you?"

"You'll see. You hear me. How do I sound?"

"You sound just fine." By then, my hand was trembling. I looked at it with distaste and propped my elbow on the telephone table.

"Well," Gideon said abruptly, "how about it?"

"What?"

"Next week." His irritation suppressed, his voice patient.

"I don't know if I'll be here next week."

This time, his silence.

"I was planning to go up to Vermont," I said.

"I see."

"I'm not working, so I've all this time—"

"You're not working?"

"No."

"And your husband?"

"We're separated." Not that this was any of his business.

"Do you need any money?"

"Of course not." No, you don't, I thought. No, you don't. Not now you don't.

In contrast, his voice was mild. He'd sensed my rage. "It's not such a terrible question, you know," he said softly. "I'm your father."

"I don't need anything."

"All right." And then, after another moment of stiff silence,

15

while I tried to think how best to end this and he, I suppose, tried to think of things to say or to ask, he said, "I was just wondering. Did you get my letter? You knew I was coming?"

I didn't want to lie. That's what I told myself. I didn't want to lie again. "Yes, I got it."

"Just wanted to know—that's all."

I hesitated. Then, I said, "I've been planning this Vermont trip for a long time now—"

But I never got a chance to finish that particular lie because Gideon changed the subject. For several more minutes we talked, about Caroline (his regards), then about Avigal, my half-sister, and her husband, who were now in Cambridge, England, for a year after their two years in California (best regards from them, he said). They had not, I noted, stopped off to see me on their way back from Palo Alto. Perhaps, after that first time, they'd no desire to see me again, or thought I would have no wish to see them. Unlike Gideon, who was sure that people would see him, would always want to see him—or, I reminded myself, had always been sure before.

"They're calling my flight," he said.

"About next week. . . ."

"It's all right. I understand."

"I'm not absolutely sure," I said. "I mean, if the skiing's no good, I might not. . . ." And my voice died away. I hated myself for that—it was capitulation, wasn't it?—I hated myself as much for that as for the first lie. More.

Gideon's tone had become brisk. "Good," he said, "I'll try again, maybe. Take care of yourself." Then he hung up.

I remember thinking, well, that's that. He won't call again, not for a long, long time. Maybe never again. I remember watching my right hand. It was no longer trembling, of course, but rested limply on the cradled silent receiver. I looked out the window—the grimy window which, a little earlier, had been streaked with the silver of melting snow. Now the windowpane was dull, opaque with frost.

I remember, too, how big the room suddenly seemed, as if the walls had receded, the floor and the ceiling, too. What had once been so small, so stuffy, so confining to me, had become

16

so vast now: a huge empty space in which I seemed to dangle, a doll suspended from invisible threads.

After all, I said to myself much later, isn't that what you wanted? Didn't you want to be left alone? Or isn't that what you wanted? What is it you wanted, anyway? But I didn't know the answer to that, and I stopped thinking about it.

I never knew if he did call again. It had not been my intention, but I went away after all. I can't remember now where I went.

4

WHILE GIORGIO WAS IN THE MEN'S ROOM, I TOOK THE POST-cards from my purse. I'd bought seven in all: views of Rome or its environs, in color, in black-and-white, one even in sepia. All wrong, all of them. I held them in my lap and flipped through them. Meanwhile the waiter laid a fresh top cloth on the table, wine stains not quite faded out in the last wash; he folded napkins, set out glasses and silver, retreated, then returned with a bread basket and menu, retreated once more.

A plump, graying man sitting alone at a table near the right wall was staring at me with great interest and, at the same time, paring an apple. The peel spiraled downward from the fruit knife. Dangerous; he might slice off a thumb. But what I was doing on my lap, below the edge of the table and out of sight—that must have been intriguing. All surreptitious acts are.

I put the postcards on the table; then I smiled at the man, and he smiled back and nodded. We'd seen each other before, familiar faces. He was one of those—a bachelor or a widower—who ate here every night, had his own napkin ring, his favorite reserved table, and paid by the month. As for me, when Giorgio and I

18

ate out—not nearly often enough—we almost always ate here, at this *trattoria* in a small street off Viale Trastevere, not far from my apartment. A small place, ten or twelve tables, and respectable. Men came with their wives and children or with mistresses of long standing. That sort of place. Only one guidebook had ever mentioned it, and this accounted for the occasional tourist earnestly searching out authenticity. The food was good, the guidebook said, and it was cheap; but, most important, the place had a true Roman atmosphere—which meant, I suppose, that on rainy nights like this one the air inside was warm and moist, the windows flanking the front door were misted over, and there was a layer of sawdust on the floor. The mirrors that lined the rear wall must have counted for something, too. They had come, each of them, to the proprietor in lieu of two months of dinners from an impoverished *principe*. The prince never ate here anymore. Three tall rectangles of scarred, yellowing glitter, they tilted forward slightly, dangerously, to reflect everything in the room foreshortened and framed ornately in tarnished gilt. They were Rome in her essence, in her grandeur and her decay. I preferred to sit facing them, but I knew Giorgio also liked that seat, so usually I gave it up to him. I twisted around to look at them once, but then I turned back, picked up and opened the menu.

The daily specials were in an artistic European hand, in blurred purple ink on a slick paper insert—hard to read. I gave up very soon and went back to my postcards. When Giorgio got back, I had them all laid out, like tarot cards, on my side of the table.

He gave them only a glance before opening the menu and ordering for us both. I shifted the cards around for a while, but when the waiter came back with a liter of red wine, I propped them against the bread basket—the top one, a photograph of Piazza di Spagna in spring, in color. Too funereal, perhaps, but I was now considering that one for Gideon.

But we did not talk about that, Giorgio and I. We talked about the weather, then I talked about how much gloves had gone up in price, that took ten minutes at least; then Giorgio explained why I hadn't seen him for the past three days. He seemed relieved to be able to explain at last. Details followed in profusion. He had been on an errand of mercy, this time comforting the family of his favorite godmother, who had died suddenly. He went on to describe the funeral, where he, too, had been overcome by grief—his favorite godmother.

I don't know what moved me, but I observed that everyone he knew seemed to be dying. (In the past three months of the approximately six months I'd known him, Giorgio had lost five close relatives and two friends. Each time, Giorgo had been away from two to five days; each time, he consoled survivors.)

He looked at me balefully.

"They're dropping like flies," I added. I said that in English and in a thoroughly neutral tone of voice, as I shook a tablespoon of grated Parmesan over my *fettucine*.

I did not expect him to understand, certainly not to react as he did—he usually ignored sarcasm or did not recognize it. This time, though, he said nothing for a while, apparently hurt. Then he took little, contemplative sips of his wine, his eyes narrowed and fixed at a point somewhere above my head.

"You have no family feeling," he said after a minute or two.

I smiled at him in a placating way. Then I picked up the top postcard, the one of Piazza di Spagna, turned it around so that Giorgio could see the picture, held it up and asked how he liked it. *"Bella."*

I then held up the photograph of the Catacombs of St. Callistus. Again he said, *"Bella."*

In fact, he said that about all of them: Hadrian's Villa, Castel Sant'Angelo, the Forum, the statue of Marcus Aurelius astride his horse in the Campidoglio. Only about the naked nymphs dancing in the spray of the Piazza Esedra fountain did he say something different. About them he said, *"Bellissima."*

By then the restaurant had emptied a little, the dinner hour almost over now. The man who'd been watching me with such interest had left. There remained a large and noisy family group at the round table in the corner, and at the smaller tables an obviously illicit pair and two bored, maybe married, couples; at a table near the door a girl sat alone. She was having an *espresso*, which had been brought from the coffee bar two doors away. Few Italians ever ordered coffee at such restaurants; only Americans did it in the evening.

I glanced at Giorgio. He was staring again at the wall above my head. For a moment I thought he must be studying himself in the mirror, indulging himself. But then I realized his expression was not quite right for that; it wasn't assessing and approving, it was merely assessing. He was watching the girl reflected in the mirror.

A tourist. There were several maps, neatly folded, lying beside the coffee cup, and she was reading a guidebook—*the* guidebook —and making little marks in it with a shiny gold pen. On the chair beside her lay a giant leather purse, half-open, all but spilling its contents. You could almost hear the little gears shift in Giorgio's skull, and the little hammers go click, click.

He was considering whether she would be around long enough to make the effort of conquest worthwhile—worth spending money, worth the energy needed, worth, after all, ditching me. Maybe she was rich—but this was a cheap little restaurant. His eyes moved down to her shoes, just visible under the edge of the tablecloth. They are usually a good indicator—shoes. Yes, after all, she might be rich, but liked local color. It was hard to tell. And impossible to say if she were going to stay in Rome three days (hardly worth the effort) or three weeks (rather more like it) or three months (too long, perhaps). And maybe she was rich but stingy. That would explain the restaurant. Then, of course, it would not be worth it. He never doubted that he could pull it off if he wanted. You could see that. This self-confidence of his was very seductive.

The girl looked up, finally, and in our direction, and Giorgio was ready. He flashed one of his great welcoming smiles in the mirror—a smile compounded of interest and surprise and feigned recognition. She saw that reflected but looked puzzled. She glanced at me, then away.

It was a wasted effort, after all; wasted on her at any rate. A diffident, very freckled, very plain young woman. She couldn't believe that Giorgio's smile was meant for her.

The girl was paying her check now, waiting for her change. Giorgio shifted in his seat restlessly. Six months before, when he'd picked me up outside a restaurant near the Trevi Fountain, he had watched me first in much the same way; he must have made the same rapid calculations. I could now imagine him following her out the door as he had once followed me, so I tried to think of something to say that would distract him. I had my mind, if not my heart, already set on the night and on the acrobatics we always indulged in after one of his absences. If he went out and then came back—even if he came back soon —it would be difficult to regenerate the ardor. I felt mine already seeping out of me.

The waiter returned to the girl's table with a plateful of change. Giorgio watched the tipping with interest. The waiter then helped her on with her raincoat; she was gathering all her things together. Giorgio looked as though he were about to say something to me.

I anticipated him. "I'm sorry I've been so—"

"*Non importa,*" he murmured.

"I've a lot on my mind now," I said.

She was going out the door, into the wet street. The waiter let the door swing shut behind her. Giorgio's gaze slid downward and met mine.

I immediately felt friendlier toward him. "I'm trying to choose a postcard," I said, and waved with my fork toward where they all were, propped up against the bread basket. "I want to send one to my father."

The thing about Giorgio—what I liked best about him—was that he wasted no time on regret. He made the best of things.

"You have a father?" he asked with interest.

"Doesn't everyone?"

"I mean, your father, he is not dead? You don't speak of him —I thought he was dead."

"Not yet," I replied. "Not yet. But he's sick."

Giorgio patted my hand. One corner of his mouth drooped in sympathy.

That's how it started—my talking about Gideon, telling Giorgio about him. Once I began it was easy. I told him everything I knew—admittedly not much, and not, as it turned out, the most important thing—but Giorgio shook his head in commiseration, looked sorry for me, in fact. I wondered uneasily how all this would affect what I called our relationship. Finally, because I wanted to end the conversation, I said, "Well, it really doesn't matter. I haven't seen him in fourteen years. I only know him from that one time, when I visited him in Israel."

That, it turned out, was the most important thing.

"He is in Israel?"

"Yes."

"Then he is Jewish?" There was a note of awe in his voice.

I nodded warily, beginning to feel a little uncomfortable.

"And you, too? Then you are a Jewess?" But of course he said, "*Ebrea?*" In times of stress Giorgio's English deserted him. And it wasn't really a question, but more a whispered statement of fact that ended on a rising note.

"Half."

There may have been a tinge of defiance in my voice then, because he hastened to reassure me—I didn't look Jewish. Nevertheless, he insisted, he knew all along. He *knew*. It was the passion, he explained. He savored the word, seemed to roll it around on his tongue. He claimed inexperience himself—did not expect me to believe him and would, in fact, have been insulted if I had—but he'd heard, he said, about Jewish girls, about how . . . ah, hot, they were, and desiring. And desirable. (I hope I lowered my eyes modestly at that.)

"Of course," he hastened to add, "they are grasping." He believed this as fervently as he did the other. "*Ma, molto sensuali!*"

He leaned over and began to stroke my arm; his skin was absolutely fevered, in contrast to mine. But, now, he was really appreciating me, and that always worked, I always found that very exciting.

Giorgio was very good that night, very efficient, and he'd hardly rolled off me before I was asleep. Gideon's face flashed into my mind then, but just for a moment—just for that one moment before I dropped off.

As for the talking, I found that hadn't helped much. It hadn't clarified anything. I was still struggling over which postcard to send, still trying to decide what to say. For three days all the postcards remained blank, then in desperation I chose one—the statue of the stoic Marcus Aurelius on his horse, which I hoped Gideon would not be too far gone to appreciate. I turned the card over and stared at the small blank space. Still too much space to fill in, I thought, too big for any message I might send. As for Giorgio, I had his orgiastic appreciation for a time, but that wore off.

Three days later he announced that he had to be at home that evening—his father's sister's daughter's little girl's something. He was gone quite a long while and was not around when I received the thick envelope from Israel.

I thought at first it was a letter, a long letter, but when I slit the envelope open, I saw there was only an airline ticket inside, and stapled to its cover a small slip of paper on which were typed the words "Please cable date of arrival." No signature.

I sat and looked at these for about five minutes—or longer. Without moving. Then I flipped open the ticket. Rome—Tel Aviv, I read, and on the next page, Tel Aviv—Rome. In other words: Come. Go. A command performance.

I went to get my handbag. The postcard was still inside, and I'd finally written something on it. I'd written, "I've heard you were ill. I hope you're feeling much better now. All the best, Sara." Inept, but I'd thought it would do.

I considered putting this card on top of the airline ticket, stuffing them both into an envelope and mailing it back to Gideon. I don't know how long I sat there considering this course of action, but half an hour, at least. I wasn't angry. I didn't even feel resentment. I think—I hope—what I felt was pity. But obviously not enough pity. In the end, I just put the ticket back into the original envelope, slid the postcard in as well, and left it on the dresser. As soon as I got a larger envelope, I decided, I would mail it, but it stayed there on the dresser for a while.

A day or so later, there was another letter from Caroline, writing this time to tell me that she was arranging a ticket back to the States for me, since I was short of cash probably. Quite as though she understood everything—these adolescent foibles, my hand-to-mouth existence (an idiosyncrasy that, no doubt,

24

I'd outgrow by forty?)—and, while she didn't approve, she loved me nonetheless. . . . She did not mention Gideon until the end, where she again expressed the mild hope that I'd write to him. Her handwriting—it was the only letter Caroline had not dictated to a secretary—was small and neat and very careful.

I found this letter, which I read over a solitary breakfast, strangely nourishing, though not in any way Caroline would have wished. Then I reread it. All correspondence, it seems, requires careful rereading, rethinking. I know why that is, but I don't often dwell on why. I also know why I wanted to send the ticket back to Gideon, and in that way, and why Caroline wanted me at home. Thinking about all this depressed me.

5

CAROLINE DIDN'T LIKE THINKING ABOUT WHY, EITHER. IT was not important to her. That's what she would have had me believe.

I once asked, "*Why* did he go away?" I must have been five or six then.

"What does that matter?" she'd said. "Aren't we fine this way, just the two of us?"

A nod. It was expected. Of course we were. We were just fine.

Caroline rustled her papers, smiled her brief, patient smile. My turn now—to retreat, to retrench; sullen, however. Time to rest, to prepare for another onslaught. I really wanted to know why he'd left me. Caroline put on her glasses. That was my cue to find something to do, something constructive: my homework, read a book, anything, anything except bother Caroline. To bother, at last resort, the woman she'd found and paid to be bothered—whichever woman was cleaning the apartment just then, cooking our meals, looking, in a manner of speaking, after me.

Those first few years, it was Brownie—Mrs. Ruby Brown—

26

slopping around as usual in tattered and greasy carpet slippers, once either brown or gray, in thick white lisle stockings accordioned down her sticklike legs from knobby knees to the huge arthritic bulge of her black ankles. Her aura, I remember well, was distinctive, the perfume fruity and alcoholic (12%), but not dabbed at throat and wrists. The yellow-whites of her doleful protuberant eyes were blood-streaked. She shook her head whenever I appeared at the kitchen door, muttered something, sighed. Exuded the forgetfulness of California vineyards and shook her head.

Was she sorry for me? Could she really have been sorry for me? I never asked. I was afraid to know if and why. If she articulated it, I knew, it would be humiliating, so I backed off, I never questioned Brownie. When I pursued the truth, I pursued it in safer places—where I would never find it.

I looked to Caroline for it. She did not shake her head. She just grew impatient. In the end, I no longer feared her impatience, no longer feared her at all. There was, I concluded, little or nothing to lose: her displeasure hardly differed from so many of her other moods. (I don't remember actually thinking that, but surely I must have felt it.) I moved from those first timidities, through the minor hesitations, and came finally to the nagging (that's what she called it).

By the time I was nine, I was halfway through that process. But now I was secretly certain—or was it merely hopeful?— that I shared the blood if not the fate of certain royal bastards (having read history, the more tawdry romances, and anything, in fact, I could lay hands on; having just finished the purported autobiography of some French mistress of kings). How else could I explain Caroline's silence—stubborn, unalterable, but punctuated now and then with "Why does it matter? Aren't you happy?"

Sure. Sure, I was.

Still, it was royal blood for me, even if she would not admit it; even if I myself could not quite believe it. That long narrow body, that long narrow face, those horn-rimmed walls of glass to shield gray eyes, those eyes so thickly fringed with pale moth-brown lashes—I could never imagine her away from her desk,

27

or playing. As, of course, she would have had to—play among the crowned heads of Europe, however impoverished in exile. But I kept asking. And oddly, I never doubted that she was my mother.

She was working at her desk in the living room when I broached the subject of my name. She turned, moist eyes resting on me. The conversation—if it was that—gasped, died. Then was, dutifully, revived.

"What about your name?" Her voice was weary.

"It's different."

"*How* is it different?"

"Your name," I pointed out, "isn't Steiner."

"Of course not. Steiner is your father's name."

I commented, then, on its foreignness. My teacher had said it was German. Was it? Those were bad years for German names. Even so, I still hoped for Prussian blood, ducal at least, even as my classmates and I squatted out mock air raids beneath our desks, arms crossed over our fragile skulls, awaiting the approach of the Luftwaffe. Our school, it was thought, must be a prime target—being so progressive, so private, so Jewish. It was at least fifty percent Jewish, in student body and in faculty.

And I too, I now discover, am fifty percent Jewish. I am then told. Or, maybe, now that I think of it, I knew already, as children do, without knowing they know. After all, there were those seemingly endless summers of my early childhood with my grandparents in Vermont . . . and hadn't I heard things? On calm afternoons, hadn't the words drifted toward me, across the lawn, reached me of their own accord where I sat, in a moving swing near the front gate? As if on a ribbon of smoke they rose, escaped the cage of other sounds: the clink of ice cubes in a pitcher of lemonade, the creak of wicker chairs on the porch, the peeved, nervous rattle of my grandfather's newspaper. They'd drifted toward me; I let them drift past.

"She doesn't look it." That's Mrs. Vining, who lives next door, my grandmother's dearest friend. She peers at me. My surface is minutely observed: my forehead with its slick of perspiration—it's very hot—and the stick-straight brown hair, the newly skinned or scabbed knees—the surface entire. Yet I feel pierced through as well. I feel she can see beneath my skin, where the blood threads delicately through the flesh, and can tell what sort of blood it is. She adds a qualifier, "Not particularly."

"Neither did he, particularly," my grandmother reminds her. "Quite good-looking, wasn't he? I'll give him that."

Mrs. Vining nods. My grandmother lapses into a short-lived silence. Then she says with a sigh, "It's a mistake—marrying out."

"Like to like, I always say." Mrs. Vining is always companionable.

"Even in New York, it's a mistake. I told her." Here my grandmother pauses, but only for a moment. "And all that talk? About what good husbands they make?"

"Yes, I've heard that, too."

"Utter nonsense!"

My grandmother folds her hands and places them in her lap. She says something else, but that is lost even before I hear it. Do I really remember such a conversation? It seems to me I do. I'm five years old. Or six.

Another time. My grandmother says, "Of course, I've got nothing against them. You know that." I'm eight or nine.

Mrs. Vining has nothing against them either. She's a Gold Star mother—the eloquent white satin, gold-fringed banner hangs in her front window. Her youngest son fell fighting the Nazis. People might say because of *them*. But (Mrs. Vining says) it's not their fault, not really.

"It's the waste—that's what I can't stand." My grandmother is a little agitated now. "When I think of all the wonderful, *wonderful* boys that Carrie could have married! When I think of them. . . ." She ticks off a distinguished list of the eminently suitable. If it's a delusion, it is fed by Mrs. Vining. She nods and nods, even adds names to the list.

"Well," my grandmother says hopelessly, "you know Carrie."

Mrs. Vining nods again. Of course she knows Carrie. She knows my mother very well, saw her grow up. But if she doesn't

29

know her, I certainly do. I should know better, shouldn't I? I shouldn't provoke her. I shouldn't ask so many questions. I shouldn't pretend, even to myself, that I do not know. What do I want, anyway? Refutation? Elaboration? Confession? Caroline has nothing to confess.

She turns back to her desk, moves some papers from one side to the other, opens a book. Snaps it open, snaps the exchange shut. "Really," she always says, in a colorless voice, "really, I don't want to talk about it anymore." Her mouth widens in a kind of smile; it thins, and the thinned lips whiten slightly. She waits me out. She has always waited me out, she will always do so.

That winter, though, she took one more step—strangely enough, a step not taken before. She arranged for my name to be changed, anglicized Steiner out of existence, making me Stone, Sara Elizabeth. The final step in the effacing of Gideon. Her father's law firm handled it. Then she went off, alone, to Texas for her sabbatical year and left me with her parents, in the town with all the stigmata of idealized New England: white pickets, green lawns, several requisite village idiots, the D.A.R., the annual rummage and cake sales for the church. She left me to ask questions of her mother who had always obliged with information and something more—with homilies, asides, resentments, details of the Barnett-Fowler family genealogy. It seems we went way back on both sides, but very dully. And something about my mother.

"Headstrong," my grandmother said, yanking my hair almost cruelly into one long plait, as though it were Caroline who stood at her knees, not I. As though she'd succeeded, at last, in making a point.

As for my father, what I knew about him I learned from her. "The wandering Jew," my grandmother called him, for he shared with the rest of his nomadic race, she said, that insane desire to keep moving.

"Why, there's even a plant named after them, isn't there, Frederick?" And she smiled at the front and back pages of the open afternoon paper behind which, she was certain, my grandfather, the family gardener, was smiling back.

30

So that much was given, at least: what my grandmother thought she knew and maybe not all, but only what she thought it proper to tell me; where Gideon had gone or, rather, where he'd come to a halt; the fact that he wrote to Caroline about me; that sometimes he sent money. Otherwise, nothing. I didn't even know what he looked like. She tried to remedy that. She had pictures to show me.

At first she couldn't find the family album. We, both of us, looked for it and found everything else neatly slotted into place. A month or so later, it turned up in Caroline's old room, in the drawer of her dresser. My grandmother wiped the dark leather cover, sat down beside me on the gold brocade sofa in the living room, and began to turn pages. Some photos seemed to be missing. There were oblong spaces, mounts at the four corners, but no pictures. Two pictures had been cut—one neatly in half, the other a third of the way in. My grandmother passed that page very quickly, but I caught glimpses of Caroline smiling out at us. Caroline, lanky, in a pale, satiny one-piece swimsuit on some nameless beach, her companion gone. Caroline on a warm fall day, a little plumper, quite pregnant, her mother beside her, and beside her mother, part of a hand, male probably, holding a cigarette, disembodied. Beside each of these, beside the cut and uncut edges, loomed the blank, black page.

I remember, now, how my grandmother shut the album, the way she slid her thin blue-veined hands over the smooth cover. I even remember what she said. She said, yes, now she remembered. They'd disappeared, just fallen out one day and got lost, nobody knew where. "That happens," she said, as though she'd seen disbelief in my eyes. For the other two pictures, the photographs that had been cut up, she offered no explanation. She forgot those; she expected me to forget them, too.

By then she'd risen. She picked up a small porcelain figurine and set it down again an inch to the right. She smoothed the antimacassar on one arm of the sofa, then those on the smaller armchair. She ran a testing forefinger along the edge of the table. All the while she kept talking about how it didn't matter really, because probably I'd never see my father anyway, because there was no connection between us at all. "Anyway," she

31

concluded, "aren't you Caroline's little girl?"

And I nodded. Sure. That may have been the only thing I was sure of.

Caroline must have been sure, too, that I was her little girl. Otherwise the summer in Israel might never have occurred. She might never have told me what my father had written, that he wanted to see me, that he'd sent a steamship ticket.

She sat on my vanity bench watching me from across the room. I sat in the middle of my bed and brushed my hair. It was 1952; I was seventeen. Palestine was now Israel, but it was still a dangerous place; those were dangerous times.

"I'm just telling you what your father wrote. What he wants," she concluded.

"All right," I said. I tried to sound indifferent.

"I won't tell you what to do about it."

I remember thinking: why not? But when I looked at her face, I saw why not. She was sure of me, she was very sure. There was no reason not to be—I'd stopped asking questions, I hadn't mentioned him in years. I'd decided that if he did not exist for her, he would not exist for me either. What I wanted was to please her. I did not want her to look at me and see in me my father. I remembered the pictures, I remembered what she'd done to them. I had never had any doubt about who had wielded the scissors, just as my grandmother had no doubt. Now she seemed to be waiting, sitting very quietly, her hands in her lap, palms up, expectant. As though something would soon be placed there—what was due her, a gift. I suppose what she expected was loyalty, that she equated it with love. But I felt helpless suddenly, too tired to get up and go toward her, even in my imagination, too tired because I'd tried too hard to please her, and now I remembered how often I'd tried and how often I'd failed. I thought: I don't want to try anymore.

I was sitting cross-legged on my bed, holding onto my ankles, bent over, folded up, smaller than usual. I was almost afraid to look at her, but I did look at her.

"Oh, I don't mind going," I said. "I'd like to. A change—it'd be nice."

We were both silent. Caroline still sat on the bench, but her

32

hands were turned over now; she slid her palms downward on her thighs, as though she'd just washed her hands and was drying them like this, on her tweed skirt.

"But if you don't want me to go," I said. "If—"

"It doesn't matter to me one way or the other." She wasn't smiling anymore; there was no trace of even the vaporous smile. You couldn't tell what she felt or, indeed, if she felt anything.

"You're quite old enough," she said, "to make up your own mind. And you have, haven't you?"

I said, yes, I had. She was at the door now, opened it, closed it softly behind her.

I remember how I stared at the door, but not for how long I stared, how I picked up the hairbrush and hurled it with all my might at the door, and how the brush bounced back to fall with a light thud on the carpet, and the nick in the white paint on the paneled wood—I can see it still.

33

6

So there it is, my past. Not, after all, particularly illuminating. It explains nothing—not how I got from then to now, nor from there, that large apartment on Riverside Drive I shared with my mother, to here, this small, furnished one in Rome that I now shared, off and on, with Giorgio.

That period can be capsulized, my whole life can, but I think that's true of everyone's life. I went to visit my father that summer, then I returned. In the fall I went to college in New Hampshire and did well; four years later I graduated. I got my first job, as typist-receptionist, with a Madison Avenue ad agency; then I went to work for another agency, then for a public relations firm. I did very little, however, to polish my own relations with the public (or, for that matter, with the private sector), but I smiled a lot: my teeth were good.

During this time I lived alone; then with Jerry; then with Don (a mistake—he turned out to be bisexual); then with Peter. Finally, there was Rob, and I lived with him the longest. I even married Rob, but that was at the end, in an irrational moment. About four years ago, long after the divorce came through, I resumed using my own name, Stone, and left New York. Since then I've been in Europe.

Such biographical detail explains nothing, of course, certainly not why I lived as I did now, as though I were on one of those trains that rattle across Europe at night, passing over or pausing on viaducts on the edges of towns, over streets of shuttered, sleeping houses, chalked yellow with lamplight and white with moonlight. It does not explain why I walk the long platforms of certain stations as though it were just for the exercise; why I sit in my seat through the short wait at others, or why I'm in Rome. This was a long stop in any journey, even one going nowhere.

Well, then, why Rome? It must be because nobody asks why. To ask is to miss the aesthetic point, to brand yourself Philistine. But say someone is fool enough and asks. You need say nothing in explanation. You wave your hand at it all: at the vast, streaked, tawny façades of old palaces, the fountains, the broken pillars, the tufts of grass sprouting among the stones, at the hungry descendants of the cats of ancient Rome prowling the ruins. What can you say about all that? Nothing, of course, the answer is obvious: Rome is glorious, past her best maybe, but still beautiful, and you appreciate her. Besides, you like the Italians, you say; they know how to live.

I blundered into Rome, recognized it at once: a refuge of sorts. I was living in Paris at the time but had no job there, had given up my room, and practically everything I owned was with me on that journey.

I mentioned Lucio before, and said I stayed in Rome because of him. Not true, not quite. It was because nobody asked questions, and therefore you needed no answers. And because the sky and the street and the sounds were wholly strange, and the people alien, and because I'd never been there (a good reason) and because, at the beginning, I understood practically nothing, did not need to understand, and when, finally, I did understand, I could shut my ears to the voices. In short, I was there because I was, and could remain, a stranger.

The Romans, of course, led their own lives, parallel to mine: lives lived intricately, hierarchically, closed, meshed into one

35

another. I lived mine, in a manner of speaking, on the periphery of theirs. I was part of their lives insofar as I watched, and was watched, with interest; insofar as a man, standing idle for a moment on a corner, murmured *"Bella!"* as I passed and then followed me for a block or two. It was enough, it seemed to me. Giorgio was enough, Lucio had been enough—too much, almost.

About Giorgio. Did I say that I believed almost nothing he said at the beginning and, at the end, absolutely nothing? Did I say that I did not care that he lied? Truth would have taken too much out of him, and out of me.

Did I say that I was often bewildered at how curiously empty he seemed? Did I also say this emptiness seemed to mirror mine to perfection? Did I speak of his desires? Not his sexual desires, which were quite ordinary, but the others—well, more like dreams. He had his dreams. He saw in the future infinite possibilities, all open to him, and he had faith in himself, in God, in the perception of women—especially in the perception of women, and in their appreciation. Women like me, but much richer; women who knew his worth. He was always testing perception in me. He would point at things in elegant shop windows on the Corso, at shirts, sweaters, ties, scarves. He would speak of how much they cost now and how much more expensive they would be later. He looked both jaunty and wistful as he spoke, as he searched my face for a sign of my appreciation, as he talked of how much—or how little—he earned at his bank and how expensive the doctors were (sometimes it was his mother who was the chronic invalid; at other times, his father).

But he understood me, he read me very well with those eyes—those black eyes like ripe olives, the light lost somewhere inside, giving off a sort of dull luster. He saw hunger in me—a simple hunger for the flesh, and for nothing else. So he fed the hunger and I was grateful, and I sometimes bought him things. Once, an expensive pigskin wallet. And after one night, when he'd done exceptionally well and given me a great deal of pleasure, I would have bought him a watch, except that the one he pointed out cost far too much. I bought him a scarf instead. He was pleased.

Well, it was payment for services rendered. Did I say this

seemed perfectly natural to me? And that when, occasionally, he bought *me* a gift, it seemed wholly unnatural? I wanted to pay. Payment absolved you, it freed you to feel nothing. Indeed, I felt nothing.

It took me thirty-one years to achieve that.

I offer no excuses or explanations for what followed. Gideon sent me an airline ticket and, in effect, summoned me to Israel. Caroline must have thought about it for a while, guessed he might do that, so she wrote and, by indirection, in her usual sidewise, scuttling, sandcrab manner, summoned me back to New York. I didn't know what their motives were precisely, but among hers, there was hatred surely, even after thirty years. As for mine, if I had any motive, if it wasn't just the simple desire to keep moving, it may have been something equally simple and much more discreditable—I may have wanted to spite her.

7

I TOLD THE SIGNORA I WOULD BE LEAVING BUT THAT I WOULD
finish the week. At first the news seemed to distract her and she
was even more short-tempered than usual when her mother
phoned. By the end of the day, though, she remembered there
were salesgirls as good that she could hire for even less money.
When I said good night, she murmured something kind about
the illness of parents, reached over and pressed my hand. On
Saturday, my last day, she paid for my late morning *espresso*
out of the cash register.

I'd set aside a few days to prepare for my departure. I had,
somehow, accumulated far too many things, and now I called
the few people I knew to say that I was going and to mention that
I had certain things which I wanted to sell. These were people
in self-imposed exile—English, Australian, American. They
lived precariously in glorious Rome, ate *pasta* for lunch, *pasta*
for dinner, and paid for it with private English lessons to ambi-
tious waiters and bored housewives. There was no ready cash
anywhere. I had to be rid of these things, however. I felt possessed by my possessions, weighed down with them, liable to

drown in a sea of clothing, books, crockery, bits and pieces of furniture. I gave everything away. Now, unencumbered, I'd be free to bypass Rome if I wanted. I could go wherever I wanted, and whenever.

There was my landlady to see. I spent a futile hour and a half with her, going over the flat and wrangling over my deposit. I lost. She would check the apartment once again, after I left, she said, to see if there was any damage. She would wait to see if there was a phone bill. Whatever was due me I would get, she assured me, when I returned.

Then, of course, there was Giorgio. He had not yet returned, and it was over a week. Some of his clothes and belongings were in the flat: two freshly laundered shirts, one soiled, some socks, some shorts, a razor, a toothbrush, a pair of gold cuff links (from some other appreciative lady), an old bathrobe, slippers, and one of those hard-boiled American detective novels, translated into the usual execrable Italian. Either his other suit was at the cleaner's, or he had spirited it out of the flat without my knowing.

Still, I thought he might return before I left, so I packed my own things, everything in two suitcases. Then I wrapped Giorgio's things in brown paper, tied the bundle with string, and waited some more.

The day before my flight I decided to mail the package, but I didn't know his address, and when I went to look it up in the phonebook—I assumed his family had a phone—I realized that I did not know his last name either, or could not remember it. I had a whole day—more than twenty-four hours left—and nothing to do with it. I had seen everyone I wanted to see, done everything I had to do. Besides, I might never see Giorgio again, and that seemed a good enough reason. I decided to go and see him at his job.

Not that I knew where he worked, exactly. He'd once said that he was a clerk in a bank in Piazza Bologna, and I remembered that, but that was all I remembered. I don't think he said which bank. Piazza Bologna was on the other side of Rome. The trip itself, going and coming, was good for more than a couple of hours, and when I found Giorgio, it would probably take care

39

of the evening—of the night, too. In fact, the trip might take care of the entire day; it would be a day without need for thought.

I took up the package, which was bulky and awkward to carry, tucked it as well as I could under one arm, and took the tram, the *circonvallazione*. It would mean a walk at the other end, but it was a sunny morning, the air was cool and crisp, and you can breathe easily on such a morning and go long distances before you know it.

I can't imagine now why I assumed there'd be only one bank in the piazza. Rome is full of banks—almost as many, it seems sometimes, as coffee bars. Piazza Bologna had a full complement of each : four bars, three banks.

In fact, it had four banks, that is, if you count one that was not in the piazza itself but just off it, on the boulevard that runs into it on one side, swerves around the traffic island in the center, and out again under a different name. But I decided I need not worry about that one, at least for the present. There were three others in the square itself, larger and more likely.

I started with the largest. I hadn't planned anything, not my approach nor what I would say when I saw him. It didn't seem necessary. I'd go in; if I saw Giorgio, I'd wave at him. Naturally, he'd come over. We'd talk. I knew that he might not like it— my coming to seek him out like this, at work—but there were reasons, perfectly legitimate reasons. It would be simple enough to explain.

But I'd chosen a bad day for this bank and, evidently, a very bad hour. The lobby seemed to heave with people, agitated little clusters of them at the long counters, at the cashiers' cages, each one intent on impossibility—snagging the attention of a clerk, then holding it. There was, therefore, a good deal of signaling over the heads of those in front, an inching forward, a more insidious elbowing aside; apologies, offhand or effusive; smallish or full-scale retreats; even, now and then, a flirtation, nothing very serious, a gay smile, a flutter of the eyelashes, a bold appreciative look. And, of course, as always—talking.

I knew what it was like to be in the middle of that. I'd grown accustomed to it in my two Roman years, but I still didn't like it. I hated it, in fact: the tangle of arms and legs, warm garlicky breath on neck and cheek, the scent of perfume, brilliantine, the smell of sweat. But I liked the sounds—the soothing, liquid sound of Italian. *Permesso, signora. Prego. Si accomodi.* Like a spill of warm syrup.

Now, of course, I was not in the middle of it. I stood near the entrance, two steps above the main lobby. From there I could see everything and everybody—clients and clerks, both those behind the counters and those at the desks farther back. No Giorgio. And since it seemed unlikely that Giorgio had the office behind the one frosted glass door at the far end of the room, I decided this was not the place after all. I departed. I felt fine. I'd not needed to speak to anyone, not needed to explain and, further, had eliminated one of the banks. Two—at most, three —left to go.

The Banco di Sicilia was less crowded, but just as noisy. Every footstep, every word ricocheted off surfaces of shiny black marble. No Giorgio at the counters, nor at the desks behind them. But, in addition to the desks, there was a high wooden partition at the rear. It could be that Giorgio worked there, behind it, hidden from view.

I came away from the door, walked down the counter to the very end where a small metal sign hung on a pillar. *Cambio*, it said. I thought that I could maneuver around the edge of the counter and from there see all the desks behind the partition, all the people, but I couldn't quite manage it. As I pushed the gate open, a smallish man in a buff-colored jacket looked up, saw what I was doing, detached himself from a conference of bank clerks and calculators, and hurried forward to meet me. I withdrew, putting the counter between us.

M. Peruzzi—his name was printed, under cellophane, on a bar pinned to his right lapel. Above it and a little to the left, his mouth curved into a half-moon of smile beneath the inverted, spread V of moustache.

"*Prego, signora?*"

I did not respond, not at first. You could say that I ignored him. For a minute or two I looked past him, at the desks and the people at them, at the counter and, just behind it, at the clerks; finally, at the opaque partition.

Signor Peruzzi tried English. "Please, Madam," he said. "Change, Madam?"

I shifted the package. The paper was starting to tear, and the string was loose already. Any minute a sock might fall to the floor, or Giorgio's razor, or his toothbrush.

I said that I'd like to see Giorgio, and was he in. He could assume from this (as I wished him to) that I knew Giorgio worked here, but that I also knew he might be busy or out at the moment, or perhaps ill and at home. But it didn't work with this man.

"Giorgio?" There was genuine puzzlement in Peruzzi's voice, and he seemed to be waiting for something else. A last name, maybe.

I shrugged. I must have, because I had nothing to say.

Peruzzi then repeated the name, but louder this time and without the question mark. Much louder—loud enough for everyone in the bank to hear. There was a sudden, fortunately very brief, moment of silence. All business came to a halt, and everyone—clerks and clients—turned to look at us. This was immediately superseded by a great deal of noise, though there were some who continued to stare. Meanwhile, the name, spoken like that and reverberating, had brought someone to his feet and someone else had emerged from behind the partition. The first fellow had been in full view all along. The second gave us a cursory look, saw that it had nothing to do with him, and returned to his business. Neither of them was Giorgio. Not the right Giorgio. I hesitate to say it—not *my* Giorgio.

The first man came forward. He, too, wore a buff jacket, which was obviously a bank uniform, and the same kind of bar on his lapel (his name was G. Bruno), but his supercilious smile was all his own. He stood beside Signor Peruzzi, and now there were three of us, staring at one another. Or, more precisely, they were staring at me, and I was looking at the floor, at the counter, and wondering how to get out of there with grace.

Then I stepped back and inadvertently gave M. Peruzzi a better view of my figure; his eyes skipped down the front of my loose raincoat, paused for a moment at the hem, slid upward again to the collar. It was obvious what he was thinking. One of those crazy American girls who come to Rome for fun—for which, read sex (wasn't there any in the U.S.?)—and who had gotten herself into the usual kind of trouble in the usual way, with a phantom who had called himself Giorgio.

Now that he'd figured it out to his own satisfaction, Peruzzi turned to Bruno. "This young lady," he said in Italian, in a lower, more confidential tone, "is looking for someone called Giorgio who is supposed to work here." Under his breath and barely audible to me, but surely audible to Bruno, he added, "*La poverina!*"

To which his colleague responded by looking sympathetic, smiling at me, the poor little thing, and raising his hand so that we could see the golden shimmer of his wedding band. But he may have sensed danger, for he then backed off and, with a meaningful glance at a coworker, sat down at his desk and became very busy. He looked up and over at us now and then, but his interest was merely academic.

It remained for Signor Peruzzi to deal with the matter. I would have liked to have helped him, but my mind was blank. I could remember none of the proper Italian phrases, those I needed to ease myself out of this—the bank, the situation.

In careful but very bad English (which I kept correcting, an unfortunate habit), Signor Peruzzi informed me that I'd seen the Giorgios that worked in the bank, in this particular branch at least. Was I sure that Giorgio worked in the Banco di Sicilia, and did he say it was this branch? (There were more than a dozen branches in Rome.) He wanted to help, but he could not, not unless he had the family name. Here his voice died away tactfully, and he left the last question unasked: Did I *know* the family name?

I gazed at him helplessly. He then asked me to describe Giorgio. I did this—I don't know why—then my voice died. Giorgio sounded, I realized, like everybody or anybody.

"Mia dispiace, signorina," he murmured. With betrayal, I had lost my more respectable title. In his eyes I was seduced and abandoned, probably beyond redemption.

And now, I too was beginning to feel like that—a poor little thing. Betrayed, deserted, with nowhere to turn. Ridiculous, but for a ludicrous moment I didn't know whether to laugh or cry and realized, with a shock, that I was much closer to the tears. Meanwhile Signor Peruzzi seemed to be undergoing some emotional upheaval of his own; there were tears in his eyes. Middle-class and middle-aged, he had, no doubt, had adventures of his own and was now, perhaps, feeling a twinge of guilt.

At this point I just turned and ran, I think. I know I got out of there without crying and, for that matter, without laughing. Out in the street again, I felt foolish, then shaken, then annoyed. Finally, in retrospect, I felt scared.

My God, I thought, what if something had happened to Giorgio while he was in my apartment? What if he'd fallen and cracked his skull in the bathtub? What if he'd electrocuted himself one night as, barefoot, he'd so meticulously ironed his trousers? Who would have come to take away his body? Whom could I have called then? (I had a swift but very vivid image: Giorgio's new wallet, his keys, and his coins heaped on my dresser. Did he have an identity card? I'd never seen it.) What would I have told the police? Would I have had to arrange his funeral and pay for it? That is, if I could not find out where his family was. And, if so, what could I have put on the headstone? "Here lies Giorgio"? "About twenty-six years old"? In place of the usual sentiments—"Beloved Son," "Of Dear Memory"—what could I have put? There were several things I knew for certain: we had met near the Trevi Fountain, he thought he was photogenic, he was usually good in bed. But these were hardly appropriate sentiments to have carved in marble.

I made one more, monumental effort to remember his name, but I could not. Could not, I realized, because I'd never heard it properly. He'd mumbled something soon after we'd met, something which, to my uneducated ear, had sounded sufficiently Calabrian or Sicilian. I'd never asked him to repeat it. And now

44

that I thought of it, I'd never asked for the name of the bank either, and he had not offered it. Nor had he given me a telephone number where I could reach him, if I needed him. But then I'd never needed him. I'd been sleeping with him for six months or more—and for all I knew, he wasn't a Giorgio at all. For all I knew, he was a Paolo or a Vincenzo or a Cesare.

(But here I misjudged him. He was a Giorgio. I found that out very soon.)

I didn't know what to do next. I stood on the sidewalk outside the bank for just a moment, then crossed to the traffic island in the middle of the piazza and stood there, with this clumsy package of Giorgio's under one arm, and wondered whether it had been worth all this trouble—these few things of his, even the prospect of another night with him. Better to depend on the *portiere's* honesty, I decided, and trust the old man to give Giorgio his things if and when he ever came back to the apartment again. Better to do that, certainly, than stand here in the middle of the square, the package about to come apart and Giorgio's things about to fall, one by one, into the gutter and come to a bad end under one of these vicious little white or cream Fiats that hooted their way past me, racing their motors. Yes, better, I decided, and then I decided to have a coffee, to sit down somewhere and think this over once more—at least before I ventured into any more banks.

There was a large bar just across the street, on the other side of the traffic. I managed the crossing and chose a table out in full sunshine, one with a bright red cloth that snapped in the breeze. I placed the package on the empty chair across from me and, turning my face up to the sun, leaned back and closed my eyes. After all, I thought more calmly now, it was over. Giorgio had survived our little affair. Someone else would have to bury him, when the time came.

A moment later I opened my eyes. Someone was standing in my sunlight: a boy, like one of those that can be seen any weekday morning in any busy Roman street, hurrying from the bar to the shopkeepers in their little shops with trays of sugary *espresso* in little glasses. He might have been a scrawny, ill-fed twelve-year-old, but he looked, and might have been, an equally

45

ill-fed ten. His blue sweater was torn at the elbows, but he wore a long white apron and a napkin was draped over his arm, in parody of waiters at the more expensive *osterie*.

Normally, I would never have noticed him. These boys are like mailboxes; they're everywhere in Rome, part of the scenery. But this boy was rather nasty. He had unilaterally declared war on me. The sun, he seemed to be saying as he stood there blocking it, belonged to the working classes. He would stand where he was as long as he possibly could, creating shade for me to sit in; the warmth was not for the likes of me.

He looked blandly at me as he took my order. I hoped he'd go away with it. I wanted a *cappuccino* and a brioche, one of the yeasty kind, with a faint tinge of cinnamon and a flaking, fragile skin of melted sugar over its virtually tasteless doughiness. I had not had breakfast. But the boy didn't move; he took my order and relayed it, leaning back a little so that he could stay in the sun but, at the same time, peer into the shadowy interior of the bar. Above the din of traffic, he called it out.

"Hey, Giorgio," he yelled, or some drawn-out Romano equivalent, something like "*Aheee, Giorgio! Caffé latte.*"

You know my first thought. I rejected it. Another Giorgio—that was my second thought. I reverted again, however, to the first thought, for I'd had a sudden image, very sharp: Giorgio at the foot of the bed on the morning I'd last seen him. Giorgio looking incredibly clerklike, white collar, gray suit, plum-colored tie. His bony wrists, always slightly and mysteriously reddened, protruding from starched cuffs. A fleeting image. But I knew. When I looked into that café, I would see Giorgio.

And sure enough, when the boy had finally decided that I'd been deprived of the sun long enough, when he'd flicked his napkin across the tabletop, wiped and centered the little glass ashtray, and gone to fetch my coffee and—instead of the brioche I'd ordered—an Italian counterfeit of the French croissant, I leaned over to look inside.

And there was Giorgio.

In fact, two Giorgios, one in the flesh, the other reflected in the long bright blue mirror behind the bar. Giorgio in double handsome profile, and in graduated rank behind him, the usual bar bottles, brilliantly colored, some also doubled. Only the highly polished chrome of the elaborate *espresso* machine near the end of the bar was, most of it, out of mirror range.

Giorgio was making coffee, and very efficiently, too. He pressed down on the little lever, produced a tiny cup with a flourish, placed it in a tiny saucer on the bar. I saw him flip open the lid of the steel bowl, scoop up a heaping spoon of sugar, hold it poised, waiting for assent. He smiled; his teeth and his white jacket gleamed.

The woman standing alongside the bar nodded. Giorgio stirred her coffee for her. One of those tightly packed Roman matrons in close-fitting tailor-made of thick purplish wool, dark hair wrapped sleekly around her head, one ringed hand on hip, the other on the bar. A customer or, perhaps, the lady he now entertained on husbandless afternoons, or maybe both. They stared at each other: *molto sensuale*, as Giorgio would say.

Do I give the impression that I watched for a long time?

Not at all. One furtive look sufficed. I was still holding onto the back of my chair. I lowered myself into it again, bringing the picture with me whole, then scraped the chair back from the doorway. That was automatic. Poor Giorgio, I thought.

Well, not exactly. First I thought: You liar—you lying bastard. Then, another minute passed, and I thought, or perhaps *felt* is the better word: poor Giorgio! When the coffee came, I drank it at once, took one bite of croissant, paid the boy, left him far too large a tip, rose and walked away. Almost ran, I'm afraid. And I was very careful not to pass in front of the open door of the bar.

I took the first bus out of the piazza, caught it just as it was pulling away from the curb. My heart was banging in my chest, my throat dry. I fell into a seat by the window as the bus swung into the street. I felt curiously light, though, as if I'd divested myself of something—an illusion, maybe—but five minutes later, I realized that it was something more substantial. I'd forgotten the package, left it lying on the chair in front of the coffee bar.

The boy would see it. He would bring it into the café. He and Giorgio and the cashier would see the name scrawled on the brown paper. They might not open it at once—there are so many Giorgios in Rome. They'd put it away for a while, perhaps behind the counter, wait a day or two for the *signorina* to come back and claim it. Finally, they would open it, and Giorgio—*my* Giorgio—would recognize his things. He'd know I'd seen him. Poor Giorgio.

That's what I felt then. I wasn't angry. The lie was so foolish, so unnecessary, and his aspirations—poor Giorgio—so limited that I felt sorry for him. I may have felt other emotions—the more normal emotions, I suppose—but they fluttered through me so quickly that they were gone almost before I fully realized their presence.

I thought about him again later, and felt sorry for him again. It was as though I had betrayed him, exposed all his secrets to some cold-eyed, pitiless stranger. Really very silly. Until this minute I've never spoken of it to anyone.

8

"GEVERET STEINER?" VERY SOFTLY.

I reluctantly opened my eyes. I'd not slept very well the night before; my lids felt gritty, my eyes dry and hot.

The stewardess was sorry; she hoped she had not wakened me. She waited for some kind of answer, a yes, a no, leaning forward a little, holding onto the forward seat, her smile professional. The plane rocked, and it seemed she might pitch forward into my lap, but she steadied herself.

"No," I said.

"You're not Geveret Steiner? They said. . . ." She made a vague gesture toward the nose of the plane.

"Stone," I said. "My name's been anglicized."

"Oh." The plane lurched. The soft, almost plump, white hand gripped the blue plush. "But you *are* Professor Steiner's daughter? Gideon Steiner?" The pronunciation was Hebrew; for the first name, two syllables minus the "e"; the second like German, the intrusive "h" between the first and second letters. As I remembered.

I nodded, but as there seemed nothing else to say, I closed my eyes again, felt the air move, knew without looking that she was gone.

Beside me, Mrs. Perlberger, who had earlier told me all about her late husband, her married daughter who lived in Beersheba, her daughter's two beautiful children, a boy and a girl, and her son, married to an American girl and working as an engineer in Pittsburgh, Pennsylvania, in the U.S. of A.—Mrs. Perlberger said, "That's what he did, too."

"Who?"

"My son. He changed his name, too. You know, made it American. He changed it to Perry." She sighed. By now, the exchange with the stewardess had begun to trouble me. I should not have closed my eyes. I should have asked why she had wanted to know. Worse, I could not now remember what the girl had looked like—only that white hand gripping the top of the forward seat. I turned to Mrs. Perlberger for help.

"Oh, she's very pretty," Mrs. Perlberger said with pride, as though I'd asked about her daughter.

"I know. But what did she *look* like?"

Mrs. Perlberger was vague. "Oh, you know—blonde. . . ."

Another stewardess was passing. I stopped her in the hope that it was the girl who'd come up to me earlier, but this one was dark. I asked for something to drink and decided that, after all, I was being apprehensive about nothing. What could it matter, anyway? What if they did know I was Gideon Steiner's daughter?

"Orange juice?" the second stewardess offered. "Coffee?"

"No, something alcoholic. Scotch."

Beside me, Mrs. Perlberger commented on this, too, now smiling; her heavily powdered face, an imperfectly set plaster mask, seemed about to crack. She talked about the drinking of "you young American Jews" (I said nothing; I hadn't the heart to correct her, the energy or desire to explain) and how different these habits were from those of their parents, who in Europe seldom drank at all. "Except for wine on Friday nights and at the seder and so on. And on Purim, of course. But that's different, you agree?"

I agreed, though I didn't know what she was talking about.

She watched as I undid the seal on the miniature bottle of Scotch and poured the liquor into the clear plastic tumbler, over the ice cubes; declined politely when I asked if she, too, would like a drink; felt she could now discuss the drinking habits of her Americanized son and his wife, Mr. and Mrs. Perry.

"You know," she confided in a very low voice, afraid perhaps of being overheard by the lady sitting in front of us or the young man in the long black silk coat and velvety black homburg who was sitting behind, "they drink every day now. Martinis. Before supper." She turned to look out the window, as though in the turbulence out there she could find a more comprehensible world.

The plane lurched. Ice cubes bounced off my front teeth, and the rim of the plastic cup shivered against my lips. Mrs. Perlberger gripped the arms of her seat and commented, once more, on modernity—negatively, but in a more general way. She wasn't against progress, no one could accuse her of that, but the past almost always seemed better to her, and if she treasured anything, it was her memories of that past. She supposed it was because she was young then; she sighed and said nothing more. The plane shook. A few minutes later we climbed above the storm or had passed through it, and Mrs. Perlberger leaned back in her seat and closed her eyes.

And left me to deal with my own past—not nearly so distant, and my memories of it—not nearly so pleasant. Jarred loose in the vibration of flight, the images were torn free of their moorings, and I'd always thought them secure, anchored forever in lost, long-forgotten coves. But they rose and fell on the tide now, thrown up, thrown back, battered, sinking, and rising again. . . .

My first glimpse of Gideon . . . the last time I'd seen him. The first and the last. Fourteen years before. A hanging sign, and on it the letters "R" slash "S," and beyond it, running down to a long table, an untidy line of suitcases, trunks, and cartons. There was a tall man moving along the line, a man with sunburnt arms and legs and, when he squatted to read a label or examine a luggage tag, his thighs were ropy with muscle beneath beige shorts. Almost a uniform, the shorts and shirt.

51

With the exception of passengers and crew, every man in the customs shed seemed to be wearing that.

I thought: that's my father, and he looks like everyone else. Then he came to the red plaid suitcase and stopped to look at the tag, and I was certain.

That's how I knew him—because he was smiling as he straightened, because he looked around expectantly and took off his sunglasses, tucking them into his shirt pocket, and because, all the time, his eyes were moving restlessly from face to face.

My suitcase, I thought numbly, therefore my father. That's how he'd know me, too—when I came forward to get it. But I did not move. I stood in the huge doorway of the customs shed and watched him. Behind me a heat haze shimmered over Haifa bay and a hot wind moved in over the water. My dress clung to my back in damp patches, and sweat trickled slowly down the back of my legs; a bad year for me, a fat year, the flesh too ample, straining the skimpy fabric of summer dresses. I wondered what I'd say to him, how I could approach him, and whether it was best to start forward now or to wait, perhaps to wait forever.

He'd stopped a porter and gestured at the suitcase. The other man shrugged and moved on. Gideon lit a cigarette, then stood there smoking it. He looked at me, then looked away. He'd not moved from my suitcase. He knew he had only to wait there. Claimed suitcase, claimed daughter—whom, otherwise, he might not know.

My father. He looked at me again but did not recognize me. A rather hesitant smile—I was the right age—but then I did not return it. I licked at my dry lips and pretended to stare past him. Finally he turned away. I started forward.

I came up behind him, said "Hello" to his back, and he swung around quickly to face me, already smiling. I could see his eyes —the chill, clear green of his eyes, and now the look of puzzlement in them.

"Well," he said after a moment, "I should have recognized you."

I thought, how could you? But I did not reply.

Then his voice, almost tentative, "Sara?"

I nodded, barely moving my head.

"Yes," he said, "of course." He searched my face, took a very short step in my direction, then—nothing. He seemed to be waiting. For me? Did he think *I* would embrace *him?* I thought of putting out my hand, but my hand was damp, trembling. Lips drier now, too. I ran a dry tongue over them. At last he did it—took the step forward and put his arms around me, pulled me close. I thought he'd feel my heart beating as I felt the small, round buttons of his shirt on my right breast, right through the thin materials of my dress and bra. Then I felt his lips on my cheek, and his special odor invaded my skull—the compound of soap and sour sweat and tobacco. Not unpleasant, but I winced, I pulled back and stood rigid before him, and thought incoherently of other men—boys, really—of their different, urgent mouths (not gentle) and tongues and furtive hands; of the "everything but" tangles on the backseats of family cars borrowed for the evening; of the excitement, if not, precisely, the pleasure, of doing it—"everything but" and, finally, every-thing—on sofas in dark living rooms. Perverse thoughts. Gideon versus Bill (who had acne) and Chuck and Davey.

"It's been a long time," Gideon was saying.

Never, I thought; really, it's been never. I think I felt a little sorry for him after that, though. Nothing he could say or do would make it better, easier, or different. He knew it. I knew it.

Inauspicious, that beginning, and after that all downhill. He picked up my luggage and brought it to the customs officers. There were a few perfunctory pokes into the contents of my suitcase. My passport had been stamped earlier. His car, which had been sitting in the shade of the customs hall all morning, was nevertheless hot and stuffy; its imitation leather seats seemed to be melting and burned the backs of my legs. He sat there for a minute staring at me, half-smiling, then leaned forward, turned the ignition key, and drove for a long time without speaking.

When he did speak again, he asked first about Caroline. I told him how she was when I last saw her, at the ship in New York—the surface things only, of course, for he had no right,

I believed, to anything else. Then he asked a few questions about me and about what I was doing and when I had to be back in the States for the fall semester and so on, and I felt he wasn't really entitled to that information either—or wasn't sure if he was entitled to it—but I supplied it, anyway.

By then, the port and Haifa were behind us; we were driving south along the coastal road. On one side, on the traffic island just outside Haifa, stunted, dusty-looking palms; on the other, my side, hillocks of shifting sand, and beyond this chain of dunes, a narrow strip of beach and then the sea, glittering, blue and green and streaks of purple, calm that day; there seemed only faint ridges on its surface, and the waves broke almost softly with a froth of cream on glistening brown sand, on wet shells and pebbles. I remember, too, the stabbing light of the sun and the way my eyes ached, that I took my sunglasses from my purse and put them on, and that before I shut my purse I saw the packet of cigarettes and, remembering my new habit, took a cigarette and inexpertly lit it.

Gideon glanced at me as I did so, but said nothing. How could he? He was smoking, and the car ashtray was full of his own stubs. An old habit of his (there were yellow nicotine stains on his fingers), but, for me, one I'd picked up about ten days earlier, aboard ship, after a necking and petting session with the ship's second engineer. I was prepared to be defiant about it, but Gideon seemed amused and looked at the road again. His profile was sharp and clean, the nose thin and straight and long; his dark hair sprung up and back from a high forehead. I stared at him, then looked away.

Now he was talking about the pleasures of sea bathing and about Avigal, how he was sure we were going to be friends as well as sisters, and how the three of us (the four, as it turned out) were going to go places and do things together. Yes, he saw it as a summer of reunion—father and daughter, sister and sister. But I knew it couldn't be that or *re*-anything, since it hadn't been anything before, certainly not a union.

In all, the drive to Gideon's house took about an hour—it was closer to Tel Aviv than to Haifa and past the seaside town of Natanya—and what I remember most clearly of it was thinking that about reunion and Gideon talking about the house and telling me that, when he'd bought the land originally, it had been on an unpretentious strip of coast which threatened to change now, to become what he called "ritzy." "But I told you about the house, didn't I?" He glanced at me. He'd mentioned it in one of his early letters, he said; maybe I remembered that.

I said nothing for a long moment and just stared straight ahead. What letters? But he went on about them, said he was now sorry that he had written so few (none, I thought, none at all), but he'd tried anyway, to keep me posted on what was happening to him. Perhaps, he said, I didn't get all of them (none, none). But, after all, most of those early years had been war years. He'd been in Africa during World War II, and then there was the '48 war, after the partition of Palestine. Perhaps some of the letters were lost. Anyway, that was a long time ago. I had been too young, maybe, to remember most of those letters, certainly the earlier ones. Or did I remember?

"Sure," I said coolly. But I thought that these were really stupid lies. Didn't he realize I'd remember? Not the letters (which he'd never written), but that none had ever come, that he'd never written any. Did he think I was feebleminded? I'd remember letters, wouldn't I? His letters. A scalding anger spilled through me.

He'd stopped writing letters, he was saying, because I'd never answered. Why not? He did not take his eyes from the road as he said this. His sunglasses had slid down a little; he used his forefinger to push them tight to the bridge of his nose. And that's what I would always remember—this recurrent, finally familiar gesture, and the fact that he had actually looked angry as he spoke. As though he had a right to be angry. All right, I thought, let's pretend. I said that I'd not answered because I was really too busy.

For a minute or two, he said nothing, then "I see." And I wondered why I had come, that is, if it was going to be like this all summer, if we were going to go on lying to each other, if I hated him, as I did at this moment, and if I was going to hate him even more, as seemed certain. All right, I thought once again, we'll do it your way.

"Anyway, it's easy," I said coldly. "Letters."

He glanced over at me then, unsmiling. "I suppose so."

I closed my eyes against the searing sun, and we drove on in silence. When I felt properly distant again, when I'd stopped shaking inside, I said in a calm voice, "I don't know why I came. I don't think we can be friends."

"I've plenty of friends," he said. I glanced at him. "More than enough friends." He was smiling at the road, a curly, slightly sardonic smile.

"What shall I call you?" I asked a moment later. And when he just looked at me, his dark brows rising in surprise, I added, "I call Caroline . . . I mean, I call her Caroline."

"I'm more conventional," he said. And he suggested "Father" or "Dad." "Not Daddy, I don't like that much. Besides, you're too old for that now."

When I didn't answer, he said, "Well, how about it?"

I shrugged and closed my eyes and kept them closed. In the end I compromised on "You." Or nothing. I didn't call him Father or Dad or even Gideon.

I leaned back then, suddenly weary, and fell asleep. When I woke, I remember, it was just before we came to a halt in front of the beach house. Batya was coming down the path. I was unprepared for her. And then Gideon was getting my suitcase out of the back. . . .

Beside me, in the window seat, Mrs. Perlberger had dozed off. She slumped against me, her head resting on my shoulder, snoring. I tried to shift her weight, but could not. She settled against me even more heavily, her hairdo still lacquered into place. Finally I sat very still, afraid of waking her, and closed my eyes.

At least, I thought, he will not be at the airport. I'd sent no wires, written no letters. I did not want him there to meet me, not again. I needed time, more time than I had now—to think, I suppose, or prepare myself. And once again I wondered why I had come. The future might be no better than the past. Nothing had changed, I knew nothing could change. How could it?

9

WHEN WE SET DOWN, IT WAS RAINING—A HARD, DRENCH-
ing rain that pounded on the tarmac and filmed the plate glass
windows of the reception hall as though with moving sheets of
heavy translucent silk.

At passport control, I answered the usual questions, said I was
a tourist but did not know how long I'd be staying, nor where.
The man in the dark blue uniform behind the desk looked
skeptical, so I took back my landing card and in the appropriate
place wrote something arbitrary—three weeks, I think it was.
Then I asked him the name of Tel Aviv's largest hotel and
scribbled that in as well.

He seemed happier now, and smiled, made various purple
marks on the card and in my passport and, remarking that it
was not the best time of the year for touring, hoped I'd get to see
some Israeli sun. I thanked him, passed into the customs hall,
and suddenly felt that heady, free-floating buoyancy I always
feel when I need be nowhere in particular, when there is nothing
that needs doing. An almost terrifying, cut-loose feeling. As
though there is nothing that can stop the drift.

Except, I reminded myself, there was something to do—Gideon. Wasn't that why I'd come—to see him? And in a day or two, I'd do it. I'd telephone, we'd make an appointment, meet. Not now. In a few days. By then, I'd have a new airline ticket, I'd know where I was going next. That was most important—knowing all that before I saw him, the way left open for retreat. Meanwhile, I'd arrived as I'd wanted to, as I did everywhere—as though I'd stumbled into this country, yet another.

There were very few people in the customs hall: the passengers, someone with a clipboard from the airline, some Israeli officials, all of us looking sickly under the fluorescent strip lighting. From the other side of the luggage carousel, Mrs. Perlberger, her navy suit visible through her plastic raincoat, waved at me and smiled. Before we'd landed, she'd written her name and address on a scrap of paper and pressed it into my hand. I supposed she was lonely—wasn't everybody? I smiled back at her over the distance. The carousel, still empty, went round and round between us.

It was easy in such circumstances to pick me out of the small crowd: only a few youngish women, most of them chattering in Hebrew, another with a small baby in her arms, still another who frowned and shook her head when the young balding man in dark blue uniform approached her. After that, he made his way toward me. I should have been prepared for it, for the "Geveret Steiner?" said in just that way. Yet it took a moment or two before I could go into the routine again, the difference between Stone and Steiner. He listened to me with ill-concealed impatience and broke in when I paused for breath.

He said he'd come to help me get through customs. I thanked him but said it wasn't really necessary. Someone was waiting, he said—and my heart plummeted. He gestured in the direction of the far-off railing, behind which people stood and waited or milled around. No one I recognized. At least, no one I could recognize from where I stood. I started to say as much, but he'd turned away already, toward the carousel, just as the first suitcases came jolting out.

"How many bags have you got? Is that yours? And that? I'll get it." He took over. I watched helplessly as he examined labels,

58

lifted my suitcases off the moving belt, strode forward. I hurried after him, angry now. The sides of my suitcases were chalked, the customs declaration collected; someone else waved us through, and he was past the barrier with my bags. I could do nothing but follow.

Another man came forward then and stopped. The suitcases were deposited on the floor before him. Not Gideon. I felt relief; also, strangely, resentment—I'd been bracing myself for Gideon. This was someone younger, shorter, narrower. Also grayer than I remembered. In that light, his thick blond hair was almost silver. But grayer than when? I knew him—of course, I knew him. At least I thought I should have known him.

He was saying, "Thanks, Moshe," in English, then the rest—a very short but animated conversation—in Hebrew. I stood there, looking from one man to the other, still unable to remember who he was, vaguely uneasy now and a little afraid, too, because I did not know him; yet somehow I knew things about him, things I could not name. I thought of picking up my suitcases and walking away. Or running, just running. Maybe, like a wild animal scenting danger, I always sense the snare.

They stopped talking. The man called Moshe turned to me, trusted I hadn't smuggled in anything much, laughed, shook hands with me, and left. But we did not touch, the other man and I; for a couple of minutes, we didn't even look at each other directly. I looked past him and saw only the jut of his cheekbone. I don't know what he saw. His first words were apologetic. He was sorry that he'd talked so long to Moshe, neglected me. I reassured him. All around us people embraced, walked off together talking, laughing, even crying. We talked, too—about my flight, the delay in Rome, Roman weather. His manner throughout all this was formal, almost ambassadorial: he was too finely bred. At some time in the past, I realized, I must have noted that. I might even have admired it. But when?

Then a blast of female voice and static issued from a loudspeaker. I winced, he turned his head, I glimpsed the bone-hard edge of his profile—and knew suddenly where I'd seen it—*him*. In the doorway of my kitchen in New York, seven years before: Avigal's husband.

59

I felt a surge of relief—remembering at last—but that ebbed too quickly. The uneasiness returned. I said, "How did you know I'd be on this flight?" It sounded less a question than a challenge.

"That was Gideon," he said. The tone was mild. "He managed to find out."

"How?"

He shrugged. "I suppose through El Al. How else? He has friends there—high and low." He smiled at the lame joke. A multitude of fine lines radiated from the corners of his eyes.

"And if I'd changed airlines?"

"You didn't," he pointed out.

"But if I had?"

He gave me a long, curious look. "Well, Gideon has lots of friends."

"You, too," I said.

He nodded in amiable agreement, his smile broadening. "Except," he corrected, "Moshe and I were in the same army unit once, that's all. I was lucky he remembered me. So he's hardly *proteksia.*"

I looked at him blankly.

"You Americans call it 'pull'," he said.

"And Gideon has it."

He nodded again.

"How nice for him."

My sarcasm gave him pause, but only for a moment. An awkward moment. Our eyes met and locked. His slid away first. The next thing he said was that he had his car, he'd drive me. He didn't say "anywhere," and I wanted that made clear. I said I wanted to go to Tel Aviv. That is, if it were not out of his way. I'd take a cab otherwise. He did not quite respond to this. At least, he said nothing, but he seemed to be waiting for something more, an alert, thoughtful expression on his face—the smile had faded—and his head tilted, almost birdlike, a little to one side.

All right, I thought, all right. I said I had a hotel reservation. He wanted to know which hotel. I gave the only name I knew, the one provided by the passport official—a grandiose establishment. I saw the amusement flicker in his eyes. I flushed, looked past him. That's when he stooped, picked up my bags, and carried them over to the plate glass wall of the terminal, close by the doors. He told me to wait there—that's all he said. I wanted to ask again if it was out of his way, but the doors had swooshed open, he was outside, and already out of reach of my voice. He stopped for a moment under the overhang—I watched him— and put up his jacket collar. Then he sprinted across the streaming pavement and disappeared around the far corner of the building.

I thought about his eyes then. The pale irises were a most peculiar color, and maybe no color at all. Hardly blue, yet not gray. Like water when it rises from a bed of quartz, out of crystal only faintly blue, all the impurities lifted out—and the whites luminous. They had disturbed me then, too—seven years before, I mean—his eyes. They were eyes that judged; utterly impersonal. Gentle, perhaps, but also rather cold. So clear they seemed transparent.

But maybe all this is imagination. Maybe I did not think about his eyes then; maybe that came later.

The rain stopped, started. The car window, rolled down on his side a scant inch or two, leaked cool drafts, and now and then I felt fine spray on my cheek or hands.

We plowed through deep pools of rain. The splash of water, the intermittent whine of the windshield wipers—those were the only sounds for a while. He was the one to break the silence. When we were about fifteen minutes on the road, he observed that it was just as well, the weather being what it was, that Gideon would not be leaving the hospital that day. This confused me. The fact is, I had not really thought about where Gideon might be. I'd just assumed he'd be at home—at home and waiting. But Gideon was in the hospital; it was the second time, he said, mostly for tests. He relayed this information without apparent emotion and without taking his eyes from the road.

I managed something vague to suit the occasion. I said something about calling Gideon very soon, as soon as I got settled and maybe looked around a little. When he did not reply, I was going

61

to say something more—something inane about sightseeing—
but I stopped in time. There was silence again. I looked out the
window on my side at fields stretching, it seemed, for miles,
sodden and empty.

Then he asked if I'd mind if he rolled down his window a
little more, and I said no, the air would be nice and, anyhow, it
could not be much longer—could it?—to Tel Aviv. I'd already
asked that question. Now I looked at my watch and asked how
much longer. The second time, or the third.

"Not far," he said.

Our conversation, such as it was, ground to another halt.

Five minutes later, the huge green and white sign loomed up
beside the road. Tel Aviv, it said, in Hebrew and English; there
was an arrow, a number. So now I knew. No comfort in that,
however. We drove past the sign, then past the turnoff, where
other cars went right and were gone. It began to rain harder.

"You passed the turnoff," I said.

"I know."

"Is there another one up ahead?"

He shook his head.

"You'll have to turn around then, won't you?" I said. He
could hear the anger in my voice. He could not have known,
though, how trapped I felt at that moment—as if all the doors
to the outside were swinging shut at once, as if every key in
every lock were turning. . . . Or maybe he did sense it—the
panic rising in me. He turned his head for a moment, to glance
over at me. I looked away, down at my hands clasped in my lap
—ungloved, cold, damp, the fingers stiff. "If you didn't want to
drive me," I said, staring at my hands, "you should have said so."

"I want to drive you."

"Not where I want to go," I said.

"But you won't jump out of the car, will you?" He almost
whispered this.

I didn't answer. A moment passed; another. Finally, in the
same soft, very agreeable tone of voice, he asked, "Why did you
come, Sara?" As if he truly desired enlightenment.

"You know."

"I wish I did."

"All right," I said, lifting my head and twisting around to face him, "let's just say I had nothing better to do." As soon as I said it, I was sorry. Though it was true enough, wasn't it?

Another minute passed. "I can't go there," I said.

"Where?"

"To Gideon's."

"We're going to my apartment," he said, "to Avigal's and mine. There's no room at Gideon's."

"I meant, I can't see him," I said. "Not right away."

"Why not?"

"I don't know why not!" It was a wail, or a whimper, I don't know which. I know I felt foolish afterward. I said then that what I needed was time to think; just a little more time.

"You've eighteen hours," he said briskly. "More or less." And when I did not reply, he went on as though that were now settled to everyone's satisfaction. He said Gideon wouldn't mind not seeing me at the hospital. He'd be at home tomorrow. "You'll see him there," he concluded. "He'll like that better."

And I made no objection at all. I thought no, not tomorrow, but I did not say it. I turned and looked at him. He was staring straight ahead now, at the road before us, and I remember noting that the sandy hair was clipped too close to the nape of his neck and that the exposed neck was too tender, almost fragile. Yet steely, too, unyielding. I felt revulsion—I remember that. Or was it anger? No, I felt repelled by both the hardness and the softness in him.

"You must really enjoy that," I said coldly.

"What?"

"You know," I said. "Directing other people's lives."

But my accusation, I saw, did not upset him, nor did it surprise him either. Others must have accused him of this before, I thought. And maybe it was true. Indeed, he seemed to be considering it carefully, turning it over in his mind.

"As a matter of fact," he said finally, in a neutral tone, "I don't like it much."

"Then you think it's your duty."

For answer this time, he smiled. An aloof, infuriating smile. I looked away again, taking his face, that smile, with me.

63

Ahead, over the road, was a broad span of footbridge—newly, brightly orange, shiny wet. I gave all my attention to that. Even today, I can summon up that bridge, the precise curve of it, the steel ribs in the ceiling, the car entering the shadows, sliding out again into the shimmering, silvery light. I can summon it up, and that smile, too. And that lingering silence.

"I don't remember your name," I said after a time.

He glanced over at me. It seemed to amuse him, what I'd said, and he did not supply it, not until much later. By then, though, I had remembered. Joshua.

10

I OUGHT TO SPEAK OF AVIGAL . . . MY SISTER . . . MY ALL-
Jewish half-sister . . . my baby sister: Avigal is three weeks
younger than I.

We were not friends, Avigal and I, could not have been. In
a sense we are children of the harem—ancient, biblical children,
whose connection is one of diluted blood, whose natural condition, I suppose, is rivalry. . . .

We were born, as I said, within three weeks of each other:
conceived, then, within days—maybe within hours—of each
other. Maybe on the same dark night. I am the older, but it
could just as easily have been Avigal. Gideon, even at that tender
age—he was no more than twenty-four—may have fancied himself the patriarch, moving between the separate and (I imagine)
the widely separated beds of our mothers, a Jacob mounting his
Leah from a sense of duty, since he was married to her, then
going to—or, more likely, coming from—the more heated, the
more desired bed of Rachel. That is the way it must have happened, but I can't be sure. I have not asked many questions, nor
have I been offered many answers. As for Avigal, I did not even

know she existed, not until the day I sailed for Israel, the summer I was seventeen.

You expect a father. I mean, you know that somewhere there must be, or must have been, a father—even if you have never seen him, not to remember. A sister, however, or a brother . . . no, there is not, as far as anyone knows, a brother.

Avigal—or the fact of Avigal—was a going-away gift from my mother. Or my punishment, maybe: having been given the freedom to choose, I had then inexplicably chosen to do the wrong thing. Or she may have thought it politic to inform me on that day, so that I would have plenty of time to think about it on the way over.

She told me about Avigal, and then about Avigal's mother, Yudit, whom Gideon had married when Avigal was three years old (it took that long, apparently, to get a divorce from my mother) and whom he had divorced also some nine years later.

Caroline speaking softly, sitting across from me, the little table between us, in the crowded tourist-class lounge of the small Israeli liner; twisting her head toward some new burst of laughter, toward others at other little tables, their paper cups foaming farewell champagne, Caroline did not look unhappy. She was wearing an absent-minded smile, in fact, the smile she employs when there are truths to tell which have nothing to do with her. In choosing to see my father, I'd chosen this too: the sordid personal history, this unknown sister, these people, all this noise. None of it her business; all mine now, her smile suggested, and welcome to it.

Now that I think of it, she smiled like that often: the pale thick lashes lowered, eyes gone a trifle blank, as though she could not quite focus on the object before her but was peering at, and seeing, pleasanter things. She may smile that way in her laboratory, as she slices and lifts away layer after layer of tissue, folds each back so neatly, even in welling blood; as she reaches and notes the still faintly beating heart of some small animal; as she comes, at last, to the tumor—the always induced tumor—which now lies exposed. Or, perhaps, the smile is a little more sympathetic. For tumor, read truth: Caroline, I think, reads it that way.

66

Now, having told me about my father, she went down and stood on the dock with others and waved. One slim white arm, lightly dusted with freckles, which soon she let limply fall. I did not wave back; I don't know why, exactly. After all, I did not blame her. Avigal was surely not *her* fault. We stood and looked at each other over the distance, I at the rail, she down on the dock, not smiling now, not calling out to each other. Long before the ship began to move into the river, I turned away. Or she did —she turned first and walked away. The culmination, you might say, the last in a long, long series of non-events. The alteration almost too subtle for detection, but we both recognized it, knew it for what it was. Characteristically, we marked it with silence.

So it was that I came to Gideon armed and armored. Divested of certain things, newly possessed of others, steel plating still intact. And those first hours, which I have since relived too often—that sparse dialogue, that dumb choreography—that was a collaboration. I must give credit to myself as well as to Caroline, and surely Gideon deserves some, too. He was always a principal actor, wasn't he?

We were alone that first week, Gideon and I—that is, if you don't count Batya, his roommate that summer and for a year before and several thereafter. Batya was slightly taller than Gideon, quite a bit younger, with long legs almost too slender for her breadth of flat hip. She was, or had been, a secretary at the institute where Gideon did his research in physics; but now, seemingly, her main occupation was what the zoologists call "grooming"—intent and intensive care of the body. A great golden cat. I remember looking up once and finding her eyes— like a cat's—fixed unblinkingly on me. She, too, said little that week, and by the eighth day, the day that Avigal came, Gideon himself had also almost retreated into silence, and into silent watching.

Every once in a while, though, he tried again. Perhaps he could not bear it that the only voices should issue from the radio —the classical music announced, the hourly newscasts. And maybe the other noise—the whistle of the kettle, water running in the kitchen sink, the clink of china against silver, the clatter of Batya's wooden clogs across the tiled floors—maybe these sounded ominous to him against a background of unnatural silence. Not so for me. I found these sounds, this silence, comforting. I was used to silence.

We were sitting, the three of us, on the stone terrace at the front of the house on the day Avigal came. It was late afternoon, a little cooler, and Gideon got up and went to turn on the sprinklers on the front lawn. When he came back he began his questions again: What had I decided? (His voice, at first, gentle.) Where would I like to go, once Avigal arrived? What would I like to see?

I shrugged. And turned another page of the book in my lap. "You don't have to entertain me," I said.

"No?" He lit another cigarette and stuffed the burnt match back into the small box it had come from, half-full of burnt matches already. There was a canvas chair on the terrace, empty, but he remained standing, his legs apart, as though bucking a wind. "Isn't that why you came?" he asked me. "To be entertained? To see the country? Do a little touring? Round out that expensive education?"

I said nothing. I didn't even glance up from my book.

"You certainly didn't come to see me."

I wasn't accustomed to that, to such unmistakable resentment, such anger. It frightened me a little, and excited me, too. Almost pleasurably.

One more word, I thought, and I will answer. There were no other words. I licked at dry lips and then lit a cigarette of my own .

After a while I said, "I guess I'd like to see the Galilee. You know, where Jesus walked on the water. Since I'm a Christian." I put my hand up to where a tiny gold cross hung, for show, close around my unbelieving neck. To check that it was there.

There was a short, explosive laugh, utterly humorless. Gideon's.

Then Batya turned her head—she was sitting on the edge of the terrace, her back to us, her legs dangling in the grass. She turned and said something sharp to him in Hebrew. His reply, in Hebrew also, was sharper still. I glanced from one to the other. They weren't looking at each other. Batya was now removing yesterday's nail polish, Cardinal Red, with a small wad of soaked cotton wool; the odor of acetone was pervasive. Gideon stared at the road.

Another minute passed. Then he said, "Very witty."

I turned the page, though I hadn't as yet read a word. "I wasn't trying to be funny."

If he was going to say more, it is lost forever. Just then Yudit's car turned into the road and came to a stop in front of the house.

We'd been expecting them, of course. Yesterday, the day before that, tomorrow, or the day after—when the spirit moved Yudit, apparently. There was no knowing when it did or would, since there were no telephone lines to that street and, consequently, no phone at the house.

Neither Batya nor I moved, but Gideon was off down the path almost before the car stopped, and Avigal out of it and halfway to him. They met in the path, she threw her arms about his waist and he hugged her; then, resting his arm on her narrow shoulders, he walked back to the car with her and opened the door in front on the driver's side, but it remained open only a moment. Yudit said something, and he pushed the door closed again, very carefully. He stood in the road now, one elbow braced on the roof of the car, the other arm around Avigal. He was talking to Yudit; he kept talking, but she did not even look at him. She just sat there, in stony, unresponsive profile. The slightly aquiline nose, her full lips, made her an ugly woman, with a honed blade of a face. I could not imagine what Gideon had seen in it, or in her, what he could have loved so much for even a short time, much less twelve years.

A minute or two later she turned toward us, Batya and me. Full-face, she was a little softer-looking, but still ugly. She glanced at the terrace, in response perhaps to what Gideon had said, or to some gesture he'd made. She gazed at Batya, now at another stage of beautification—lacquering her toenails, this time with a shade called Orange Sherbet—then at me, with the open book in my lap. Between us, between the road and the house, the sprinklers clicked around, then back again. Spray fell in the tall grass and wet a rough semicircle of the cement

69

path and the stones at the far end of the terrace. And Yudit's dark eyes—like Avigal's eyes—noted what had once been hers, and then the usurpers; briefly looked up at Gideon—he was leaning forward, being friendly.

But it was obvious she did not want his friendship. She said something to Avigal, who leaned forward and kissed her mother on the cheek. Gideon, meanwhile, opened the back door of the car and took out Avigal's suitcase. Then Yudit turned the key in the ignition, and the car jerked forward. More smoothly, it drove on. The road was unpaved then, a small side road of shifting sand; the sand rose in dust, then settled. The two of them stood watching until Yudit's car turned the corner. Then Gideon picked up Avigal's suitcase, and they came up the path together, ran forward together, laughing, to avoid the spray, then walked more sedately the rest of the way.

That's when we first met, Avigal and I, one late summer afternoon. We looked at each other, and we took full, careful measure. And maybe we saw, each in the other, aspects of the self, qualities we would have wished away or denied, or even destroyed, had we the will and the sense. Or is that too melodramatic? Perhaps we only stared at each other and were thankful that, after all, we were so different.

For we *were* different. Gideon had been judicious with his genes. He'd apportioned them between us as he had no doubt apportioned himself between our mothers. To Avigal, his almost black hair, the texture and weight of raw silk. To me, the ice green eyes. So we did not look much like him, nor like each other, though we did have some physical traits in common. The heavy-lidded eyes, for instance, the almost Oriental slope of cheekbone, the wide, full-lipped mouth; but these features were either softened or coarsened or intensified by the admixture in one or the other of us. Originally, the eyes and mouth and the cheekbones, too—these belonged to our common grandmother; they could be seen in sepia photographs of Gideon Steiner's mother taken in Frankfurt long ago. She was considered beautiful, I suppose. Neither of us partook of this peculiar beauty. Still, we shared those features.

Just as we shared other things that summer: the small bedroom in Gideon's house, his fitful attention for my few remaining weeks there, Gideon himself. At least, it was what Avigal feared—that we shared him. I knew better. He was hers, her father. Certainly not mine.

And now, some fourteen years later, I found I could recognize other of her possessions. The room in which I stood, for instance, the whole apartment—they bore her stamp, were Avigal's unmistakably. Even the man. As much, I told myself, as much as that kind of ownership is possible, even the man.

He'd left me there alone to drive to the hospital to fetch her. Before he'd gone, he'd brewed some strong, dark tea and stacked records on the phonograph. The third and last of these dropped into place, the arm swung forward over it and settled. I stood with my back to the long uncurtained window in Avigal's living room and listened. Mozart again, I noted—two out of three. I was standing there still when the music stopped; a moment or so later, I heard their footsteps on the stairs.

11

I DID NOT EXPECT IT TO GO WELL, AND IT DID NOT GO WELL. Her first words were querulous. "Why is it so dark in here?"

I didn't know. That was too facile an answer, however, so I made no attempt at an answer. I hadn't realized how dark the room had become, but I didn't say that. The only light slanted in from the foyer or filtered in through the front window from the street lamps. I'd been standing there for longer than I cared to think.

"Why don't you switch on the lamp?" She gestured. "Over there." She meant the tall brass lamp on the end table near me, and I was happy to do it, of course, happy to do anything at all just then, however trivial. I went to the table, bent, switched on the lamp, turned my head for an instant and saw the dark window transformed into an imperfect mirror and, in it, all of us reflected. I saw us all at one remove: Avigal, in the full light of the foyer, Josh behind her in the open doorway; saw the timed stairwell light go out and Josh shut the front door. I knew I'd have to straighten, turn, face her, finally say something, but she spoke again before I could.

"You knew, didn't you," she said, "you knew we were waiting for you at the hospital?"

I had no answer to this either, real question or not. Nothing I could say would be acceptable, neither the truth nor the lie. The only sound came from Josh—a loud, irritated sigh—and Avigal twisted around swiftly as though she meant to silence him. She'd got her raincoat off by then and held it out to him. No, she thrust it at him. For a moment neither moved. Then he took the coat and disappeared down the hall with it, to hang it in the bathroom, I supposed, beside mine in the shower. Meanwhile, Avigal kicked off her sodden shoes. On silent, stocking feet, she crossed the living room.

I felt my body stiffen and looked down. The first glimpse of her face had numbed me. Far easier to watch her unshod feet make wet marks on the tiles, damp indentations in the soft, thick plush of the blood-orange carpet—to watch her footprints form and fade—than to look at her face or into her eyes.

I did not meet her eyes. From beneath my lowered lids, though, I watched her, saw her sink into the far corner of the long sofa, her head drop back against the cushions, her eyes close, and found then that I was staring at her, at the skull beneath the skin. I seemed to perceive that already: the chalk-white bone beneath the fine, flat pad of flesh. Not that the face had changed so much, I thought, not that it had thinned down so much; rather, it had drawn nearer to an end, to what it must ultimately become. As though, in fact, Avigal were close to death. Closer, perhaps, than Gideon.

That was the fault of the hairdo, I decided, the dark hair skinned back like that, the double length of scarlet wool knotted so, at the nape of her neck. Not flattering. She was a long sinuous black line against the blood-orange of the sofa, with her narrow hips encased in tight black slacks, breasts small and pointed beneath the cling of ribbed black sweater. Yet, all in all, she had the look, both old and young, of a haggard little girl.

Josh reappeared in the living room doorway. She lifted her head, glanced at him, then turned back to me. "What did he tell you?" she asked, as if he were not in the room with us.

I hesitated. "I don't understand."

73

"Did he say it could wait?" she demanded. "That you didn't have to come to the hospital today? He didn't tell you that *Abba* wanted to see you, did he? That *Abba* was waiting?"

"No." I didn't look at Josh. A moment later I said it really was my fault, I was the one who hadn't wanted to go—not today.

"Why not?" she asked.

But I didn't know what to say then either. In desperation, I said I had been too tired.

"Then you'd better sit down," she snapped, "if you're so damn tired."

I did. I took the armchair nearest me, from which I could see Avigal and Josh, where he stood, still silent, still motionless, in the doorway. I got my cigarettes out of my jacket pocket, lit one, then placed the half-empty pack on the low coffee table before me and a few inches away, exactly parallel to it, the cheap butane lighter. I did this carefully, as though I were laying out weapons.

She found that amusing, I think. I saw that she was watching me and smiling. "Maybe I ought to apologize," she said. There was, of course, no hint of apology in her voice. "I'm not the diplomat in this family," she went on and waved in the direction of the doorway. "My husband—he's the diplomat. So much tact." Her tone suggested that tact was overrated. "Me," she said, "I just say what I think."

"Really."

Her smile broadened for an instant, then disappeared. She said, "*Abba* went to a lot of trouble to find out when you were coming."

"No need." I leaned over to tap cigarette ash into the large ashtray.

"He wanted to see you."

"I would have phoned," I said. "Soon, when I got settled."

"He wanted to see you today." She was studying my face now, dark eyes intent on my mouth, expecting lies, maybe. Or as though she'd never quite seen me before. There was a strange, almost calculating look in her eyes. When she spoke, a grudging wonder filled her voice. "All afternoon he kept thinking he heard you. He got up maybe ten times to go to the door. He thought he heard you in the corridor."

No, I did not imagine that—her surprise. I saw it in her look, heard it in her voice. It surprised her that Gideon should be so eager to see me, so disappointed when I did not come. I shrugged. Of course. I felt surprise myself—then something else, something altogether different. That means he's sick, I thought suddenly, he's really sick. I'd not believed it, not fully, until that moment.

The cup I'd drunk from earlier was where I'd left it, on the coffee table. I reached for it now—no reason, really—just to be holding something more solid than a burning cigarette. I saw my hands were trembling, the cigarette between my fingers, too, and now the cup, no matter how hard I gripped it. The tea remaining in it sloshed around—cold, black, bitter, but still floating that fragile, almost transparent cartwheel of lemon. I stared into the cup. Josh took this to mean that I wanted something more to drink. He came toward me, took the cup from my hands, and retreated with it into the kitchen.

We watched him go, Avigal and I. We knew he'd left us, gratefully; left us alone to get on with it, but without him as witness. To continue and end, I suppose, what had begun fourteen years before. No—much longer ago than that. Not an argument, not a confrontation. I don't think either of us could say what it was exactly, and perhaps, after all, it was better nameless—the things we had to say to each other better left unsaid.

She may have thought that, too. In any case, for a while after Josh had gone, neither of us spoke. I stubbed out one cigarette, took another, then offered her the pack. She ignored it, opened the small copper box on the table, extracted a cigarette of her own instead, lit it, leaned back against the cushions, and in that posture, with slightly narrowed eyes, watched me. I think she watched me. I can't be sure. She might have been watching the smoke curl upward from the end of her cigarette, spread, dissipate.

I know I didn't look at her. I looked past her. Earlier, when Josh had first left me alone here, I'd prowled this room, wan-

75

dered from one side of it to the other, one corner to the other, restless, constantly moving, careful to touch nothing in my passage. I'd resisted the desire to sit in it—to steep in its essence. Avigal's essence, after all. But I felt saturated anyway, heavy. I sat almost motionless, my palm on the pebbly surface of the upholstery, my eyes fastened on the huge vase set on the floor beneath the window. It hypnotized me, the opulent curve of it, the jewel-like glow of deep blue-green glass, the pale bouquet of wild wheat, dry grasses, yellow thistles—the kind, I reminded myself, that leave sharp little spines in your flesh. I stared at all this and waited . . . for the lassitude to pass, I suppose . . . for something to happen, maybe . . . for Avigal to go on. Yet when she spoke, her voice startled me.

She said, "He knew you'd be like this."

"Like what?"

"You know. Like you are." Her eyes were reproachful. "But I told him—I said it would be different. You had to be different."

"Sorry," I said.

She took one long last drag of her cigarette, then leaned forward and crushed it out in the ashtray. The gesture was angry, her face also angry. "What's the matter with you, anyway?"

I said I didn't know what she was talking about.

"Don't you *feel* anything?" she demanded.

I asked what it was I should be feeling.

"You don't even ask how he is."

"How is he?"

I thought she would begin to cry then. I saw her eyes redden, and then her shoulders hunch a little, as though she were warding off a blow, and I looked away. I didn't want to see her grief. It was none of my business. I could not comprehend it, nor did I wish to. But she didn't cry. When I looked at her again, I saw she was comforting herself in another way. Her body had jack-knifed together, the knees up, heels close to buttocks, her arms around her legs, her toes curled into the edge of the seat cushion. She was hugging herself now, swaying a little. A familiar posture, one I'd seen in modified form several times that long-ago summer.

"I told him," she went on, "I told him he had to write to you. He had to ask you to come. He had to try. So he got the address. But then—after he got it—he said he couldn't. Not anymore. He couldn't be sure that you'd even read his letter. He said he'd feel foolish writing." She stopped and looked up at me. She seemed to expect something from me, to be waiting for a denial. But I did not deny it, no.

I felt the blood rush to my face, then, as swiftly, drain away. And it was once again that morning, most vividly that morning, and I held—I seemed to hold—the ticket in my hands again. I'd not felt anger then—that's what I'd told myself—but I felt it now. It was as though long dead soil had come suddenly alive. A new volcano, tremors. My hands were shaking, and my voice. "But he didn't write, did he? He didn't bother. Why bother? Anyway, it was just what I'd expect. A round-trip ticket—that's all. No letter, nothing. No 'Please come.' Why bother? It's only Sara. She'll come."

"No," Avigal said, "not *Abba*."

I laughed rather bitterly.

She said, "*Me*. I sent it. I'm sorry." She looked stricken. "Really sorry. I didn't mean it in that way. I didn't mean to insult you."

I did not believe her, of course. I thought she was lying. Not that it mattered, anyway, who had sent it.

"All right," I said, finally. "I'm here now. Since I'm here, what am I supposed to do?"

She didn't answer at once. I supposed she was composing instructions. At one point, she rose from the sofa and moved around the room. My eyes followed her. Her fingertips skimmed the rim of the vase, the top of the sofa, the edge of a bookshelf. As if she'd felt it slip away, as if she were repossessing it all. A minute or two passed in this way; then Josh came in with some glasses of vermouth he placed on the coffee table. She came forward, picked up a glass, sipped.

I asked again what it was she wanted me to do. Since she'd sent the ticket, she could call the tune—that's what I implied.

"Nothing," she said.

77

I looked up from my drink.

"Really," she said, "nothing. Except—don't tell *Abba* I sent you the ticket. All right?"

It wasn't all right. But I said only, "I see. In other words, I came on my own, is that it?" It was funny, in a way, and I found I was smiling.

She nodded. I don't suppose she saw the joke.

"I want you to know something," I said.

"Yes?"

"I can't feel about him the way you do." But even as I spoke, I saw that she didn't believe me. She thought that couldn't be true—or if it were true now, that it wouldn't be in the future. It would be as she'd told Gideon—it would be different. A delusion, I told myself.

A few minutes later she said she was going to change, since we were going out to dinner that night—there was absolutely nothing to eat in the house. And did I, too, want to change or wash up or anything? I shook my head. She left me sitting there opposite a resolutely silent Josh. He'd turned the records over and switched on the phonograph again, and we listened to Mozart, were lapped gently by the cool, measured grace of the music. Once I thought of asking Josh what it was about Mozart, why him and not Bach, say, and I glanced over at him, but then did not ask. He did not look very communicative just then.

He was scarcely more so later on over dinner. No doubt he regarded all conversation that evening as ours exclusively— Avigal's and mine. He drove us to the restaurant in silence, too. It was at the far end of the town's main street, an Oriental place that smelled pleasantly of charcoal smoke, filled with rickety tables and chairs. Otherwise, the room was almost empty—certainly of diners—but a number of young men sat at two large tables at the back, thin, dark-skinned young men, most of them in open-necked white shirts more suitable for midsummer. Like the tense and hungry young men in the bars of Rome, I decided, though these were distinctly less glossy. In any case, they'd eyed us with interest when we'd first come in but were now discussing women in general (Avigal said) and, between sips of arak or brandy or Turkish coffee and rather more heatedly, soccer.

As for us, you might say our conversation was also conventional—more so in any case than our earlier exchange. Over shashlik and crisp but oily chips and an Israeli salad of finely diced cucumber and tomato and onion, we walked a sedate round dance of memory. A change of subject was like a change of hands, mostly about the seven years since we'd last seen each other. That was in New York, when they'd stopped off on their way to California. At one point—we were then talking about Rob—Avigal suggested that I might afterward have regretted it. She darted a long sideways glance at Josh.

"Regretted what?" I said.

"The divorce." She seemed perfectly serious.

I laughed. I did not say it had hardly been a marriage and therefore hardly a divorce. "No, of course I don't regret it," I said. "It's better this way.'

"He was nice," Avigal said.

I must have looked astonished. Then I lifted my wine glass in mock salute, took a long sip of the dry red wine and said, "If you thought so." My voice was firmly noncommittal.

"I did," she said as firmly. "He was. I remember."

And I did, too, I remembered. It took all my strength to press memory back, to hold it in check for a while. The conversation then came around to Gideon, of course. Came back to him, as it had to, via something or someone. As it happens, via Batya—or rather, something Avigal said that had nothing to do with Gideon at all.

"You're thinner," she said suddenly. She was staring at me, and I hate that.

"You, too." My voice was stiff.

She said yes, she knew, but really she had to lose even more weight—it was the modeling she did. Her elbows rested on the table, her hands on her cheeks. She'd spread her fingers, and now moved the fingertips upward to the corners of her long eyes, rubbing gently, then harder, all the time talking about how she'd begun modeling, how Batya had helped her break into it at first. Batya, who had once been so much in demand by the knitwear manufacturers of Tel Aviv. That was after she'd left Gideon. Unfortunately she was past it now, Avigal said, past Gideon, too. She'd married someone else, but never him. Her one distinction, not marrying Gideon.

I asked then about Gideon's wife.

"Oh, you'll meet her soon enough," Avigal said. "Tomorrow, when we go over to *Abba*'s."

I put down my wine glass. The same nameless panic had seized me. I thought I'd spill the wine.

"About that," I said, and then could not go on.

Avigal just watched me. She waited. And watched me.

For a little while, I said absolutely nothing. Then, quite calmly, I said, "All right. Yes." And I thought, yes, tomorrow. Or better—tonight. Why not tonight? (But I did not say it.) Just go, I thought. Get it over with. That was all I wanted—just to get through it, past it and out. I must have looked toward Josh then for some response, for I can remember his face. He was staring down into his wine glass, with a faintly bemused expression. The desolation I felt then—no, that's not too strong a word—was worse than the earlier panic. And silly. Ridiculous to want or to expect his approval. I didn't even like him.

Nor her.

My mouth was rather dry. I took a last sip of wine and said, "Look, I just want you to understand something."

She did not speak, but her eyes were still on my face.

I said, "It can't be the same for me. I can't feel the way you do."

"You said that."

"But you don't believe me." I sounded angry. "I don't think you believe me."

"But it doesn't matter," she said, simply. "I'm glad you're here, anyway. I'm just glad you're here."

12

I WAS SUPPOSED TO SLEEP IN JOSH'S STUDY. I LAY ON THE sofa, which Avigal had made up into a bed, and tried to sleep, but their voices filtered in through the wall between this room and theirs, the hum of their voices reached me—the sound, but not the sense. Fortunately. The actual words did not matter, anyway. The night songs of insects are like that for me, a reminder that life is going on somewhere else, and this was a reminder, too, that there were people alive in the world with me. I lay in the dark, but my eyes were wide open. Finally, there was a silence. I wondered if they were making love, if she found comfort in his body and if he—if he looked for and found it in hers. Then I willed myself to stop thinking about it, and I did stop. On that first night, it was not hard to stop.

But still I could not sleep. The past crowded into this present: Rob (whom Avigal thought she remembered) and the night Avigal and Josh had come to see me. A seven-year-old memory. I thought I had forgotten it, that evening, but it came back now, all of it unsummoned, as such memories do.

I remembered my apartment in New York, and Rob, and

earlier that evening Avigal's voice on the telephone—which had startled me : so unexpected. "We're just passing through," she'd said. "My husband and I. We're going to California tomorrow." There was a long pause. "My husband and I," she'd said. My wonder that she'd married at all—had found someone enough like Gideon to marry. Of course, I invited them to dinner. She brought her husband, and also Gideon's present, one of a double pair of antique gold chains that once belonged to his mother. Avigal wore the other. Gideon was being even-handed.

As for Avigal's husband, he'd surprised me. He didn't look like Gideon at all, as I'd half-expected, was nothing like him. He hardly spoke, and was not, it would seem, easy with people. Avigal did the talking. All the while her eyes darted around the room, from one piece of furniture to another, one ornament to another. She made some comments but said nothing about the lumpy divan on which she sat. Nothing about the scarred, almost lame maple rocker. (Both of which had come from the Salvation Army Store on West 86th Street.) Nor did she mention the perfectly good bookcase that had been salvaged from someone's trash and painted. Very tactful. She commented instead on the handmade hooked rug (a gift from my Vermont grandmother) and the Swedish crystal (Georg Jensen). She knew good things all right, but she could not understand the bad ones, was finally bewildered by what I myself would call a weird melange.

She looked softer than I remembered. The dark red jersey dress clung, was cut low; her skin was a rich coffee cream. And Rob appreciated her. Of course. As she did him. In fact, the only thing in the room she fully understood, I thought, was Robert.

At one point, as she peered at the bookcase, I wanted to say—I suppose I could have said it—"I'm in the middle of moving." Or "I'm going to redecorate as soon as I get some money." Or "I really don't have time for interior decoration." Nasty, this last. With an effort, I controlled myself, said nothing. I could also have said, "My tastes are eclectic." But would she have understood that? That would have explained it all, I knew—the furnishings, and Rob. Yes, even Rob.

He was acting the host that night. He mixed the drinks, and

told two smutty stories he knew I'd hate. I think the first one embarrassed both of them, but Avigal, at any rate, laughed. She glanced at Josh, her face flushed, but she laughed. At the second story, too. Josh didn't laugh that time either. By then Rob had lifted one white silken ankle and brought it to rest on his knee. As the evening advanced his face grew pinker, he smiled more, leaned back, grew more expansive.

And Joshua became more silent still.

Then I went into the kitchen, and Josh followed. He paused in the doorway, leaned against the frame, and watched the final preparations for dinner. I felt uncomfortable with him standing there, watching; I felt clumsy and wanted to hide. And then, too, I thought he must have misread the situation. He must have seen the shirt on the bedroom chair when he'd gone to the bathroom, seen the robe on the back of the bathroom door and thought—he must have thought it—that Rob and I were married. I wanted to tell him I would never marry Rob (but, of course, later on I did). I wanted, I realized suddenly, to confess to what he might think far worse. Yes, there seemed something priestlike in him, something that evoked in me an unlikely desire for confession, for absolution. I'd never—ever—thought my life and what I did with it was anyone else's business. It was his profession, I decided. His goal, like Gideon's, was truth. Truth, at least, in physics, but truth still. As far as I could figure out, Rob's goal was membership in the Playboy Club; he wanted a go at the bunnies.

I took the casserole from the oven. A new burst of laughter came from the living room. For a moment, Josh and I looked at each other without speaking.

"Does he have many more of those?" he asked.

I knew exactly what he meant. The jokes.

"Unfortunately."

I started toward the door. He let me pass, then went to the counter, picked up the salad bowl, and followed me to the table.

We ate on white Melmac and yellow plastic place mats (Woolworth's: twenty-nine cents each) and drank white wine from my crystal. By then, however, Avigal was high with the gin in

83

Rob's martinis and with Rob's admiration and was no longer interested, I saw, in my strange tastes. Rob kept talking, and no matter what he said, Avigal laughed.

That was what she remembered, I knew—her own laughter. She could not remember what I did. That happened afterward, after Rob had walked them to the subway station, when he'd come back and taken off his jacket. There were half moons of sweat under his arms—I remembered that, and Rob pouring himself yet another drink, coming over to me at the sink, Rob grinning.

"Hey, your sister," he said.

"My half-sister," I corrected.

"She certainly has got the hots."

I glanced at him and put another dish in the drainer.

He said, "She practically grabbed my dick."

"So?" I must have sounded bored—I *was* bored.

"So? So nothing." His arm dropped, he moved away. Another sullen moment, and he said, "You know something?"

"Sure," I said, "you've got a terrific imagination."

"And you're a bitch."

I may have laughed.

"Your sister, too."

"My half-sister."

"You gotta feel sorry for that guy—nice guy—married to such a bitch. Why, she practically had it out—my dick—right there on the street." He was grinning. The memory—if it was that—gave him pleasure.

"What did she do, exactly?" I asked.

He shrugged. It turned out to be nothing—nothing you could see, anyway. Just her manner. "You know—the way she acts?"

"No, I don't," I said, now half-smiling. "But was it exciting?"

He caught hold of my shoulder, spun me around. He was really angry now; he hated sarcasm. He slapped me, very hard, and I took it. Then, because that always excited him, pushing me around, he had me up against the kitchen table and then down on the floor, and my skirt up around my waist and my slip rooked up, and he ripped my pants as he pulled them off and unzipped his, all it seemed in one frenzied movement. By then, I wanted it. I helped him. That's where we did it—under the kitchen table. That's where we made the connection: the only way to put it. I can't even use my euphemisms; a connection was all it was. But it was good. I had my legs wrapped around his waist, and I was moving with him, my hands soapy, still wet. I rocked back and forth with him. Because those times—they were the only times it was any good.

That was the night I got caught, the only time, because I wasn't prepared, though I should have been. I just wasn't expecting it to happen that way. I shivered, now, remembering my panic. Felt nausea, again, remembering that nausea. . . .

I sat up and switched on the lamp that hung on the wall over the sofa. The light, scooped into a cone by the flared metal shade, breached the narrowness of the room. It was not a room for pacing. Ten steps in any direction, and there was a closed door or a window wall or open shelves of books. Across from me, the long table Josh used—all his neat, scholarly paraphernalia. A thick book stood of its own accord, the leather spine rigid. A pile of scientific journals. A jar of pencils, a slide rule. Dead center, a stack of papers, edges perfectly aligned, held down by a small resident rock, cut wedge-shaped to a glittering purple quartz heart. A large ashtray and a pipe, bowl downward, in a litter of cigarette stubs and burnt wooden matches. An almost empty, crumpled paper packet of Israeli cigarettes. All illuminated, everything in sharp outline.

I groped for the lampshade, already almost too hot to touch, and pushed it down and back with my fingertips, tilted it so that the light fell against the wall and was reflected from it, diffused, softer. Then I got up and went over to Josh's table and took one of his last cigarettes. I went around the corner of the table to the window, pushed aside the curtains, and stood there, staring into the darkness.

No moon out there, no stars, only a solitary streetlamp near the front gate. It had stopped raining, but the pavement still shone like black satin. The pine trees creaked in the wind; the pine needles shook and glistened.

I pressed my forehead against the cold windowpane, turned my head and pressed my hot cheek against it, too. Now I could

85

see the top sheet of the pile of papers, beneath the paperweight, and the name in English, Dr. Yehoshua Weiller. For a minute I did not know who that was: Joshua, of course. Josh. Beneath the name his neat, precise handwriting—mathematical symbols, esoteric equations, row upon row of these. They were the connections, the numbers, the knowns of the universe. To find the unknowns. The mysteries might be revealed to him. But not to me, of course. I had many questions for him, and they all needed answers.

I suppose I stood like that for some time. Then I heard a door opening somewhere in the apartment, another door opening and closing. A moment or two later someone passed under the trees in the front yard. It wasn't raining anymore, but the wind was fresh and whipped at his trousers, at his hair. At the gate, he turned right and began walking away.

I wanted to tap on the window. I wanted him to look up and see me. And wait for me, maybe, so that I could go down and walk with him. Walk wherever he was walking. And talk, or be silent—whichever he wanted. Both. Either.

But of course I did nothing. Something in me would not let it happen, or something in him. And, anyway, when he'd turned at the gate, he had glanced up at the window. I knew he had seen me standing there, watching him. But he made no sign at all.

13

Avigal knows about propitiating the gods. She tries to do it, to make "Please God if only" bargains. Of course, she fails in the end, as we all do—errs, perhaps, in aspects of ceremony, fails to make the proper sacrifices. Or just fails. Offers too little, maybe, and asks too much.

On that morning, for instance, her first sacrifice was frenzy. I, too, woke to frenzy that morning, but it was my own, another sort entirely, and not sacrifice, like Avigal's. Watching, hearing, bearing witness to hers—oddly enough, that soothed me.

In the early morning, she beat the carpet, sloshed water over the tiles. Then she knocked on the study door. Had to speak to someone, she said. I thought: in between her phone calls. She'd made several already, though it was not yet ten-thirty: to her mother in Jerusalem, to several friends; to Josh, though he had left only a short time before; even, she admitted, to Gideon's wife, Paulette.

"I'm sorry," she said when she saw I was still in bed. "Did I wake you?"

"I was up."

"Did you sleep well? Was the couch comfortable?" But she did not hear my reply, wasn't even listening, or listened with only a small part of her brain. Already, she was moving away.

The rest of the morning passed that way: Avigal restless, making and drinking innumerable cups of instant coffee, smoking one cigarette after another, talking at length in a breathless, disjointed way; then sudden, heavy silences: the radio, pop music and news on the hour. When the living room floor was dry, Avigal replaced the carpet and shifted pieces of furniture. Then she changed to another sweater, put on her raincoat, left me alone to go shopping for groceries, returned, did some more cleaning, drank more coffee, talked some more. And then her surprising request—that I call Josh for her.

"Can't you?"

"I can, but I don't want to. He'll be mad if I call so soon again." She did not look at me as she said this, or as she gave me the number. I dialed it, gave the operator his extension.

When he lifted the receiver, I said, "Good morning." Behind me, Avigal whispered again what I must ask him.

"This is Sara," I began.

"I know. Good morning."

"Is there a change in plans? Avigal would like to know—"

"I know what she'd like to know," he said. Then he repeated what, he made clear to me, he had already made clear to her: that he wouldn't be leaving for the hospital to pick up Gideon until one, and maybe later. We were to stay at home and wait for his call. "And tell her to calm down, will you? Tell her to calm down, for God's sake."

I hung up and relayed this message. Avigal listened and smiled absently at something over my shoulder. Maybe his irritation was what she wanted; perhaps it was another sacrifice she made, part of the bargain. After another minute or two, she went into the bedroom, and when she came out I saw she had changed her clothes again. She was wearing a different pair of pants now and a pale blue-and-white striped sweater. Then, despite what Josh had said, she pulled on her coat, waited impatiently for me to get mine, and we left the apartment. Too early, of course—and each of us still pursued by our private and singular furies. We hurried forward.

When we reached Herzl, the main street, Avigal suddenly and deliberately slowed her pace. Defiant of her furies. And of mine. Now we stopped often, too often. We stopped at almost every shop. There were many, large and small, strung out along the street, one after another, the merchandise on display in their windows like the things you find for sale in lower-middle-class neighborhoods all over the world: men's underwear and socks, women's nylon blouses with superfluous mother-of-pearl buttons, sweaters of bright synthetic yarn, cheap shoes and boots and slippers, gaudy strips of fabric. In a pharmacy window, Tampax, imported, and tubes of toothpaste nestling in faded crepe paper. In a bakery, a tray of sweet, frosted buns. In a stationery store, thin notebooks, pencils, crayons. The blind, curtained window of a Sick Fund Clinic. A driving school. A real estate office.

I'd say we talked, but the truth is it was Avigal who did most of the talking. She commented on everything we saw, was impatient with everything and denigrating about the town itself. "If you want style," she said, "you won't find it here. Not in anything."

Who wants style, I wondered, but I suppose she did. And what she said was true enough. The town was not pretty. It had a makeshift, almost ramshackle air about it; vigorous, yet at the same time, curiously apathetic, as though the surge of energy and purpose that had set its founding in motion had given out too quickly, and each succeeding surge, though different, was equally short-lived, the energy dissipating, the purpose decaying —even as the buildings all these generations had left behind were decaying. The town, it seemed to me, had not changed much since I'd seen it that one summer morning fourteen years before, when Gideon had driven me in from the coast. It was more crowded now and noisier, and some of the buildings were new, of course, and others older; but the town still sprawled like a huge, injured centipede, this main thoroughfare, its long body, and the fine, hairlike legs, these little streets that were roughly

89

perpendicular to it. Streets like the streets in all the small towns we had driven through then, and bearing the same names—the names of the heroes of Zion: Herzl, of course, and Ben Yehuda, Jabotinsky, Dizengoff. . . . The same sorts of apartment blocks, too, buildings of uncertain vintage, their stucco walls peeling away in large patches; balconies, their tattered awnings flapping in the damp wind; in the front yards, heaped pine needles, creaking trees, gaunt hungry cats prodding at the wet newspaper, the muddy coffee grounds, the orange and grapefruit peel and pulp in uncovered garbage cans. Here and there, there was an attempt at order, at beauty, but it was not often sustained, not very often successful. Unlike the institute, of course. But then, that was almost a suburb; it sat on the edge of the town like some great estate, outside but attached to the squalor of this, well, peasant community, elegant in the cultured, middle-European tradition. At least, that's how Avigal saw it. And that's how I, too, vaguely remembered it, from that one visit.

"But Josh won't live there," she said. "They offered us a flat, and he refused it."

"Why?"

"He says he doesn't like it—living in somebody's pocket, and everybody knowing his business."

A private man, I thought, a very private man.

"But I don't give a damn," Avigal went on. "I don't care what anybody knows about me. Or says. Or thinks. *Abba* doesn't mind either," she concluded.

"Nothing to hide," I said drily.

She gave me a peculiar look. "Neither have I," she said.

We were across the street from the bus terminal now, facing it—a narrow space slotted between the shiny black marble façade of the Israel Discount Bank and a small kiosk selling papers and candy and carrot juice, from which huge, shabby buses lumbered into the street, went northward to Tel Aviv or south to Jerusalem and beyond, to the desert and Beersheba. We watched one of them belch out of a narrow archway, swerve and go north. Avigal turned away. Behind us was a small radio shop, its window full of transistors and two or three television sets with blank screens. Avigal went into the store, and I followed.

The proprietor was a young man with a cloud of black, frizzy hair, who seemed to be an acquaintance of Avigal's. She did not introduce me at first, and we did not appear to be together, I suppose, for he glanced apologetically at her and turned to me first, sensing the foreigner at once, launching into unconvincing sales patter in laborious, fractured English, something about the wonderful TV reception I could get from Lebanon and Jordan just now (if I were lucky in where I lived), maybe even from Cairo and Cyprus (if I were luckier and the elements were not against me). Unfortunately, he said, not yet from Israel. Or not quite yet, not until the next year, for they'd promised television by then, by 1968. Well, maybe; but by 1969—that was for certain. The very latest, 1970. He looked at me expectantly. "If now you buy, you ready," he said.

Avigal listened to all this with what seemed the greatest interest, a faint smile on her face. She waited until he'd stopped talking, then she caught his sleeve and leaned forward, said something close to his ear, something in Hebrew, in which my name was embedded. And something else besides, I thought, for he did not look embarrassed but held his hand, regarding me with unabashed curiosity, murmuring his apology all the while ("*Sliha, sliha!*") as I took it and shook it.

For an instant I felt as though I'd lived through all this before. At least, I'd seen that expression before. Not on his face, of course. He could not have been there, his could not have been one of those sun-darkened, oiled young bodies, one element of that random composition on a blanket on the beach, one of those poised against the brilliance of sky and sea. He could not have been one of those who'd brushed sand from ankle or calf and looked up with curious eyes squinting at me through dark glasses. He was too young for that, six or eight years too young to be one of Avigal's old friends from back then, one of her *hevra*—the boys and girls she'd be with, was with, in the army. To these, years ago, she had introduced me: Sara, from New York, her half-sister, seventeen. Her own age, exactly. Gratuitous information, utterly unnecessary—no one had asked. Besides, it had bewildered several of them, those who could not be sure they had understood Avigal's English (spoken for my benefit alone). Delighted one or two others. One girl with dark hair had wriggled her flower-bedecked bottom in the soft, hot sand and giggled *"Be-emet, Avigal, ha abba shelakh—hoo hatikh!"* And indeed, Avigal's father—and mine—*was* a piece. (I'd learned that phrase on the ship coming over.) The admiration for his sexual attractions, his sexual prowess, too, was merited.

But Avigal's face had hardened, and she'd turned away. Then another of those friends—a tall, lanky boy—had murmured *"Nu?"* and that Yiddish-Hebrew equivalent of "So?" or "So what?" or "So what else is new?" put everything back into the ordinary, into the unexceptional. Depending on intonation or rhythm, *"Nu?"* expressed all shades of impatience, skepticism, boredom. Interest, too, sometimes impatient interest. But not then. Then, that one word had seemed appropriately bored.

But this was not that young man, nor was he one of the others —he who stared at me now. I flushed. *Now.* Odd that reaction, for I had not done so when I was seventeen. Then I'd kept my face expressionless, like Avigal's; I'd spread my beach towel, lowered myself, rather clumsily, onto it, and lay back, my face up to the sun, once again pondering, with satisfaction, on how very different we were, Avigal and I. She with her demented need to make everything known, to leave nothing open to more imaginative constructions. I—well, I supposed I was more like my mother. Hugging my secrets, keeping them locked away in silence until revelation was politic or essential or could be avoided no longer.

I remember opening my eyes and looking at her, sitting near me on the edge of the towel, turned away from me slightly, her knees up, arms across them, head lowered, forehead resting on her forearms; then only her head raised and tilted backward so I could not see her face but only the sharp line of her cheek, chin, and jaw, and down the length of her glistening brown back, stippled in the skin, prominent, the row of vulnerable little bones, from the nape to where the white jersey swimsuit began, just above the gentle swell of buttocks. Those tiny bones were eloquent, were so much better than words; they told me she was

92

a victim. And I, the opposite—a victor, if anything. I felt very strong, safe, and perhaps more than a little superior. Now, fourteen years later, she was victim again. Vulnerable. The same Avigal. As I was the same, the same Sara.

She was now asking the young man for the time. He held his arm out in response, and she, pushing back the sleeve of his bright green sweater, caught at his wrist and held it a trifle too long. Only 12:30. The young man patted her shoulder, comfortingly, comfortably, as though he knew he must do it, and knew why he must, as though he'd done it often. We left the shop.

And went to another, and then another. Avigal bought a lipstick, which she swiveled up and spread on her pale lips, a toothbrush, a bar of soap. At the bookstore, two newspapers—the English *Jerusalem Post*, which she handed to me, and *Ma'ariv*, an afternoon paper in Hebrew—and a paperback novel; she spent a long time choosing a birthday card for a friend. Then, in a small confectionery, she bought a long bar of halvah, wrapped in oily silver foil ("*Abba* loves this"). Here, she asked me the time, but I wore no watch that day, either. The saleswoman heard her, though, and told her—12:55—and Avigal stared blankly into a smudged glass case of noxious-looking pastry. By the time the package was ready and we left that shop, it was one o'clock. The shoe store next door was already shuttered for the midday break. But it was still too early. Gideon was not at home yet, not waiting. If we went there now, the house would be empty, it would be silent. That might be an omen of something evil. It might suggest that this was a natural state of affairs, and accepted. And Avigal could not accept it. So we stopped again. This time at a café at the corner of Gordon, a place veneered in orange and white formica, with a few wet, slightly grimy white tables set out under the marquee. We went inside and took a table at the glass wall.

It was drizzling again, and the few people who were out in the street were hurrying by, intent on their business. Inside there was a middle-aged couple whispering at a back table and a counterman who proved hopelessly inept with the espresso machine. There was the hiss of the machine and the radio, of course, tuned to the army station. Music, news. It was one o'clock, and there was news every hour.

We drank the bad coffee, we smoked, and we agreed we would not smoke at the house, at least not in Gideon's presence. (That was Avigal's idea, but I went along with it.) Then we sat silently and stared at the street, at the scraps of wet paper lifted by the wind, and two torn plastic bags plastered against a narrow tree trunk, then blown into the gutter, to join sand and tiny pebbles whirling around in circles. After a while Avigal got up and went to telephone again. This time there was no answer at all—not from Josh's office or lab (though she had the institute operator ring there several times), nor from Gideon's house. She paid the counterman for the call and for the coffees and asked him the time. One-twenty now. "So we can go," she said. She scooped up all the packages and stuffed them into her large handbag. Her face had a strange greenish pallor. It was almost phosphorescent in the gloom of the café, and she looked exhausted.

We walked slowly, but not slowly enough, it seems. We got to the main gate of the institute in minutes. From there Avigal called the house again; still no answer. But it was too late now to turn back. She tried to waste time, I think, talking to the two guards, each of whom wore a peaked cap by way of a uniform. She introduced me to them—they'd know me in the future. No, they'd seen nobody come, and nobody go, for that matter; not that they could remember, there were so many. So, in the end, none of it mattered—what we'd done that morning. We entered the grounds of the institute, a manicured landscape, walked between clipped hedges under tall, rustling trees, passing one building complex after another, laboratories and libraries. We walked first along the main road, and at the sound of every far-off motor, Avigal turned and stood at the curb of the narrow sidewalk and waited until the car had passed us. Finally we veered left into a part of the grounds I'd not seen before or could not recall. Left and then right, down a small wooded path, past a sad-looking wall fountain and huge circular flowerbed without any flowers, and we came to an area of gardens and small houses and, looming up behind them, several apartment buildings.

94

Gideon's one-story bungalow was still empty, still dark, still silent. Naturally, or unnaturally. We sat on the front porch, on metal chairs slightly rusty, pushed a foot or so back from the edge, protected, while the rain dripped steadily from the ivy clinging to posts and lintel. We sat in that dank cold, shivering, huddled in our raincoats. Avigal had a key, but I did not know it then, and perhaps it would not have mattered to me either. Perhaps I'd have wanted to do this, too—sit here outside and wait until Gideon came home. It began to rain harder.

"I hate this, you know," Avigal said.

"The rain?"

"This." She waved at the empty path, the gate, the empty curving road up which the car must come. "The way it is now. The way I have to live. Having to be here. Or anywhere. Waiting."

"You don't have to do it," I said.

"No, I don't have to. Nobody says I have to." She pushed her hands deeper into the pockets of her trenchcoat, her chin down into the upturned collar, into the scarf around her neck and the warmth of her own flesh.

"Then why do it?" I asked reasonably. "If you say you hate it."

She was silent for a moment. Then she said, "Because I have to." Her voice was muffled in the silk scarf. She was not looking at the path then, nor at the road, but at herself—at the shiny gold buckle at her waist, at the black corduroy knees under the hem of her raincoat, at the tips of black leather boots. She was studying herself, and I know she was feeling sorry for herself. I know that feeling.

The rain slackened, then stopped altogether. Avigal leaned her head against the back of the metal chair and stared up into the darkness between the struts of the porch ceiling.

"Do you know what I want?" she said. "What I keep wishing for? I want it to be like it was for me. I want to live the way I used to live. Just that way. I hate change." Then she turned toward me and said, "That's really stupid, isn't it? I know things change, they have to. But that's what I want—I want nothing to change ever."

"Not me," I said. Or I thought I said it—I'm not sure now. Probably I didn't, for Avigal did not reply. Yet a dissonance flooded my brain, the "not me, not me" like a cracked bell gone wild. Not me, I said inside my skull. Not me. Please. God, *not me.* I want everything to change.

14

SHE HEARD THE CAR BEFORE I DID, AND SHE SAW IT EVEN
before it turned into the road leading to the house. Glimpsed it
through the wind-lashed shrubbery and was out of her chair and
had reached the gate almost before Josh stepped on the brakes.

As for me, I stood up, but otherwise I did not move. I waited
on the porch, behind the drip of rain from the ivy. Gideon was
first; they were behind him. I glimpsed their faces over his
shoulder—Avigal's face and Josh's, and a round face I did not
then know, Paulette's face.

Gideon paused on the porch step, and they urged him forward.
But he didn't move. I was the one this time. I stepped toward
him. It was a short, hesitant step. I tried to smile. I don't remember what I said. "Hello," probably. "Hello," again. Whatever I said, I remember now, it sounded strange.

Then, of course, there was no time, no time to step back or
to think how to meet his embrace. I did not pull away, though;
I did not grow rigid. My arms—as though they were not mine,
not attached to my body, or directed by my brain—my arms
went around him, my palms flat on his back. I was fully aware

of this reaction—mindless, automatic—and I was watching my-self doing it. Paulette's face appeared again, then blurred be-hind him. Avigal put her key in the door. Josh stepped around us and opened it.

So we were not condemned to repetition after all. It was different this time. I pulled back at last, nervously, but just to look at him. He had not changed at all, that's how it seemed to me. Thinner, perhaps, but that might be just the passage of fourteen years. His hair seemed as thick as it had been and as dark; there was only a little gray in it. He was far less gray than Josh, I thought, though he was at least twenty years older. And his eyes, too, as I remembered them—as critical, it seemed to me, and as dispassionate, the same cool, green eyes. I shivered. His arms tightened around me. My chin bumped against his wet shoulder. I let go. I dropped my arms, but imprinted on the skin, layer upon layer of fabric—his coat, jacket, sweater, shirt —all of it burned into the skin of my arms. Through my own clothing. Even, it seemed to me, the flat ribs (which, of course, I could not possibly feel) and the attenuated, weakened flesh.

Avigal did all the rest. She urged us inside with almost grim efficiency, took Gideon's coat, hung it up, maneuvered him down the one shallow step into the living room, into an armchair. He let himself be led. She even contrived, somehow, to tuck a blanket around his knees. To all of which he said nothing. He watched her, however, with a vague, rather irritated look on his face. When she had finished, she leaned over the back of his chair and put her arms around his neck and kissed him.

I watched all this and felt embarrassed, then strangely ener-vated, almost fuzzy. As though the hard edge of me—the hard, sharp edge—were already going. As though the shape I'd fash-ioned for myself, the only shape I knew, were melting. For I remembered the heat of Gideon's body and thought, yes, that was it, I'm wax, but it's all right now, he is halfway across the room.

He was patting Avigal's arm and stroking her wrist, but she must have felt his impatience, because finally she moved away. She knelt beside the electric fire, busied herself with switching it on and positioning it, and asking if that were all right. "Are you warm enough, Sara?" And she asked him that, too. Then she went off to find Josh. He had wandered into the kitchen, Paulette in his wake, for a quick bite of lunch; he had to go back to the lab.

So now we were alone, Gideon and I—he in his chair, I on the long, low sofa across from him, surely far enough away.

I said, "We won't stay long today." I don't know why I said this, perhaps just to break the silence.

"Why not?"

"You're tired."

"Is that why?" He smiled. "I'm also sick, but that isn't a good reason to go either. The fact is I may be dying. So there isn't much time left." His tone of voice was matter-of-fact.

I hadn't expected this cool little speech. My reaction to it, I suppose, was stiff. "I'm sorry," I said, and then I wondered why I'd said that. He was asking for nothing, really, that was obvious —certainly not for my automatic pity. Nothing except that I stay a little longer. Not much. "I'm very sorry," I said. Then I realized that I'd said it again and reddened.

"That's definitely what your Vermont grandmother would call 'good manners.' The proper thing to say now." He supposed it was nice to hear even from me, even if insincere; then he began to laugh. Then it was suddenly no longer a laugh but a cough—a hacking cough. He leaned forward in the chair and pulled a handkerchief from his pocket, held it against his mouth. I didn't know what to do. I watched him helplessly, glancing now and then at the door. They must have heard this in the kitchen. Paulette. Avigal. But no one came.

Then he said, looking up at me again, "It takes a while, they say, before the treatment takes effect. That is, if it's going to work at all. But it will work, you'll see."

"Yes."

"I don't want your pity, ever." Now he spoke sharply.

"I don't pity you," I said. "Why should I?"

"Good," he said. "That's not what I want from you." Then he pushed aside the blanket, which fell in a heap on the tiled floor, and stood up. He began to move around the room, pacing the floor as though it were a deck with the sea rolling beneath

99

it. I thought once, in fact, that he might fall, but I made no move to help him. After a while, I got up, went over to the chair, picked up the blanket and began slowly to fold it. This time he watched me—even as I'd watched him. He caught the edge of the library table, perhaps to steady himself, then stood there as I walked back to the sofa.

"Well," he said softly, "that's surprising. You're domestic."

"Not very." I suppose I sounded annoyed.

"All right." He was reassuring now. "I'm not judging you, Sara. I'm just trying to find you."

"I'm not lost," I said, and I laughed.

"Aren't you?" He gazed at me for a long minute or two. I looked away. He said, "But, anyway, I mean discover you. Know you. I think you must know what I mean."

I shook my head.

"Last time," he said, "it didn't work out very well, did it? But we're older now, both of us. I think it will be easier—you'll understand more."

"There's nothing to understand." It was very simple, I thought. I'd always understood it.

His smile was rueful. The grooves that went from his nostrils to the corners of his mouth seemed much deeper, darker, as though in the seams of his face night was trapped. He looked suddenly older. Old.

There was a moment of silence. Then he said, "You're un-forgiving, Sara."

"Are you asking for forgiveness?"

"No, I'm not."

Then I can be what I want, I thought. I began to resent him once more, as I had that first time, and each time he'd telephoned me. What did he want, I wondered. What had he wanted? I felt myself slipping back into the past. I was on the side of a huge glacier; I could catch hold of nothing, could not stop the slide. I looked up to meet his eyes—dark green, brooding.

"I didn't think I would see you again," he said. He sat down on the sofa beside me.

I said nothing.

"I didn't know if I could travel to see you. I didn't think you'd want to come and see me, here."

Perhaps that was the time to tell him. I had promised Avigal nothing. I could have told him then and made it clear why I had come. I could have mentioned the ticket Avigal had sent me and Caroline's letter and Rome and how bored I'd been there. I could have shown him in that way that I had not changed, that I'd grown no older, no wiser, no warmer. But there was no real struggle in me at that moment. I hesitated. Instead, I said, "I guess you were wrong."

The voice, of course, was not mine. It was false, the voice of some other woman, someone weaker than I. Or kinder.

At the front door, Josh was putting on his raincoat. I looked up at him; he said good-bye and left. Paulette appeared then, her dark, graying hair smoothed up and back again, the shiny face matte, once more powdered, and lipsticked. She said lunch was ready.

Gideon rose before I could. He held out his hand. I took it. He pulled me up. I glanced at his watch. I don't think I believed it important then, the precise time, the day, the year. But I did note it, I have remembered it. It was 2:35 exactly. A Wednesday in early February, 1967. And too late, I knew, to add anything to what I'd already said. Too late to tell the truth, whatever the truth might be.

15

THE TEXTURE OF THOSE FIRST FEW DAYS ELUDES ME. THEIR color, for instance, the smell, the very feel of them. The days sift through me, through my memory, my senses, over and over again; become a silky powder, hang for a moment in the air, then settle. Perhaps this is the reason I cannot remember what those days were like exactly. It changes every time.

It seems to me now that they were always wet. There may have been a day or two of sun, but I do not remember that. The elements of the electric space heaters glow red, then orange, then yellow-white. The afternoons are short, the dark comes early. Gideon's living room is not very large, but it has dusky corners. There is a table lamp at one end of the library table, another on the end table beside the sofa, a standing lamp to the right of the window. There is the long, low, oatmeal tweed sofa —where I sat the first day—and three or four armchairs. An ottoman of dark red leather, an Oriental rug. Paulette and I sit facing each other in front of the big window, our feet extended, our toes almost touching, sharing one of the heaters. The odors vary. There is Paulette's scent, spicy or sweet heavy, depending on her mood. The odor of garlic sometimes, or cinnamon, or coffee, or sometimes chocolate: Paulette makes a lovely mousse. These odors linger. And, of course, there is the rich earth smell rising from beneath the wet shrubbery. It is almost any afternoon after that first day.

I flip through the pages of Paulette's fashion magazines. They seem to come in every mail. French, English, Italian. She knits—something white, bulky, like Gideon's sweater. For Josh. But Josh is not there. He is present, anyway—present as an absence. He's there but also somewhere else on the institute grounds, in one of those cinder block buildings across the road, sitting in a small, bare office, working in a laboratory filled with the hulk of apparatus, with switches, gauges, and dials. This image—like the black-gray-white transparency of some never-to-be-seen photograph—drifted before my eyes as I sat reading one day, perhaps two weeks after I'd arrived. And it returns. Again and again, it returns.

As for the rest of them, they are in the room with me. Or I in the room with them. Gideon and Avigal are at the library table, playing chess. So this must be the third or the fourth day, for that chess game began early and went on from day to day. Gideon is talking about the lab now, about going to his office and taking me with him.

"You can meet the lady who knows everything," he says to me. "My secretary. No, let me correct that. The departmental secretary—not mine. I don't want you getting the wrong idea. I'm not so important that I rate my own secretary."

"Aren't you?"

"Of course not. I can't even get you a job. Not unless you type. Do you?"

"Yes." I've answered without thinking. "I don't think I'd like it though," I add. I turn another page of the fashion magazine.

At the library table, Avigal says, "Don't do that, *Abba*." She sounds annoyed.

"What?" Gideon's voice is mild.

"Tell Sara what to do. She doesn't like it."

There is a moment or two of silence, the only sound the steady

103

click of Paulette's knitting needles. Gideon has already wandered away from the chess game, is behind Paulette, leaning forward, arms on the back of her chair. He's waiting for me to speak, regarding me steadily over the smooth mound of Paulette's hairdo.

Finally he says, "Sara doesn't mind."

I say again, "I wouldn't like it much—typing." My voice is cool. The truth is, I do not mind. I don't mind being told what to do. I'm four or five years old again, and trying to please my daddy. A regression. It really is grotesque. I shudder, but I don't realize that until Paulette asks if I'd like a shawl or a sweater.

My reply has satisfied Avigal. But, actually, I have said nothing, only that I would not like being a typist: true enough.

"Come on, *Abba*," Avigal says. "It's your move."

No, it can't have been one of those first days. It could not have happened on the third, or even on the fourth day. The chess game is well along. When it began, Gideon had asked me if I played chess.

"I can't think far enough ahead," I'd said. And don't want to, I thought. I was reading another of Paulette's magazines, an elaborate article about how to strengthen and beautify fingernails, grow them long and lethal-looking. I'd come to the diet part, about gelatin in fruit juice. Or maybe it wasn't an article about fingernails, but about skin or hair. I can't remember now.

Avigal, Gideon observed, was an interesting player. "Inconsistent. But that's what makes it interesting. At the beginning of a game, you can never be sure if she's obeying an impulse or engaged in a classic opening. In short, you never know if she knows what she's doing."

Avigal said briskly, "Excuses."

Gideon moved a white pawn forward: the game had begun.

On that day, too, he'd looked toward me and asked how long I could stay.

"As long as I like," I said.

"And how long will you like?"

I shrugged. It must have irritated him. "A week or two," I said.

"But you can stay longer if you like?"

104

I nodded.

"Nothing you've got to return to—a job, an apartment?" He paused in the questioning. Then, "Someone important?"

I laughed. "I might not go back at all," I said. "I was getting rather bored with it."

"What did you do?" He'd once again begun an aimless circuit of the room.

That question took me by surprise. "Do?"

"For a living."

So simple a question, after all, that I could answer it easily. I told him, but the answer did not please him. Still, did I detect along with his displeasure, a flicker of relief, too? That I was not one of those tarnished doxies, the ones that stand in dark doorways along Via Viminale, swinging their handbags and umbrellas?

"Your mother didn't write that."

"She didn't know."

What, he asked, did she think I worked at? But I didn't know what she thought. I didn't tell her things like that, nor ask what she thought. But it was hard to explain this to Gideon, so I didn't try.

"Didn't that expensive college prepare you for anything?"

"I've got a degree in philosophy," I told him.

"Really?"

"Really." Then I said something quite foolish—I even felt foolish as I said it, but by then I couldn't stop. With honors, I said. And yes, there I was showing Caroline my kindergarten paintings again. Momma in her laboratory with her test tubes, her white mice; the mice were so white they were not even on the paper. Clever. I liked all the laboratory paraphernalia, but I didn't know what happened to those mice. "Nice," said Caroline when I brought my pictures home and showed them to her. But, of course, that wasn't enough for me. I was greedy. I wanted admiration—I needed admiration—lots of it. So I must have painted ten pictures like that, with minute differences. "Can't you draw anything else?" she'd asked at last. A good incisive question. It ended my career in the arts.

Now I flipped nervously through the magazine on my lap

105

and wondered why I'd made such a fool of myself, and with Gideon this time. He seemed, however, to have forgotten it already. He certainly made no comment. Instead he asked, "What kind of work can you do with a degree like that?"

"Sell gloves." My kind of talk again. I almost smiled.

And Avigal giggled. Gideon ignored her. "Can't you teach something?"

What, exactly, was something? But I didn't say that. I said, "It would bore me. I taught once in a high school, and it really bored me." I turned another glossy page.

He was standing between Paulette and me then, between our chairs, staring into the electric fire. He wore the same dark blue tweed jacket he'd worn that first day, the day he came back from the hospital, but the jacket did not hang so loosely now from his bony shoulders. The slack was taken up, by more flesh, I supposed, or by the heavy white sweater. He looked much better, too. An illusion maybe. He took his pipe from his jacket pocket and sucked at it. Unfilled, unlit, yet another illusion. His "pacifier," he called it.

For a moment or two, he said nothing. Then, "You shouldn't say that. Or, for that matter, even think it."

We both looked up at him, Paulette and I. "Say what?" I asked.

"That you're bored. The divine sense of humor is malevolent," He seemed perfectly serious.

Avigal looked up from the chessboard.

"Don't tempt them," he went on. "Don't irritate them."

Paulette tried a little smile. She pulled her feet back from the fire. Her plump legs, still shapely, bare where the ruby velvet gown had fallen away, were now an unhealthy-looking pink. She asked what he meant by "them."

"The fates," he told her. "Or the gods. Or, as the *rebbitzen* instructed you, Paulie, God. Jehovah. *Yahweh.* Who knows? In any case, you're supposed to be grateful for everything. Every minute. Certainly, not bored."

"Were you bored?" she asked. Unafraid of the answer, surely.

"Just a little."

The answer did not distress Paulette. She said nothing. The

106

knitting needles clicked on in unbroken rhythm. "Weren't you?" he asked her. This did not distress her either.

"Never," she said placidly. "I'm never bored with you."

She's a very confident woman, Paulette. A woman who can give up a life that is comfortable if too conventional, leave Paris to follow a transient Israeli scientist home (after a two-month affair, Avigal said, unasked). Such a woman must be confident. She'd left a whole life behind her: two grown sons (she sometimes spoke of them); the carefully tended grave of a respected, wealthy husband (now it was Paulette who was wealthy); a large apartment, many friends; a suitor or two; even, in the end, her religion. Until the day she'd met Gideon, Paulette had been a Catholic, practicing more from habit perhaps than out of conviction. Still, that was something, the ritual; she turned her back on it. She'd followed Gideon here and waited. And waited. And was eventually rewarded. She's a Jewess now—I wonder, sometimes, if that troubles her—and she is also Mrs. Gideon Steiner. The fourth Mrs. Steiner. (I never met or even saw the third Mrs. Steiner.) Probably, in fact, the last Mrs. Steiner. Perhaps, I thought, more than anything else, this makes her feel secure.

I do her less than justice, though, I know it. She's attractive: full-breasted, small-waisted, wide-hipped—yet almost dumpy if the truth be known (Avigal says so), for she's quite short, and the velvety hostess gowns she wears for warmth in the house, though dark and long, do not lend her much height. Neither do the tweed skirts that sometimes seem sausage-tight around her bottom. She surprised me that first day. Nothing like the others. Not Gideon's type—or what I had imagined his type to be. Still, she *is* pretty, in a lush, though somewhat matronly way. And Gideon perched on the arm of her chair now and put his hand on the bare nape of her neck, letting it rest there.

"Contentment," he said very softly, "can get boring, too."

"No," she smiled. He began to caress her neck.

It is embarrassing to watch them sometimes. Often.

Avigal, still at the chessboard, said, "And I thought you were an atheist, *Abba*."

"Where did you get that idea?" he asked her. "Not at all—

107

I'm not arrogant enough for that. Me, I'm one of your old-fashioned Jewish agnostics. One of many." He laughed. At least, no longer trying to pacify what gods there might be. Imagining they could do no more or had already done their worst. Paulette reached out and lightly touched his knee. Avigal kept her eyes averted from this. Dampening her own jealousies, I supposed, sacrificing them to her own gods.

I don't know what day that was exactly. It was, I think, very like the others. The same texture—the soft, small, dense patches of quiet; the talk—more talk than I'd ever heard all at once, more than I myself had ever done. I was raised in a genteel semi-silence.

"We are a wordy people," Gideon said once. "There is a superabundance of hot air in this country which has nothing to do with its subtropical weather." I remember I laughed at this, skeptical. Every newscast, however, proved him right.

Every hour on the hour—only five minutes of news but full, it seemed, of what somebody—or everybody—had said. All the government ministers talked, it seemed, and all the time; all the members of the Knesset, too. Every occasion, from the opening of a crèche to a Hadassah tea, became the occasion for a speech of some sort. All this was reported, of course. And also what Nasser said, and Hussein and the Syrians, Iraqis, and Saudis. The Americans, the British, and the French. All the rhetoric, warlike or pacifist, and some of it was analyzed at great length. Words. And also national calamities. There were plenty of those. That day, I remember, a boy had been killed when he stepped on a land mine on the edge of a playing field up north. A traffic accident near Jerusalem. These and dark hints of other imminent disasters. Apprehension filled the air like fog.

The other sounds were pleasanter. There was music some-times—Gideon was partial to Beethoven, Paulette to Berlioz, and in her more romantic moments hummed along with Piaf. Chairs scraped back or were pulled forward to the table. A tea-kettle whistled. And, of course, the telephone, with its persistent double ring. It was Paulette who answered it, usually. In those first hours, she said, "Yes, I'll tell him. Yes, he's fine, but he's resting now. Yes, tomorrow maybe. I'll tell him." She lied even

108

more, later on. She did it easily, gracefully, her firm voice candid. She promised messages would be relayed but never relayed them, promised vague future invitations, promised to call back, and said Gideon could not be disturbed, was working or resting or sleeping. Not tonight, maybe tomorrow. We'll call you. She put herself between Gideon and the telephone. It did not always please him.

"Who was it?" he'd ask.

And she'd say, "Professor Climmer, he'll call again." Or Baruch. Or Mr. Cohen. Or Avner. And, he wants you to call him in the morning.

Gideon would say, "I wanted to speak to him. Why didn't you call me?"

On that day—I can't remember what day, exactly—she said, "Arieh." Her voice had gone quite sour, and she stood in the doorway, looking at Gideon as if Arieh, whoever he was, were his fault. "He just invited himself. I couldn't stop him."

Avigal had just conceded the chess game and was putting the pieces back in the wooden box.

Paulette said, "Didn't you hear me? Arieh Berendt is on his way." It sounded ominous. He could see into this living room from his own across the way, and he'd seen Gideon walking about, apparently hale and hearty. And he'd seen women.

"Did he actually say that?" Avigal asked, with a grin.

"Actually." He was coming over to say hello, he'd said, just for a moment. "But you know what that means," she concluded darkly.

"It means," Gideon told her, "we should have invited him over before this."

"A vulgar man," she said.

And almost at the same moment—she had hardly finished speaking—Arieh appeared. He'd not knocked, just pushed the door open. If he'd heard what Paulette said, it would not disturb him unduly. One of those men who are cursed—or blessed—with a skin of leather. He took one of the armchairs as if it were his by poacher's right, sank down into it sighing, and his luxuriant rust moustache seemed to blow outward for a moment, then settled.

109

He sat, but could not be said to be still. An antic man in his speech, in all the motions that went with it. He was still bursting with the prodigious energies you associate with youth, and though not very young, he had the seemingly unappeasable hungers of youth also. His broad muscular body advertised it. Even his hair. Even that. He was almost bald, but otherwise his whole body, it seemed, must be covered with hair. It was red and curly and crisp, and it seemed electric; it was alive on the backs of his hands, on his wrists, though you could still see the freckles. On his arms, too, I imagined, beneath the sleeves of the checked sport jacket. Red tendrils sprung like live copper wire at the open shirt collar.

And then he seemed to spread—he consumed our space and light. In return, he radiated blood-heat. Paulette retreated from it, into the chair by the window, but Gideon did not, and Avigal and I, we both came forward to sit opposite him, as though we could bask in it there, what he took from us and, transmuted, returned.

He smiled at me, talked and talked, and all the while his eyes, a black coffee-brown, moved from my ankles to my knees, to the precise spot where one thigh crossed the other and my skirt was too skimpy to cover it. He managed to convey to me in those first minutes everything necessary, but I still don't know how he did it. At the end of that time, I knew he was married, the father of three, soon to be four, that he was a geneticist—and he laughed when he said it, as though that were some huge joke. For it was obvious he considered it not only his vocation but his avocation, too—improving the race. It could be with me, if I wanted. His look said that. He was available. But he did not stop with me. He looked at Avigal also, and then at Paulette. Provided, his stare said, she was still able.

And all the time, he was smiling. He had large, square, yellowish teeth and a full-lipped mouth. I could imagine that mouth moving over my body with little deftness, maybe, but with great gusto. I felt my blood rise. Maybe it showed.

I knew that type, I thought. He was my type. Any woman could have him, of course. I think that's what I appreciated most

110

about him—that anyone could have him. That's what I told myself.

But I think I was glad, too—relieved—when Paulette summoned me into the kitchen. Her body was rigid as she walked to the door. I remember getting up and following her. And I knew his eyes would follow me, would note the ungirdled flesh move under my skirt. I even knew what he could imagine. I imagined those things myself. I knew the type. My type.

16

IN ALL, ARIEH STAYED AN HOUR, ATE TWO PIECES OF APPLE tart, drank two cups of coffee, and smoked three cigarettes, the first lit while Paulette and I were in the kitchen and not yet finished when we returned.

I think she was going to protest about the smoking, but Gideon came toward us purposefully to help lift the tea trolley down the one step into the living room, also to dart a warning glance at her and shake his head so slightly that only she and I saw it. So, of course, she said nothing. She poured coffee and cut the tart, and I handed around cups and saucers and cake plates.

Meanwhile, Arieh talked; he carried the conversation. Every once in a while, he would glance toward an inattentive Paulette, but on the whole he seemed satisfied with us, the attentive, appreciative majority. He'd switched to English for me (and for Paulette, too, I imagine) without a pause in his monologue, an in-depth critique of the way "they" were running the army (no one asked who "they" were). He'd just returned from ten days of army reserve duty, the rest to come later in the year, and he knew everything.

It was just one little step from that to what the Syrians could expect if they continued to encourage and finance terrorists. From there, he went on to Nasser and Hussein of Jordan—whether either would be smart enough to stay out of whatever might be brewing. For there was something brewing; there always was in this part of the world. (In the kitchen, earlier, Paulette had said bitterly, "They're talking about war again. That's all they ever talk about. War. War and politics." She said this over the calm murmur of voices from the living room.)

And what, Arieh was now saying, could you legitimately expect of Washington? The U.S. had its own troubles. ("Right?" he said to me, as though he thought he were addressing the newest American contingent.) And what if it came to the worst —if it came to the very worst?

"All they do in Europe is complain that we overreact," he said. "As if you can overreact to murder."

Near the window the pillow on Paulette's armchair sighed as she shifted her weight. She'd already heard this conversation. In the weeks to come I, too, would hear it again—it or something very like it—at least twenty times more. Whenever and wherever people came together, almost the same words from different speakers, and ending always with someone saying, "I don't think we have a choice. We have to protect ourselves." Or, "No one will do it for us. Whatever happens here, we're all alone."

Now, Arieh said it, then added, "We'll manage."

No one replied.

It was a statement, anyway, addressed to no one in particular. Making of war a low-grade problem in logistics, in technology. Bleaching the red out of it, or attempting to; the wet and immediate blood out of it, though it would be both wet and red enough if and when war came.

A moment later, the mood changed. It was Arieh's conversation, he orchestrated everything; he moved from the international scene to the national, to the Israeli government—ludicrous, he intimated, not to be taken too seriously. If we get through anything (he said), it will be in spite of the cabinet and the Knesset. Then, something about an imminent currency devaluation; the true unemployment figures; the cutback in institute research budgets; finally, a scurrilous story about a government minister. Arieh's wife's father, a doting grandfather, was also the Deputy Director-General of some obscure government office. You could be sure that Arieh's inside information was accurate. When his father-in-law came to visit the grandchildren, he was always candid with Arieh; in turn, Arieh was candid with his friends. And we—his smile said—were, all of us, his friends.

Gideon got up about then and began to move around the room. He switched on a floor lamp as he passed it and, at the far end of the library table, the lamp with the mushroom-shaped green glass shade. There was a little coffee left in the pot, but it was now lukewarm; nevertheless, he poured some into Arieh's cup and into his own. He stood near the tea trolley as he drank it, then made another seemingly aimless circuit of the room. By the time he'd returned to his seat, Arieh had gotten around to the local scene, and Gideon looked a little bored.

It was bemused speculation, this time, about one of the institute wives and an Arab gardener. Or a Druse who'd been hired, initially, to paint her kitchen. Or, maybe, a lab technician. Nobody knew *who* for sure, but everyone knew *what*. The husband knew, too. The question was what was he going to do about it. Arieh looked at each of us expectantly, but no one commented on this tale. Unless the look Paulette threw at him was a comment. Her head swiveled round like a mechanical doll's, and she stared at him with something close to loathing. Then she turned back to the dark window and the scene reflected in it, more comforting at one remove.

As for me, I smiled back at him automatically. He looked delighted. I was the only one to smile, I think. At the same time, I stared at him, frozen—like one of the small animals the snake hypnotizes and then preys on. I remember thinking that, but not feeling afraid. After all, I'd been preyed on before and survived; I'd done my own preying. Now, across the dark inside of my skull, bright little pictures flickered. Arieh and me, us together. I, lost in the russet hair of his belly, my hands on his back or impatient on his shoulders. Or, on a field of white sheet, my throbbing heifer to his bull. He'd be clumsy, probably, but do the job well enough. After all, what more could I want? That was all I'd ever wanted—the job done with efficiency. The job. I couldn't name it. The more accurate, more precise words are not in my active vocabulary. When I need them, they elude me. My age, I suppose. I've always called it "making love."

I felt nothing much. At one point, a little sick maybe, but that wave of nausea was gone in a moment: it rose, crested, receded. And I found I was still smiling at him, still staring, still listening.

This time, to a graphic description of the fevered activities of one of his colleagues, in untiring if slowed-down pursuit of the chairmanship of the department. "Which," Arieh concluded, "he will never get."

Gideon looked surprised.

"There are better men," Arieh said, with a touch of defiance.

"Is better the same as younger?" Gideon asked mildly, now smiling at him.

Better, Arieh said stiffly, meant better. Then he pulled on his cigarette, the third one he'd had in that hour. Held it as though shielding it from the nonexistent wind and expelled quantities of bluish smoke, through which he appraised Gideon. The Old Guard, his look said clearly, about to be toppled, almost finished. Maybe, already finished—if only he knew it. (At that time Gideon was fifty-six, and Arieh, thirty-five or forty. Hard to tell his age—the sort of man whose age is always a surprise to someone.)

The next tidbit was a risk, and he must have known it. Perhaps Gideon's amusement goaded him, or Paulette's stony profile, or Avigal's impassive stare.

In any case, it was a tedious rendition—all the mistakes some female researcher had made. He wasn't mentioning names, he said, but Gideon knew her well. One of your generation, the look said. Unforgivable mistakes—the others in her lab attributed them to premenstrual tension. Arieh knew better. Given her age, he said, which she thought such a well-guarded secret. . . .

At this point, Paulette abruptly rose, gathered her long velvet skirts close, as though to avoid soiling them, and threaded her way out between Arieh's chair and the coffee table—the quickest,

115

the most direct way to the door. She moved swiftly and carefully and managed not to touch him. In her wake, she left the lingering spicy haze of her perfume and a brief, embarrassed silence.

Arieh broke it. "Is she all right?" he asked, glancing toward the empty doorway. He managed to sound both concerned and too knowing.

"Perfectly," Gideon assured him.

Then, before Arieh could say any more. Avigal broke in. It was the first time she'd spoken since I'd returned from the kitchen.

"You know what it is, I think?" she said to him. "Paulette just doesn't like you." She smiled at him very sweetly and leaned back against the sofa cushions; from there, still smiling, she gazed at him.

He left soon afterward, glanced at his watch, remembered forgotten promises, rose, shook hands all around—his hands were a surprise: strong, the freckled fingers long, slender, surprisingly elegant—and then, Gideon followed him to the front door. The "*Shalom*" was loud enough and the sound of the door closing, too, to effect Paulette's reappearance. By then, Gideon was standing in the archway, staring at Avigal and me.

"Unnecessary," he said to her.

"Maybe," Avigal replied.

"And inappropriate, too," he said, "coming from you."

She didn't answer for a moment. Then she said, too innocently, "She *does* like him?"

"Anyway," Gideon went on, grinning, "a real *shvitzer*, isn't he?"

"You always say that," Paulette said. She sounded petulant.

"And you—you sound absolutely bored with me, Paulie!" He put his arm around her plump shoulders, but she stepped away from him, down the one step into the living room, and bent over the low coffee table and began snatching up the litter—the silver, cups, plates, napkins—making a great deal of aggrieved noise. Both Avigal and I watched her. Neither of us moved or tried to help.

116

"What would you want me to say?" Gideon asked from the doorway. He sounded very patient, with the sort of male patience that either infuriates women or makes them feel ashamed.

"That," Paulette said, without looking up. "But not after he's gone."

"When he's here, you mean?"

"Why not?"

"Well, for one thing, Arieh is sensitive."

Paulette snorted and began to move with the stacked plates to the tea trolley.

Gideon turned to Avigal. "Isn't he sensitive, Avi?" His eyes came to rest, unsmiling, on Avigal's face.

"How should I know?" She stared back at him.

For a moment longer, he gazed at her, then turned to me. "And you, Sara? How about you?"

I wasn't sure what he wanted.

"Your opinion. You have one, I'm sure."

I denied it.

The careful examination, he observed, had come to nothing then?

I flushed and looked away. He had read my thoughts, I felt, seen my private pictures.

"Based on your experience, then," he prompted.

"What experience?"

"Oh, of men. You have some, haven't you?"

"My vast experience, you mean?" I met his eyes this time.

"Vast, is it?" He seemed amused. "Well, then, isn't Arieh Berendt sensitive? Almost a sensitive flower?"

I shrugged and said I couldn't know if sensitivity mattered, or if he would be offended or hurt by that word he'd used, since I didn't know what it meant, and I couldn't tell if anyone would be insulted.

He explained the word. Yiddish folk wisdom. Literally, a *shvitzer* is one who sweats—someone who works so hard at impressing you that it's self-defeating.

"The *shvitz*, on the other hand," he went on, "is what the *shvitzer* is trying to impress you with." He came down into the

117

room again and took his chair. "Everyone has a *shvitz*," he said. He made an all-encompassing gesture at the room. "One kind or another. Take Paulie."

Paulette, stacking cake plates now, did not look up, but stiffened and seemed to be waiting for Gideon to go on.

"Paulie's *shvitz*," Gideon said, "is that she's a lady. Right, Paulie?"

Paulette's full lips came together, but she said nothing. At any moment, though, I thought, she might hurl a cake plate at his head from across the room.

Gideon was unperturbed. "Well, she's not. Just as well. I haven't much use for ladies."

Paulette then thanked him from between compressed lips, and Gideon in mock surrender held up his hands, palms out, and said, "No more examples." Someone in the room sighed.

But Gideon was not finished. "By the way," he said, turning to me, "don't underestimate Arieh."

"Why should I?"

"There's always that danger with *shvitzers*. He's a first-rate scientist, among other things. Josh will confirm that."

I said I'd take Gideon's word for it. Then, because I thought he'd expect it, I asked, "What other things?"

And I was told. Arieh, it seems, was a reserve army officer of high rank who had been decorated once already. He was also a very good father, Gideon said, wonderful with his kids. Paulette, I think, was going to add something here—something sharp, and nasty, no doubt—but Avigal cut in before she did.

"I'm sick of that subject," Avigal's voice was almost belligerent. "Really," she said. "I'm really sick of it. I've been sick of it for a long time now."

"Good." Gideon was smiling at her.

"Yes. So, now—can we just drop it?"

Gideon did not reply at once.

Avigal crossed her legs, uncrossed them, and a moment later crossed them once more. The dark corduroy whispered at thigh and knee, the only sound. Then Paulette pushed the tea trolley forward; it jounced over the edge of the carpet. Cups clinked against one another, soiled silver rattled. Gideon went to her,

118

and together they lifted the trolley clear of the shallow step. When he came back to us and sat down at last, we talked about other things.

By the time Josh got there, we were talking about the reasons Israeli soldiers were required to take along their machine guns, their Uzis, when they went on leave. I'd seen them in the streets, the young boys in khaki carrying their guns, and I'd thought it more than strange. Security, Gideon said, speed, convenience. Just in case. Then we talked about the reason for the dizzying rate of inflation. Josh said it was government policy, because the government regarded itself, and was regarded, as an enemy of the citizenry. Gideon said that showed what his politics were—conservative. Josh denied it—but, yes, not socialist, anyway.

There followed what should have been a heated debate of a political naure, but which seemed, from long practice, to be proceeding rather good-naturedly. But I'd long ago lost track of what they were saying. I watched them both, but they'd lapsed into Hebrew.

Finally, when they'd exhausted that, they talked about the weather. Which, Gideon said, would be better very soon. It would stop raining and grow warmer. He assured me I'd like the Israeli spring. As a matter of fact, it was, in a manner of speaking, spring in Israel already, but somehow the sunlight was a long time in coming—in coming and staying. The winter seemed longer to everyone that year, colder and wetter.

17

ON ONE OF THOSE COLD, DAMP NIGHTS, JOSH WAS LATE
getting home. He'd been at a conference in Jerusalem, and
Avigal had said he might stay at her mother's apartment overnight. But he didn't. Hearing his car, I went to the window of
the study, watched him lock the car door and then walk away,
toward Herzl Street that night, though it was now almost midnight and all the shops were closed. It had stopped raining, and
his light raincoat was open, his hands jammed deep in his
trouser pockets, his head bare and lowered against the wind.

About thirty minutes later, he came back. I heard his footsteps on the path below but did not move, not right away—not
until he was at the door of the apartment and I heard his key
in the lock. I got out of bed, then, and crossed the study in the
dark.

He'd switched on the small wall light in the hall and was
hanging up his coat. When he turned, all I could see were the
stiff white wings of his shirt collar, open at the throat, and his
spare frame outlined, a sun in eclipse, by the light behind. He
stood in the doorway facing me, and his long shadow slanted

toward me, framed in pale yellow on the tiles of the living room floor, on the far edge of the carpet. Even so, I couldn't be sure he'd heard the study door open or that he knew I was standing there, and I did not speak: dumb, suddenly, or shy. I wasn't even sure now that I wanted to speak to him; sure only that I had wanted to see him, and no longer sure about that either.

"Aren't you cold?" he said.

Not a question. Not surprised. It sounded too offhand, too casual. As though he'd prepared for this. As if, pursuant to his fears, he'd found this—Sara, waiting.

I was suddenly aware of the way I must look: hair down, lank on my shoulders, bare feet on the cold tiles, my bony ankles just visible beneath the deep ruffle of Avigal's long-sleeved blue flannel nightgown. All of which he could see in the dimness, even if I could not properly see him.

I was naked beneath the gown; the soft fabric now seemed coarse as sandpaper, so that my flesh seemed to draw away from it, to pucker, to harden. I thought he must sense this, too—my nakedness. I shivered and crossed my arms over my breasts, as if for warmth.

He asked if I needed another blanket. I said no, I didn't.

"Can't you sleep?" His voice was low.

I nodded.

There was a moment of silence. Then: "What does that mean? You can? Or you can't?"

"I wanted to talk to you," I said.

He waited, poised in the doorway. He was not going to move toward me, not going to move away, either. The shadows lay like broad, inky brush strokes on his face, and I didn't know if his expression was kind or cruel, bored or interested, and I think I was glad, because I was suddenly afraid to know what it was, afraid to see it.

Finally, he said, "What about?"

"About Gideon."

There was an odd sound—an intake of breath, or one expelled. Relief? I didn't know.

"All right," he said. "In the kitchen." His voice was even lower now; it was past midnight, and the whole world was asleep. As he turned away, he added, "Put on something else."

When I came into the kitchen—shuffled in wearing Avigal's slippers and my own old red wool robe—he was standing at the stove, keeping close watch over a small saucepan of milk. He'd draped his tweed jacket on the back of a kitchen chair and had already pulled out the chair opposite for me. He did not look up, and at first, we did not discuss Gideon.

He did the talking—an impersonal lecture, well-rehearsed—about insomnia. Not its causes—that would be too intimate—but its cures. Pills. Warm baths. The more efficacious warm milk and brandy. (He made an offhand gesture at the bottle and two glasses that stood on the counter beside him, each glass already with its dollop of brandy.)

But walking, he told me, was the best. Long, aimless, solitary walks. They had to be all that: solitary, aimless, long. Otherwise, they did not work, did not relax you or release you, or release your thoughts. Otherwise they accomplished nothing. That's what he did when he could not sleep, when he had something on his mind. He walked. "You ought to try it," he said and, for the first time since I'd entered the kitchen, glanced at me. And caught me staring at him. I laughed and looked away for a moment. The laugh must have sounded derisive. He made it sound a panacea, I said—walking as a cure for all the random ills of mankind.

"Not all, I'm afraid." He switched off the gas, began pouring milk with great concentration and care into each glass, then stirred the mixture. Then, he put water in the saucepan and placed it in the sink, picked up both glasses and carried them gingerly to the table, where he set one before me and the other at the opposite end of the table. There, he pulled out the chair. Or, rather, he lifted the chair out, clear of the floor, careful it should not touch the tiles. At almost the same moment, he glanced toward the closed kitchen door, as though even that little sound—the light tap of the chair being lowered to the floor—might wake Avigal.

I watched this as I'd watched everything else he had done, as though we were not in the room together—his achievement. As though I were sitting at the rear of an immense, empty theater and he were a remote, flickering image on a distant screen. I felt both resentment and relief; it was as though I were in school again and a test I'd prepared for, a difficult test, had been postponed or even canceled. Then, suddenly, inexplicably, the relief was gone, but not the resentment, and I felt anger rise in me and then spill over.

"You're out of it, aren't you?" I demanded; my voice was harsh, shaky.

He looked up, surprised.

"You don't care at all, do you?" I went on. My hands were trembling now. I leaned forward, my elbows on the table, palms on my ears, as though I refused to hear his answer (he'd said nothing); then I clawed my hair back, fingers skinning it back, and sat like that awhile, staring at the tabletop and thinking how stupid I'd sounded, how irrational. What did it matter, after all, whether he cared? Gideon didn't need his concern. Neither, for that matter, did I.

"I'm sorry," he said. The words seemed to be coming toward me over a great distance.

"For what?"

"That you should think so," he said softly, his pale eyes fixed, unsmiling, on me.

"It doesn't matter what I think."

He ignored that. "And, of course, I'm sorry for Gideon."

I picked up the glass he'd set before me and sipped the milk. The fruity perfume of the brandy was so strong it stung my eyes and nostrils, and the milk was still warm. I've always hated milk, especially warm milk. I drank some more.

Josh lit a cigarette for himself, then pushed the packet across the table to me. I made no move to touch it. I found myself staring at his hands—smallish, bony, a few fine golden hairs glinting on his knuckles, a threadlike silvery white scar running from the base of the right thumb to the first joint. I'd never noticed this before, I realized (but did not question why I should have noticed), had not seen it, not catalogued it as I'd done other things, not thought about when he had hurt himself and if it had bled much and whether there was much pain. . . .

"I like Gideon," he was saying.

123

"But do not approve of him." I stared at him and waited for the denial.

"Whether or not I approve isn't important," he said.

"You're right," I said, briskly. "It's not. It doesn't matter."

"Anyway, I like him," he went on. "And there are things I respect. He does fine physics. He's good, he's very good. One of the best, maybe. A really good scientist. And there were no distractions—he never allowed any when it came to his work."

Is that what Gideon called all those ladies, I wondered. Distractions?

"And then," Josh went on, "he's a cultivated man."

"And charming," I said, as if that could make any difference, as if it were worthy of respect.

He agreed. "That, too."

"And kind," I added. As if kindness had ever mattered to me. He shrugged this time, looked skeptical, but did not refute it.

"But you do disapprove," I said, again.

He grinned. "My petit-bourgeois background, my upbringing. It can't be helped. You'll have to make allowances."

Not I, I thought, I don't have to make allowances for anybody. Then I said, "Most men are like that, you know."

"I don't know. Are they?" he murmured. The smile was fading.

"I do," I said. "They are."

For a moment, he merely gazed at me with a detachment almost scientific, as if he were studying a new specimen but one of only minor interest. His eyes narrowed against the cigarette smoke. "In any case," he said at last, "your father would deny it. He'd say he was very different."

I laughed.

"And, in a way," Josh went on, "he is. I don't think, for instance, that he ever needed women very much. Not in the way you mean. Except of course, for the obvious reasons. And not a *particular* woman. Anyone would do—any attractive woman. In fact, he'll tell you that. He'll expound on it. I'm surprised he hasn't done it already. How all he ever needed was a reasonable woman. Hasn't he told you that?"

"No."

124

"He will." He smiled. "But we're not arguing again, are we? I mean, there's no reason to argue. Gideon's life is, well, tame now."

"And yours?" I remember thinking that I should not say it. Then I remember saying it. And other things.

There was a moment of surprised silence. Then, "Very tame," he said. His voice was cool.

"And you—do you need a particular woman?" I went on recklessly, my heart pounding. "Or does a reasonable one do just as well?" My eyes were on his mouth, watching for the answer.

All this is etched on my memory as on a metal plate. I can reproduce it any time, I can re-create it. Everything. The smell of brandy and milk and cigarette smoke. The milk coating my tongue. The strange dryness in my throat. The soft flannel of Avigal's nightgown rubbing against my breasts. The fluorescent light on glossy kitchen surfaces. The no-color of his pale eyes— ice crystal and sun-bleached sky. The purple-brown bruises of fatigue beneath those eyes. And the way his hand moved forward to stub out his cigarette in the ashtray, then upward, the fingertips pinching the bridge of his nose. The way his hand opened, fingers fanning out, and the way he made a shield of that hand.

For I'd gone beyond the limits we had tacitly set. I knew it, but could not have stopped myself. I'd leaped over the invisible wall, or I had breached it. In any case, I'd gone too far. I wasn't sorry. I stared at him now. His hand moved downward from closed eyes. Then he opened them.

"I thought you wanted to talk about Gideon," he said. And then he became very businesslike. He even glanced at his watch. What was it exactly, he said, I'd wanted to say?

"Ask," I corrected, equally brisk. "When I can go."

"I don't understand. Go where?"

"Oh, you know," I said. "You know. Go. Travel. Leave." And I waved airily in the direction of the sea, or where I thought the sea must be: thirty or thirty-five kilometers due west, at the end of long white roads. Past the industrial outskirts of this town and through other towns like it. Past citrus groves and

125

orchards and green-and-earth-striped fields. Past banana jungles and silver carp ponds, right down to the damp yellow shifting dunes and over them, down to the edge of the land, over flat wind-rippled sand to the edge of the water.

"You know," I said again, "somewhere else."

"Are you asking for my permission?"

"Your opinion."

But he said nothing to this. He picked up the glass and finished his drink.

I said, "I'm disturbing you."

His eyes were strange—wary. "How?"

"There's your room. You must need your room."

"I hardly use it."

"Not now, anyway," I said. "You never use it now."

His head tilted slightly; he was studying me. "Is that what's bothering you?"

Yes. No. Maybe. What did it matter? I didn't answer.

"If that's what it is," Josh was saying, "if that's what's troubling you—it doesn't me, you understand—there's a remedy. You can rent a flat of your own."

"I didn't intend to stay forever," I said stiffly.

"Hardly forever yet. What is it—four weeks?"

"Almost five."

"Still not forever."

I did not reply. I picked up my glass and drank the rest of the milk; when I set it down again, I held onto it. My fingers slid up the slick side of the glass and down again, up and down.

"You ought to stay," he said.

"Why?" And then, again, as if I dared him to give me a reasonable answer, "*Why?*"

"For Gideon, for his sake. Because he'll need you."

I smiled. I knew better. Why even by Josh's calculations, Gideon needed no one, no one in particular. (A peculiar trait, and it ran in the family. A comfort, of sorts.) And especially now, certainly he'd need no one now—now that he was better. And he was that, wasn't he? You could see how much better he was. Yes, I knew they could do nothing with the tumor surgically —its position so bad it was hopeless. But now the first set of

126

radiation treatments had begun to work, wonderfully well, in fact. The doctors were very pleased, Paulette had told me, as if their pleasure were all that mattered to her: an amulet against the evil. The tumor had begun to shrink, was still shrinking. Soon it would disappear altogether. A miracle. Those were Paulette's words. Which I now used to tell Josh why I was going away—Paulette's emotional words. Hypnotic.

"Don't be a bloody fool," he said, but his voice was almost gentle.

And that confused me. The tone, those words. The confusion was succeeded by another wave—one of hot, unreasoning anger. He spoke, I said, as if no one ever recovered from this. But they did. Some did. And—I could barely articulate this—he spoke as if Gideon were dying.

"Maybe."

"That's nonsense," I said. But I couldn't look at him then; I looked down at the tabletop instead and sat like that for a long while, head bent, almost motionless. He was right, I knew. But how could he be right? I felt rather than saw him move, light another cigarette. This time I took one, too, and he handed me the matches and watched as I lit it for myself. My hands were shaking. We sat there for a long while smoking; my cigarette burned down, he stubbed his out.

"I don't know what to believe," I said.

I think I expected him to tell me, but he shook his head and said he didn't know what to believe either. Nor what to expect. No one did. Even in the hard sciences, he said, men and women spend most of their lives finding out what isn't so, what will not happen if you do this and this and the other. And then when they find out what will happen—it happens, say, 98 percent of the time or less, or 99.5 percent or more. The old causal relationships, in other words, were all blown to hell, even in physics. So what could you expect of medicine—which, strictly speaking, was more of an art than a science. I stared at him without speaking.

"Look," he said, as though he felt he must somehow make this clear to me, "you toss a coin into the air enough times—say, ten thousand times or fifty thousand—and you can count on it coming down heads, or tails, about fifty percent of the time. But if you toss it up just once—"

I interrupted. "What has this to do with my father?"

He leaned over to pluck the cigarette stub from between my fingers and drop it into the ashtray. "The only thing you can be sure of," he said, "was that you were going to burn yourself with that very soon."

"Unless it went out."

"Yes, unless it went out. Unlikely."

"Possible," I said.

He rose then and stood for a moment, looking down at me. "Just don't expect too much, all right?"

"I won't."

"Expect the worst, in fact. You know how that goes, don't you? Expect the worst, and you won't be disappointed."

I wondered what he could know about that. Certainly not what I did. I'd lived almost the whole of my life that way, so I knew how to do it. Expect the worst. But I didn't say that. I nodded dumbly.

He took his glass and placed it in the sink, took his jacket from the back of the chair, said good night and was gone. The door swung back again when he'd left, rocking back and forth in its frame. It slowed. Finally, it stopped.

18

THAT WAS LATE WEDNESDAY NIGHT AND EARLY THURSDAY morning. After Joshua left, I stayed on in the kitchen, sat there smoking another cigarette while, in the bony vault of my skull, I recited my litany—the chant of exotic place names. Hong Kong, I said; Shanghai, Tokyo, Bombay. An incantation, but the magic was gone.

Then I thought about reasonable men. Perhaps Gideon was right—perhaps he could have lived with any reasonable woman. And since I was my father's daughter, it must be true for me, too. Any reasonable man, loved or not, anyone would do. Arieh, for instance. Not a long-term proposition, but I didn't want a long-term proposition. Wasn't I going soon? So he was reasonable enough. If that was what I wanted. Or Baruch. I'd met Baruch at Gideon's house one afternoon, and he'd already asked me out. Yes, indeed. Very reasonable.

After a while, I got up and went to the counter, poured some more brandy, and stood there drinking it. Then I put my glass in the sink, beside Josh's, reached out and touched the rim of

129

his glass, my fingertip sliding along it, circle upon circle, over and over again, where his lips had and had not been. Quickly, then more quickly, as though safety lay in speed, in this swift, circular motion, as if I could move along the edge of a whirlpool and, if I kept moving, could escape being sucked in—if I just kept going fast enough.

Then I turned on the tap, washed the saucepan and my glass, and then I washed his.

On Thursday morning I woke early, but I did not move until I heard him leave. Then I got up and dressed, walked down to Herzl Street and waited with others for 8:30, when the bank would open. When I got back, Avigal was up. She was in the kitchen, leaning against the one window and peering out at the street, the narrow rectangle of it that was visible between the jut of this building and the next. She held a coffee mug in both hands, breast high, and the wide, loose sleeves of her caftan—a billowing coarse cotton tent, striped crimson and orange and yellow—fell back in folds from slender wrists and thin arms.

I put the envelope on the kitchen table, then went back into the hall to hang up my raincoat. When I returned, I saw she hadn't moved. I made some instant coffee for myself and took the chair that Josh had occupied some hours before.

We talked, finally, but the conversation was not memorable. About the time, and when I told her, she said yes, that's what she thought. She'd just seen a neighbor, a Mrs. Federmann, go by with her morning shopping, a green plastic openwork basket with the usual bread, milk, the six plastic cups of *leben*. So she knew the approximate time—9:15, more or less. Then she talked about how much she disliked watches, and then about the advantages of not wearing one—which consisted mainly, it would seem, in its being a good excuse for being late for an appointment or, sometimes, for not turning up at all. Then she said that if she'd known I was going out, she'd have asked me to buy fresh rolls and some milk. But it didn't matter. We could always eat the stale bread, we could make toast. That is, if I didn't mind. And, finally, she asked where I had been—it was so early. I gestured at the envelope then, still untouched on the table.

"What is it?"

"Money," I said. "About half the price of the ticket." I couldn't be sure if the amount was right; I'd asked at the El Al office a few days earlier and they'd said she must have paid the travel tax, though sometimes, for compassionate reasons, you could get a reduction in the tax or an exemption from it. I didn't know whether she had paid it or not, so I had figured it in, and the envelope held half of what the ticket cost (unless it had cost more) plus half the travel tax. I'd get the rest of it to her as soon as I could, when money came from the States. I'd give it to her or send it, whichever. I liked, I said, to settle accounts.

She darted a quick, sullen glance at me; there was disgust in her voice. "This is stupid," she said. It sounded faintly familiar.

I said nothing. I sipped my coffee.

"You don't owe me anything."

"Of course, I do."

"It was my money," she said. "I could make with it—*do* with it—what I wanted. Whatever I wanted."

At first, I thought this was mere form, acceptable family manners. A ritual unconcern, then a ritual rejection of the money I owed. And slightly silly, I thought, for I knew how small all the salaries were—Josh's, Avigal's when she worked, even Gideon's salary, a full professor's, about a quarter of what it would be elsewhere in the world, in the U.S., say, and with the cost of living as high, or higher. I lit a cigarette and said nothing, did not reply to what she'd said last, but I saw a most peculiar expression on Avigal's stiff face, a strange compound of irritation and anxiety.

"Can't you think of it as a present?" she asked.

I didn't think we had that kind of relationship, I said, we didn't exchange presents.

"We can. We could. Things can change."

I smiled.

She hesitated. Then, "Would you have come to see *Abba* otherwise?"

131

I shrugged. "We'll never know now, will we?"

She straightened suddenly, came over to the table, put down her coffee mug, then walked past me to the door. "Well, it's for him, not for you. It's *Abba*'s present."

She left the room before I could answer.

I finished my coffee while she was gone, smoked one cigarette, then another. After that, I drew the thick envelope toward me, took my pen from my purse, crossed out my name and the old Rome address (it was the envelope the ticket had come in), then wrote hers. Her full married name, in big print letters, across the top of the envelope. I don't know why, but this gave me enormous satisfaction, as though I were back in control again—in this, if in nothing else.

Ten minutes later she came back dressed for the street. She had a modeling job in Tel Aviv that afternoon, showing leather coats to American buyers, and was now dressed with the usual offhand elegance—her beige sweater close but not tight, the brown velveteen trousers sleek, hair coiled in a shining knot above the nape of her neck. Over one arm she carried a jacket—the soft, curly white lamb's wool of the lining the only soft thing about her costume—and a skirt, which she now began to fold. Still standing beside the table, she tucked it into her handbag, then took one of my cigarettes and lit it.

I pushed the envelope toward her. "This is for you," I said.

I supposed that as she had stood there, folding her skirt, she'd been rehearsing what she would say, but now, for a while, she didn't speak; she just stared at the envelope, did not touch it. The envelope gaped; inside, the bills were grimy, limp, some torn and taped together—in circulation until they fell to pieces twice.

"What about the ticket?" she asked.

"What about it?"

"Did you cash it in—the other half?"

"No."

"I thought," she said, "this money might be from the ticket."

"It isn't."

She looked down at the envelope, which carried several canceled Israeli stamps. She seemed to be studying these, to have

132

forgotten about me. Then she said, "You could always do that, you know. Cash it in. That is, if you're so worried about paying me back."

"No," I said too quickly, my voice already teetering, I realized, on the edge of panic. "I couldn't. I'll need it."

She said nothing for a moment, then picked up the envelope, stuffed it in her purse, pulled a compartment zipper closed, and shut the bag itself—a loud snap, metal meshing with metal.

"When will you need it?" It sounded almost a challenge.

"I don't know, exactly. Soon. You can't expect me to stay forever," I said. "I've got my own life to lead. But I don't know." It came down to the usual: I don't know.

"I see," Avigal said.

But, of course, she didn't.

On Friday morning, there was a listing in the weekend *Post* for an apartment in town. Avigal insisted on doing the telephoning for me and talking to the landlord in Hebrew, then on going with me to see the flat.

It was almost ten blocks down Herzl and on the other side. A new apartment in a new building of no discernible architectural style. A boxlike bedroom, with two very narrow beds, and a rectangular living room stretching toward a front balcony. A bare bulb dangled from the middle of the ceiling, and I sat on what constituted the living room furniture: a dark blue sofa with gray arms and cushions, of the sort I remembered from, and bypassed, in my Salvation Army Store days. Meanwhile, Avigal and the landlord talked in Hebrew, their voices resounding in the bare room.

Mr. Spitz wanted far too much rent. He'd bought the apartment for his daughter, for when she would get married, but she was in the army still and not even engaged; he wanted to put some money away for her. Everything had gone up in price, he said. Didn't we realize that? This was a bargain. And another advantage—the way it looked with his daughter, she was so choosy—I could have the flat for as long as I wanted, practically speaking.

133

Another advantage: it was furnished, he said. By which he meant the beds and a wall of closet in the bedroom and a three-burner electric hot plate and a refrigerator of such ancient vintage that I'd thought, at first, it was an icebox. And, of course, the sofa.

No telephone, Avigal said. And not even a place to sit and eat, no chairs, no table. Well, he could lower the rent a little—or, alternatively, get hold of a table and a chair for me, or two (one chair for a guest).

But Avigal told me the rent was still too high and reminded me of what—if I ever got a job—I could expect in the way of salary. It was out of the question, she said. Mr. Spitz followed us down the three flights to the street. At the entrance, he told us he wasn't worried, there were ten tenants for every available rental apartment. "Good luck," Avigal said crisply. On the way home, she said I'd be wasting my money. All that rent for nothing, because when the beach house was ready—the tenants had it until April 15—Gideon and Paulette would go there for Passover (the last week in April that year) and stay for late spring and summer, and would expect Sara to stay with them. Plenty of room there. Plenty of time to study the language. (There must be an *ulpan* in Herzlia; there certainly was one in Natanya—I could go to one or the other.) And opportunity, of course, since it was so near Tel Aviv, to look for a job and an apartment. Numerous jobs in Tel Aviv, she said, interesting ones, and better apartments.

Not, she concluded, as we turned into her street, that I'd need an apartment right away. T.A. was only a half-hour's bus trip along the coastal road to the beach house, and it was perhaps fifty minutes going inland by car from the center of T.A. to the institute.

I said nothing. I felt penned in already, but I just listened.

"What's the matter?" she asked finally.

I said I didn't think that would work out very well. A week or two, maybe, for the holiday. No more. Just as, I added carefully, it wasn't such a great idea my staying at her place so long.

"I don't know," she said. "Josh keeps his temper a little better with you around."

134

"It's my temper I'm concerned with," I said curtly. "And my privacy."

"Too much family?" She was smiling now.

"I'm not used to it anymore," I said. And knew I'd never been used to it.

By then it had begun to rain again. Avigal put up the umbrella she was carrying, and we both huddled under it for the last few yards to the house. Upstairs, in her kitchen, she said that if I really wanted that apartment, I could have it. No one would rush to take it, she said. It was really too depressing. We could get other furniture together, yes, but there was no phone and it cost far too much to install one and the waiting period could be years. But if I still wanted it, I could call Spitz in the afternoon. Or she would do it for me.

I did it. I called him at three, but he'd already found a tenant.

On Saturday, Avigal and Josh drove to Jerusalem to spend the day with Yudit. Gideon and Paulette and I had lunch in Tel Aviv. It was a gray, overcast day, and it began to rain, though not very heavily, just after we drove through Rishon. Gideon sat beside me in the front seat, giving extended and querulous directions about speeds, turnoffs, when to pass another car and when not, and why and why not. He obviously preferred to do the driving himself, but Paulette, who sat silently in back, had been against this little excursion from the beginning as too tiring, so they had compromised.

We walked the length of Dizengoff from North Tel Aviv to the Circle in a hesitant drizzle, shopping the windows along the way. The stores, of course, were closed and shuttered for the Sabbath. Only cafés and restaurants were open. But Gideon was already planning a shopping trip for us on some sunny weekday afternoon soon. He walked between us, one hand cupped under Paulette's elbow, the other holding my hand. When he raised his hand in greeting to familiar faces behind rain-streaked café windows, he raised mine, too.

We met Mr. Pflamm that day. Gideon introduced us with a flourish. This was the man, Gideon said, who had practically

135

saved his life when he'd arrived in Palestine in the thirties. Pflamm had gotten in touch with the right people, got him the required papers—forged, of course, but good as gold, for the British authorities had never found him out—and provided him with a sofa in the salon of the Pflamm apartment on Idelson. The old man still lived there, same apartment, same street, but alone now, a widower, and the other respectable people had long since moved away to make room for the prostitutes and pimps. Oh, yes, Gideon said, he owed a great deal to Pflamm, he who had remonstrated with him but consoled him when, at first, Yudit refused to see him or let him see the baby. We stood, the four of us, under a shop awning, and Mr. Pflamm listened to all this, smiling, nodding.

He was a tiny man, a head shorter than I, very frail and genteelly, shabbily neat. When I shook his hand, I felt skin the texture of old paper and bones that were frangible. He smiled at me and, then, with a shy, almost apologetic look at Paulette, asked Gideon about Avigal and about Yudit—and why hadn't he seen Gideon for so long, for months and months? Busy, Gideon said evasively.

He invited Mr. Pflamm to have lunch with us, but the old man said he could not. He'd just come from a synagogue kiddush, where he'd eaten too much already (pickled herring—indeed, he exuded the faint, rather pleasant aromas of vinegar and onions—and sponge cake) and had drunk too much schnapps. He would not be able to eat lunch at all. "Another time, maybe," he said.

"Another time," Gideon agreed. And they parted.

But I don't think they saw each other again. Two months later, when we were at the beach house, Gideon, reading his Hebrew newspaper, came across the death notice, two columns wide, bordered in black, inserted by Mr. Pflamm's younger sister. Gideon lowered his paper and just sat there for a long time. The sun was bright and hot on us though it was still early morning. Finally, I asked him what the matter was, but he just commented on the weather, the glorious weather. He did not mention Pflamm's death until late in the afternoon, when he spoke about the notice and about Mr. Pflamm's one son—who would be younger than Gideon now, he said, if he hadn't been killed in one of the first skirmishes of the '48 war. There were no other children, no Mrs. Pflamm either. She had died of cancer, which was why he'd not mentioned his illness to Pflamm on that Saturday afternoon. Then he lapsed into silence again; he sat on the terrace that evening until it grew quite dark.

But on that rainy Saturday, except for the few moments after Mr. Pflamm had said good-bye and he'd watched the older man's slow progress up the street to Ben Yehuda, Gideon was light-spirited, even gay.

We ate in a small restaurant in a street off Dizengoff Circle, at a small table wedged in between the sloping window of a display refrigerator case and the window that fronted the street. I remember that meal very well. Sweet and peppery gefilte fish, decorated with bright orange disks of carrot. Roast chicken, a little too well done, and *chulent*, a rich brown stew of beans and barley and great marrow bones and pieces of fatty meat, all of which had been cooking together for sixteen hours at least. Not the first time I'd tasted such food, of course. There were plenty of Jewish restaurants in New York. I'd patronized them as I did the others—the Greek, Italian, Spanish, and Chinese places. "Yes," Gideon said, "like a tourist."

Now, between mouthfuls of *chulent*, Gideon traced the East European history of the dish—a creation of the *shtetl*, he believed, for unrefined, hungry, peasant stomachs. Paulette ate with rather less gusto than we, and halfway through her portion she put down her fork, remarking that it was very heavy and must be hard to digest and that Gideon would wake up in the middle of the night with indigestion and a good deal of pain.

"That's the price you pay, Paulie," he said, grinning at her.

"Yes, for gourmandise," she muttered.

"No, no. For being Jewish." He turned to me then. "And, of course, for being middle-aged. Not you, of course." He patted my hand. "You don't have anything to worry about. Not yet. *Ess, mein kindt.*"

That was Saturday, half of it. The other half was the evening I spent with Baruch. I'd met him at Gideon's, as I said, on one of those febrile, crowded afternoons that, despite Paulette's irritation and Avigal's boredom, had become almost a custom before Gideon went back to work. There were four from the physics department that afternoon: the gray-haired secretary Nehama, who offered to find me a job; Professor Bar-On and his lanky wife; and Baruch, Gideon's assistant, also known as Dr. Amitai.

They'd lined up on the sofa, with Baruch at the far end, nearest me; they sipped coffee, talked in the usual, well-worn grooves, of defense and warfare and the cost of living. Sitting across from them, Gideon was genial and witty but serious when necessary for the first forty minutes, wilting a little in the next thirty but obviously reluctant to let anyone leave, and glazing over, finally. That's when Baruch had leaned toward me and asked if I liked the cinema. I nodded. He mentioned some experimental French film. I hadn't seen it. Neither, it turned out, had he. And would eight on Saturday be all right? It caught me off guard, I must admit. So public an invitation that I could not, with any grace and without embarrassing anyone, refuse it. Then it occurred to me that Gideon might have arranged it, and I flushed. When I looked over at him, however, I saw he was watching us with a faintly surprised look on his face. It wasn't his doing.

I relate all this—the ordinary events of that day and of others —as if they were both the form and substance of my life.

19

ON SUNDAY, I HAD MY FIRST HEBREW LESSON AT AN *ulpan*, and Gideon went back to work. Or, more precisely, since he'd been working off and on at home, he went back to his office, to his several graduate students, his blackboard, seminar rooms, and lecture halls. He walked—it wasn't far.

The physics building is about a kilometer from the house if you cut across grass and go down provisional paths, and only a little farther if you use the main road. It's named for Charles Blum, an American businessman who had thirsted for glory and found he could achieve it by donating a building. But it seems to be not one building, but several—a series of massive white blocks strung together, as though a giant child had played in that meadow and left them undulating over the landscape, snaking forward at one end as though to embrace the ornamental goldfish pond, arching suddenly back at the other as though in revulsion.

I did not remember the building from the one time I'd visited it, but I thought I remembered Gideon's office well enough. It seemed smaller, yet familiar—like rooms you live in for a long time and then leave, and to which you return after an absence.

I'd come at Paulette's behest to fetch him, to remind him, as she'd said, that the bargain he'd struck with his doctors was for half days only at first. A telephone call would not have been enough. He laughed when I repeated our conversation, got up docilely enough at last, took his furled black umbrella from the clothes hook on the back of the door and, when we were outside the building, put his arm through mine—either seeking support or lending it—and we set off at a brisk pace. In fact, I had to hurry to keep up with him; he chose the longer way home.

It had been raining earlier that morning. Now, a moist patina of pale sunlight lay on the hedges and flowerbeds, and there seemed a fine silver mist hanging in the air, and above it a layer of clear air, and above that the placid blue sky. Gideon swung the umbrella jauntily, slammed the tip to the pavement now and then, prodded wet leaves, poked at mounds of pine needles, and asked questions.

First, about my Hebrew class. I told him about the teacher, who insisted that everyone call her by her first name (Hadassah) and upon calling the students, no matter what their age, by theirs. In fact, not only did she call students Binyamin and Baila, but she changed other names to Hebrew equivalents. George became Gershon and Irving became Itzhak, and Mrs. Gold, who had reveled in Rose for sixty years at least, in the Diaspora, now suddenly had become Shoshana. Only Miriam and I had escaped, but our names were given their appropriate pronunciations. I now knew (I told Gideon) how to say my name, and "Hello" and "Good-bye," and even "How are you?"—in both the masculine and feminine.

From this, we somehow got on to Baruch. Gideon commented on what he called the ardor of Baruch's greeting when we passed him in the hall.

"That was for you," I said.

"Then it wasn't a success—last night?"

I said I didn't know, really, but I didn't think so. I then provided some details, dutifully but sketchily. The name of the movie we'd seen and the actors, the sunflower seeds on the floor of the theater and the way they'd rustled under my shifting feet, the clatter of empty soft drink bottles as they rolled screenward. ("You'll get used to it," Gideon said.) Even Baruch's enraged response to this and the fact that, for a moment, I thought he might end up taking on four or five of the town's rowdies in the alley. I even described our hour in the café afterwards—at least, some of it. Over glasses of orange-colored tea, cloudy with sugar and pulpy teardrops of lemon, Baruch strove to elicit some intelligent criticism from me. Failing that, he had dissected the movie himself, analyzed the symbolic elements (too obvious, perhaps), the story (too sentimental), and note was taken and the purpose noted of close-ups, long shots, fade-ins, and fade-outs. Finally, the movie lay on the table between us, in bits and pieces, dismembered. If it had ever breathed, it did so no longer. No (I corrected myself), it was I who called it a movie; Baruch had referred to it always as a film or cinema or, in more heady moments, either as an artistic achievement or a cinematic statement. I felt a little uncomfortable after I related all this, as though I'd been bitchy about someone undeserving of it and were receiving Gideon's approbation. He grinned and squeezed my arm.

In atonement, I said nothing about the final deliberation: *cinema verité* directors versus those of the *nouvelle vague* and the fact that, when Baruch had asked my opinion, I had agreed with him at once. This despite the fact that I had not been following his intricate argument and, consequently, did not know which group he thought inferior. Still, I'd nodded soberly.

He'd removed his glasses, then, folded and placed them between us on the shaky café table—an intimacy. The tinted lenses winked upward into the overhead fluorescence. I may have smiled at him, but I don't remember that; I do remember that his face looked naked, that anyway I smiled in his direction—at the long, raised white ridge of his left ear in a cluster of coarse black ringlets—and that my eyes moved beyond the ear to the slick curve of the counter and the large tin tray of pastry on it, and that, finally, I had smiled at the calendar on the back wall.

But I said none of this to Gideon. These were minutiae which could not interest him.

"Poor Baruch," he murmured.

141

"I guess that's his *shvitz*," I said.

Gideon laughed. At my pronunciation. First, the name Baruch, which I had not said correctly, then the word *shvitz*. He had me say them again and again until, pronouncing judgment, he said I sounded a little less like a *shiksa*.

"Jewish?"

He cast a sidelong glance at me.

"Half."

Then he said I was wrong about Baruch. Cinema as an art form wasn't Baruch's *shvitz*, not the main one at any rate. Like almost all the native-born, Baruch's *shvitz* was the authentic sabra variety. The national *shvitz*, Gideon called it. I must have noticed. But I hadn't.

"They're Israelis," he said, as if that would explain it all. When I looked blankly at him, he added, "That's the *shvitz*— they're not Jews, they're Israelis."

By then, our pace had slackened somewhat—in fact, it was almost funereal. Gideon seemed absorbed in some interior monologue and was oblivious of me, of the passing cars, of people who waved from the cars. A small red car went by, close to him, in the road. Arieh Berendt, who braked, stopped, waited. I was the one who waved him on again. Further down the road, the red car turned in under the stone arch, into the road that wound gently upward between the faculty houses.

"Well, if it has to happen," Gideon was saying, "I suppose that's the best way."

"If what has to happen?"

"The end of the Jews," he said. His mouth curled into the now familiar smile. "As for me," he added, "that's my *shvitz*— how Jewish I am."

I laughed and it surprised him; I was asked to explain the laugh. I said something lame, perhaps idiotic, about ritual observance, about the young man on the El Al plane, about the black skullcap under the homburg, and his earlocks tucked behind his ears, about the pregnant young wife beside him, who'd looked about sixteen, even with the scarf binding her shaved head. I also remembered the pungent smell of apples and oranges and the paper cups of ice water, and the boy telling the steward-

142

ess, in pure Brooklynese, that the food was not as kosher as she would have him believe—it was not *glatt* kosher. He would not eat, nor his wife either.

"I see," Gideon said, "you'd prefer a Chassid, huh?" He was grinning. "I don't look Jewish enough for you."

I flushed. There was, alas, an element of truth in that. I liked categories, and always had. The members of a category are, in most ways, graspable, comprehensible, easier to cope with. Easier, by far, than Gideon's singular reality. But I didn't say that. I defended myself with his acknowledged agnosticism, which couldn't be compatible, I said, with being a member of any Western religion. "It's just not logical."

But again he disagreed. He'd struggled with conscience for years, he said, and had concluded that it was part of the tradition—that questioning of God, even questioning His existence; even, if it came to that, worshipping other gods. After all, the Israelites had worshiped the golden calf, but they had remained Israelites. As he remained a Jew. And it mattered so much to him because he came to it so late. Only when he came to Palestine, in fact.

His own father, who had left Germany in the early twenties, with wife and child, had denied his Jewishness utterly. He always regarded himself as a displaced German. Once, before Gideon's mother had died—she'd died when Gideon was twelve —his father had informed him that whatever had been . . . he'd hesitated and then said firmly, "Whatever has been—ah— done, has been done only for health reasons." (Gideon, telling me this, said that what he had meant was circumcision—"done" was his father's euphemism.)

"He was a stiff, rigid man," Gideon said. "Everything he did —practically everything, at least where that was concerned— was wrong. Dead wrong. But I loved him."

When I said nothing to this, he said, "That's possible, you know."

I said yes, I knew. But I kept my eyes averted.

He wasn't asking for anything. I knew it. I knew if I turned my head from the road ahead, I would meet the same green eyes, as cool, as arrogant, as self-possessed as ever, with nothing of

143

the supplicant in them. For which I should be grateful, I thought. Yet I resented it—that he could and would ask for nothing, yet expect everything. Like Caroline, I thought; in that way, at least, like her.

Then almost as if he could read my mind, he began to talk about her. He said that his father had liked her and had gone to visit us—Caroline and me—after Gideon had gone. Every Sunday, he said. Afterward, he would go home and write to his son Gideon in Palestine the weekly moralizing letter: about a husband's responsibility, a father's, about Gideon's abdication of it, and about duty and, finally, about what a fine, fine woman he'd deserted. He'd praised Caroline's independence, her cool intelligence, her calm, her efficiency. "Not things," Gideon said now, "to recommend a woman to a lover." These letters he'd posted on his way to the 72nd Street Chess Club or, in the morning, on his way to the classes in philology he taught at Columbia. Then the letters had stopped, as the visits had stopped, because Gustav Steiner died. That was the year I'd turned three; I didn't remember him.

Gideon shrugged. "Didn't your mother ever talk about him?"

"Never."

And several moments later, as if he'd struggled with himself over the question and lost, he said, "And me, what did she say about me?"

"Nothing," I said. "She never talked about you, either. Never."

He thought about that for a while. Then he said, "You know? I assumed we were all reasonable people. I thought that the situation had to have some kind of solution, that we could find one—a modus vivendi—and I thought we could all live with it. Something that would do the least damage—I mean, once the damage was done."

I almost smiled. The word "reasonable" again. I wondered if he was going to talk about "reasonable" women now.

"And Yudit, was she reasonable?" I asked. He must have heard the sarcasm in my voice, but ignored it.

"I thought so—I thought she would be."

144

"But was she?"

He sounded rueful, his smile was rueful: "Reasonable women —they turn out to be very thin on the ground."

We were passing through the archway by then, and a sudden wind shook the trees. Overhead there was a rustling in the leaves, and a few drops fell. Gideon's hair was wet; a trickle of cold water spilled down the back of my neck under my collar. I shivered. Gideon still held onto my arm; he was talking about the letters, his letters to me.

I could say he was talking about them again, but "again" suggests repetition. The last time—the only other time he spoke of them—was so long ago: on that first day fourteen years before, as we drove south through the summer heat, when I sat rigid in the car beside him and thought he was lying, when I hated him for lying. . . .

Now, silently, I willed him to stop. But he went on and on. He was talking as though those early letters had absolved him, as if they had canceled out everything else, even his desertion, as if ink on paper had bought him grace, forgiveness, and ulti-i mately, innocence.

He'd dropped my arm, and his hand rested now on top of the green iron gate in front of the house. On the porch, Avigal lowered her newspaper and looked at us quizzically. I tried to push past him, but he held the gate closed. He was saying that, even if they were unanswered, his letters had served their purpose. I stared at his white sweater where it met the V of his tweed jacket.

"Haven't they?" he asked. "Haven't they served their purpose? At least, I wasn't a stranger to you."

He was so sure of himself, and so sure of what he was saying, that I could not answer at once; I stared at him dumbly. Then I said, "Yes, you were. You were a stranger."

I didn't look into his face. I stared at his hand on the gate, holding the gate. I stared at his sweater, at his jacket. And I was remembering the letters and the day I first saw them, all of them.

That was eleven years before. I was home from college. We had had another argument, Caroline and I. One which, as usual,

I'd forced on her. I could not remember what it was about, or what any of our arguments were about. "Spats," Caroline called them, and on that day, as usual, she had waited for my rage to subside, preferring conversation, she always said, when I was calmer. And, as usual, this only enraged me more.

I did not hurl the onyx ashtray at her—I might have done it once—but I hurled my father. And his letters. His "dream" letters—those letters I thought he'd written to me only in his dreams. But they would serve as well, I knew; they would be lethal. Just my talking about him would hurt her, but I *wanted* to hurt her. Or I wanted to make her look at me. I don't know which now. I wanted her to look at me differently, not as though she were viewing the aberrant behavior of some laboratory animal, to look at me and see me, Sara. So I flung the letters at her. I said she had never given them to me, and what right had she to keep them? I don't think—no, I never believed they existed. But it did not matter—whether they were or were not. They were a weapon. And a symbol. I was not certain of what they were symbolic, but of something. And she had stood there as I went through this tirade, my fury mounting, and before I had finished she turned away to her desk. I thought she was going to sit down, freeze me out again, just stop talking. As she always did. Instead she bent down and clumsily pulled out the bottom drawer, took out a packet of envelopes, turned and held them out to me.

At first, I stared at them in disbelief. Ten years—more—of letters. Most of them unopened. All of them unanswered. There were rubber bands around the packet, ten or twelve of these, like the steel bands on packing cases, crossing at intervals, as though she thought she could contain them this way. Now she held them out to me—she leaned back against the desk and held them out, but I did not move.

"Go on," she'd said, and had thrust the packet at me, upward, again and again. Her face was dead white, her eyes somehow too moist. She was shaking.

But I did not describe that scene to him. I owed her that much, at least. If not the secret kept, then to keep that pitiless exchange secret. Besides, it was not necessary for understanding. The simple statement was enough. On the porch, Avigal stood up and folded her paper.

"You mean," he said, "she kept them all?"

"I don't know about *all*."

"And you never saw them before?" When he spoke there was wonder in his voice, as though all this were really beyond belief.

"She said it was just like you," I told him. "She said you never kept a promise." I looked up at him. "Did you promise?"

"Yes." Then he didn't speak for a while. A blessed silence. But he still held onto the gate; he held the gate closed.

"Why didn't she destroy them?" he asked. "When they came."

"Ask her," I said. My voice was cold. I had my own theories, but to discuss them with him would be to betray her in yet some other way. She'd kept the letters; I think she'd kept the photographs she'd taken from the album, and also the lopped-off pieces of the photographs she'd cut in two. But you can never be sure of theories; anyway, he no longer seemed interested. He had given perhaps forty seconds of thought to the mystery and, once again, had set my mother aside.

"When I talked to you about the letters—do you remember? Did you think I was lying?" I could see he thought that explained it—that cold, stiff, long-ago and lost summer—and everything else.

"It didn't matter," I said.

"Of course, it mattered." His voice was sharp. "But I never expected you'd read them like that, all at once. How old were you?"

"Twenty."

"At that age, too. I mean, they must have seemed absolutely ridiculous to you. Those letters were for when you were six. Or eight. Or ten. A little girl, you know. I hope you took that into account when you read them."

"I didn't read them."

"You didn't?"

"No," I said. And remembered the room again. And Caroline

147

at the desk. And moving toward her. Then removing the rubber
bands, one by one, staring down at the top letter, and suddenly
—as if, after all, there was nothing else to do . . . I shuddered
and looked up at Gideon, said no again, and, "I tore them up."

"What?"

I looked away from the gray-white flesh of his face, past him,
to Avigal standing at the edge of the porch and watching this.
Two or three at a time, I remembered, once across, then again
across, and then again. Until the bits of blue and white paper,
and pieces of airmail envelopes and stamps, and the slick scraps
of a black-and-white photograph or two—until they littered
Caroline's desk. And then how I'd picked up the wastebasket and
quickly—too quickly—swept all into it, the remnants of my past.
That's what I thought they were—the minutes, hours, days of
my unknown past, my unlived life. They fell into the wastebasket, then the trembling started, and I couldn't stop. And
Caroline's face no longer seemed so tortured. When I looked up
at her at last, she looked happy. So happy. She'd never looked
happier.

"Why?" Gideon asked.

"Why what?"

"Why did you tear them up?"

"What did you expect me to do with them," I asked, "after all
those years?"

"Read them perhaps," he said gently. "And if not, then why
tell me about it? I wish, in fact, you hadn't."

"I thought you wanted the truth," I said. "That's what you
wanted, remember? To know me. Well, that's me. Was me. *Is*
me."

He shook his head. "Not is." And then watching my face—
searching for something, kindness maybe—something I knew he
would not find in it, he said, "I think I could have lived with that
particular lie."

"Not me," I said.

He ignored that. "As to the other—why you tore them up—I
think I know why. That's your *shvitz*, Sara."

It was beginning to rain now, slow, cold drops on my hair. I

148

waited for him to go on, a sarcastic, rather skeptical look carefully applied to my face.

"But it convinces no one," he said. "You're really nothing like your mother."

20

I REMEMBER THAT VERY WELL NOW—THE WORDS, WHAT happened afterward. I think about it often. The way we stared at each other. What seemed like an endless silence. And how, when I could stand the silence no longer, I asked, "Can we go in now?"

For answer, Gideon let go of the gate, put out his hand and touched my cheek very gently. His fingers were cold and damp, but that wasn't why I stepped back. No, my reaction was automatic—symptomatic. You live long enough with the pox-ridden and you catch the pox. It's a law of nature.

I stepped back then, very quickly, and one heel sank into the soft dark brown soil of the empty flowerbed behind me. But I did not fall. Gideon's gesture was futile. He grabbed at the air, as though to catch me. Then he took a step toward me, as large as the one I'd taken backward—as large but no larger—and he put his hand out again. This time I did not move. His fingers grazed my cheek; in almost the same motion, his hand fell away. Then he pushed open the gate, hinge grating on iron hinge, and held it open. But I hesitated, I could not move, so he went first, walking up the path to the house. After a moment, I followed.

Later, we were alone in the house, Gideon and I. The first time, surely. Paulette had left at four to walk over to her dressmaker's, and Avigal was at a friend's house, gossiping probably, drinking coffee. I didn't know where Josh was, but supposed he was in his office. At least that's where I envisioned him, in his office or in the lab. The image came and went.

Most of the time I stood at the living room window. The gray sky moved; I watched it move, and though I did not look at Gideon, I was not oblivious of him. I knew he was there. If I turned my head, I would see him. He sat in an armchair near the end of the library table, in the greenish light of the lamp.

He was reading a doctoral thesis. The gold pencil glinted as it moved along the lines and when he made neat little notes on his pad. He'd crossed his legs, the sheaf of papers resting on one knee. One foot swayed a little—left, right, left again. I turned to look at him and saw that he'd already forgotten it, everything I'd said to him, everything he'd said to me. Forgotten it, or put it out of his mind as unimportant.

Perhaps I was relieved. I don't remember. As the afternoon advanced, all that began to recede for me, too. It could have happened years, instead of hours, ago. At the far end of the dark tunnel of time, our silhouetted figures gesticulated at each other against the small circle of light.

Then I turned back to the window, and after a while I thought he'd looked up and was studying me as I stood there, and it made me uneasy. I kept my eyes averted, but then I determined to smile. I turned, already smiling, but he wasn't looking at me. He was still bent over his work, in the wash of greenish light. I glanced around quickly, as though there must be jeering witnesses to this scene.

My grandmother used to do that, glance around like that, to see if anyone had observed her embarrassment. As though a scene so manifestly not of her manufacture must not, on any account, be recorded. Otherwise she was serene, convinced that as she moved through her life, the camera always rolled back before her, filming it—her version of her life—through lenses smeared with Vaseline.

When I went into the kitchen to make some coffee for Gideon and myself, my grandmother went with me, the ghost, costumed as usual—as I remembered—in the grayed pastel wools of winter, the dark organzas of summer, fabric always limp on sloping, well-corseted hips, hems rippling about her meager calves and, from her young womanhood, the same elegant, high-heeled pumps, though each narrow ankle was now enveloped in a swell of mottled flesh. The stiff new leather must have bitten into her instep, but she smiled; she kept smiling. And smiling, she exhorted smiles. Even, you might say, extorted them.

"Don't mope now," she would say to me. "You can't imagine how much prettier you look, Sara, when you smile." And because I was then so solemn, so darkly saturnine a child and resistant to such flattery, she would say the whole world would surely benefit —"the *whole* world, Sara"—if there were more smiling people. Unfortunately, I didn't care about the world. Neither, I suppose, did my grandfather. But I noticed she never said that to him. Indeed, she never said it while he was in the room, not even when he sat half a room away, mute and almost motionless, within the paper fortress of his Boston dailies. Not until he'd gone into the garden and she could watch him through a pane of window glass. "I do wish," she would sigh then, "I do wish everyone would smile a little more."

My grandfather never heard that. His tall spare body was then bent over his white roses. His hands moved gently among them, his long bony fingers removing with judicious, almost reverent care the odd insect from stem, leaf, or petal. He'd dust, he'd spray. In the appropriate season, he'd mulch and compost. In fact, the roses were his religion, and a purer religion than most. The ritual was its essence; its essence was no more than this ritual. I have always suspected that the rest of his life—the tedium of Sunday sermons, for instance, his polite carving of the Sunday roast, the grave, silent consumption of the meat, the mealy potatoes, the tinned peas—these were his concessions to domestic peace and nothing more. To domestic peace, if not to bliss. But

152

when he was in his garden, when he bent over his roses, he was like a lover then—his face intent, almost dreamy—the white roses a transcendental passion. And an earthly one. I do not think my grandmother minded. But she would have liked him to smile a little more.

The last time I saw my grandmother, she was laid out in a room in the Abbot-Pemberton Funeral Home. She looked happy, I thought, but she wasn't smiling. Her skin, which had in life looked like crumpled tissue paper carefully smoothed out again, was almost flawless in death. At least, that's the way it looked from across the room—her face powdered and heavily rouged, in profile against the artfully draped white satin lining of the casket. It was midwinter then. That was a blessing for my grandfather. He hated cutting his white roses for funerals. He ordered lilies from the town florist.

The last time I saw my grandfather was on a Sunday in June of 1963. I went with Caroline on her monthly visit, just before I left for Europe. He was in a nursing home then (and still is), a small place in rural Connecticut. When we drove up, I remember, he was sitting out on the lawn in the sun, staring at the dark green hedge beside him. Remembering his lost white roses maybe. Maybe longing for them.

Caroline took a chair on one side of him, I took a chair on the other. But we spoke mostly to each other; my grandfather was very quiet that day. That is, after the first few minutes of complaint, to which Caroline listened with a show of concern. After that, he hardly spoke, and when he did, he made scant sense.

He thought, for instance, I was his wife, Margaret. He told me I was looking very well—considering. "Considering what?" Caroline asked with a trace of amusement. Then she leaned across him to say to me, "I'm afraid it's not one of his more lucid days. I'm sorry." But she didn't say what she was sorry about.

My grandfather blinked. He wore no glasses now. Then Caroline said he must realize it could not be Margaret. Margaret was gone. "Gone where?" he asked. Dead, she told him. "Is she?" Then he added, "I don't remember. I'm sorry." I suppose he meant he was sorry about not remembering, but I can't be sure.

153

The words were slurred a little, but perfectly comprehensible. A moment later, he asked Caroline who I was. "Sara," Caroline said.

Then my grandfather smiled. (My grandmother, I thought, would have been very happy.) A trail of spittle like the shiny trail of a snail crept from one corner of his mouth down his chin. Tiny tufts of silver whiskers sprouted on his fallen cheeks, missed in the morning shave the attendant gave him.

I looked away. He turned to Caroline and asked once more, "Well, who is she?"

"It's Sara, Dad. Little Sara." She threw a pity-me look in my direction. "Don't you remember Sara?"

"Of course I do."

But a few minutes after that, he asked once more. Who was I? This time, I told him. I had to say it again and again. You'd think that would make me uncertain of who I was, but it didn't. I could repeat it over and over again and still be sure.

There are perceptible patterns here surely. That Sunday and this one, that Sunday when I knew exactly who I was. This one when I should have known but, for long, bewildering moments, did not. When everything should have changed but had not. Except that I did not know for certain who Sara was and what she was.

I was still uncertain on Monday. On Tuesday, Josh left for two weeks of reserve duty somewhere up north.

I came awake as usual that morning, as I'd done now every day during the past four weeks. He was moving around out there, beyond the several walls, making small but unavoidable noises. I lay motionless on the bed, face upturned to the blank ceiling, eyes shut but not really wanting sleep, my arms aching, clamped across my flattened breasts—as though this might somehow steady the erratic beat of my heart. I listened to him as I listened every morning. . . . Then I heard Josh in the living room, just beyond the closed study door.

I could say good-bye, I thought, but I'd said that last night. It would seem odd to say it again. He would think it very odd.

Then he solved it for me, almost. He rapped on the study door
—so lightly you could believe, if you wished, that it was no
knock at all. Merely a scrape of knuckle on the wood, the
knuckle instantly withdrawn. After that, silence. I threw off the
covers and, barefoot, stumbled to the door, pulled it open. He
was across the room by then, crouching beside the bookshelves.
He rose and turned.

Now that he was facing me, there seemed absolutely nothing
to say. Nothing normal. It was, it seemed to me, much the same
scene we'd played through once before; but then, at least, it was
in the shadows, that night I'd waited up for him and faced him
like this, barefoot on the cold tile floor, in Avigal's nightgown,
he about to withdraw as he was about to do now. Except now
the room blazed with sunlight. I stared at him—I wanted to
store his image.

On the face of it, this was slightly ridiculous, since it didn't
seem to be Josh at all, but someone only faintly resembling him
and looking decidedly grubby in an old army uniform. (His
own, I found out later, salvaged for nostalgia's sake.) He looked
slightly bandy-legged. The trousers, hanging beltless from his
hips, bagged a little. The shirt fit a little better, but there was a
button under stress on his hard, almost flat middle, and its collar
and cuffs were frayed. He did not look even remotely military.
I told him so. He shrugged, undisturbed. Very few did, he said.
It was, after all, a citizen's army. And he asked if he'd
wakened me.

I shook my head; then, because I could think of nothing else
to say, I asked if he had wanted something. It sounded brusque.
From his room, I said, and gestured behind me.

"No. Just to say hello," he said, "and good-bye."

I thought, I said, we'd said good-bye the night before. It
sounded arch—I realized that at once—and I thought I saw a
glint of humor in his pale eyes. I hated myself at that moment
because I was sure I'd somehow betrayed myself. He knew—he
must know—what I was feeling. And then I think I almost hated
him for knowing.

He turned away. He had been tucking some books into the
canvas bag resting on the coffee table, and now he zipped the

155

bag closed. He put on the olive-drab parka and picked up the bag. He was going, and there was nothing I could do about it, nothing I could say that would sound less than foolish. Except, of course, ask for a cigarette. I could do that. Then his movements toward me would be natural enough, and mine toward him, natural, too. When he lit my cigarette, I could touch him. Lightly. His hand, or his wrist; his sleeve, at last resort. I had to touch him. But it must appear accidental. Casual. Perfectly logical in the situation. Now, I thought. *Now.* Ask for the cigarette. I wanted to move toward him, but found I could not do it. I was imprisoned in a block of granite—my body only half-carved out of it, the rest locked still in the safe stone. At least that—safe. As long as I did nothing. But, then, not quite safe either, for there was still the confusion to deal with—the battering emotions that he evoked. I could gaze at him in cool-eyed appraisal and still feel anguish. And desire. And the coldness that came with fear—the fear that he felt nothing of what I felt. And rage. And this strange, wild tenderness.

I still wanted to touch him. I could not think how. It will be all right, I thought, still standing in the doorway; it'll be all right after he's left. It will be a relief. He was moving toward the door. There was the sound of another door opening, and then Avigal appeared in the hall, as though to emphasize how much more ludicrous all this was than lurid.

"You're both up?" She yawned. I mumbled my good-bye— I don't know if he heard me—then backed into the study, shut the door. Through it I heard their voices. Perhaps he kissed her as he left. (Yes, of course, he did.) There was the sound of the front door opening, then closing. I did not go to the window; I sat rigidly on the edge of the bed, instead, and lit one of my own cigarettes. I heard his footsteps in the path below. Tomorrow, I thought, it will be better, easier. But I was wrong. It was worse. I lay awake that next morning and every morning thereafter, listening for him, but there was nothing to hear.

I went out with Baruch on Wednesday. Well, not precisely out. This time, the second time, we went to visit some friends of

156

his, a married couple, the husband a chemical engineer at the institute, the wife a technician in one of the biology labs. They lived in an apartment on the institute grounds; Baruch lived in the same building.

The evening was placid enough, and rather dull. I suppose the two things must go together. There was some talk—only a little —about my father and his illness; they voiced approval of hope. There's always hope, they said. Then Baruch talked about the movie we'd seen together on Saturday—he made it sound as if we'd been going together for a long time. He turned to me for confirmation of his opinions. I confirmed them. Finally, there was music. The stereo they'd bought recently was of German manufacture; the music, *Tannhäuser*.

Rather florid, as Wagner is, our host said, but he'd listen to whomever he pleased. It was his way of reaffirming the apolitical nature of music. His way of protesting the banning of Wagner from the concert halls and the opera stage of Israel, which was done, he explained, in deference to survivors of the Holocaust. He sounded reasonable enough—until he began talking about the passivity of Europe's murdered Jews. You could see he believed that if he had been there—well, the concentration camps could never have happened to him. The gas ovens? Partly, he implied, because Europe's Jews were so passive. Anyway, he concluded, we can hardly blame Wagner for the excesses of the Nazis.

Baruch nodded in amicable agreement. I think he would have nodded if his friend, out of the blue, had suggested a suicide pact. The wife nodded in an accepting, wifely way. Mentally, I filed "excesses" away for Gideon—for use in his no doubt continuing research into the sabra *shvitz*.

At this point, the wife rose to go into the kitchen, and because it seemed expected of me—I was getting very accommodating —I followed her. We discussed clothes in there—mine, mostly. She admired the green sweater I was wearing—the one Paulette had made me—and my Roman shoes. The wife said she really envied me. "You're so adventurous," she said, but sounding not at all envious—complacent, rather.

"I am?"

"All of you, your whole family." Her dark eyes were knowing, I thought; they slid toward me. I began to feel uncomfortable, not certain what I was supposed to answer.

"Of course," she murmured, "in different ways, adventurous." Then she picked up the laden tea tray and, as though riding the crest of some triumphant wave, sailed out into what she—and all other Israelis—call the salon. I followed with a plate of sugared pastry shells filled with whipped cream and strawberries.

I watched her for the brief rest of the evening, trying to decide what she'd meant. The engineer put questions to me about Italian neofascism and the Italian attitude to the Arabs. I answered as best I could but watched her. The wife talked about the Italian washing machine they were going to buy and the new stove. Once I smiled at her. She smiled back, her smile not shy, I decided, but sly. Finally, we listened to the first part of *Tristan und Isolde*, and when the record came to an end, Baruch and I left. It was almost midnight.

On the way down the stairs, Baruch seemed a little nervous. On the lowest landing, when we were outside the door of his apartment, he patted his jacket pocket and said he had another pack of cigarettes inside—and wasn't I curious, anyway, to see his place? I wasn't really, but I nodded. I could have predicted all this.

His place was on the other side of the building, and about half the size of his friends' apartment. He had a hall, one large, rather bare studio room, a kitchen, a bath. That's what he said as he unlocked the door. I stood in the doorway of the main room. He made his way across it to the desk to get the packet of cigarettes. Along the wall opposite me was his bed—a narrow, ascetic-looking sofa bed. Already made up for the night, the cover turned back invitingly.

Then he came toward me and said—I knew just what he'd say—he said, "Well, come in, sit down."

I made a show of weariness, smiling to soften the "No." He'd say I was leading him on, I suppose. Perhaps I was. I said I had a big day ahead of me. Another time, maybe. He pulled the cellophane from the pack of cigarettes. American, I noticed, expensive. He held them out to me, so I took one. I couldn't very well refuse, could I? Since it was obvious he'd bought them for me especially. He smoked an Israeli brand, and by no means the most expensive one—in fact, the sort of cigarette from which loose tobacco falls as you lift it to your mouth. He lit my American cigarette for me now, then went to bring me an ashtray. All this, it seemed to me, was done in slow motion. And I was still not sure what I wanted.

I stood where I was, in the doorway, inhaled and expelled smoke. He returned, caught my hand. I let him hold it, but almost at once, he dropped it. Now, he stood before me—he seemed to be waiting. I think I began to grow impatient then. I wanted him to begin. No, he didn't excite me much, but I felt no revulsion either, at least not for the moment. No sensation at all, in fact. I could envisage all the moves—that is, once he realized he would have to make them all, make the first move and every other—all the plays, all of them. But this would be real, at least, as Rob had been real, and Lucio, and even Giorgio. Simple, too: sexual hunger and then satiation. I think I was almost eager, by then. And like a clairvoyant, eager for confirmation, too— for my predictions to come true.

I knew what he'd do next. He'd put his arms around me and kiss me, and his tongue would push its way into my mouth, and at the same time his hand would go to my breast, he'd squeeze my breast, knead it. I could imagine the rest, too—the undressing. He'd surely fold his gray corduroy trousers, but pull off the turtleneck sweater more excitedly; he'd fold his glasses and place them on the bedside table. Then, when he was under the covers, he'd turn to me—his body would be white and smooth, already aroused—I could predict all this. I'd be grateful afterward. I assumed my body would be thankful for all his perfected movements, all the correlations he could make with his perfected cinema vocabulary—the thrust (of the narrative), the ongoing movement, the freeze, the frozen frame, the shudder, the end. I saw all this in the future, but I did not move from the doorway, and it seemed to me that it was all going to happen to someone else.

Then he actually took the last step (or the first); he stood in front of me, put his hands on my waist—and I thought, well, why not? But when he tried to kiss me, I turned my head slightly; I don't know why, really. His mouth skidded off one sharp cheekbone. I felt a little sick. I disengaged myself, stepped backward, turned toward the front door. After a minute, he followed; he had to. The ride home was silent, and he sullen; but by the time we arrived in front of Avigal's house, he was more cheerful. In fact, he tried to kiss me again.

"Listen," I said, pushing him away, "I don't think there's any point to this, do you?"

"It's all right," he said.

"What is?"

"I've got patience. *Savlanoot*. I can wait."

"What for?"

There was an awkward moment of silence. Then he said, rather stubbornly, "You know."

I did—I did know. But not what to say. In any case, he'd made one unmistakable point, and he felt he could make others. He went on.

"It would be good for you," he said. He sounded kind, as if it were only my interests he was concerned about. His arm lay along the back of the seat. Now it moved slightly. He touched my hair. I leaned forward at once, out of reach, but as though to put my cigarette out in the car ashtray. I didn't like myself much for that, but I liked him even less.

"It would calm you," he said.

I laughed as though he'd made a fine little joke.

"It would," he insisted.

"Thank you," I said, "but I think I'm really calm enough."

I groped for the door handle, opened the door, got out very quickly, left the door swinging, and walked quickly away. I suppose I was afraid to shut the door, afraid I'd slam it. He'd think I was angry. I didn't want that. But by the time I reached the staircase, I didn't care what he'd think.

160

21

THE PHONE WOKE ME. IT RANG AND RANG, AND NO ONE answered. The second awakening. At seven, I'd lain there and listened to the silence. Finally, I'd slept again. The second sleep is always heavier than the first, so when the phone rang, it was almost eleven, the living room streaming with sunlight, the hall shadowy. I picked up the phone on the tenth ring and said hello.

For a moment, there was silence. As though there was no one at the other end. "Hello," I said again.

There was now an almost inaudible intake of breath. Then Avigal's voice. "Sara?"

"Yes."

"I thought you'd be gone by now."

I stared at the phone, I remember, and wondered at the construction of that sentence. But all I said was that I'd overslept. Too late for the *ulpan* now, and I'd skip it for today. What Avigal said was that when she'd left quite early, she'd known I was still asleep but thought I'd wake by myself very soon, to go out to the Hebrew class, even if I got there a little late.

"You must have had a good time," she added.

"When?"

"Last night. You came in so late."

"Not very," I told her, and left her to figure that out. Not a very good time. Not very late. Whichever.

Avigal then asked if I'd seen her note. I saw it now—on the floor. It had, I assumed, slipped from its perch on the telephone table. I bent to pick it up. "See you at *Abba's*," in Avigal's green ballpoint scrawl.

"Yes, I see it," I said, and added—there was something in her tone that made me do it—"What shall I tell them?"

"Tell them?" There was a long pause before she spoke again. "Nothing. I'll just be a little late, that's all. Tell *Abba* I had some things to do in town."

"All right." I started to hang up, but a fraction of a second later I heard Avigal's voice again.

"Sara?"

"Yes."

"Are you going over there now?"

"As soon as I get dressed," I said. "Why? Did you want me to do something?"

"No," she said, "nothing. Never mind, just asking." And she hung up.

There was the steady buzz that follows a broken connection. For a confused moment, I stood there just staring down at the telephone, but I think I suspected even then what she was up to . . . that she wasn't coming to Tel Aviv with us. She had called to ask me to explain to Gideon and then, inexplicably, changed her mind—about asking, that is, not about the trip. The afternoon—the visiting he'd planned, the shopping—would just have to be lived through without her. Gideon won't mind, she would have said, you're going, and Paulette. But I knew that wasn't true. Gideon would mind all right.

Then it occurred to me that, in some strange and rather skillful way, she'd succeeded—she'd changed me. At least, she'd given me a role—that of obedient, dutiful, attentive, even loving daughter—and here I was acting it out. Not that I liked the role or felt comfortable in it. No more, in fact, than I liked the other—that of the officious, proper lady with nothing better

162

to do than remind others of their sometimes onerous duties. As I'd been about to do, I realized.

I had my coffee, a cigarette, then got dressed. As I was going out the door, the phone rang again. This time I got it on the third ring, but there was silence now at the other end of the line, then a click, and the connection was broken.

I locked the door. It was early still, but that was all right. It took fifteen minutes to get to the institute. A leisurely walk. I'd have been there in fifteen minutes if it hadn't been for the letters.

Two of them, deep in the mailbox. Through the openwork of the mailbox door I could see my name, typed very neatly on the envelope in front. Caroline's letter. I had no mailbox key— they had only two between them—so I tried a pen first, poked it through the horizontal slot at the top, tried to press the first envelope against the back of the box and so slide it upward. That worked until the envelope dropped back again when I tried to catch hold of it. I thought of tweezers—mine, which were in my purse. I fished out the first, longer letter—Caroline's— pulling it toward me through the narrow slot, then the second, Rob's, in the same way. Both letters were rather battered now, but that didn't matter. I folded them once, stuffed them into my jacket pocket. I'd read them later.

I was halfway to the institute when I decided suddenly that, no, I must read them at once. Another time, I think, and I could have waited forever, but this was the first mail I'd received in Israel—in response to my short notes. And I had time; it was still quite early. I was walking along the main street then, following the route I usually took, but I turned off into another smaller street, the first street that I came to, and then off into another, still smaller winding road. Very quiet. I was still walk-ing in the direction of the institute, but now toward the side entrance. There was a low stone wall on my right, fronting a straggly garden. I sat down on it, pulled both letters from my pocket, opened Caroline's first, and smoothed it out on my thigh.

The letter was almost sunny. First, she was pleased I'd de-cided to stay in Israel "for a short while," and then how "in-telligent" it was of me "to try to become friends, at least, with your father." As though friendship were a course that she, for

163

one, had been urging upon me for years. "Before it's too late," she added.

And then something about getting bored ("It's such a backwater, I hear, culturally"), and why she'd not written sooner— there had been some legal matters to attend to. So time-consuming, but she did them gladly for my sake. On one of her monthly visits to the nursing home in the environs of Greenwich, she'd noticed how very frail her father had become. "But, of course, he can live for another five, or even ten, years yet. His own father lived to the age of ninety-five in just that condition, and people live so much longer these days—that is, those who do not become mortally ill."

Anyway, though he was frail, he was, she said, rather more lucid that day than usual. Surprising. She had again broached the subject of giving away some of his money "before decease." She had no doubt used those same dry and unsentimental words to her father, counting on his legal training to overcome the understandable feelings of resentment. She was afraid, she said, that he would not respond in a reasonable way, and of course, she could have done it without his knowing—she had power of attorney, after all—but she had wanted everything to be above reproach, with no possible question about the validity of a transfer. Finally, he had agreed. He'd signed the papers and the check she'd brought to him, arranging for the transfer of funds to my name. I now had thirty thousand dollars in the bank. At least that, she said, would be safe from the tax men. "And when you get back," she had dictated to some typist, "it will be a measure of security—you won't have to take the first job offered." The rest of the letter was financial advice. She suggested I invest the money. She'd do it for me, if I wished. G.M., Du Pont, Minnesota Mining—they'd done very well by my grandfather. Her final words were strange: "It's foolish, isn't it, to hang on and on. My regards to your father." I still don't know what she meant exactly. I don't think she knows either.

I refolded the letter, put it back in its long white envelope, and then into my purse. Then I opened Rob's letter. There was the usual check inside and a note somewhat longer than usual. He was, he wrote me, "seeing someone." A divorcée with two

164

young children. Serious, he said. He mentioned "mature love." He also mentioned the present cost of living, his financial commitments, the length of our marriage, the years we'd been separated, divorced. My eyes skimmed the rest of this. I was looking for the logical next sentence. But no. Instead, he assured me I'd like her. (As if I were his mother.) And then how surprised he'd been to get a letter from Israel. "If Candy and I go to Greece this summer, we might just drop in there to see you." I stared at this letter, aware of what it had to be. A plea. I turned the check over. "For Deposit Only." I put both letter and check into the envelope and into my purse, extracted a cigarette, lit it, smoked, and thought about the dangers of generous gestures. About the fact that Gideon would definitely be against alimony—of course —and that he'd approve of what I was thinking of doing. Not that I cared what he thought anyway. Or, for that matter, that I had ever insisted on the money Rob sent me. If he felt he needed a statement to the effect that he could stop sending it, however, I'd send him such a statement. I'd have it notarized. I didn't want to stand between him and his ex-domestic airline stewardess, now a hostess at the Playboy Club. But there was a danger in all this, I knew. They might, the two of them, in an excess of gratitude, actually come to thank me, "drop in" when they went to Greece. On the other hand, if I did not return this check and write that he could forget all others in the future, they might drop in anyway, to plead their case. Either, or.

In the end, I deliberately turned my thoughts back to Caroline, to consider whether the money she spoke of was in the nature of a bribe. Would the whole thing evaporate like so much morning dew—the entire thirty thousand dollars—if I chose not to return to New York or, more precisely, if I chose to stay here? And should I feel guilty? She would never, I knew, never have done that earlier. She expected, then, to be loved for herself —or perhaps in spite of herself. We had done this together, Gideon and I—and that expectation had at last withered away. It was very warm in the sun, but I pulled my jacket closer, got up and began walking again, following the road.

I felt rather stiff now, as though I had been sitting on that stone wall for more than the actual ten minutes. The street was sunny, but the sidewalk and patches of grass were flecked with the shadows of moving leaves. I stared at the façades of shabby houses, daubed with tar against the winter rains. They looked, in fact, rather like friendly faces: blank, impersonal perhaps, but generous and understanding—even, in a way, forgiving.

I followed that winding road to its end, and realized I was lost. Now I was in another street—at least, it had seemed a street, but short, more a lane, I suppose. Four houses on my side, three on the opposite. A few large old trees, one in the gutter. And at the very end of the road, a small red car, with Avigal in it.

I didn't know her at first. I saw the back of her head through the rear window. She seemed to be leaning forward, her shoulders hunched a little, but when I was almost halfway toward the car, she turned to whoever was at the wheel, and the profile was unmistakable. As was the soft rolled collar of her favorite white sweater, and the way it dipped away from her long neck; and her loose dark hair, forward at first, a thick fall, and then, when she lifted her chin, sliding backward.

She was talking. I thought she seemed upset about something, but I still couldn't see the other person; there was a tree in the way. I saw nothing but his heavy shoulder. Then the way his right arm snaked along the back of the front seat, and his hand, of course, when it touched Avigal. Her hair first, then moving downward into the collar of her sweater. And Avigal—tense or angry. Or excited. Then she laughed, and her head fell back again, her eyes half-closed. The hand came up and touched her throat once more. A disembodied hand in a brown and white checked sleeve. It came away.

But I think this registered only on the surface of my mind. I kept moving forward. I was almost abreast of the car before I realized what I was witnessing. It seemed to me, until that moment, natural enough to see Avigal sitting in a car—even Avigal where I least expected her. The other things, not natural, of course; but I hardly took them in. Only Avigal. I think I was actually going to say hello to her.

And then I saw him. Not all of him. The shoulder again. The elbow on the rolled-down window. His hands resting lightly now on the steering wheel. The long slender fingers. Strangely elegant, I'd thought, when I first saw them. The smudge of springy ginger hair on each finger below the knuckles, the extravagant splash of freckle on both broad-boned, hairy wrists. I remembered those hands all right—Arieh's hands. Arieh, in fact, all of him.

I bolted then. I turned quickly, looking for a way out, a way back, before they could see me, before they realized I'd seen them. I am not a woman for that kind of confrontation. There was an open gate on my left. I turned into it quickly, went up the path to the house, which had a thick-walled entrance—solid, dark even in the daylight—so that the hall, bricked in, could in an emergency serve also as a bomb shelter. I went through this hall and out the open door at the back into the yard, then through a clump of pine, overgrown with ivy. But I didn't have to stand there and wait until they'd gone. There was a break in the old chain fence between this house and the next. I passed through it into the next garden, then walked around to the front of that house. At any rate, I was a bit farther up the street now, back the way I'd come, nearer the corner. And farther away from the car.

Just before I turned the corner, though, I looked back at them. Still absorbed, still sitting there. But not for long, I knew. Soon, Arieh would start up his car, and they'd go to find a telephone. She'd phone the apartment again. This time, of course, there would be no answer. Or maybe they'd just drive to the house, unable to wait any longer. He'd sit outside; she'd go up, hoping all the while that it was late enough, that I'd have left. As I had. And that the apartment would, at last, be empty. As it was.

22

WE WERE ALMOST FINISHED WITH LUNCH WHEN AVIGAL called. By then, Paulette had also detached herself from the afternoon's excursion. Maybe she'd never intended going—though when Gideon had first broached his plans, she'd seemed amenable enough. In her case, it might have been the chilling prospect of visiting Batya, whom Paulette perhaps still saw as a rival. She may have decided, for the sake of her own peace of mind, not to meet any rivals, ex- or not, married-off or not. In any case, her excuses were varied, legitimate but perhaps excessive, though Gideon listened to them all without comment and without expression.

There were the French scientist and his wife, she said, coming for dinner the next evening. On Saturday, an English couple, also guests of the physics department, were invited to tea. On Friday morning—tomorrow—there was to be a new *ozeret* from the Labor Exchange. If she came. And Paulette would have to help her clean or, at the very least, supervise everything. And the shopping, the baking, the cooking—that would all have

to be done that afternoon. Besides, there was the impossibility—
she had tried—of getting any other than her usual Thursday
afternoon appointment at the hairdresser's.

Then the phone rang, and Gideon went into the bedroom to
answer it. We heard him, Paulette and I, from the dining room.
His voice carried. Cool after the hello, then rather curt. Finally,
his footsteps returning.

"Another desertion," he told us. He sat down, spread his
napkin in his lap again, picked up his fork, and began to eat.

Paulette's eyes met mine across the dining table, but the expression in them was unreadable. After a few moments she
observed to Gideon that it wasn't so terrible, after all. "You
don't need a harem everywhere you go," she said tartly. "You're
not a Bedouin sheik."

He reached over and caressed her wrist, held her plump hand
for a minute, then let go. And said to me, "It's you and me,
Sara. That is, unless you've changed your mind."

I shook my head. He took that for denial and nodded.

Soufflés, Paulette had sniffed before we sat down for lunch,
soufflés did not wait upon people, even the most favored.
Which was why, though Gideon was against it, we'd started
without Avigal, but not why we were finishing without her.
I ate what Gideon had said was a superb soufflé. At that moment,
it could have been a display in a shop window, made of Styro-
foam or papier-mâché; but I lifted my hand automatically, reg-
ularly, to bring spoonfuls to my mouth. No one was watching.
Paulette was looking at Gideon and asking what Avigal had
said. She spoke in an idly curious voice, but Gideon answered
sharply, and I knew at that instant that they knew—both of
them—what I knew. Or more.

"Something rather novel this time," he said.

Paulette waited.

"A toothache," he said. "She needs a filling."

"*Drôle*," Paulette murmured. Her face was expressionless,
and her voice, too. Then she stood up, leaned over to take
Gideon's empty plate, then mine. She stacked them on hers, and
on these, the round, fluted oven dish in which the soufflé had

169

risen to such glorious heights. She did not speak, but the way she did this, the very act of setting china upon china, though done gently, seemed somehow to strike sparks from them.

"Well, who is it?" she asked.

"The—ah—dentist?" Gideon's smile was distinctly sour.

"Yes. Someone new? Or one of the old ones?"

"I don't know," he said. He was irritated suddenly, and angry. "Do you *really* think she tells me?"

At which point, Paulette hefted the dishes. "I thought she told you everything," she said. Her tone was spiteful. Or maybe jealous. I suppose you could forgive her that. She pushed the kitchen door inward with her shoulder. It swung back again. Gideon and I sat staring at the door long after she had gone, listening, without speaking, to Paulette dissipating her frustration in the kitchen, or her fury, or some hurt which I knew nothing about but could perhaps imagine—knowing my father. Then the noise died down. Finally, it ceased altogether.

Gideon glanced at me. "She's very fond of Josh," he said.

As though I must surely understand this statement—as, of course, I did—but I looked at him blankly. He could not tell if I understood or not. Obvious, though, that he wanted me to say something . . . and I had nothing to say.

"By the way," he said, "Avigal said she mentioned that to you."

"What?"

"Her toothache."

I stared past him, to the dark polished wood of the sideboard.

"I told her," he went on, "that you'd said nothing."

I did not reply.

"She said you must have forgotten."

I picked up one of the teaspoons then and began turning it between my fingers, noting dully the dull luster of the stainless steel, the manufacturer's name on the back of the shallow bowl, and the shape of the bowl—austere, sleek. Not Paulette's taste, judging from her cherished tea service. Hers ran to the baroque, if not downright rococo, to opulence. And in the manner of the French middle-aged middle class, to a stiff and correct code of behavior, very Victorian, both on the surface and in substance.

I turned the teaspoon between my fingers, as though it were endlessly enthralling, but did not see it. Saw them instead. On Josh's bed, on the spread, in the sheets. The rank odor of their rut would cling to the cloth forever; the sheets would never again be clean enough for Josh. That image persisted, defied obliteration. And yet the next moment, I heard myself saying that yes, now I remembered, Avigal *had* complained of a toothache. And I'd forgotten. I was sorry. And then I think I said it again, in another way, and looked at Gideon squarely. I don't know if I expected him to believe me. I didn't even know if I *wanted* him to believe me. That was his choice: to decide that I was lying— at Avigal's behest, conspiring in her betrayals; or that I was telling the truth and Avigal had lied to me also.

I looked down at the teaspoon again. Gideon's taste, I decided. Such cold, clean lines. Or else reminders of some reign other than Paulette's.

He reached over and snapped the spoon from my fingers. His face was dark now, suffused with the suddenly risen blood of anger—anger under strict control, of course. "That's very touching," he said dryly. "Your loyalty to your sister. I didn't know you had it in you."

I didn't answer. That didn't require an answer. Instead, I reached over and picked up another spoon.

"It's misplaced," he said now, looking at my hands and the spoon. "But I think you know that. Avigal goes through the motions, but she's transparent. She doesn't really care."

"All that trouble for nothing then," I murmured.

"Of course, she'll return the favor. If you need it." His eyebrows rose. "Will you?"

"I don't know," I said. "I might."

For a moment, he merely looked at me. Then, "So there are two of you," he said.

"No," I corrected. "Three. Three of us."

I didn't look at him when I said that; I don't know what expression crossed his face. I know that a moment later he leaned back in his chair, his hands resting on the table's edge, his eyes still on me. Was he hurt? I don't know. I won't say I didn't care. I did, a little. This was another truth, of course, but perhaps one

171

truth too many. I studied the small squares where the bands of red crossed each other on the luncheon cloth. The dark red of blood. Most appropriate. A reiteration. Blood to blood, sharing it. Whatever. You could not escape after all, none of us could. If it were there, if it were there from the very beginning. . . . But could you—should you ever—talk like this to your father? Even if what you said was true? I didn't know. I'd never had a father.

"Anyway," I said, looking up, "they don't stone you for adultery in this country. It's a free country, isn't it?"

"A small country," he said. "People talk."

I think I smiled then. So that was it. I said, "But who cares anyway? Who gives a damn?"

"I do."

I laughed.

"That's funny, is it?" he said.

"Very."

"You mean, *considering*," he went on. "And people who live in glass houses, et cetera, et cetera."

"Yes."

A moment of silence then, before he said, "I don't think I'd care to defend myself today." He sounded annoyed.

I flushed. "Another day perhaps." Because I couldn't stop.

He nodded. "Another day, maybe."

Gideon did the driving; he picked up speed as usual outside of town. I know what we passed—I've made the same trip many times since—but the trip that day is still a blur, indistinct, as though it were not experienced at first hand. I can't even remember what we said to each other in the car, or if we said anything. There was news, I remember. But afterward, could we have sat for so long in such companionable silence? After that exchange—for it wasn't a conversation.

I know one thing—I didn't think about Gideon at all. I thought about them: about Avigal and Arieh—and about Josh, of course. About Josh. But by the time we'd reached the decayed streets on the periphery of Tel Aviv, I'd worked up a hedge against them all, against delusion. This has nothing to do with you, I reminded myself. Nothing. It changes nothing. It does not concern you. A tribal chant for those who belong to no tribe. But it did not work all that well. Whatever Gideon's formula was, it worked better. I turned and saw his mood was fine now, even eager.

Avigal might not have existed, for all he thought about her. He'd once forgotten me in the same way. And my mother, and Avigal's mother. As for Paulette, when we dropped her off on the main street near the supermarket, he'd kissed her full on the mouth—and, I imagine, had promptly forgotten her, too. Which explained everything. How he reconciled things that mattered with other things that mattered.

In Tel Aviv, we parked on Hayarkon Street, across from one of the huge luxury hotels which loom up in front of the sea and sand and cast long shadows on the shabby houses opposite. From there we walked the two or three blocks to Dizengoff, where the shops had just opened for the afternoon hours. We wandered from one to the other, collecting things, all Gideon's choices, his whims. A long silk scarf for Avigal—the color of wild clover honey. At the Librairie Française, two new novels for Paulette. And then the record for Josh—Haydn this time, because Mozart, Gideon thought, had become too much an obsession with him. And then the dress for me.

We saw it first on a mannequin in a shop window: an olive-green silk jersey dress that clung to the figure but was somehow also demure. He went into the shop, and I followed. He insisted I try on the dress. I argued, then saw it did no good, went into the small dressing room at the back of the shop, put it on and came out to show him. Approached him quickly, felt rather silly, then retreated, saying it was not a dress I'd wear much. Why not, he wanted to know. I went back into the dressing room room and put on my own skirt and sweater. When I came out again, Gideon had already paid for it, and the salesgirl was putting the dress in a plastic bag with little handles. I said again I didn't want it. "Of course, you do," he assured me. "It looks very nice on you." He took the package from her, and I followed him out of the store.

When we sat down to have some coffee, I brought the dress

up again. We'd found a café table on the sunny side of Dizen-goff, back a little from the continuous stream of people. Gideon deposited all the packages on an empty chair, then signaled the waiter to come and clear the table—the glasses in their metal holders held the dregs of someone else's tea, the saucers, their soggy brown tea bags.

I said, then, that he'd wasted his money.

"On what?" he wanted to know.

I motioned toward the packages. "Well, wasted it on me," I said. I told him I wouldn't wear that dress. "It isn't me."

"And your version of you, you think, can bear no altera-tion?" he asked. And gave me a sidelong glance.

I asked, rather stiffly, what he thought was wrong with my version of me. He said nothing, nothing, I was perfect, of my kind. But he—he was sentimental. "The thing is that I wanted to buy you something," he said. "I never bought you anything when you were little."

I pointed out that I wasn't a little girl anymore.

"That isn't a dress for a little girl," he said.

I had to agree, it wasn't. I thought it made me look over-ripe, but I did not say that. Instead I said that I would not wear it and added, as an afterthought, "much."

"Suit yourself," Gideon said. "But you will, I think." And then a moment later, when I did not reply to that, he ventured, "But if you really don't like it, we can go back, and you can choose another." Then, eyeing me, he asked, "Do you want to do that?"

But by then I'd come to terms with it. I said no, I'd keep it and wear it for special occasions. I don't think he believed that at first, but he wanted to believe it and then, despite himself, seemed pleased. I leaned back, kicked off my shoes, and pressed my aching feet to the cool, rough pavement. Gideon again tried to snag the waiter's attention, and this time succeeded. The young man, wearing a white shirt and rather dusty-looking black trousers, came forward, addressed Gideon rather familiarly as *Habibi*—"my dear," in Arabic—took our order, and then went away. Then, before I realized what he was doing, Gideon

174

bent down, lifted one of my stockinged feet to his knee, and began rubbing it. At first quite gently, but expertly, then harder,
pressing the sore flesh firmly with his strong fingers until I
purred like a sensuous cat. Then he set that one down and lifted
the other foot and did the same with that one.

"Is that better?" he asked.

I nodded gratefully.

"Judging from those shoes of yours," he observed, "I'd say
that dress was just your sort of dress."

I didn't answer. No use talking anyway, for at that moment
a bus heaved to a stop at the curb, disgorged several passengers,
and the radio newscast came on. Everyone turned toward it to
listen. Afterward, the pop music, just as loud. A young woman
passing saw a friend of hers at one of the tables and called out
to him; they laughed, hugged each other; chairs scraped back,
then were pulled forward, setting my teeth on edge. A huge
old taxi honked, stopped, took on two other passengers, picked
up speed again and, when it passed, a cloud of black exhaust
hung in the air.

Then the waiter returned with our coffee, with the cake—he
hadn't asked us if we wanted any cake, I noticed, he'd asked which
cake we wanted, and Gideon had responded automatically. It
was then I saw the sleek blond woman at a table to the right of
us, sitting with a man but staring at Gideon as if she thought
she knew him, knew him from somewhere, but could not quite
place him. And then she did place him and rose abruptly to make
her way to our table.

"I almost didn't recognize you," she said as Gideon got to his
feet. He took her extended hand. A very thin hand, almost a
birdlike claw, with long silvery fingernails that curved downward at the ends, and clanking above a bony wrist, a multitude
of metallic chains dangling coins, medallions, charms—all of
some monetary value but also, she would point out sweetly, I
was sure, of sentimental value, too. That kind of woman. So
many different kinds, I thought.

"How are you?" she asked Gideon.

And Gideon, in the usual manner of Israelis, merely said,

175

"Thank you." Not an answer to the question—which, indeed, never seemed to be answered. Thank you, presumably, for having asked.

Her eyes moved over his face. "I'm glad to see you looking so handsome, *Motek*. I've heard all sorts of stories."

"Lies," Gideon said a little too jauntily. "All lies."

She squeezed his arm. "I'm so glad."

Then she noticed me. I was still sitting, my face upturned, watching them both. Her glance might have seemed, to a disinterested observer, merely a superficial flicker. But in that instant or two, she'd noted if I was pretty, just how pretty I was, or would be if I had a different hairdo, calculated the prices of my sweater, my skirt, and my shoes, then resting on their sides almost out of sight under the table. But she *knew* my age—I could see that.

She waited, her eyes on me still. Gideon introduced us reluctantly; told me her name, too, but I've long since forgotten it.

"Oh, the American daughter," she said. "Yes, yes. I can see the resemblance now." She leaned back slightly as though to get a better perspective. "Like Avigal."

"Not really," Gideon said, and for some reason he sounded offended.

"Well, only a little," she conceded. And her eyes, after that one bemused glance at Gideon, were on me again. I hate being stared at or studied. But this time it was not my ordeal, it was Gideon's. His face had gone stony, his eyes were cold.

She went away right after that—sensitive to the chill, perhaps—but pecked Gideon on the cheek unexpectedly, before she returned to her table and her escort. She sat there talking animatedly to him but still watching us. Gideon sat down again; we finished our coffee in silence and left most of the cake—too sweet, too doughy. The Gideon called for the check, paid it, bent over to retrieve our packages, and took my arm. "*Shalom*," she called out as we started to walk away, reminding us, I suppose, that she'd not forgotten. "Be healthy." Gideon merely nodded and walked faster.

We must have walked for almost an hour at this pace, and in

176

somber silence. Turned off Dizengoff, came to Ben Yehuda, parallel but quieter, where the strollers were less concerned with being seen or seeing. We walked north on that street, almost to the end, crossed over, went south. Gideon looked neither right nor left, I remember, but held onto my arm tightly and clutched the packages; he had lost, it seemed, all interest in the shop windows and did not wave to anyone, did not even nod when someone came toward us smiling recognition. Finally, we came to the bottom of the street, where Ben Yehuda meets Allenby and where the Levant begins. Where no one knew Gideon and did not know of him and did not care. I think that's what he wanted. On the wide shallow steps that ascended to the main entrance of the Mograbi Cinema, young men stood about in small clusters smoking, talking, eating, chewing on polly seeds, spitting out the hulls. And calling to the girls who passed, who also traveled, it seemed, in packs—either enticing them or insulting them, I couldn't tell which. I only know the Hebrew spoken here was thick, soft, deep in the throat, reminiscent, I suppose, of Arabic. Indeed, they all looked like young Arabs— thin and dark-skinned—or Greeks, or Sicilians. But somehow tougher-looking.

It was dusk now, and the streetlights came on. Gideon and I sat down at a sidewalk table of a café near the corner. Three or four blocks to the right were the seafront and the wall above the beach, where the prostitutes loitered. To the left was Allenby, mostly shops; it would be dark soon, closed down, its shops, its offices, its cafés. When the waiter came, Gideon ordered two brandies. We stared past each other. The wind rose. The smell of the sea mingled with the odors of frying steak from the formica-lined caves which housed the small snack bars and falafel stands. I pulled on my jacket. Gideon asked me if my feet hurt. I said they did, a little. "One at a time," he said. And I raised my foot; he rubbed it again, this time more absent-mindedly, however. When the brandy came, Gideon drank his quickly and ordered another. I asked what was the matter. He said, nothing. "What should be the matter? And wear low-heeled shoes next time." I nodded.

I mentioned the woman again. "Your past?" I asked.

His eyebrows rose. "Why do you think every woman we meet must be out of my past?"

"I don't," I said. "Not every woman."

"As a matter of fact," he said, shifting on the small iron chair, "in a way, she's my future. She writes a gossip column —idiocies, mostly—for one of the afternoon papers. Monday and Friday. Next week, surely, she'll mention Avigal—Avigal doesn't seem to mind—and you. She'll note your age. And hers. And mention me—she'll have me at the gates of the cemetery or, at the very least, with the *Hevra Kadisha*, the burial society, waiting." He picked up and drank this brandy quickly, too, then ordered still another. Drank that, too, but not entirely. And said he was too tired to visit anybody. Did I mind?

I shook my head. He went into the café then to telephone Batya and cancel our projected visit; he came back looking a little more cheerful and gave me Batya's fond regards. We finished the brandies—my first, his third—and then walked back up Ben Yehuda and two blocks over to the car. I took the keys from him and did the driving, took refuge in that, in following his directions, taking turns smoothly, driving very carefully as though there were something infinitely fragile in the car with me—something which might shatter without special care.

For a long while it seemed to me that it was this silence that I wanted, that above all else I wanted this silence unbroken. But, after a time, I realized that it unnerved me, the wordless quiet, the heavy sound of his breathing in the seat beside me. And then, because it was so quiet, I thought he must have fallen asleep. We were passing through a traffic intersection. I glanced over at him and saw his eyes were wide-open, staring at the road ahead. No, not staring. Merely looking at it, as though he knew well enough what was up ahead, as though it was just what he expected. I think then I wanted to ask him what was the matter. I wanted to ask, "Is anything the matter, *Abba?*" But I couldn't.

23

No, I never called him *Abba*. The word was Avigal's possession, as alien to me as "Father" would have been. I never used that word either.

We were adversaries. We confronted each other—besieger, besieged. I made my stylized, almost formal sorties, fended him off, withdrew with more, or less, hesitation. And warily we circled each other. Sometimes, of course, the circles went wrong; when he came closer, or too close, or I pulled back too far—then the circles went berserk, becoming wild, unpredictable ellipses. In short, we were like pieces in some monumentally ill-played chess game. Each move seemed aimless, but we must have been up to something, must have been trying for something. Some way in maybe, or out. But we never found it—what we were looking for. At best, now and then—as on that afternoon—we achieved a kind of fragile, febrile peace.

While we were having supper, Avigal called again. She'd called several times before we came home, Paulette said. Gideon went to answer the phone, then returned to the kitchen but said nothing about the call, only that it was Avigal and that she'd been waiting supper for me. He had told her not to bother.

He then returned to the description of our day, for Paulette's benefit. A short, rather sketchy version of it, I thought, with no mention of the lady with the many chain bracelets and his flight from her. He said only that he'd canceled his visit to Batya because he had wanted to get home early. She smiled. Just the thing to say. And was as pleased with the novels he'd bought her. Gideon's kindnesses were all like that. Prodigious, an abundance of them, automatic, careless, impulsive. He offered kindness, in fact, when you might want something else. In other ways, though, consistent, he remained what I'd come to expect—acerbic, critical, suddenly, brutally outspoken. He sometimes thought of it as teasing. If there was a softening anywhere, a giving-way—in either of us—it was imperceptible. Like the softening in the flesh you do not notice until early one awful morning you rise and look at yourself in the mirror. But the time was not yet ripe for such revelation. Even the threat of extinction does not alter the basic character that easily. I think, in fact, it must reinforce what there is in us to begin with.

In any case, I think he thrust that from his mind. He felt fine, he said. The disease seemed to be in remission. And he worked now almost full-time, sometimes staying at his office until after six or seven. He worked at home, too, though Paulette fussed a little. Earlier in the month, there'd been an international conference on high-energy physics and structure in Rehovot. Gideon had given a paper. He was doing more work on it and planned to attend another conference in September, abroad this time, in Zurich. Paulette would go with him. He may have been thinking about that as we sat there that night listening to the new Haydn record first, then to one of Paulette's Edith Piaf records. I knew he was unaware of us. At one point, he rose suddenly and, without a word, left the room, went to his desk in the bedroom and stayed there almost an hour. I suppose Paulette was used to this. She smiled at me but said nothing.

When he came back, it was eleven. He switched on the radio for the news. Of course. There'd been an attempt to sabotage the national water main in the south near Arad. The Arab League wished to expel Jordan. Sartre and de Beauvoir had arrived in the country for a visit. In fact, the usual.

I left soon after and walked back to the apartment slowly, through the same quiet streets I'd walked that morning. Avigal would be up, I knew. She'd want to talk. I saw the light of the brass lamp in the living room from the street. Avigal was on the sofa, in her usual half-closed jackknife position, heels drawn close to her buttocks, toes curled over the edge of the cushion, her toenails glistening through the nylons. She wore the sweater she'd worn earlier that day. No mistake then. I sat down opposite her in the armchair and worked my shoes off, toe to heel, and pressed both my feet into the resilience of the thick blood-orange carpet. Then I took a cigarette from the copper box, lit it, leaned back and stared at the coffee table. We sat like that, in silence. Beyond "Hello," I'd said nothing. Neither had she. The question, I knew, was—who would begin now, who would break this silence? Not me, I thought stubbornly.

"About today," she said a moment later, then paused, uncertain. Without looking up, I knew she was staring at me and waiting for a response. Another moment passed, two, three. She began again. "Look," she said, "I'm sorry. I want you to understand what happened. I need—"

"Don't." But that burst out of me before I knew it. "Don't— please don't tell me about it." My eyes rose now to meet hers.

"About what?"

"Your needs." A moment later, I said more calmly, "And I promise not to tell you about mine."

"I wouldn't mind," she murmured.

"I would. Very boring."

I leaned forward and carefully knocked the ash into the large ashtray.

"All right," she said, "if you want it that way."

I did not reply to this either. I took another puff of my cigarette, and then another, and remembered the presents. When I'd hung up my jacket, I'd left the large plastic bag on the little table in the hall. I now went to get it. The other two packages were in the bag, nestling now in the folds of my dress. I put

181

Josh's record on the shelf beside the rack of records. Flat, though, so he would see it at once when he returned. Then I put the little package for Avigal on the coffee table.

The silk scarf, folded small, was wrapped in silvery paper, with slivers of scotch tape where the paper came together and was folded under. A crinkly purple ribbon divided the upper surface into neat little silver squares. I stared at it for a moment before I went to put my dress on the bed in the study. When I returned, I saw Avigal had not moved.

I gestured at the package and said it was hers—her present.

"I know." But still she made no move to open it.

I sat down again.

"What is it?" she asked.

I told her. As far as I could, I kept my voice expressionless. Then she thanked me. I said, coldly, that it was Gideon she had to thank. It was his present. He'd only sent it with me.

"No, not for that. For—well, for going along with it."

I must have looked blank for a moment.

She added, "With the story."

"No one believed it," I said.

But she was unconcerned. "Thanks, anyway."

I stood up abruptly and walked to the door of the study again. "Anytime," I said. I meant that to sound contemptuous, I think, but it did not quite come off. My voice was shaky with bottled-up rage. I hated her for expecting that of me, expecting me to conspire in her betrayals. And I hated myself for fulfilling her expectations.

Four days later, when we were having breakfast in the kitchen, she said she had a favor to ask of me. I waited for her to go on, and this seemed to exasperate her. Could I stay away from the apartment that afternoon? Her voice was almost belligerent. She may have expected me to refuse.

"Until when?" I asked.

"Oh, about five-thirty. Or six maybe." She now seemed rather pleased with me. And with herself.

I finished my coffee and rose. She must have realized then that I had not really answered. "Well?" she said.

"It's your apartment."

182

"Don't say that." She sounded annoyed again.

"Isn't it?"

There was a long pause, then she decided to be conciliatory. She had a friend, she said. She managed to convey to me that it was a woman friend but did it, I noticed, without mentioning sex at all, without using "he" or "she." This friend had a problem and needed to talk with Avigal. Privately.

I smiled. "All afternoon?" And then I picked up my Hebrew book and my notebook and walked to the kitchen door.

The kitchen was rather dark—its one window, the wrong exposure, with tall trees just outside—I could hardly see Avigal in the dimness. I touched the switch beside the door. The fluorescent ring on the ceiling above the table hummed, flickered, then came on full. Her face was flushed, I saw, the clever dark eyes fever-bright. Yet she looked somehow innocent to me, so full of guile as to be almost guileless. Transparent, as Gideon had said. The light seemed to shine through her, you could see to the other side. Not the dark side, as it would be with me. Maybe there was no dark side to her. I knew, of course, I suffered from delusion.

For a few bewildering moments, I stared at her and felt the hard core of hatred inside me liquefy, flow outward; I was cleansed. I wanted only to reassure her—she could go anywhere, do anything, do it with anybody. All would be forgiven. Everyone would understand. I wanted, in fact, to say *I* understood—though I didn't, not anymore. And even wanted to say that I forgave her, though she'd not asked for forgiveness, not from me. Yes, I still resented her. More than ever, in fact. She had it all, I thought—she'd always had it all, and held it all too lightly. It didn't seem to matter much before, but now it did—now that I wanted something at last. Someone. She had what I wanted. What I needed. And she'd betrayed him. And continued to betray him. Still, it wasn't rage that made me tremble this time but the fierceness, and this protectiveness, this strange mixture of feelings rushing through me—which exhausted me, too, and left me limp. I describe it as best I can. I can't say I understood it. Or ever will.

I cannot remember the Hebrew class that morning. I know

183

it finished at quarter of twelve as usual . . . and that Mrs. Shapiro walked with me toward Herzl Street, talking, talking . . . and that I called Paulette from a café and told her I was going to Tel Aviv and would see her later. I knew Gideon wasn't at home that day. He was in Beersheba, doing his little bit for the military—that's what he called it. I climbed aboard the intercity bus, sat down and leaned wearily against the streaked, dusty window. Half-dreamed my thoughts—they ran into one another. Avigal's transparency. And opacity—mine. My dark side. My light. If there was one. And, of course, Josh once again. The deceived, the undeceived. I didn't know, and didn't know which I wished for him. Not that it made a difference. Joshua, Yehoshua, Josh. Oh, yes, the many names of God, I thought wryly. No doubt I'd spoken the name far too often. No doubt I needed to hear the name spoken. No doubt it was dangerous.

Once Gideon and I were talking about the Hebrew language, its concrete splendor, its logic, the economy of its vocabulary or the poverty—whichever way, he said, you wanted to look at it. We were talking about the difficulty of learning it. I asked him if he had had any difficulty. And Josh—had he? I spoke in such an offhand manner, so naturally. And he said no, he hadn't had too much trouble—he'd known three other languages by then. And Josh, he imagined, had had none at all. How could he? He'd come to the country when he was only four.

I stored the fact away. Another fact. But then I realized that Gideon was studying me with a bemused expression. He said, "But Josh is nothing like me, you know."

I froze. I knew he wasn't speaking now about languages or learning them. I didn't know what to reply. Numbly, I said, "Why should he be like you?"

"I don't know," he said. "Somehow I've got the impression that is what you think."

I didn't think so. "No," I said.

"Anyway," Gideon went on, "I suppose we *are* alike in some ways. I expect moral perfection, of course—expect it, too, I mean. But, mostly, I expect it from others." He smiled now. "Josh, on the other hand—Joshua expects it only from himself."

"Is that unusual?" I asked, my voice stiff, my face expressionless.

"Yes. And arrogant. Don't you think so?"

I think I nodded. And did not mention Joshua in his hearing again.

I found the apartment three weeks later. One large room that would have to do for both living and sleeping, a small kitchen and smaller bath, and an even smaller balcony which looked out upon the window of the top-floor flat in the house next door and down upon the garbage pails in the garden below. And I grabbed it. I even liked it. It reminded me of some of my other refuges. By then, maybe, I would have liked anything, rented anything.

It had its advantages, of course. It was central—that's what the rental agent said—very central. Two blocks south of Arlozoroff, four east of Dizengoff—and four blocks beyond Dizengoff, there was the sea. The landlord, Mr. Levi, said it was fully furnished. Hardly. Unless you regard two cots with wafer-thin mattresses, a battered wooden sideboard, a kitchen table and four slatted folding chairs as full furnishings. In the kitchen were a rusty three-burner electric hot plate and a waist-high refrigerator. These, it turned out, were also considered part of the furnishings. There was no phone. A phone, Mr. Levi informed me—he was perfectly serious—would have made this a luxury apartment and doubled the rent.

I signed a six-month lease with various options, mine being that I could paint the kitchen table and the chairs in some appropriate kitcheny color and, if I wished, renew the lease for six more months. The landlord's options had to do with money: he could raise the rent if the Israeli pound was devalued or if prices rose enough (and one or the other of these was bound to happen). Then Mr. Levi gave me the key, but with the understanding that I could not move in to live until the first of May. Meanwhile, he would remove his two suitcases from the loft and replace the broken mirror in the hall. And I—well, I'd be spending the latter half of April with Gideon and Paulette at the beach house. That meant there were only eight days left at Avigal's. Eight nights, eight mornings. . . .

I celebrated the signing of the lease rather modestly. I had an espresso in a café on Dizengoff. And let a husky young man pick me up. After the extended preliminaries, of course—the time, the weather, how I liked Israel, how long I'd been here, how long I intended staying—I let him buy me another dreadful espresso.

He said he was an artist, and dressed the part: paint-daubed jeans, white T-shirt, and a full rusty beard he seemed to wear both as badge of his calling and a disguise. My face, he said, interested him. A classic Russian Jewish face. I may have laughed, but he took no notice, so intent was he on discussing the broadness of my cheekbones, the full-lipped mouth, the heavy-lidded green eyes. That conversation, I must admit, buoyed me. The coffee was bad coffee, but might well have been good, intoxicating wine. A few of his blunter questions I evaded; others I answered with half-truths. In answer to questions I did not ask but which he thought perhaps I ought to, he told me some earnest truths. Or perhaps little lies. I didn't care. I accepted his invitation to dinner, and afterward an invitation to his studio in Jaffa, where I gazed at his canvases and made encouraging noises, appropriate but insincere. And then he came up behind me and embraced me. I felt sorry for him—I don't know why—and sorry for myself. I turned and put my arms around his heavy body; we necked a little standing there in front of his paintings, then I asked Eli—that was his name, Eliezer—to drive me home. All the way home. It so startled him, I think, that he agreed. I felt a little guilty but felt also that I'd earned it. The buses, both local and express, swayed back and forth, and my flesh was mercilessly battered and bruised. Earlier that day, coming in, I'd not had a seat. The trip had seemed purgatory to me then. And that evening, I felt almost safe from envy, less covetous of Avigal's possessions. Sinless. Relatively.

I made Eli stop the car in front of the institute. That surprised him. I clambered out of the little Fiat, and as I shut the door, he leaned forward, looked up at me through the open window, and said he didn't know where to reach me. Didn't even know my last name. I said I didn't know his either, but not to worry, I often went to that café, I'd see him there. (By then, I didn't remember which café it was or exactly where it was.) Then I hurried across the road and walked through the front gate into the institute grounds. Past Gideon's house—there was a light on in the bedroom, though it was almost midnight—and out the side gate. And then slowly through the dark and quiet back streets to Avigal's apartment.

Josh's car was at the curb. I was later than he that night, for once. The hall light was on, and after I locked the door, I switched it off. Now the only light was the streetlight filtering in between the slats of the blinds. I could see my way across the living room, see the door of the study. I took off my shoes and carried them. The door was slightly open. I pushed it inward.

He was sitting at his desk, in his room. Or was it my room? Sitting in the dark, then standing in it. When he heard me, he rose; then, a moment later, he switched on the lamp. The light was harsh. I winced.

I'd seen him three times in the sixteen days he'd been back—this was the fourth. That's what I thought—how often I'd seen him. How little. And how he avoided me. How in the midst of some conversation when we met at Gideon's those three times, I'd look up and meet his eyes and then, an instant later, he would turn away. But do it naturally. So elegantly. The way, in fact, he avoided me. Coming home later and later each night and, in the mornings, leaving earlier. I knew then, of course, that it was not my doing at all, but his, and noted also how, in contrast to my own clumsy, nervous efforts—from which the purpose too often ebbed away—how elegantly he always went about it. How very effective he was.

He didn't look effective now. He looked exhausted, his face stiff, with brown bruises of fatigue beneath his eyes. He held onto the back of the chair, for support—or because he might need to put something between us. I sensed this and felt like laughing. It would have been bitter, that laugh, for I'd come to terms with it already. I'd accepted that I had my reasons for avoiding him, and he had his for avoiding me, and that they were different reasons. I wanted to tell him that, to reassure him,

187

but I couldn't, of course. I stood there, hesitant, in the doorway, and could think of nothing else to say—nothing right. I stared at him, then past him, and thought how much I wanted him, how much I wanted to touch him. God, how I longed to touch him! But I couldn't do that either.

"Where were you?" he asked.

"Why?"

"You're late. You didn't phone." I thought I could hear anger in his voice now.

Automatically, I responded in kind. "I forgot," I said, too quietly. "Do I have to report in to you?"

For a long moment, he didn't speak. I saw something very cold in his eyes. I looked away confused. And then the hot blood rose in me again—higher. I spoke without thinking. The words sounded stupid even as they came from me, but I couldn't stop. "Do you want to know where I was? *Everywhere?* And everyone I saw?"

"You don't have to account to me," he said evenly. "It's none of my business."

"That's right."

"It's your father. He's worried. He's called three times this evening." Then, as he brushed past me, an order: "Call him."

I heard the front door open and close; a moment later I heard his quick footsteps on the garden path below. I stood there, motionless, a long time after he'd gone. Then I walked over to the divan and put down my purse, went out into the hall again, and dialed the institute.

Gideon answered on the first ring. No, I hadn't wakened him. He didn't sound upset or worried, or anything, in fact, except curious. Where had I been all day? I told him.

Then I went back to my room and lay down on top of the bed. I still wore my street clothes, but I was too tired now to undress. Yet I couldn't sleep. I lay there for what seemed hours. The sky was beginning to grow light before I dropped off, but long before that he'd returned. I'd heard him. Heard him go into their bedroom, knew he got undressed in there, and then knew that he climbed into bed beside Avigal.

And maybe she'd wakened when he came in. Maybe he woke

her. And was making love to her now, their bodies locked together, the one straining against the other, holding each other hard. Then, gently. Maybe they smoked and talked and held each other in the darkness, on the other side of the wall.

It was not a voluntary thought. No more willed than when your tongue probes a broken tooth to find the exposed nerve. Something you do to remind yourself of the facts. Or of what is real. Of what to expect.

24

I WAS TALKING ABOUT THE BOMB SHELTER, I REMEMBER, about how Mr. Levi had used it as the last, and, he must have believed, the most compelling reason I should rent his little apartment. It was downstairs, off the lobby, and he'd unlocked the door to show me a small rectangular room without windows, filled just then with the detritus of middle-class Tel Aviv life: two huge old wooden trunks banded with strips of iron, an ancient icebox, a baby carriage, two broken kitchen chairs, and an upended iron cot without its mattress. The storeroom, in fact. He said it could be cleared out at a moment's notice, though where all the junk was to go, he didn't make clear. I related all this with an attempt at humor. Paulette laughed a little, but not Gideon, and not Avigal, who interrupted me in midsentence.

"What is so funny?"

I don't think that surprised me. We were almost bloody now with abrasion. What I did and said irritated her almost beyond endurance, and had been doing so for weeks. Just the fact of her existence grated on me. But I'd fought the feeling down when I could. . . . I'd tried to quell it.

I remember smiling coolly at her, and saying rather reasonably, I thought, that what was so funny was this constant preoccupation with war. Or it would be funny if it weren't so sad. I talked then about Mrs. Levi—an emotional type, and not very well educated. Her belief was that war might begin tomorrow, or even tonight. The Arab armies would rise up in their millions and swoop down upon us, the nameless *fedayeen* in their checked *kefiyahs* coming along for the ride. Carrying axes and long knives, they would—if they could, of course—kill all the men, rape all the women, and who knows what they'd do with the children. And certainly burn down everything. *Everything.* Starting with the American Embassy. Obviously this vivid recreation acted as catharsis. And Mr. Levi let her go on, and on, and on. I'd already signed the lease.

"That sounds impossible to you?" Avigal asked.

"Improbable, let's say." I did not elaborate.

But she would not have that. "Why? Why does it seem so far-fetched?"

So I told her; or I attempted to tell her. It seemed to me that, except for the threats and counterthreats—none of which materialized—and the citizenry playing at soldier but with real guns, and an incident or two at the border, everything seemed quite normal. I mean, I said, what *is* normal anyway? Dizengoff is normal. Like any other such city street in the world, allowing for climate, of course, and customs and language. And those newscasts. In fact, you might even say peaceful.

An unfortunate word. Avigal jumped on it. "Peaceful!" She was scornful.

"Not at war, in any case," I snapped.

"What do you know about it?" she demanded.

And she was right, of course, I knew nothing about it.

Now I half-turned to Gideon, for his opinion maybe. She did the same. But he'd not said a word, and it looked as if he were going to maintain the silence. In the interests of peace, he would say, at the luncheon table. Avigal gave him up, turned back to me at once.

"Well, this country is at war now," she said. "Even you have got to see that."

"I'm not afraid." God, I must have sounded unbearably smug.

191

"Neither am I," she retorted, "but not because I'm stupid."

Paulette broke in; her voice was plaintive. "Can't we talk about the weather?"

"Warm, isn't it?" Avigal said. She picked up her wine glass and drank. It did not mellow her at all.

I hoped it would mellow me; but in any case, it was cool, tart, and wet and I was very thirsty, having walked there from the *ulpan* in a thick amber-colored haze. I'd be fuzzy all afternoon, I knew—but it didn't matter. The day would accomplish that, anyway: a hot day, when the sunlight seemed to have acquired physical weight of its own, and the wind—you'd think a wind would be welcome, but not this one—hot, dry, and gritty. The *khamsin*, Gideon had explained, which came from the east, and carried with it the sands of the desert. The windows were closed tightly against it, but if you went into the living room and ran your finger along the top of the library table, you'd make a glistening streak in the coating of fine yellow dust. And, worse ——the *khamsin* always gave Gideon a raging headache. He looked as if he had one now. His eyes were dull with pain. "All right," he said abruptly, "apologize!"

"Who?" Avigal asked.

"Just do it," he said, "and go and get me some aspirin."

She got up at once, left the table, and returned from the bathroom two minutes later with a silver foil packet that she put down beside his plate. By then, he was describing the general effects of a *khamsin*. It worried away at the nerves. On the third consecutive day, he said, when the wind had become unendurable, a man could kill a nagging wife and get off scot-free. He put two aspirin on his tongue and washed them down with the last of the rosé. He assumed, he went on, that this extended to other female relatives as well, since any female—especially to the Muslim—was a possession and as much a source of irritation, perhaps, as of pride. As was true of any possession—of his donkey, for instance, which he might well value more than his wife or his daughter.

"They call it temporary insanity," he said. "An enlightened people."

Avigal giggled and reminded him it was only the first day of *khamsin.*

"So you're safe for a while," he said.

He lay down after lunch. The headache still raged. Aspirin didn't help much, or not for very long. Paulette made a cold compress, then went into the bedroom with it and, I suppose, lay down beside him. In any case, she disappeared. Avigal called the office—as he'd asked her to—to say he wouldn't be in that afternoon and where he'd be. Then she came out to the kitchen, and together we finished the dishes, talking about the apartment all the while, the bits and pieces of furniture that were available, the linens I'd need, and so on, and what she could let me have, and what Paulette could let me have, and what I'd have to buy for myself. All very friendly.

We continued the conversation out on the front porch, where we smoked and talked—a dull, almost sleepy conversation—and finally fell silent. It was hot outside. Even in the dense black shadow of the porch, behind the leafy vines. The air was so heavy you could scarcely breathe. I felt perspiration start, then crawl slowly down my thighs under my jeans, dry, start once again. I rolled up the sleeves of my cotton shirt, undid the two bottom buttons, and pulled the shirttails forward to tie under my breasts. It was what Avigal had done earlier, though she'd come better prepared, with white shorts to change into. She wore them now and, leaning back with a sigh, stretched out her legs —long, almost coltish in their slenderness, already darker with sunburn.

We didn't talk for a while. Avigal crushed out her cigarette, put the ashtray down on the floor between our two chairs, leaned back again, and closed her eyes. I hardly expected a conversation then; I thought, in fact, she'd fallen asleep. I closed my own eyes, foggy enough with wine for sleep, too.

"He's right," she said suddenly. "I ought to apologize."

I opened my eyes and turned to her.

"I mean," she went on, eyes still closed, "it doesn't matter what you think, really."

"Doesn't it?"

193

"No. Because when it happens, you'll be on the first plane out of here anyway."

I suppose that I ought to have felt anger then, but I didn't. What I felt was shame, the kind that comes with an offhand, perfectly gratuitous insult. A thoughtless one. As though the other knows you—knows you so well that she can say this and knows you'll accept it as true. Then you begin to wonder yourself whether you deserve it.

I said stiffly, "You don't think very much of me, do you?"

"No, that isn't it," she said. She opened her eyes and twisted around to look at me. "I'm not judging you. I meant, why *should* you stay? You're not an Israeli. Not a Zionist. You're not even a Jew. Your mother isn't—that decides it, you know." She looked away after this little speech, and said nothing for a while. Finally, "Anyway, why should you get involved? And maybe— Who knows? It can happen—maybe die."

I snorted. It sounded ludicrous, self-pitying, overly dramatic. But she didn't see the joke.

I said, "I'm not going to die. Not in battle, anyway. Neither are you."

She nodded. "Not me. But others. I knew a woman who died in forty-eight. And a friend of mine, a girl--she got blown up by a mine a few years ago. Women die like that, too. It's not only the men. But there'll be men dying, too. Plenty of men dying." She sounded somber now, no longer ridiculous. I didn't laugh. I said nothing. I lit another cigarette and smoked it in silence.

"But you're right, not me. I'll probably live forever." She was serious now, too. "Or, anyway, much longer than I want to. I'll get old. And ugly. No one will want me."

"You don't believe that either," I snapped.

"Sure I do."

"That there'll be no one?"

"Oh, Josh, I suppose. There's always Josh." She smiled at me, moodily.

I nodded. "Of course."

*　*　*

It was past four when the army captain drove up and got out of his car. He'd been to Gideon's office first, and there was told Professor Steiner could be found at home and just where his home was.

We were drinking iced coffee, Avigal and I. She offered to make him some, went inside to knock on Gideon's door, came out two minutes later with a tall glass of dark coffee, a lump of ice cream floating in it. She set it down on the little metal stool before the officer and sat down in her chair once again, still smiling at him. She began talking. In Hebrew, of course. I thought she knew him, the way they were talking together and laughing. Then Gideon came out on the porch, his cheek still creased from sleep, took the large brown envelope from the young man, and went back into his own room.

Now Avigal was talking very rapidly. She rose, went around the young man, leaned over to get the empty glass, bent very close. She wore no perfume; it was her true odor in his nostrils. Her breast brushed against his arm.

He was about twenty-five, I imagine, very tall and lanky, with hair that was almost yellow and bright blue eyes. He looked, in fact, like a Swede, the way you expect Scandinavians to look, though they so seldom look that way; not Jews, though they sometimes do. In any case, Avigal found him attractive—that was obvious to me and to him—and the captain responded in appropriate fashion, by smiling, talking a lot, and watching her with a faintly lecherous expression on his otherwise wholesome face.

It was a mating dance, but without music. Set to words. I watched it through the expelled smoke of yet another of my cigarettes. The Jewish rites of spring. By the time Gideon emerged from his bedroom, sucking on his dead pipe, Avigal had decided the captain was, anyway, driving to Jerusalem, or through it—as he'd said—and she could not miss the chance of hitching a ride, of seeing her mother.

She had, in fact, already gone to the bathroom, leaving the captain with me. We sat silent, smiling emptily at each other, until she returned. She was in her slacks again, but with her midriff still bared to the sun. Now, in front of us, she undid the knot of her shirttail, did up the bottom two buttons, and tucked the shirt into her slacks. She'd already wound the silk scarf around her dark hair—the scarf that was Gideon's gift to her. The final part of the ceremony was to call Yudit in Jerusalem. She did that before Gideon came out of his room.

So when he did, at last, it was *fait accompli*. She was going. The captain took the envelope of papers from Gideon with an apologetic air and walked slowly to his car, but he did not drive away. He sat in it, waiting. And Avigal told Gideon where she was going and what she was going to do. At least, told him what could be told. He had nothing relevant to say to this—no more than I had had. He was reduced to saying, rather helplessly, "Is that the way you're going? Just as you stand?"

"Why not? I look all right, don't I?"

"It'll get cold soon. You know how cold it is in Jerusalem."

She laughed and said she had something at her mother's house that she could wear in a pinch.

"Does she expect you?"

"Yes." She sounded triumphant. "I telephoned."

And as if that were the last hurdle, she fairly leaped off the porch, impatient to be gone. But then, she hesitated. She turned in the path, glanced up at Gideon, who stood on the porch steps, and me, still in the chair, as if she were awaiting our blessings.

"It would be a shame to waste this ride, *Abba*," she said. "It's a wonderful *tramp*. Right to the door." She gave us both a dazzling smile, sure she'd now made her point, such as it was. A free ride like that ought not to be missed. But there was still, I noticed, a hint of supplication in her voice when she spoke: understand, it almost begged, please.

"You have a guest," Gideon said.

"Oh, Sara doesn't mind." She glanced at me, as if for assent. And as if we shared secrets.

"And Josh—what about Josh?"

"What about him?" She sounded impatient.

"What did you tell him?"

"Nothing. I don't have time to call him. You do it, *Abba*, O.K.? And Sara," she said to me, "make Josh take you out to

196

dinner. Make him take you out." And her head swung around again, to make sure the car was still there, the captain waiting for her. "And you'll call him for me, won't you, *Abba?*"

"You call him," Gideon said.

"But I don't have time now," she cried. "Really, I just don't have the time." Then she turned and almost skipped down the path to where the army car was parked in front of Gideon's white car.

Gideon, speechless, stared after her.

She smiled at us once more before she climbed in beside the army captain. She said something to him that made him laugh, and they glanced—rather guiltily, I thought—toward the porch. Then he started the car, drove to the end of the road, swung around there, and went past the house again. Avigal waved at us as they drove by.

At the screen door, Paulette said softly, "I'll call him." I hadn't heard her come up, she'd done it so quietly.

Gideon said no. "What's the hurry?" he demanded. "He'll know it soon enough."

"I will," she said again. "I'll invite him to dinner." And she did—but he refused. He had work to do, he said.

A few minutes after that, I rose and began gathering my things together. Gideon asked where I was going. I said I was going home, I was tired. I don't know if that surprised him. I avoided his eyes. I don't even know if I said good-bye properly. I remember none of that now. Only that they watched me as I prepared to go, and said nothing and did nothing. What, after all, could they do?

25

I KNEW HE WOULD COME. I TOLD MYSELF HE WOULD. LET'S say it was my blood that knew. It did my thinking.

But an hour passed, and I began to be afraid. Perhaps he would not come at all—perhaps my blood was wrong. I still believed then—at least a part of me did—that I just wanted to talk to him. But talk about what? Or just see him, and sit there and talk. And, of course, look at him for as long as I wished, and have him look willingly at me. It seemed to me that this was perfectly possible—at least, to part of me it seemed possible —but the hour passed and then another started, and he still hadn't come. And that part of me that knew there was no reason for him to come took over.

I enumerated for myself all the reasons he would not come and all the things he might have chosen to do instead. Work, as he'd told Paulette. He could stay late in the lab again. Or he could go and have dinner with them, he could say that he'd changed his mind. Or visit friends. Or go to a movie. Or for a walk. Or a drive. He might even drive to Jerusalem to fetch Avigal home. It was hardly an hour's drive—he might be there already. I almost wished that had happened. It would solve things, I thought. A perverse desire, but a certain part of me would have settled for that—for just seeing him when he came home with Avigal.

But the other part—the part that said he will come, he will— that part would not let me rest. I bathed and I dressed. In fact, I dressed three times over. First in the dress Gideon bought for me, then in another, finally in Gideon's dress again. At one point I stood in the bathroom and stared at the stranger in the mirror, whose eyes seemed somehow darker; darker and strangely wet. Whose skin was flushed. Whose throat had gone quite dry with fear. I turned on the tap and cupped my palm under the stream of cool water, and I bent and lapped at it like a cat. A cat in heat. A thieving cat. A hungry cat. I stared at myself again and tried once more to comb my hair, but my hand shook uncontrollably and I dropped the comb. When I bent to pick it up, I found my knees were buckling. I sank to the bathmat and knelt there, still trembling. I pressed my forehead against the cool white edge of the tub. I thought, this is ridiculous. I'm thirty-one years of age. I'm too old for this.

Then, I thought: please. But I don't know to whom I addressed myself. Whether to the gods, Gideon's arbitrary gods. Or to God. Or the cosmic forces. Or to Josh. Perhaps, after all, to myself. And if I didn't know from whom I begged, I was equally ignorant of the other—for *what* I begged. An end to this? Or a beginning? I cannot, even now, be certain.

But I'm certain of other things. It does hammer—the heart. It hammers at the layers of flesh and fat and bone and skin that contain it. The romantic novels are right: no other word is so apt. It hammers, batters the flesh. If you look, you can see it move. I looked at the person in the bathroom mirror, down to where the white lace bra made an oblique slash in the swell of her flesh—I'm sure I saw it move.

But about the blood—they're wrong about that. It gushes forth, yes; the heart contracts, there is that first spill into the artery, but it does not race. It lurches forward, it slows, it pools. Slides back, slips forward. Only one thing is certain: its course, though confined, is erratic. And it sweeps everything away—

199

everything else in the world, everyone else. In a sense, you are cleansed. And one other thing: you are always aware of your blood, of its passage through your body. A constant lisp in your ears, an endless whisper. A sigh. But the sigh is inside you, and it goes on and on.

So the blood doesn't race. And when the waiting is over, the trembling stops. I noticed that, too.

I was in the far corner of the sofa when he came in. I'd been sitting there for more than an hour. I heard his step on the stairs outside the door, then the key turn in the lock, and when he came in—when, finally, I could see him—in the first voluntary movement I could make, I rose. The turbulence ended. In that instant. One moment I had been both the storm and mercilessly buffeted by it; the next I was at the eye of the hurricane, and it at the center of me. As if the high wind dropped, and everything, all at once, had ceased moving. A sweet calm filled me. A peace. And I was waiting again, but it was a different kind of waiting.

But this new waiting went on and on, too. For long moments, it seemed, he stood just inside the front door, his eyes avoiding mine; his gaze looped around me, it seemed to take in everything else—the furniture, the carpet, the wide, uncurtained window. And the part of me that imagined this moment and other things —an embrace maybe, gentle, chaste, a holding on to each other, a coming together—that part faltered, froze. It made wordless, whimpering animal sounds in my skull. For it saw desire recognized, communicated, unreturned. And it saw embarrassment, too, and a determination, nevertheless, to meet it head-on. The situation. For surely that's how he saw it. An unfortunate situation—which had, however, to be faced. I was halfway across the room then, and I stopped.

Then, as if he'd just seen me, he said, "Come on. Let's get something to eat." He turned away and walked out of the apartment before me, moving very quickly. I followed, pausing only to switch off the light and lock the apartment door, which I did almost automatically. When I reached the street floor, he was already in the car, in the driver's seat, and he leaned across to open the other door. Only then did he look at me, his pale eyes

200

met mine. But it was safe now. I stood on the sidewalk, in public. I would do nothing embarrassing. But it would have been safe for him up there, too, I knew, up in Avigal's living room, for there was nothing in his eyes for me. Nothing at all. I don't know what I felt. No, let me reduce this to the irreducible. I should not speak of feelings. I was numb.

Later, of course, when I could draw back a little, I could feel along with the numbness a mild, slightly bitter amusement, but that took the whole long drive to the seacoast to achieve. And meanwhile, after a short silence, he had initiated conversation. Impersonal, amiable, about books and music and movies. But the conversation died from an insufficiency of response, from the very thin trickle of monosyllabic answers, my dull "yes" and "no." I could not help myself just then, and maybe he knew it. He was very patient. He grew discursive. He was most educational on Jewish history, on international and national politics, and when that threatened to dry up, there was the radio, music. In fact, Mozart. He looked content.

By then the part of me that had postulated friendship, that part turned toward him and tried to smile. But we'd reached the restaurant. The proprietor met us at the entrance.

I was introduced: the American daughter of my father. The proprietor, smiling, took my hand in his warm, plump, moist one, held it for far too long, and said in English that, yes, he knew my father. A great man, he said. I thanked him. As if that were all my doing. As if, indeed, it were true. Then led us through the narrow steamy restaurant to the large flagstoned terrace beyond, and over to the far end of it, to a small, rickety table set, as though for support, against a wooden balustrade. Below, the sea lapped against huge boulders; above, the vines twisted under and over a roof trellis. Leaves rustled in the sea-wind, and bare bulbs, hanging from a crisscross of exposed wire, swayed now and then in the damp breeze.

The proprietor then lit the candle on the table. He did it with a flourish, bringing the match cupped in his hand to the rim of a ruby glass bowl and dipping it down to the wick, which caught and swelled with flame. I watched, hypnotized. He reached up and switched off two or three of the colored overhead bulbs and left. We sat, silently now, facing each other in the dimness. We were alone.

But not for long. The waiter came to tell us what Saleh had ordered for us, and then Saleh returned, carrying three glasses in one hand and a bottle of white wine in the other. He sat with us through almost all of our dinner, talking and talking, smiling at Josh and at me, smoking his cigar, sipping wine. The arak he pressed upon us at the last, he said, was also with the compliments of the house. An orthodox host, in fact, but an unorthodox Muslim. As it turned out, an ultraorthodox Palestinian.

He spoke in Hebrew to Josh, with occasional lapses into Arabic. Of course, I could understand neither, but then he would turn to me occasionally, to make some comment or other in his facile but not quite correct or colloquial English, his eyes swerving from Josh to me, his smile seductive, his forefinger forever smoothing the thick shiny black moustache outward, downward, afraid it would get mussed.

For the most part, his tone was hectoring, but hectoring in a rather gentle way. He was enumerating Arab grievances to Josh, who responded with a shrug, a skeptical smile, a grimace of dismay—whichever might be appropriate to the moment. But also with serious advice about where to write, whom to call, or see—all of which Saleh rejected. "No, my friend," the proprietor said, "this is not a just society for the Arab. That is only in an Arab state. A democrat Arab state."

"Like Jordan, you mean, or Egypt?" Josh was smiling at him. "Or maybe like Saudi Arabia?"

Saleh laughed at the little joke, but without much appreciation. "A Marxist state," he said, "which will come into being when we receive our country back."

"Of course," Josh said.

Not that he belonged to any organization, Saleh said, turning to me. He was a law-abiding citizen, and these were all illegal organizations—even if illegal only in Israel—and he did not believe in carrying arms; but his sympathy was always with his brothers in the cause.

Josh said he understood that—both the Arab cause and the Arab case.

"You cannot understand it, my friend," Saleh told him. "Or understand *us*. We love our land."

"The tragedy in conflicts like this," Josh began, almost ignoring that, and speaking now very slowly, very carefully, "is that there is right on each side. Someone wiser than you and me said that once. I'm just repeating it now." It sounded as if he'd memorized it, as if it were his set piece for the evening.

It was. For, after they smiled at each other—though these were, for the moment, no longer very easy or comfortable smiles —and after a waiter appeared with the rest of our dinner and whispered a message in Saleh's ear, after Saleh rose reluctantly, to follow the waiter to the kitchen, Josh said that they always had this sort of conversation, the same one, more or less. And it always came down to that, to Saleh claiming to belong to no organization but expressing great sympathy for the revolution and the cause. And Josh saying what he did, and then both of them smiling at each other.

"Does he belong?" I asked.

"I don't know," Josh said. "Sometimes I think he does, and it's a good cover, saying that. And it *is* very clever, I must admit. He's clever. But I don't know. Anyway, I imagine that he's watched. And that isn't what I feel frustrated about—it's that we never seem to get past that point. We never discuss any compromise, for instance."

"You're not very good at that," I said quickly. I knew that somehow even then.

He stared at me for a moment. "Why do you say that?"

"Are you?"

"As a matter of fact, I'm not. Not very. But neither is he."

"Not much hope then, is there?"

"Not much," he agreed.

We were quiet after that. Eating, drinking, not looking at each other. Pointedly looking past each other. But it would now be easier, I knew. My heart had already stopped hammering. I was back to acceptance again, to things as they were. Or to something close to it. I looked at the sea, leaning over the railing to watch the black water frill white on the rocks. Then Saleh returned and broke the silence. He sat down again, lit another cigar, and after a while leaned over to knock a fat cylinder of ash into the ashtray.

Josh complimented him on the food, on the grilled fish, the salads, and the chips; then, on the coffee—so thick it had first to settle before we could drink it—sweet and dark and very strong, with fragrant seeds of *hel* floating in it. Turkish coffee, Josh had called it.

"Arab coffee," Saleh corrected. "You see how you always are insulting us?" Then he turned to me and said, "But I like this man. Even though he is European. He is not like the others."

"What others?" Josh asked, looking up.

But Saleh merely smiled, and anyway we could supply the answer for ourselves. In other words, the Jews—not like other Jews. We neither of us replied to this, and the proprietor went on, "But you mustn't worry," he said to Josh. "I will come to defend you myself. You are like my brother. I can say anything to you."

Josh asked why he should need defense, but I imagine he already knew what Saleh would say.

"Before the tribunal, of course—the Palestinian revolutionary tribunal. Jews will need defense. Except for, maybe, members of Rakah." This was the name of the Israeli Communist Party. "But I will defend you, I promise. Because I like you so much. Because I can speak so honestly with you."

"Thank you," Josh said, and raised his arak in a toast.

"I will also defend your father-in-law," Saleh added expansively. "A man who can produce beautiful daughters must be preserved at all costs. And he is almost a Muslim, isn't he? Four wives. Not at the same time, of course. We can't have everything." And he laughed heartily.

I wondered how he could know that, who might have told him, where he might have read it. Though everyone seemed to know. I supposed Gideon was right: it *was* a small country.

Josh smiled at this, I saw. I did, too, though I no longer thought him amusing. Then he lapsed into Hebrew again, and I watched them both in the flickering light of the candle: the round, comfortably plump face of the Arab and his dark liquid eyes, and then Josh's bony jut of cheekbone, his pale, rather cool eyes, and the distant, polite but very attentive smile that played around his mouth—the way his eyes met mine, and turned back to Saleh. And then Saleh rose once more; there was really much he had to do, he said. Josh said something to him in Hebrew, and the other man laughed. He glanced over at me, said something to Josh in return, lifted his thick shoulders as though something were past understanding, and reached up then to switch on one of the overhead bulbs. The one directly above us; in fact, full on us now, its yellow light illuminating everything, swaying now and then in the seawind and casting long, slanted shadows.

I blinked. Saleh blew out the candle and took it away with him.

"Does the light bother you?" Josh said.

"Did you ask him to do that?"

"Yes, the candle was giving me a headache." He glanced up at the swaying bulb, then back at me. "This doesn't seem much better. Does it bother you?"

I said no, very curtly.

There was a moment or two of strained silence. I said again that it was fine, that it didn't bother me.

"I told him the candlelight was wasted on us," he said.

"Is that why he laughed?"

"Yes." He paused—no, it was more a hesitation, considering whether he ought to say more or not. Then, "You've made a conquest."

"Have I?"

"He says you have beautiful eyes."

"Everyone to his taste," I said. "What does he say to Avigal?"

But he didn't answer that. He merely stared at me, and I'm not sure he heard.

"He said another thing or two, but I'll spare you those."

"No, please. Tell me. That was nice to hear."

"The other things are not so nice."

"Tell me."

"If you insist." But he paused again as though he had to phrase it the right way. "He said he'd be proud to make love to you—if I wasn't up to it."

205

I dropped my eyes at once, stared into the glass of arak. My hand was now shaking a little. I felt his eyes rest on my hands. If I look up now, I thought, I'll see cruelty in his pale eyes; he will see the pain in mine. I didn't look up.

After a moment I asked, "What did you say?"

"That it was up to you. Your choice."

I moved the glass around and watched the colorless liquid swirl, coating the sides of the glass. The scent of licorice was overpowering—I could drown in that smell and never need to look up again. I saw his hand holding out a pack of cigarettes, but I shook my head. My hands would tremble uncontrollably, as they were trembling now. I put them flat on the table, palms down. And we sat in silence as he smoked. It was a long, tense silence.

In the car going home, he talked about Arab politics. He mentioned names, he gave dates; the whole thing was very complicated. But I wasn't listening anymore. I heard only the rush of sad blood in my ears and the slowed, almost funereal throb of my heart.

"Please," I said suddenly.

"What?"

"Could you be quiet now?"

He glanced at me. "I haven't said anything for at least ten minutes." He looked at the luminous hands of his watch. "No, twelve minutes."

I was sorry. I said so.

"For what?"

"For everything. That's all. Just for everything." I think I was going to cry. My eyes burned, I couldn't look at him. "I'm not myself this evening, ' I said. And, again, that I was sorry.

"You said that," he reminded me. "Who are you then?"

"What—*what*," I corrected.

"All right," he said. "What?"

"I'm a cat. A hungry cat."

"I see. Nine lives and all? One of those? Landing on your feet?"

"Of course. I always land on my feet." I said no more after that. No more until we turned into the street where he lived and he drew to a stop before the darkened apartment house. I looked up at the living room window. Still dark. Did I think Avigal was home? I don't know. And I didn't care.

I thought: I must thank him nicely for the dinner. It was a good dinner. But I couldn't speak for a moment; I just sat there, staring straight ahead. He leaned across me to open the door, groped for the handle, never found it. Instead, he put his hand on my shoulder and pulled me around. He touched my cheek first, then held my face between his palms. He kissed me. His mouth was trembling. Like mine. It was almost an awkward kiss, innocent even, but I held on to him convulsively. He pulled away.

But I wouldn't let him go. I pressed my face into his throat. His hot flesh against my lips. I could smell and taste him now. So fevered his skin, I thought, it could not be his. Could not. Was. When I opened my eyes again, I could see his eyes—glittering sapphire blue, narrowed—and his mouth spreading into a slow, sensual satyr's smile. I held on to him with both hands, my arms around him. But he caught hold of my hands.

"Yes," I said.

"That's an answer," he said. "What's the question?"

"I want you."

"Not a question," he murmured. Then he placed my hands in my lap and turned away. His face against the darkness, his profile, was like a carving on a coin. Regular, rigid, unalterable except by eons of time. I don't know how long we just sat there: I in my seat, staring at him; he in his. We did not speak. But it was real now, at last. It had happened. I hadn't dreamed it.

Finally, I said, "Do you want me?"

He didn't answer. I think I began to be afraid then.

"Do I—do I disgust you?" I asked. "Does my wanting you so much disgust you?"

"You're a bloody little fool."

"Do I want you too much? Is that it? Am I supposed to play hard to get?"

"Shut up."

I caught hold of his hand, but he shook me off. It didn't matter. He could have slapped me then; it wouldn't have mattered.

207

Then he shifted in his seat; he faced me. It was I who looked away then, down at my hands twisted together in my lap, the knuckles white.

"Your terms," I said.

"You're not a cat."

"I am." But I still dared not look at him.

And when I did—when I looked up—everything around him had blurred, had lost its outline. There was only Joshua, very sharp; the rest of the world was his aura.

"I'm in love with you," I said.

"I know."

"Do you—are you in love with me?" I'm not sure the question took any courage. Or maybe it took superhuman courage. I had to know, that was all. But I thought I knew the answer already, and it hardly mattered what he'd say. But, still, I think I wanted to hear it . . . to hear something.

"What difference would it make?" he asked. He spoke to the steering wheel again.

"It makes a difference to me," I said. "Do you?"

"I don't even know if I like you." His voice was low, the tone flat, expressionless.

"You don't," I said. "I'm not likable. But the other—do you?"

But he said nothing, and his swift glance told me nothing.

A minute later, he said to the steering wheel, "Go on up, Sara. Go upstairs." He sounded weary.

"You think it'll just go away, is that it?"

"I hope it will go away," he said. "I hope so." He sounded hopeless. He lifted his head and stared through the windshield. The hood of the car was misted over. He said, "It's insane, isn't it? Taking you out was insane. I thought it would be all right, but it wasn't. Kissing you was insane. Insane. I'm crazy. It was better to do nothing. And to say nothing."

I reached out then to touch his cheek. I lay my palm on the side of his face, made him turn and face me so I could see his eyes again, see it there again, in the pale sadness of his eyes. What we should not speak of, what he did not want to speak of, what he hoped would just go away. I did see it. It was there. I

208

have to remind myself of that now. That I saw it; he did love me.

I leaned forward and put my mouth to his cheek. He touched my face with his fingertips, very gently. I felt his mouth touch mine again, in a very innocent kiss. But then I pressed myself against him. I wanted to hold him, to take him into me, into my body. And, at that moment, I was aware of him only, of him and of me, and of no one else, and of nothing else.

He said, "Now. Go on. Go on, now. Go on up."

I stared at him in bewilderment and didn't move.

He said, "I'll be up a little later."

"I'll wait," I said. But I felt panic rise even as I spoke, and he must have heard it in my voice, because he reached over and lifted a wisp of my hair and laid it back, smoothed it back slowly. "Go on now," he said.

"I need you," I said.

"I know. I need you, too." But he wasn't looking at me anymore.

So I went upstairs and waited again. I waited in the living room. I sat down in the dark living room and I waited.

After a while, I went to the window and looked down at the street. The car was still parked at the curb. I don't know if he was in it. I stood there a long time, I remember, staring at the car. I thought, any moment he will open the door and come up to me. I did not know if he would want to make love to me then but that didn't matter either. I longed just to touch him, to hold him for a while, and nothing else—not if he didn't want it. But I thought he would want to kiss me again, at least. At least that.

Then I went back to the sofa and sat down again. I waited an hour. I closed my eyes. And I saw Josh on the dark inside of my lids. Perhaps I slept then, I don't know. But I heard something—something in the street. I jumped up and stumbled over to the window.

I did it, I think now, merely to confirm what I already knew. That the street was empty, the car gone.

26

WE LEFT FOR THE BEACH HOUSE TWO DAYS LATER: THE DAY
after the winter tenants had vacated. A week earlier than originally planned. That was Gideon's decision. He'd been very
moody after I'd left; too late, he'd said, but the sooner now, the
better. And had prowled the house for an hour or so before he
finally settled down to some work. This Paulette told me the
next day—and having told me, regarded me silently as if I
held the key to his behavior, as if she expected an explanation
from me if not from him. But I could not believe she did not
know—she looked too understanding, too calm and sane. I got
up and, on some pretext, left the kitchen.

I must have called the institute ten times that day. I stared
down at the empty street and called the institute. I don't know
how many times exactly, because quite often I'd lift the phone
and replace it before dialing. Or before I'd finished dialing. Or
dialed and then hung up before the switchboard answered. I
got through enough times, though, for the switchboard operator

to come to recognize my voice. The fifth or sixth call, I think. She was beginning to think me insane. I was beginning to think myself insane.

"*Ain tshuva, geveret*," she said each time the call was completed, each time she rang and rang Josh's room and got no answer. Once she cut me off without even telling me this. And each time I hung up I wondered what I would have said—if he had answered. What could I have said that would not have sounded foolish? Foolish after that night, foolish now—in the bright yellow light of day?

It was very clear what he wanted. Wanted from me. Nothing. I put down the phone each time, and each time I was shaking inside. But still frenzied: toward the end, though, I called but did not expect him to answer. Did not now even want him to answer, I think. For if he had answered, what in the world could I have said to him that would make any difference?

Still, I kept telephoning. The girl at the switchboard sounded impatient now; then, without asking, she switched me over to the physics office. But the secretary there didn't know where Dr. Weiller was or when he'd be back. Sorry. That was at two. I got dressed and walked over to Gideon's house.

At four, I was helping Paulette pack the china and glassware we'd need at the beach house. I'd gone into the living room to fetch some of Gideon's old newspapers and was on my way back to the kitchen, passing through the hall, and there was the phone. An internal phone, this time. I would not have to speak to the girl at the switchboard. I remember putting down the newspapers and lifting the receiver. I do not remember the act of dialing. At the other end, the phone rang five or six times. I think I was almost relieved there was no answer. And was about to hang up when someone did answer.

Not Josh. Another male voice. "Dr. Weiller?" I said uncertainly.

The man at the other end was very helpful. The phone had been ringing on Dr. Weiller's desk all day, he said, and he'd wanted to answer but had restrained himself. But Dr. Weiller had called in just a while ago to say he was in Jerusalem, at

211

his mother-in-law's, in case anyone asked or called. And then, "Do you want the number?"

I said no, it wasn't important, I'd call again. And after that, I don't know—I suppose I said good-bye. I hung up and stood there for a minute or two, staring down at the phone but maybe not seeing it. That's how I found out where he'd gone. And to whom. As, of course, was right and proper.

In the kitchen I kneeled beside an open carton, wrapped tumblers in newspaper, placed them on a bed of crumpled newspaper. Then, in a smaller carton, the wine glasses: I made a ritual of it, almost a ceremony of wrapping, of crumpling the newspaper, of placing it just so in the carton. At any rate, it was something to concentrate on. On that if not on Paulette and what she was saying. Something, of course, about Gideon. He'd changed, she'd said—and looking at me—didn't I think so? I didn't.

"Not physically," she said. "Inside, inside."

I said again that I didn't think so. But what did she mean exactly? She meant that he always wanted people around him now. Lots of people, almost all the time, even when he was working. He wanted people sitting with him or nearby in another room. And he kept inviting people to the house—even though he'd never done this before, invited people he'd never liked especially. "Even strangers." The last word she bit off as though it were a loose, hanging thread. He was, she said, talking about a party—a big party.

"He likes parties," I told her.

"Not this kind."

I didn't say anything for a minute or two. I finished packing the wine glasses, closed the carton, and said that as far as I could remember Gideon had always needed people. Needed to be charming. Perhaps he wanted now to widen the Gideon-charmed circle.

She looked angry. "You don't understand me."

"You mean," I said, "he's always been a hermit before this? And now he's a bon vivant. In one giant leap?"

"He's never been a hermit," she said stiffly, her eyes dull with pain.

212

I said I thought I understood it. "He doesn't want to be alone now, doesn't want to think."

"He isn't alone," she snapped. "He thinks."

"About physics."

She didn't answer.

"But not about dying."

I don't know what prompted me to say that. I don't even know if I meant to be so cruel. Perhaps I did—perhaps I wanted to hurt in my turn. Even so, I felt wretched. I put my hands over my face.

"What's the matter?" she asked with concern.

"Nothing." The next moment, I was crying.

She came over to me then and crouched beside me, put her arms around me. We were both crying now, both of us. I suppose she thought I cried for the same reasons—for her reasons. For Gideon. And maybe, after all, she was right. I cried for him, too, surely. And for myself. Not as she did, for what she'd had, for what she might lose now. The grief that wrenched out of me was for what I'd never had. For what had been within my reach, though, for what I had myself pushed away. Or lost irretrievably in some other way, for some other reason; not because I'd held back. No, for reasons I thought I would never understand—or for no reason at all.

When Paulette spoke, at last, she was calmer. "What are we crying for anyway?" She rose and stood looking down at me. "It's silly. He's fine now. Come on, let's have some coffee." And when I didn't move, "Come on, now. Come on."

Gideon drove with his usual skill but concentrated on his driving. For the first half hour or so, he was unusually quiet. Paulette sat beside him with the small carton of stemware in her lap, peering at him anxiously now and then as he honked and maneuvered his almost abandoned way through the heavy traffic.

The cars that passed us flashed sunlight from their shiny metal roofs—the light hurt my eyes. But when I closed my eyes, I saw Josh again. I kept them resolutely open. Paulette twisted

213

around to look at me. She wanted to make sure I was holding onto the carton of china beside me on the back seat. Her face shone rosily. She knew how to protect herself from this sun— her forehead and cheeks were filmed lightly with cold cream. Now she leaned over the back of the seat and held out the tube of cold cream. I shook my head.

At the beginning of the trip, Gideon had said it would be uncomfortable. Too hot to drive. We should, he said, have started out in the early morning; but he had had to go to the lab to see to a few things and did not get back until after one. We could have gone in the evening, but he wouldn't wait. Now he said nothing about the wind that blew sand off the dunes, or the glare of the sunlight—the harsh light that filled the sky seemed to fill the universe.

At three o'clock he switched on the news and translated for us. For me, I should say. Paulette said she wasn't interested.

A boy sitting on a balcony in East Jerusalem had been shot by a Jordanian soldier from his position on the ancient wall of the old city. There were the usual reverberations from a speech made several days earlier, a rather bellicose speech I'd thought at the time, in which the prime minister had warned the Arabs that it was dangerous to test Israel's patience. (I'd once seen Eshkol's photo in the newspaper—he looked like the mild-mannered owner of a dry goods store in a medium-sized town in the American Midwest.) Then there were some samples of Arab rhetoric, bits of a strident newspaper editorial published in Damascus. When the news went off the air and the pop music came on, Gideon switched off the radio. In the silence, I said the news was depressing, as usual. And overheated.

"You mean," he said, "we Jews talk too much?"

"Arabs, too."

"It's a Semitic flaw, then?" he persisted.

I said I didn't know. In any case, it was a good way of just letting off steam. And cooled things down, somewhat.

"You think so?" And then, a moment later, catching my eye in the rear-view mirror, "That's because you don't believe them. I believe them all right. Respect them enough to do that.

They are very clear about their intentions. And this is a way of bringing things to the boil."

"There you go again," Paulette moaned. She threw me a scolding look, as if it were my fault—bringing up that subject. She maintained it was the most popular subject of conversation in the country.

"The only subject," I said.

But Gideon said, rather dryly, that there was at least one other, jostling that one for popularity, too: the dreadful state of the economy.

Then, to me, he said, "I could go into the many reasons you ought to believe them, Sara—our neighbors. But I won't. Paulie doesn't like it." And he glanced at Paulette with a smile. "And when I think how different you were," he said to her. "Was it only five years ago? Night and day. The things you said to me then." His voice trailed off.

"What did I say?" she demanded.

But he merely smiled at the road and overtook another car. Paulette, pink under the sheen of cold cream, made a weak attempt at coolness, saying she would never have said those things —she didn't say which things—if she'd known how this sort of conversation would affect her digestion.

Gideon laughed and said that I could take that as fair warning. The dangers of falling in love with one of the French. "The French are a passionate people, but practical," he said. "Love, in the end, always takes a back seat to the liver."

Paulette giggled, mollified by his humor, perhaps, or by memory. She looked at Gideon now with such naked hunger that it embarrassed me.

But he wasn't finished. He was talking about the Arabs again, about being a Cassandra in the Middle East, whom only other Israelis believed—because they, too, were all Cassandras. But that was inevitable. "You'll see," he said comfortably, obviously expecting me in time to become a seeress, too.

"Anyway," he said, "when it finally happens—"

I interrupted. "If—don't you mean?"

"When," he said firmly, eyeing me in the rear-view mirror.

215

"But don't worry—when it happens, it'll be over, one way or the other, almost before you know it. A short war. We couldn't survive a long one."

He lapsed into silence after that, giving himself over, maybe, to a contemplation of the near or distant future: of the Arab armies close at hand; of those as far away as Iraq, but brandishing the weapons from their Czech and Russian arsenals—guns, missile launchers, planes, tanks—and ominously silent about other weapons, like the one the Egyptians had, their not-so-secret weapon, the poison gas they had used on rebels in the Yemen. After that, his thoughts perhaps turned to the beach house, situated on the narrow coastal strip and so near the Jordanian border—perhaps twenty miles away or less—that Hussein's well-trained army, his British officer-trained Legion, could reach the sea in a matter of hours, or less, and cut the country in two. Grim thoughts—I didn't know if he thought them. I know I did, in spite of myself. He said, in the silence, "Did I upset you?"

"Yes," I said, "I'm a coward."

He laughed. Paulette, however, looked unhappy and shifted restlessly in her seat.

"We have, of course, one distinct advantage," he told me. "It's this," and he waved at the white road, the fields, the houses. "Or that," and he gestured at the sea, the blue and emerald sea beyond the dull yellow-gray dunes.

"Not much of an advantage," I murmured.

"We must be grateful," he said, "for little things. At least, we know the alternatives."

This must have further depressed Paulette; her head drooped. It may even have depressed Gideon. He was quiet again, after that. I know it depressed me—or would have if I had not already been so deep in misery I could sink no further. And the house, too, depressed us when we reached it, ten minutes later.

First, there was the scorpion that fell out of the mailbox when Gideon opened it, which tried to scuttle away, but which he killed with one whack of a rolled-up newspaper. And then the fact that Paulette's worst fears had proved well-founded. There was a long crack across the bathroom mirror, a broken chair in a corner of the dining room, and a horde of flies buzzing around the grease-encrusted stove in the kitchen. She stared at this last with patent disgust. Then she did some sketchy sweeping; this, while I made up the beds and dusted the bedroom furniture.

When I finished in the room that Avigal and I had once shared, where I would sleep now, I went to the window and saw Gideon in the backyard. He was crouching beside the flower-beds, poking among the clog of weeds—looking, I supposed, for the flowering perennials of last summer. But they seemed to be gone, all of them, or dead. The tenants, an American professor and his small family, had been as careless of the land as of the house.

But the flowers were not the only things gone. Other things, too, were gone or changed utterly. There'd been large vacant lots at either end of the lane, but now both were hedged-in gardens, with large houses set within. The only field left was the one just across from our house, two lots back to back extending to the main road, which was parallel and led to the sea: a sandy field, full of rocks and pebbles, thick with a tall, tough, dusty green tangle of weeds. But the road in front of the house—that was no longer sandy. It was paved now. You could only kick up a choking cloud of dust if you went down into a ditch. And the house itself seemed smaller, shabbier.

I mentioned this to Gideon later. I said that I missed the old soft sand road.

He looked at me curoiusly. "I didn't think you'd miss anything."

"Neither did I," I said.

We were having supper at one of the new resort hotels that lined the beach, among the ladies in pastel slacks—apple green, powder bluē, peach—with sweaters to match and mutation mink stoles draped over their shoulders, among the men who smoked thick cigars, wore madras jackets or cream flannel and flowing, flowered sport shirts. Very gay, in gorgeous multicolor. Dressed as we were, we might have been three dun-colored sparrows among a strut of peacocks. I think all this amused Gideon. He looked around curiously, smiled at everyone. They stared back. He was even amused by the waiter who ignored us for as long as he could, recognizing the local nontipping breed when he saw it.

"When the time comes," Gideon said, with a sardonic smile, "this hotel will be emptied overnight. And I can't blame them." He meant, of course, the tourists, who would sprout wings, fly away. Paulette looked as if she wished he would shut up. He dropped the subject and began talking about Zurich in the fall and of maybe going to Paris, too, so that Paulette could see her children and her grandchildren. At which point, Paulette took out photographs to show me, naming them for me: Corinne, who was six, and Thiery, three, and Solange, two.

Later, when we were alone on the terrace, I thanked Gideon —for me and for her, too. For dropping the all-important, pervasive subject. I spoke lightly.

He peered at me. "It won't go away," he said, "just because I drop it."

27

EACH NIGHT IT WAS THE SAME: I PLUNGED INTO A BOTTOM-less well of sleep, into the blackness as if I wished to drown in it, as though sleep were the black water and my thirst for it otherwise unslakable. And then each morning, too early, coming awake, certain that there was something I'd neglected to do, unable to remember what it was. Someplace I had to be. Not here. Though I didn't know, for the moment, where "here" was. Or "there."

Afterward, I could not sleep again. There was the blank white ceiling, the blank white walls, the sky growing lighter, the first birdsong, the sun rising. And with them the ghosts of morning, the ritual unfolding of the past into the present, all of them crowding in—where Josh had been—to fill the void. The void, nevertheless, remained. Peopled: Giorgios and Lucios, those who came after Rob, before him. Nameless now, some of them, some faceless. Finally, Rob himself. Retribution.

The day I discovered I was pregnant. How sick I was, vomit everywhere. After, not before. And then, for some illogical reason, getting married. The office of the justice of the peace;

Rob's mother red-eyed, though she never, she assured me, cried at weddings. He had done right by me. That was important to her. The baby—he had to.

Except I didn't think of it like that. Not as a baby, not mine and his. But, rather, as something inside me, some faintly obscene growth, getting larger all the time.

A week later, I woke up sick again. It was a Saturday morning. I vomited into the toilet. Then I sat down in a chair beside the bed where Rob lay sleeping. I watched him. I thought he'd wake up soon; then I thought I'd wake him, shake him awake. That is, if he didn't wake soon. I sat there thinking that, staring at him, willing him to wake.

After a while he groaned, turned over. He opened his eyes, saw me, patted the bed beside him invitingly. My mouth filled with bile, and I stumbled back into the bathroom. When I came back this time, I told him. I was sorry, I said. I couldn't. I'd made a mistake. I couldn't.

Couldn't what?

I didn't want it. I was rattled now; my voice rose. Why hadn't I thought of this before, I wondered. It didn't matter. I'd thought of it at last. I couldn't have it. *It.* I said this over and over again and almost slammed at my belly with my fists.

He watched me at first with an air of amazement—then one of anger. He watched my hands moving.

I began to talk about a girl I knew—she'd been in trouble, too. This girl, I said, had gone to Mexico City, to a doctor there, on the outskirts of the city; he had a little hospital, nurses; it was clean and safe, cheaper even than one of the hole-in-the-wall and, of course, illegal places we'd have to seek in New York. We had to get the money. We had to go. On Monday. At the latest on Monday. It was very late, I told him. It couldn't get any later. It wasn't safe. I didn't want it. I couldn't have it. I wouldn't. That's what I kept saying—and *it*. He must have recognized hysteria in my voice, and the loathing.

Even so, I don't think he believed it. Not at first. Not quite. A stubborn look came into his eyes. I was afraid he would refuse to help me.

I said I was sorry again. Abjectly. It's all right, he said. He just wanted to understand, and it was very hard. But I didn't want to be understood. I just wanted to get rid of it. My voice went out of control. Can't you understand that? I screamed at him. He'd never heard me scream before or seen so much emotion from me, in fact, at one time.

He looked confused. He couldn't understand. He'd married me, hadn't he? What else, the tone implied, could I conceivably want?

I had to be sick again. I left the bathroom door open this time. He heard me retching. When I came back, he was on the telephone. He made call after call, persuasive enough everywhere for small amounts. Finally he called his boss. By noon, he'd gotten promises for almost all we needed. One friend of his said he knew a doctor in New York. Another knew one in Pennsylvania, very safe. Did we want the name? He looked at me. No, he said, Sara has set her heart on Mexico City. As though it were a vacation we'd planned together.

He left soon after that to pick up some of the promised loans. The others he'd have to pick up at offices on Monday morning, after the banks opened. While he was gone I phoned the girl who'd gone to Mexico City; she gave me the doctor's name and address and his telephone number. I ought to call, she said— perhaps he was in jail, these things happened, one never knew, best to be safe. I did, New York to Mexico City. The doctor spoke English, it was arranged in the most arcane of vocabularies. I told Rob all this when he got back.

I saw it then : how he could hate, how much, at that moment, he hated me. All through dinner, he was unnaturally silent. Afterward, he undressed and told me to undress. He wanted, he said, to make love to me, and he communicated his hatred of me that way—in copulation. Exercising his conjugal rights, he said afterward. He hurt me. He hurt the "it" inside me. It didn't matter. Indeed, it was no worse than it had ever been— no worse, perhaps better. His hatred little different from his love.

On Sunday, when he went to see his mother in New Jersey, I packed a suitcase. He came back at eight. His tone at the beginning of the evening was almost conciliatory. He wanted to talk

221

about the baby; I would only talk about "it." I told him he didn't need to go to Mexico with me. He insisted. Between eight and nine, he packed a bag for himself, then sat and watched television; he went to bed at midnight. As far as I could tell, he fell asleep at once. He didn't touch me. I can't say if I would have minded. Probably not. We left at five in the afternoon that next day, Monday, and came back four days later.

Six days after that, I came home from work in the afternoon and found that he'd taken all his clothes, the few other things that were his, that he'd brought with him to the apartment when he'd moved in some months before, and left. There was a note. He couldn't live with me anymore—I wasn't normal. He'd spoken to his analyst about me—that was the decade for analysts—his analyst had agreed: I needed an analyst. He'd pay, he said.

What I remembered was reading that note and thinking that, of course, he was right. Then going into the bedroom and staring down at the bed, remembering us in it, when we were not on the floor: our couplings, pleasurable enough sometimes, always loveless. Thinking that now I could strip the bed—pull off the sheets, the pillowcases, the blankets—that I could wash them, wash them right away. And in a sudden frenzy, doing it, ripping off the linens. The last thought I gave my marriage was which soap I should take with me to the laundromat on Broadway; that was the very last thought.

Until now. Until those mornings of the silvery-gray light, when the sun had not yet risen and the house was very still but I lay wide awake in the room I'd once shared with Avigal—the room with blank white walls.

The days are harder to recall. As though a brush laden with color had snaked its way across the rough spongy texture of the daylight hours, followed by another and another, and the paint bled into the bright yellow margins, and one muted color into another. . . .

Except for the days I telephoned Josh. But, of course, did not speak to him. The first time was seven days after we'd come to the beach house. His office phone did not answer. I put the phone down, relieved.

The second time was three days later. Gideon was home that afternoon but out in the garden. Paulette was busy in the kitchen. I gave the extension number to the switchboard girl at the institute. Josh picked up the phone, said hello. I wanted to speak, I think, but speech had deserted me. My mouth and throat were dry, my tongue thick, and anyway I did not know now what to say. That I wanted to hear his voice? Needed to hear him? Or that I needed him?

"*Mi zeh?*" He sounded impatient.

I didn't answer.

Then he said it in English. "Who is this?" I didn't answer that question either. I couldn't.

There was a moment when all I could hear was his breathing. Then his voice again, but softer now, "Is that you," he asked, "Sara?"

I put the phone down quickly and held it down. The hammer blows of my heart vibrated in my bones. Then I turned, and Gideon was there, in the doorway of the kitchen. I did not know how long he'd been standing there. Or what he had heard. Or not heard. He never said.

28

I DON'T KNOW HOW TRADITIONAL GIDEON'S PASSOVER SEDER was. Not very, I suspect. I don't remember too much of it, in any case. I drank too much sweet red wine so quickly that I saw everything and everyone through a desperate pink haze.

I know Batya's little boy asked the Four Questions—traditional—and Gideon led off with the recitation of the story of the Exodus from Egypt, but chunks of the Haggadah were missing. He skipped these, and the little boy didn't notice. Having painfully but successfully delivered the questions, he was tired now and unconcerned about the answers. It was Batya's little girl who objected. She was almost eight, and took after her father—the same longish, thin nose and pale frizzy hair, and what the Israelis call *pedanti*, a stickler for detail. She complained. Gideon, at the head of the table, merely smiled at her —a very sweet smile, I thought—and plowed on.

I glanced at Josh then, sitting across the table but off to my right. He seemed absorbed in something Paulette was whispering to him, in the book open on the table before him, in Batya's now restless little girl. His gaze swept past me without pausing.

I picked up my glass and drank more wine. Now everything seemed eerily distant but in fine detail, as though I were looking through the wrong end of a telescope. Or were off in space somewhere, watching everything from there. Even better.

We came to the part that was a recitation of the plagues visited on Pharaoh's Egypt, and wine was dipped out of the glasses. Afterward, I drank more wine. Traditional, too, I told myself.

As for the meal, it was not traditional. Paulette had made a Gallic-type feast instead, with a clear soup for the first course. The young American couple whom Gideon had invited—I don't know where he'd met them—looked betrayed. Batya's husband took it upon himself to explain. Delicious, he said to Paulette, waving at the soup. But where were the *kneidlach?* Paulette, flushed. Josh broke in; he said he hated *kneidlach.*

Otherwise, though, he did not speak. Neither did I. He did not look at me, nor I at him. And no one, I think, noticed. Why should anyone? Notice. Or care. I lifted my glass again.

Throughout dinner, Uri, Batya's husband, went on at some length about how the Israeli government chooses its military attachés. Was misleading, I'm sure, about embassy life abroad —I forget to which city in Europe they were going. Batya looked on, a half-indulgent, perhaps half-bored smile on her face.

She hadn't changed much—her face was untouched by the fourteen years—but she'd put on at least thirty pounds since then, all concentrated between her magnificent shoulders and thighs. Her legs were as slender, as elegant as ever, her hands as graceful. I could see again, in that instant, the row of nail polish bottles on the edge of the stone terrace. That night, I remember, her nails were silver-white, like fish scales in the moonlight.

I glanced at her husband. At the way he moved his hands when he talked, how he heaped the matzo crumbs beside his plate, the way he rearranged the silver, the glasses. Beside him, Josh seemed monumentally still, as well as silent. I turned to the young American wife, who sat beside me. Pregnant. Wary. She was gazing past me at Avigal, at Avigal's long silver-and-coral earrings swinging, glinting in the candlelight. Avigal was talking to the husband and laughing. This may have made his wife uneasy, but I don't know.

The main course was *boeuf à la bourguignonne*, made, of course, within the restrictions, with potato flour. Afterward, a dark chocolate mousse and some fruit, and a glass of wine poured out for the symbolic visit of the prophet Elijah.

The little girl went to hold the door open for him, to hold it open to the night—and feeling important for the first time that evening, held it open far too long. The wind made the candles flicker, they almost went out. Batya had to rise at last, go and take her hand and close the door herself, very firmly. Everyone laughed. Well, almost everyone.

The American couple left first—the wife rose—to make their ten-minute trek to the other side of the Haifa–Tel Aviv highway. Then Batya and her husband, though I cannot remember the precise order of events: whose good-byes, where, nor the how of the progress across the living room, out the door. The children were listless now, sucking on chocolate Paulette had provided. I've a vague memory of the cold outside and then walking down the path beside Batya, and ahead of us, already at the road, in the light that shone from the living room windows, the children, and Uri and Gideon shaking hands, then car doors opening and slamming shut.

Batya slackened her step and caught hold of my arm. I felt the swell of yielding flesh around her middle. She smelt nice—something expensive, French, but not very subtle. She'd never expected to see me again, she said. She was pleased. She even kissed me on the cheek.

At the car, she kissed Gideon. It was meant, I suppose, to be a sisterly kiss on the cheek. It came very close, however, to the corner of his mouth, and he put his arms around her; they held on to each other.

In the car, Uri said impatiently, "*Nu*, Batya?" She opened the door beside him and climbed in, and Gideon let go of her hand at last and shut the door for her.

We both stepped back as the car pulled away and stood watching it till it turned out of the lane. Then Gideon said it was cold,

we'd better go inside. He put his arm across my shoulders. We
turned and started up the walk.

By now my feet were heavy, almost dragging, my head
spinning with the wine. I stared down at the ground, I remember, as though fearful I'd catch my toe, stumble, pitch forward.
And when I looked up, I saw Avigal standing at the window,
framed in the parted draperies, silhouetted against the light—
slender, black, almost featureless in the broad column of light.
She stood very still. Even the long dangling earrings seemed
to have frozen in midflight. We were halfway to the house,
Gideon and I, and I was conscious suddenly of having been here
before, seen this before. Somewhere, sometime.

It was not night then, of course. It was late afternoon. It was
summer, not spring. And I was not walking up the path with
Gideon. On that day I was watching them—as she watched
us now.

I heard them debate waking me; I heard Avigal say Sara
would want to go to the beach, and then after a little more of
that kind of talk, I heard them leave. I waited. Then I rose and
went barefoot from Gideon's study, where I'd slept, to the
other room—my room, after all—to get some clean clothing
from the dresser.

At first, I kept my eyes on the contents of the drawers. I
got the bra and shorts and cotton jersey, and then I straightened. The dresser mirror was before me, reflecting the rumpled
beds behind me, Josh's trousers draped neatly over the back
of a chair, and flung across its seat, Avigal's mauve nylon
nightgown with its edging of ecru lace. I looked down again at
the dresser top. They were there, too. Their things. Avigal's
silver earrings, collapsed, looking somehow forlorn. Her silver
bracelet. Her wedding ring—a wide, plain band of gold. The
coins from Josh's pockets, his wallet. A cigarette lighter. His.
Or hers. I didn't know. I turned and hurried from the room.

I dressed in the study and went into the bathroom to comb
my hair, to stare at my face in the mirror. It did not look

rested. The wine, they'd say, the late morning waking—they'd say something. In any case, it was an unfamiliar face, which I washed in cool water. Once I had to grab hold of the edge of the sink, and I held on until the dizziness passed.

The note was on the kitchen table, one corner of it held down by the sugar bowl: directions on how to find them. I had merely to walk down the main road to where the beach began; they'd be somewhere near the water, under a big sun umbrella. Gideon's angular handwriting—at least, I supposed it was his. I stared at it until the kettle boiled, then I folded the note small and tucked it in a pocket in my shorts. I made myself some instant coffee, which I drank black. Then I smoked a cigarette, then another. The kitchen curtains bellied out in a sudden breeze once while I sat there, then collapsed, the slugs of lead in the hem bounced against the window frames. The refrigerator heaved, started up again. There was no other sound, the house being empty, silent. And waiting, as I was waiting. It seemed a perfectly natural thing to do, in fact, what I'd been doing all my life, though I'd not been aware of it. In constant, almost frenzied action, but at the core of me very still, and waiting.

When he came at last—when the waiting was over—the appropriate sounds preceded him. The front door stood open already, but the screen door creaked, then slammed shut. His rubber beach sandals slapped against the tiles as he came down the hall. Then he was in the kitchen doorway, and I turned toward him.

That first glimpse was like a blow to the breastbone—swift, almost lethal. It was all I could do to breathe normally, to remain where I was.

"Good morning," he said cheerfully. Just the right amount of geniality. I looked away, looked down into the coffee cup on the table in front of me. I don't remember speaking. I could not have spoken, anyway. All I could have done then was rise and move blindly toward him and put my arms around him, my face against his throat. But I just sat there, very still. Waiting.

"They're wondering what's happened to you." He was standing on the other side of the table now. Half-naked. Khaki shorts pulled on over his wet bathing trunks. I shut my eyes for a moment. When I opened them again, he was sitting, very close to me, just across the table, his elbows resting on the bare wood. I could see the long blue veins move in the flesh of his forearms, the tufts of coarse sandy hair in his armpits. I could smell him— the salt smell of the sea that emanated from his flesh. The heat of his body came in waves toward me, lapped against my skin. I knew I could touch him, he was that close. I wanted to touch him. I reached out my hand . . . but I caught a glimpse of his eyes. Don't touch me, they said. And he leaned back, very quickly, out of reach. He sat perfectly motionless now, his arms folded across his chest, his head bent a little. My face burned as though he'd slapped me. No, it was almost worse than a slap. A slap showed emotion of a sort. This— nothing.

So I touched the cigarette packet, instead. I twisted it between my fingers, around and around. I turned it over, read the English words, then turned it over again and read the Hebrew. My heart slowed finally, and my blood. Minutes passed that way. The refrigerator shivered to a halt. That was the only sound.

Until he said, "Well, what about it?"

I looked up, startled at the sound of his voice.

"The beach." He seemed impatient now. He shifted in his chair. "Are you coming? They're waiting."

"Is—is that why you came?" But halfway through that short sentence my voice failed me. It died away completely. I had to start again. This time I added something. "Or did they send you?"

"I offered." He sounded weary. "I wanted to talk to you, Sara. We can talk on the way."

But I didn't move and said nothing. I was waiting again.

And he didn't talk. Not then. At least, he seemed resigned to sitting there. He leaned over, took a cigarette from the packet on the table, and lit it. The match flared in the brilliant sunlight, the stench of sulfur blossomed for a moment in the air. I watched his every movement. I watched him drop the blackened match into the ashtray. His hand trembled then—I did not imagine that—but for only a fraction of a second. The next moment it was steady, as his gaze was steady when he lifted his eyes to meet mine : direct, utterly candid, steady.

"I'm sorry," he said. "That's what I wanted to say—that I'm very sorry. It should never have happened."

"Nothing happened," I snapped. "Absolutely nothing. You forget."

"You know what I mean."

Yes, I knew. "Why?"

"Why what?" Irritated now.

"Why didn't anything happen?" I asked, watching his face, his eyes. "Why did you run away?"

"That's self-evident, isn't it?"

"No, not to me."

"All right—I didn't want to hurt you."

"Hurt me?" I laughed. "God! You don't know me, do you? I don't get hurt."

And when he didn't answer, I said, "Anyway, why me? I mean, you can get hurt, too, can't you? Or are you immune to that?" My voice had risen as I spoke, to another pitch altogether. I stood up abruptly—the chair crashed backward to the floor. I moved away from the table and turned to face him.

He hadn't moved.

"I was just playing," he said. "That's all, Sara. Just playing." He spoke very slowly, so that I'd get every word. But he didn't look at me. He stared at the burning tip of his cigarette.

I didn't believe him, of course. "You were afraid," I said.

"Yes." He rose then, too. His chair scraped back. He came toward me where I stood at the sink. "I was afraid of hurting you."

"You're lying!"

"Yes, I did lie."

"No, not then. Now. You're lying *now!*"

My eyes were burning; his face had blurred. I looked away.

"Sara?" He was in front of me now, very close again. I could have reached out and touched him. I wanted to. In fact, he touched me, put his hand gently on my arm. I shrugged him off. Where it had lain for that one instant, my skin was very tender.

"Go away," I said.

He didn't move.

He said again that he was sorry.

"You're repeating yourself," I said. And then, looking up, I said that, anyway, there was nothing to be sorry for, was there? Since he hadn't touched me. No harm done. No harm.

"I'm not Sleeping Beauty, you know. It takes more than one kiss to wake me." And then I pushed past him to the door. I turned to look at him once more, one last time. He, too, had turned, but his face was absolutely blank, his eyes hidden for a moment behind thick pale lashes, as if he did not wish to look at me again. I could tell nothing from his face, or from the way he stood. Nothing.

I walked into the study and shut the door. A few minutes later, I heard his footsteps in the hall, heard the screen door slam shut, and then his footsteps in the path.

And it was over.

29

IF I EVER REALLY HATED HIM, IT MUST HAVE BEEN ON THAT day, and in that hour after he'd left, when the things he'd said to me still burned on my skin and in my brain like acid.

Later, I would grow confused. I would not know what to believe, and I would begin to weigh both sets of words, think about and re-create both conversations—the tender one of the night, the other of the morning. A normal woman would, perhaps, have chosen to believe the last, been forced to believe it. I was not normal. I did not know which to believe: these words or those, that conversation or this, or both, or neither. . . .

Finally, I knew it did not matter—that I felt rage and even hate for a while, and still I felt the longing.

I walked for miles that afternoon. When I started, the sun was high; later it was directly overhead and hotter. By then I was on a road lined with old eucalyptus trees—I walked in their dense shadow. At the intersections, if you looked right, you could see a patch of glitter on the water and above it, in the intense blue of the cloudless sky, a burning sun.

I remember walking down to the beach—an empty stretch

by then, in late afternoon—and sitting in the warm soft sand, smoking, staring at the sea; and not thinking at all: empty, dull. Then I got up and walked toward the water, carrying my sneakers by their laces. I walked along the margin of the sea and into the surf, over broken shells, pebbles, and looked down to watch the water rush toward me, break into foam around my legs and the foam disappear in an instant.

As far as the line of the horizon, the sea was empty that afternoon. The gulls had vanished and left an empty sky, too—the blue-gray, misty sky of early dusk. The water came in and went out, and the sand streamed away from my toes. The earth had seemed so solid a moment before, but now it seemed to shift beneath me, to slide away. And my first fear, and all the others— then and later—was of falling, of giving way. . . .

Josh's car was gone when I got back to the house. Gideon was alone on the terrace. He never asked me where I'd been that day, nor did Paulette. After a while, I offered an explanation— I'd been for a long, long walk. It seemed to satisfy them. And Gideon relayed Avigal's regretful good-bye: they'd had to leave before I returned. They were expected in Jerusalem, at Yudit's house. They were sorry, Gideon said, to have missed me.

About ten days later, Gideon asked if I wanted to drive to the institute with him the next day—Avigal had asked about me. I could spend the day with her, he said, and come back in the evening with him. I didn't answer at once, but let him think I was considering it. Then I said I couldn't—I had some shopping to do in Tel Aviv, which I'd planned to do tomorrow. When, a moment later, I glanced at him, I saw that he looked unbelieving. I knew then that Paulette had told him what I'd been doing with my days . . . or not doing.

It was dusk then, I remember, growing dark very quickly. The subtropic twilight is fleeting, the dark blue night seems to leap out of the earth. Paulette had turned on the terrace light before she went in—to start supper, she'd said, but in reality to leave us to it, to a discussion of what I was not doing with my life. It worried her. The long hours I disappeared, when I

233

went, or seemed to go, nowhere. Was I at the beach all that time? What did I do there? I never went into the water—she would vouch for that. My swimsuit was never wet. What on earth, then, did I do all day on the beach? Or, for that matter, in my room? That was the worst of it, she would have said to him. It sometimes happened that, though she didn't know it, I'd been in the house all day, in my room, sitting silent in the shuttered darkness. Or lying there. Not reading, surely: it was so dark in there. What, she would have asked Gideon with a hint of puzzlement in her voice—what could I be doing? Sleeping, he would have suggested. Not all day, surely. Not day after day.

But, of course, Gideon did not tell me this. He just stared at me now with that skeptical look, and this forced me to begin enumerating all the things I had to buy for the apartment. To dispel his doubts, to dispel my own, for I hardly believed I was going anywhere, going to do anything.

Then he asked when I could move into the flat, and I had to tell him that I could move in anytime. I could, in fact, have moved in the week before. But couldn't. Or didn't want to. I wanted to stay here . . . wanted nothing more than that. But I couldn't say that to him. He was asking about money now: did I have enough money for all that, because he had some for me . . .

But I said no, it wasn't money. I jumped up and went into the house to get Caroline's letters: the first one, which had been at the bottom of my purse for weeks now, and a second letter, which Gideon had brought from Avigal's three days before and laid on my dresser.

"I'm an heiress," I said lightly, handing the letters to him. The first reeked of spilled cologne. He sniffed at it before he took the letter from the envelope. I watched as he read it, held it up to the light, then as he read the other one. His face seemed almost impassive. Afterward he folded each again, slipped each into the appropriate envelope, checking the date against the postmark. Meticulous. He reminded me of Caroline. Then he handed the letters back. "Your scent?" he asked.

"She doesn't use any."

"Yes, I remember now." And then, quite without warning, he said, "Have you ever wondered why I married her?"

So unexpected, I was confused.

"Who? Paulette?"

"No, of course not. Your mother."

I shook my head. And then said I never thought now about why people married each other. Not after I'd married Rob. They seemed to marry for no logical reason—none I could see.

"Oh, there's logic somewhere," he assured me. "Always a reason."

"And yours?"

He grinned at me. "She was the *shiksa* of a Jew-boy's dream."

I think I must have winced, because he asked which one of those words I didn't like. I said I liked neither.

"Well," he said, "that's what the boys in Yorkville called me before they pounced. I like it better than kike, don't you? My father, by the way, could never understand how they knew. They knew, all right. And as for the other word, *shiksa,* that was what a friend of mine said when I told him I was going to get married. He said Caroline was the *shiksa* of my dreams—but actually maybe more of my nightmares." He paused. "I put it down to jealousy, of course."

"Of course."

"Yes. I knew she was the *shiksa* of his dreams, too."

I laughed, but he said at once that it was really no laughing matter, "a delusion like that." Downright dangerous, he said. To imagine that whatever is foreign, or exotic, or forbidden is by its very nature infinitely desirable. To believe that you cannot live without it—the object of your deluded desire.

I began to feel a trifle uneasy and shifted in my chair. That little lecture, I thought—no, I *knew*—was meant for me. But I held my tongue. There were too many dangers in contradiction. He went on, in the same musing tone.

"In my case," he said, "exotic was a New England Wasp. Also, of course, she was forbidden. My father didn't care, but I knew my mother would have—if she'd been alive. And Caroline's parents were dead-set against it. So for a while, it seemed she was something I couldn't have. Then it turned out she was also something I shouldn't have had. We were a *very* bad match." He wasn't smiling now, seemed rather pensive. "As for Caroline," he went on, "she may have married me for the same deluded reason."

"Or," I retorted, "because she loved you."

He seemed amused. "Nonsense."

No, I insisted, it might be the other—the other that was nonsense. I was a little angry now, and arguing a case—I realized that as I began to speak—but I was uncertain still of what I was trying to prove. The obvious, surely. That he knew perfectly well it wasn't always a delusion. He seemed happy with Paulette, who, after all, was just as exotic, as foreign, as what have you. Certainly, forbidden—before she converted. He'd chosen her, and it wasn't a mistake, not for either of them. She was what he seemed to need. So it wasn't a delusion. As if to underline what I was saying, we heard Paulette in the kitchen just then, humming a rather melancholy French song. She sounded happy.

"There must have been plenty of women you could have married right here in Israel," I said. "You had no difficulty in finding women before."

"Why do you make it sound like an army?" he asked. He sounded irritated.

A moment later, he rose and went down into the grass and over to the side of the house to switch on the sprinklers. The time to water, he'd once said, was in the evening, when the water could soak into the earth. The sprinklers clicked their way right, then left. The spray glinted silvery in the dim light from the terrace. Under the rhythmic click of the jets, there was a continuing whisper as the water fell on the grass. Gideon came back, through the grass, skirting the spray. He took the same chair, picked up the threads of what he'd been saying, talked about Paulette now. He supposed he'd been less of a romantic when he'd met Paulette. And he'd been lucky, in spite of the pitfalls.

"I'm an egocentric man," he said.

I nodded. He saw that and laughed. "I'm glad," he murmured, "that you agree with something." And then, "My tastes are simple, and my needs. Paulette takes care of all that and of me. Makes me happy. That, I suppose, is because it's her only concern, right now, making me happy. She's a good housekeeper and a very good cook. She's pretty. All right, a little *zoftig*, but so what? Most important though," he concluded, smiling a little, "she always wants me. In bed, I mean."

I looked away, faintly embarrassed. He didn't seem to notice.

"In short, she pleases me," he said. He glanced at me, almost apologetically. "That's a Biblical turn of phrase, I know, but it's very apt. What a woman ought to do. Be." But, an instant later, he amended that last. "Anyway, what a wife ought to be."

"But not a daughter?"

He nodded. "Not *my* daughters, anyway." He was smiling at me broadly, his teeth glinting in the half-light of the weak terrace lamp. As though, at long last, I were living up to his expectations—or, better, his hopes. Indeed, absolutely delighted, I could see, with this perception of mine. "Yes, you're right, that's the split in my personality. I want something better for you. And for Avigal. Or something more. I'm not sure, you understand, if it *is* better. But I'd like to think so—that the life of the mind is better. I'm not sure if you'd be any happier that way—either of you. On the contrary. Or, maybe, what I really want is that you be both—like Paulette and also like your own mother." He stopped, his eyebrows rose. "Or isn't that possible?"

"It isn't," I said with certainty—more than I actually felt.

"Well," he sighed. He leaned back and extended his legs, giving up the fight. "It's your life. You live it the way you want."

"Thanks," I said. "It's not always a matter of choice."

"Maybe not."

A minute or two passed. "You should have had sons," I said.

"Too late. This is absolutely my last marriage."

I smiled what could be construed an approving smile. I can't imagine, now, why I thought it any of my business. Any more than my life was his business. But I liked Paulette.

On the lawn, the sprinklers clicked around once again. The

237

grass whispered under the onslaught of cool water. In the kitchen, Paulette, unaware she'd been reduced, or elevated, to a woman made for the pleasure of one man, called out, "Almost ready. Are you hungry?" Neither of us answered. That wasn't a question either—merely Paulette reminding us she was there. Both of us stared at the grass. I felt sure the conversation had ended, this time on a pleasant note, that we were not going to say any more about anything, but he surprised me.

"As it is," he said abruptly, breaking the silence, "you're, both of you, very much women. Unhappy women."

I stiffened.

He said more. "Avigal seems to find relief, though. She prances down the runway at the Hilton and makes the other ladies envious. Or she finds relief in other men, I suppose. Not much relief, I imagine, but some. Or, maybe, she isn't unhappy—I can't always tell. But you. You, Sara—"

I jumped up before he could finish the sentence. I took the two or three steps to the edge of the terrace, knew I could leap onto the grass, walk away—no, run away. I fumbled in my sweater pocket for a cigarette and tried to light it. One match went out. I struck another, lit the cigarette this time, but now held two blackened matches in my fingers, unwilling to turn to the ashtray on the little table beside my chair, unwilling to come face to face with him. He hadn't yet moved from his chair, which creaked a little as he shifted his weight. "I want to say something to you," he began in a circumspect tone. "You won't believe it, but I want to say it anyway."

"Say what?"

"Everything passes," he said.

"Does it?"

"Yes, if you let it." He'd risen, come toward me, was standing beside me. Now he put his arm around my shoulders.

"And if I don't?" I said dully. "If I can't?"

"Look at me, Sara," he said.

I did. I turned my head and lifted my eyes.

"You must," he said.

After a minute, I looked away. "You're right," I said. "Of course."

"Good." He squeezed my shoulder. "Good."

"And about the other, too. I don't believe it."

The next morning, on his way to the institute, Gideon dropped Paulette and me off at the Arlozoroff intersection in Tel Aviv, and we took the bus from there. We went to the apartment first, so that Paulette could see it and measure the windows for the curtains she'd said she would make for me.

I remember how she turned round and round in the living room: she put me in mind of the lawn sprinklers at the beach house, but instead of drops of water, she radiated dismay. I felt dismay myself when I saw the room again. She made her way through the flat, with me at her heels. I held the other end of the tape measure, and she made notes of the length and width of every window. I glimpsed a moue of disapproval when she saw the kitchen. That stove, she said, that refrigerator, would have to be scrubbed down; otherwise I'd get sick. And that table, that would have to be painted. I assured her I was planning to do just that, and she looked mollified. Afterward, we took a bus to Allenby Street, where we bought fabric for the curtains and some heavier material to make into spreads for the two cots.

The next week, I went to Tel Aviv alone two or three times. I would shop before I climbed the four flights up to the flat, then I would clean. Stripped down to my underwear, I cleaned for hours. It was very hot in the flat those afternoons, and afterward my bra and panties would be soaking wet, sweat trickling down my scalp under my hair. Then I'd go over to the window and stand there a while hoping for a breeze—which never came—and staring at the side of the building next door, at the empty balconies, one above the other, and the windows still shuttered against the sun.

That's when the lassitude would overtake me. I'd beaten it back for a while; now, contrary to its very nature, it rushed toward me again. Like a tidal wave, it crested, and it crashed down; it overwhelmed me. It was useless to fight it. Useless, in fact, to do anything. I would close my eyes for a moment, but it did not help. Josh's face was there always, on the black-red inside of my lids. . . .

Then I decided to call him . . . except "decided" is not the

239

right word, perhaps. Let's say I knew I would call him. I didn't think about whether I ought to. I knew I had to—and that I was going to do it. That nothing would stop it now.

It was four o'clock in the afternoon, the last day before the Independence Day holiday. Behind me, as I stood looking out the window, the tiles of the living-room floor gleamed wetly. I made my way across them; I showered, dressed very quickly, then locked the apartment, went down to the street, and walked blankly through all the streets until I reached Arlozoroff. Once there, I went to the nearest café, the one next to the supermarket, but by the time I'd entered, my resolution had died. Instead, I sat down at one of the tables inside, near the phone, but with my back to it. I ordered coffee, paid for it, drank it, smoked one cigarette, crushed it out in the ashtray, got up and went to the back counter, where I picked up the receiver and dialed the institute—or began dialing. I never finished dialing, that first time.

A few minutes later, I picked up the phone again, this time completing the call. The phone rang five or six times before the institute switchboard answered. I told the girl the number of his phone. It was past five then, he might not even be in his office—that hardly mattered. What I wanted, I thought, was the illusion of doing, of dialing, of asking for the number and hearing the phone ring in his office. Where he might or might not be. Whether he answered or not. If there'd been no answer, I knew I would have hung up with a feeling of relief. If he hadn't answered, I know now, I would have called again. But on the fourth ring, he picked up the phone and said, "Hello." I did not speak. Then he asked, "Sara?"

I said yes, that was who it was. My mouth was very dry.

"How are you?" He sounded so normal, and as if he'd been expecting me to call.

I remember staring at the phone. Then I remember saying that I'd called to apologize. For the scene I'd made, I said. I had to say that. Otherwise, what was the purpose of the call?

"Yes," he said, "I'm sorry, too."

I wondered if he, too, were lying.

240

"Why are you apologizing?" I said. "You—you acted like a perfect gentleman." Midway, the bitterness crept into my voice. He heard it.

There was this long, stiff silence. I was sure he was going to hang up.

I said what I'd never planned to say. Not that I'd planned anything carefully, but I blurted this out : "I—I just wanted to hear your voice."

"Yes," he said.

"Yes?"

"I mean," he said hastily, "I'm glad you called. I was thinking of calling you."

"Why?"

"We mustn't leave it like that." He sounded strange.

"Why not?"

"You know why not." Now he sounded angry.

"No, I don't. I don't know anything." My voice was shaking now. I knew the woman behind the counter heard me, saw me. I didn't care. "I don't know when you lied. When you didn't. Maybe you can convince me of when you lied. I need to be convinced."

He did not reply to this.

I said, "Will I see you?" I loathed myself for asking that.

"Sure," he said. And then, "We'll be at the beach house next Saturday maybe."

"I meant alone," I said. "Will I see you alone?"

"Is that what you want?"

"Yes."

"When?" he asked.

"You—you say when."

But then there was silence again, and it went on and on. Finally he said he didn't know when he could manage it. He was very busy.

"I see." What else was there to say? I did see.

"Anyway," he said, "I think it would be best to wait for a while."

"Would it?" I asked woodenly. Hang up, I thought, hang up.

241

"Yes." He spoke firmly. As though he'd just given it all the thought it deserved and had decided.

"Will that change anything?" I asked.

He did not answer.

I thought: Hang up. *Now.* But I couldn't.

After a while, he said, "Sara?"

"Sorry," I said. "I'm sorry I called you. Good-bye." Then I hung up. I reached over and dropped the receiver into its cradle. There was a short, sharp ring as the connection was broken.

The curtains for the living room were blue, green, and mauve stripes; the ones for the kitchen, green-and-white checks. After we'd hung them up, we arranged the dark blue covers over the bare mattresses on the cots. Paulette felt she'd done a good week's work. I thanked her. Then we sat on the balcony, drank cold orange juice, drew up yet another list of the things I had still to buy, and discussed how much they'd cost.

She was still talking about how expensive household things were when we boarded the bus for home. We were ten minutes out of town, moving along the coast road, when the hourly newscast came on. Very loud, this time. Not that this mattered —I'd never heard anyone complain. But this time a lady who sat behind us leaned forward, suddenly, to shush Paulette. Up near the front of the bus, after the newscast was over, there was a good deal of talk, even an argument of some kind.

"Something's happened," I said to Paulette, but all I knew was that it had something to do with Nasser of Egypt. I remember now leaning forward to talk to a young boy sitting directly in front of us; all he did was smile and make some chopping gestures with the side of his hand which I could not understand. He knew no English, and I couldn't make myself understood in Hebrew. Paulette refused to try French. She felt silly, she said, and could wait. She was tired, anyway, of hearing about Egyptian and Syrian troop movements. There'd been more than enough of that over the weekend. I saw a soldier rise then and pull the bell cord. The bus stopped. The soldier descended

242

and crossed the road to wait at the bus stop there. Going back. I turned around to talk to the lady who had shushed Paulette, but she was slumped against the window and seemed to be crying. I turned back and sat very still. And Paulette, too, sat very still.

30

I USED TO CALL IT THE TIME OF WAITING—THE WAR OF waiting—and it was that for a few days: the days between the time Egypt requested that the UNEF troops be removed from the border, from Sharm el Sheikh, and the time that the Secretary-General removed them. After that, it was more a time of watching and listening, a time of shifting around—of what might seem aimless movement, but movement which was really quite purposeful. We did not know what would happen, but we acted as if the worst must happen. We prepared for the worst.

Paulette and I taped all the windows in the house. We made blackout curtains. We stayed home, and listened to the programs we could understand. We heard Cairo radio a lot and Jordan. English broadcasts. Martial music, for the most part, and shrill splenetic voices addressing the Jews. "We will drive you into the sea" was one vivid message—one of the less strident, in fact. That was the second week of waiting. Jordan had allowed entry to Saudi and Iraqi troops. On the 29th of May, the Straits of Tiran were closed to Israeli shipping. On the 28th or 29th, Nasser promised total war if anyone meddled in this. On the 30th, Egyptian troops fired from Gaza. Egyptian troops and equipment were being pulled out of Yemen. They were preparing, of course. We were preparing, too. Meanwhile, the U.S. government asked Israel to wait—just wait for the U.N. to do something. Which was what we were doing. We were getting good at it : waiting.

I did not go into Tel Aviv. It was hard to travel. The buses had begun to disappear from the roads, and there were far fewer taxis. When Gideon went to the institute, he took his car. He took it farther south when he went to Beersheba at the behest of the army, but he always picked up soldiers, he told me. It was no time to be driving alone—no time, in fact, to be living alone. Especially, without knowing the language. "Besides, he said, "what will you do in town?"

Look for a job, I said.

And he laughed. Did I think anyone was hiring now? Or even interviewing? No, I'd have to wait until things quieted down. He didn't say *how* they would quiet down, and I didn't ask. Paulette was sitting there. She was nervous enough by then.

Avigal called one day. "Oh, you're still here," she said when I answered the phone.

"I hope that's a joke," I said. "But if so, it's not a very funny one."

"All the other tourists," she said, "are at the airport."

"Are they?"

"Yes. Screaming or crying, I hear, to get out. The smarter ones, of course, are gone already."

"I'll keep away then," I said. "I hate noise of that kind."

She giggled.

She was calling from Jerusalem; she was still visiting her mother. She gave me the news, but it turned out there really was no news. Some of the professors at the institute had been called up, a lot of the engineers, almost all the students. Not Josh, however; he hadn't been called, not yet. He'd phoned someone at army headquarters, but was told he had to wait. When they needed him, they would call him. He was going crazy, she said.

Gideon took the phone from me. When he heard where she was, he exploded. "Are you insane?" he asked. "Why don't you

245

take your mother back with you to *your* apartment?" She said something to him that made him angrier still, so she hung up in the middle of the ensuing tirade. I'd never heard him so angry. He tried to call her back at Yudit's flat, but the lines to Jerusalem were all busy.

"All right," he said, "her problem." He turned away from the phone then. He'd washed his hands of her again—for the tenth time in almost as many days.

The next day, Gideon went to the institute, and Paulette went with him. I chose that day to go into Tel Aviv. To visit the apartment, I told them, just to make sure it was still there. I'd take the bus because they were leaving too early.

I waited at the bus stop for an hour and a half. Three buses had passed, but none of them stopped, and even if they had stopped, I could not have climbed aboard—they were packed so tight with passengers that not another one could enter. I was just about to give it up when a middle-aged woman driving a small French car stopped for me. She already had two large young soldiers in the back, complete with machine guns across their knees, and the car springs creaked ominously. Still, she stopped, leaned over, opened the door, and I climbed in. All the way to Tel Aviv, we listened to music and news and the army code words used for call-ups.

Then, while I was in the flat, moving about restlessly, uncertain of what to do—whether, in fact, to do anything—I had two visitors, one right after the other. The first, a man who lived with his family in the flat beneath mine, came to inform me of where the bomb shelter was and the necessity of turning off the gas in the event of an air raid and pulling the electric plugs from the sockets, and of keeping fresh water in jerry cans. "The water supply might go," he said in English that dated, I think, from Mandate times. He concluded with an invitation to tea the next day, but I had to decline. I did not know where I might be the next day.

He smiled, his round face damp with perspiration. He said, "No, nobody knows." But the invitation still stood, he said, and when things quieted down, I must come for his wife's wonderful strudel.

The old lady from down the hall was next. She had a telephone, she said, and if anyone needed to reach me, she would
be glad . . . glad. She had a plate of cookies for me. The phone
and the cookies—that was all I understood. She spoke only
German and very bad Hebrew. So we smiled, and she retreated,
leaving the cookies.

Then I lay down on my cot, on top of the new spread, and
stared up at the ceiling for a while. In the end, I fell asleep.

When I awoke, it was dark, my forehead was damp, my
clothes felt clammy, and my watch had stopped. I went down
to a café to call Gideon, to tell him it would be impossible to get
back to the house that night, that I would be home the next
day. That's what I said: home. That must have placated him, or
pleased him. He'd obviously been upset not to find me when he
returned from the institute. He said as much and then decided
he would come himself and fetch me home the next day, that I
should wait for him. "I want to see this place of yours," he said.

I remember how he moved around the flat that first time.
His expression was one of sheer delight. His hands resting on his
lean hips, he turned and turned as Paulette had done, but not in
dismay. He lifted one of the straw mattresses as though he could
not believe it.

"That's a kibbutz mattress," he said, "but not the kind they
have today." He dropped it back on the flat lozenges of the steel
springs. "Did you sleep on that last night?"

"On top of the spread."

"Ah, the pioneer life," he said and grinned. He began to talk
about the first room he had had, and then about the room he'd
lived in with Yudit and Avigal. Both rooms with furniture like
this, he said. He gestured at the cots, at the long sideboard.

"Awful, you mean?"

But, no, he liked it. That was the past. The thirties, the
forties. You didn't have to lock your door then. You had nothing
to steal, and no one else had anything to steal either.

"I feel downright nostalgic now," he said. "I wish you'd been
here, Sara. I wish I'd taken you along."

I said nothing. What was there to say?

"Do you hate me for it?" he asked. His eyes were on my face.

247

I shook my head.

"I didn't try very hard, you know. I just assumed she wouldn't let you go. And, anyway, what would I have done with you? You were three months old. I was all alone here at the beginning. And I was here illegally."

"I know," I said. Somehow, these did not seem very good reasons; but, then, no reasons would have been good enough.

And perhaps he guessed what I was thinking. He turned away, walked to the window, then out onto the balcony—which he proclaimed a luxury : "We never had it so good."

He saw me smile and smiled himself. "I sound like a crochety old man."

"About ninety," I agreed.

Then I sat down on one of the chairs on the balcony, expecting him to take the other, but he remained standing. He leaned against the railing, his brown arms out, bracing himself. He stood in the hot sun and created welcome shadow.

He gazed at me. "You came too late, Sara," he said abruptly.

"Too late for what?"

"Oh, too late for the banquet, I suppose."

I heard myself laugh. It didn't sound as if it had been much of a banquet, I said.

But no, he didn't mean the food. Not food for the body, at any rate. Yes, I was right. You can ask anyone, they'll tell you —the food was awful, and what's more, as awful as it was, there was never enough of it. The eggplant made in a hundred and fifty different ways, but still eggplant. The coarse bread, the margarine, the *leben*, the olives. But it wasn't that kind of food he'd meant, anyway. Not food for the body. He'd meant food for the soul.

"Or do I sound pompous now?" His eyebrows rose with the question.

I shook my head.

He said nothing for a moment.

"Are you sure it's all gone?" I asked.

"Not gone, maybe. But rotting—or burnt to a crisp. I haven't decided which yet. It's this hot sun. But it's not the fault of the sun. It may just be in the nature of things. Bodies decay . .

248

vegetation . . . buildings . . . machines . . . ideals . . . dreams. Everything decays."

"Or burns," I said.

"And is no good to anyone," he said, looking up. "No good that way to anyone."

"I don't know. You can make a feast out of ashes," I said, "if you're hungry enough."

I remember now that we looked at each other. I don't know what we thought we were talking about—whether of hunger and satiety or of living when one could, the best one could. Or about the life he wanted to give me now, the identity he held out to me, such as it was. I don't know. He straightened. I stood up and went to get my bag. When I came out on the balcony again, he was sitting in my chair. He had his head in his hands. I thought something was wrong. No, he said, nothing. Just a headache. Philosophizing too much. The confounded *sharav*, which always affected him that way. It would pass. Should we go now? I drove us back home, I remember. He sat in the seat beside me, leaning back, his eyes closed against the yellow morning.

In the end, I prevailed. Gideon drove me back to my apartment. That was at the end of the month. Nothing, it seemed, was happening.

There were conferences in foreign capitals, of course. Nasser continued to deliver his bellicose speeches and to move his troops and equipment around. The Israelis spoke of the pledges made ten years before, when they withdrew from the Sinai, the pledges upholding the presumed freedom of international waterways. One evening, two youngish women from the neighborhood came to the door with a petition for what they called a "wall-to-wall" government: that is, one which would include the leaders of the opposition parties—and therefore, one hoped, strong enough to take action. Gideon engaged them in conversation, flirted a little with the prettier one, and finally signed it.

Meanwhile, other things also went on as before. At night, late, if we were sitting on the terrace in the dark, we could hear

249

the rumble of huge trailer trucks on the highway, their cargoes draped with canvas, traveling north and south. The cleaning store was still closed because the man who owned and ran it was somewhere in the Negev and his wife was at home diapering her baby. There was only one cashier now at the supermarket, so the checkout line was endless. Buses ran even more irregularly; on their way to Tel Aviv they were so full of passengers that they always went right past our stop. By then, I suppose, many of the drivers had been called up, and the Egged buses pressed into use as troop transport.

On one of those days, I was a reluctant witness to an argument that ended with Paulette crying and Gideon banging his way out of the house.

Paulette had been doing what all the other women were doing: laying in supplies for a dull siege that threatened to go on forever. No need to hoard, the government spokesman had stated, but everyone was hoarding. And what's more, being encouraged to hoard by the storekeepers, one of whom had offered Paulette sacks of flour and rice and sugar that day, too many tins of sardines, and finally—what had started the whole argument—several bars of milk chocolate.

"Go on," the storekeeper's wife had said, "go on. You must keep up your family's strength."

I was in the kitchen having coffee when these groceries were delivered by one of the younger boys of the neighborhood. Paulette unpacked the carton so that the boy could take it back to the shop. She piled everything on the kitchen table, then tried to find room for the things in the cupboards.

That was when Gideon walked in. He saw the rice, sugar, and flour in their superfluous abundance. And the six chocolate bars.

"What is all this?" he asked, his voice still quite calm, still even.

Paulette glanced up at him, then hastily away. She said something vague about being prepared, that the storekeeper's wife had urged all this on her. Just in case.

"In case of what?" he wanted to know. His face had already darkened with anger, but he'd not raised his voice.

Paulette gave him a baleful look, then tucked the two bags of rice into the cupboard, next to the sardines.

He watched this without speaking. When she turned back to the table, he asked her again, "In case of what, Paulie?" His voice was contemptuous now. "In case of famine?"

"Don't talk to me like that," Paulette said. "I have lived through a war also. I know what it is like." Her voice was very stiff, very formal, and full of misery.

"Not in this country, you haven't," he said, as though there were no other country like it. "In Jerusalem in nineteen forty-eight, we ate grass. I stand before you now. You see, I survived. I'll survive again. So will you."

"This isn't nineteen forty-eight," she said. "Everyone is doing this." She gestured at the remaining groceries.

Perhaps this made him angriest—the fact that what she said was true. Everyone *was* doing it.

He picked up the chocolate bars and said, "Do you really think I would eat these? Or let you eat them?" He waved the chocolate bars in the air, the silver foil flashing in the sunlight. "Tell me, Paulie, when was the last time you ate a chocolate bar? Did you take it from one of your grandchildren?"

Then, still holding the chocolate, he pushed his way past her. The screen door flew open, and he let it bang behind him; we heard him cross the back porch, go down the steps. Then we heard nothing more. I supposed that he'd gone through the break in the hedge, to the back door of the next house, where there were three small children. Where he knocked, and the door was opened, and he entered the kitchen. We could hear none of this, of course. By then, Paulette had sunk into the chair opposite me, her face in her hands.

I didn't know what to do. I reached over and touched her arm. She cried harder. Then she lifted her face, her eyes red, her face swollen. I said it was all right, that he'd forget about it as soon as he gave the chocolate away.

"But I won't forget it," she said. She rose clumsily and went into the bathroom. I heard the water running and supposed she was repairing her makeup. When Gideon came in, he asked where she was—as if nothing had happened. I looked at him, but did not speak. He asked me to get him a cup of coffee; I poured him some. When Paulette came back, she even got him a piece of cake. Then they sat at the table together, but said nothing, either of them. This lasted for the rest of the day, their silence, their studied indifference to each other. I suppose, though, they made it up that night, for the next day things were back to normal, or as close to normal as they could be.

What they needed, of course, was to be alone. And I wanted to be out of it, anyway, not observer of their infrequent arguments, nor their more innocent lovemaking. When Gideon stroked Paulette's arm and she practically purred with pleasure, I looked away. Not jealous, of course—or maybe jealous, I don't know—surely embarrassed. And lonely. Sure then of what I should be doing now—living my own life, such as it was.

So I asked Gideon to drive me to the flat. There was no other way to get there. The next month's rent was due, and the landlord would think that I'd left with the tourists. Anyway, I said, I ought to be living there now. I'd paid for the whole month of May and slept there only one night. Besides, it looked to me as though the armies were going to sit at the borders forever, while the Arabs made their martial, blood-curdling noises, but in the end would do nothing. They'd withdraw, we'd withdraw. That's all that would happen. He listened to this, an expression of disbelief on his face. He must have thought me naïve, or a political innocent, or crazy, perhaps.

But I insisted on leaving, and finally he agreed. I think now it was because of Josh, because Josh was going to be at the beach house on the 4th, 5th, and 6th of June. There was a scientific meeting at the university in Tel Aviv, planned long before; it would start quite early in the morning, and anyway Avigal was in Jerusalem with her mother now. So Josh had been invited to stay; he would come the evening before and drive in to the meeting with Gideon and back with him each night. And it was best, Gideon must have thought, if I were not there at all, if we did not meet, not so soon again.

No, I don't know what Gideon thought, of course. I assumed that. I knew only that he seemed almost eager to take me to

town on the Wednesday, after the reluctance . . . after that
real reluctance. He said that if anything were to happen, of
course, I must return to the beach house at once, but he piled
my suitcase into the trunk without another word, with the carton of sheets and pillowcases and some of the disputed groceries
as well, and drove me into town. He helped me take the packages
up to the flat. I came down with him again and watched him
start up the car. At the corner, he stopped for a moment, looked
back, waved at me.

I went shopping the next morning and slept in the afternoon.
That Friday, I went to see Mr. Levi, but Mr. Levi had been
called up. In place of the once-cowering Mrs. Levi, there was a
lady who seemed to be spoiling now for a fight. She was surprised
I was still here, she said, but glad, she was glad.

"Nothing to worry about," she told me. She patted her newly
washed hair into place. "It will start very soon—you'll see. It
must start soon. But I say—what I say, is—the sooner the
better."

I handed her the rent. She gave me a receipt. "Don't you
worry," she told me again. "You're perfectly safe."

On Saturday, the 4th of June, Paulette and Gideon came and
took me out to lunch but left early. There was a *khamsin*, so
Gideon had a bad headache. On Sunday, Soviet warships were
reported in the Mediterranean, and the new Israeli minister of
defense was quoted as saying he preferred a diplomatic solution
to this problem.

31

THE SOUND OF SIRENS WOKE ME, WRENCHED ME INTO THAT hot morning. Out in the hall, there was a hurrying scuffle of feet, the whimper of a baby warming to more tears, a woman's crooning, calming voice, and several other voices, frightened, more strident, female voices mostly and those of young children. The man who lived downstairs—the one in *Haga*, who had given me instructions on what to do in case this happened—must have left for work already, because I did not hear him. There were quick steps on the stairs going down, then silence.

There was no need even to turn on the radio that Gideon had given me. It was obvious what had happened. I got out of bed and went to the window, looked out at an empty street, at a world made suddenly still and waiting.

Nothing moved. Even the leaves on the trees seemed motionless, preserved in the sultry silence as though they were ferns in amber—or as though it were a stage set, I thought, floodlit by a merciless sun, and I was the audience waiting for the play to begin—audience and, it would seem, actor. And it would begin, I thought, as soon as I heard the planes, the drone of their engines moving in from the north, or from the south, or from the east—perhaps, even, approaching from the sea, dipping, swooping out of the sun, swinging in low over the houses on the shorefront, over the big hotels, empty now except for the international press . . . then it would begin in earnest. We waited for it now in silence, like the unmoving leaves, silently waiting. Except for one lonely gray cat, half-grown, nudging its hungry and determined way into a brown paper bag that someone had dropped or flung in the gutter.

About fifteen minutes after that first siren, the all-clear sounded. I'd heard no planes, nothing, and nothing now, either, for several minutes. Finally, the voices again, echoing in the stony shaft of the hall and stairwell, a trill of unrelieved or nervous laughter, footsteps, doors opening and closing.

In the apartment next door, I imagined, the radio was switched on, though I could not hear it. In the house across the hedge, in the apartment almost level with mine, a young woman passed in front of the open window, the panes of which were taped. As mine were not. I'd forgotten. I'd been standing there at the window throughout that first alert, in an almost transparent nightgown. Hardly protection. Splinters of windowglass can be lethal, bloody. I backed away. Now that there was no danger, when it no longer mattered, or so I thought. And yet the little twist of fear inside me seemed to wind in upon itself even tighter, and when it could go no farther, snapped, loosened. Then I went into the bathroom to take a shower. I dressed. Before I'd finished combing my hair and twisting it up off my neck, the siren started again, boring its way into bones, into teeth. . . .

I was afraid, of course, as much as any of them—those who descended so quickly, so efficiently, to the bomb shelter. The baby was wailing now, like the siren, the mother less calm. I heard them hurrying past my door. Then other footsteps. Someone paused, knocked, waited, then went on.

I knew I had to be alone with it—with my fear. I'd always known it. I sat out the second alert on the cot farthest from the untaped windows. I turned on the radio—the transistor Gideon had given me. Music. Pop music. And I could not understand

255

the news, except that the announcer's voice was slow and calm, soothing. I tried vainly to get the English program from Jordan, or from Cairo, then sat with my bare feet pressed flat to the warm tiles. My body and face were damp with perspiration, and I was shivering.

For it had occurred to me that the whole of what had always seemed a rather aimless life might not be so aimless after all. It might have been leading me to this—to dying. The way all life leads to dying, of course. But to dying here, in this flat, and now. Now that I no longer wished to die. Ironic, and slightly ridiculous, too. I looked toward the white ceiling. Outside, above the flat tarred roof, the sky was brightly, benignly blue, empty of clouds, empty of everything but the sun. Then the all-clear sounded again. I snatched up my purse, let the door slam behind me, and hurried down the stairs, brushing past people coming up.

There was a little café on Arlozoroff, next to the supermarket, but I couldn't be sure it would be open. It was. For the moment, I was the only customer.

The woman behind the counter was patiently polishing glasses when I came in. She placed them in an exquisite, sparkling, carefully balanced pyramid on the glass shelf behind her. I took the stool at the back counter, ordered coffee, then asked for a line and dialed the beach house. At the other end, the phone rang eight or ten times. I didn't know whether to hang up or not. Perhaps it was not as quiet there.

Finally Gideon answered, out of breath. They'd been in the trench in the empty lot across the road—the trench the neighborhood boys had dug the week before for just such a contingency. He was not going back there, however. Ten kilos of shifting sand for each occupant, ten thousand hungry sand fleas. If necessary, he said, he'd get under the bed. Or, maybe, on top of it. More fun. Then I heard Paulette's breathy laugh. She must have been standing very close.

"Are you all right?" I asked.

"Headache," he said. "The heat." And then he asked me about the shelter. Was it very hot?

I said no, that it was bearable. Did not, in short, correct his impression that I'd been with the others. No need to do that, really. I didn't have to tell him everything.

He asked if anyone had translated the news for me.

There'd been no radio, I said, and then, what had happened—did he know what happened?

Yes, he knew. "I think what happened was we managed to get most of their planes before they left the ground. Otherwise, they'd be bombing Tel Aviv now. Or are they?"

I said no, they were not. In fact, everything seemed quiet. An alert or two, that was all. The café was open for business, I said. I was having my breakfast now, in fact. And calling him.

That, he went on, had been the plan as he'd understood it. Of course, he was assuming now that the plan had been executed successfully. He sounded relieved, not happy.

"The radio," he went on, "has it that we were attacked. Of course."

"We weren't?"

He laughed. "Oh, yes, of course we were. Three weeks ago. I'd say we've been damn patient."

Then he said it was better for me to be at the beach house, with Paulette, since he had things to do. It was, in any case, safer. They might try bombing Tel Aviv, anyway, as a last resort with their last planes. And then, that Josh was coming for me. The meeting at the university had been canceled, but Josh had some business to do in town. He was on his way now. Or maybe he was there already. He'd come by for me in the afternoon. About five or six. He knew the address.

And to my stricken silence, Gideon said, "That's all right, isn't it?"

I said yes, that was all right. And that I'd see him later. I hung up. A cup of pale brown, foamy coffee was set before me. I saw that. The round, pale, placid face of the woman—she smiled at me now. I smiled back. And saw the rest, too: the frizzy gray hair, the blue tattooed number of the concentration camp on the inside of her white forearm, which, I supposed, explained a few things. The way she stood there now, a glass in one hand, a towel in the other, and stared impassively through

257

the open doors of the café at the silent and empty street. For the wail of the siren had sliced through the air once more. But it no longer terrified me. As it had never terrified her.

I didn't wait for the all-clear. I paid for the coffee, the telephone call, the half-eaten cheese bun, and left. It was then past ten-thirty. Too early. Or too late. And what I imagined was not a day of waiting. I thought he was there, already, that he was waiting for me. Improbable. Still, I hurried through the silence of the sultry morning.

His car was parked in front of the house—or, I told myself, some car that looked like his car. My heart was pounding now, my throat dry, but I took the steps very slowly. I counted the steps as I ascended.

Yes, he was there. I couldn't see him for a moment. All I saw at first, in the dimness, was the glowing end of his cigarette. He sat on the top step of the last flight, next to my door, leaning against the wall and smoking. He didn't move when I came around the newel post, nor when I just stood there, at the foot of the last flight, staring up at him.

My face was stiff, but he couldn't see that. Then it was as if a giant hand had pushed its way through the wall of my chest and placed itself gently upon my heart. I felt it and felt my heart slow. There was a pool of stillness at the center of me now. He is there, I thought. I spoke from where I stood. I said the door was open. He rose without speaking, tried the knob. The door swung inward. He glanced at me, surprised, but still said nothing.

I reached him finally. The steps had multiplied, it seemed, and now stretched endlessly upward, but finally, I reached the top. He entered the flat first and looked around it quickly, to satisfy himself perhaps that there was no one there, no intruder, because after that he turned back to me and went to shut the door. He asked in a carefully neutral tone of voice why I'd left the door open.

But I didn't know, except that I'd been in a hurry. I remembered what Gideon had said about people never locking their doors. I said it.

"Thirty years ago," Josh snapped. "Times have changed. He locks his door now. Ask him."

I turned away, feeling rather foolish. At the same moment, the all-clear sounded. I heard my neighbors coming up the stairs again. But Josh, oblivious to this, was moving around the apartment again. Curious, polite. Yes, very polite. He always asked before he opened doors, and always I nodded. The very few doors. Finally, he stood in the living room, but did not ask when he bent at the sideboard to read some titles in the row of paperbacks. Nor ask either when he picked up my hairbrush, which he did almost absently, and turned it over. Nor ask when he pulled one long brown hair free of the tangle of the others caught in the bristles. I watched him. I felt my skin burn at this intimacy. I didn't want him to do it; nor, now that he was doing it, did I want him to stop. But he replaced the brush where he'd come upon it. Turned away. And it was as though he'd abandoned me once more.

Finally, he walked over to the balcony door, opened it, glanced at me—for confirmation, I think—went outside, and took the chair at the far end of the terrace. He folded his long, lean torso into the chair, his shoulders hunched a little, his head bent. I took the chair beside him. That was the way we sat. We sat there without speaking for a long time. He dropped his cigarette into the ashtray on the floor, where it smoldered, charred, turned black, went out.

"You're early," I said.

"Didn't you expect me?"

"Yes," I said automatically. Then, too quickly, "No. Not yet. At five or six. That's what Gideon said."

He was gazing at me, thoughtfully now. "Somehow," he said, "somehow I thought you expected me to be here now."

"No," I said. And looked away, embarrassed. "Do you want to start back?"

"Not yet," he said. And then, "I wanted to talk to you, Sara."

"Not again." I said this abruptly, and then I laughed. A brittle, bitter laugh. My eyes met his.

There was a long moment of silence.

259

"Shall I go away?" he asked. His pale eyes seemed somehow paler now, softer, oddly gentle. I couldn't speak. "Shall I go away," he asked again, "and come back for you later?"

"No." Almost a whisper.

"No what?"

"Don't leave."

He expelled a held-back breath, looked down at his hands.

"Unless you want to leave," I said. I closed my eyes for a moment.

"Yes," he said. "That's the way it should be, shouldn't it? I should want to leave."

"So go—why don't you?" I said, my voice toneless.

But he didn't move. In the moments that followed, neither of us moved. Nor spoke. Nor breathed, it seemed. Then, quite suddenly, he rose. I thought, dully, he's going now, he's going. I felt helpless.

But all he did was walk the length of the balcony—three or four long strides—to grip the railing, to lean forward and stare down into the tops of the two trees at the back, and stare also at the gray walls of houses rising on every side, it seemed, at their windows shuttered against sun and war. Finally, he turned; he gestured at the houses. "Nice view," he said.

I didn't smile. "Thanks," I said. "I'm glad you like it." And then, because he said nothing, I added, "I had to get out of your house."

He said nothing to this either. I stared past him then, past his shoulder. The cloth of the white starched shirt shone, the sheen so bright it hurt my eyes. The shirtsleeves were folded back, rolled neatly above the elbows. The scrolls of golden hair on his forearms glinted in the sun; the thick ridge of vein moved under the skin.

"Anyway," I said, "Gideon likes it."

"Yes, he said that."

"When?" I glanced up at him.

"Last night."

"You—were talking about me?" I asked, with a surge of shame, or fear—I'm not sure which. I know only that I felt exposed, perhaps betrayed.

"No, no," he said mildly, "not about you. As a matter of fact, we talked about him. His life. Your father, if you've noticed, is very nostalgic these days."

I watched him. I did not speak.

"I suppose it's a way of reliving his life," he said. "And maybe, living it better." He smiled. He went on then to tell me about the rest of that conversation, which, it turned out, was about the perfectibility of man's moral nature—or rather its imperfectibility. And also about time.

"According to your father," Josh said now, "if there were no limit to our time on earth, we could—or would—be as moral, as ethical as God expects. Maybe. Not as He *is*, of course. Since God is above all that—morality. I think we must have debated that, too—the meaning of goodness. And God."

"What were your conclusions?"

"Whose? His? Or mine?"

"I know his."

"But not mine?"

"No, not yours. Why should I?" I kept my voice very cool.

"I thought you knew me, Sara," he said gently.

I looked away from him, from the pale eyes. I looked down at my hands.

"For one thing, I'm weak," he said. "You know that, don't you?"

After a moment, as calmly as I could, I said, "Is that supposed to be an explanation?"

"No." And then, "Yes. And it's one of the things you will have to know about me."

"What are the others?"

"That I won't leave her," he said promptly. "She married me because she knew that."

"I didn't ask you to leave her, did I?" I said, incensed. "I never asked you to, did I?"

"You expected it," he said.

I shook my head. But he was right, perhaps. Perhaps I did expect it. Not now, though. Now it didn't matter.

"Is this going to be enough for you?" he asked.

"What?"

261

"This." And he lifted his arm and made a sweeping gesture encompassing it all—the buildings around us, the balcony, even the room inside. "If I come here to see you like this," he said, "to see you. And talk to you."

I was afraid to look at him. "Why should you do that?"

"Because you want it," he said. "Why else? And because I want it."

I don't want your pity, I thought. And then said it, my voice barely audible, but he heard me.

He merely laughed. A moment later, impatient, he said, "Can't you answer a simple question?"

"Can you?" I countered.

He stared at me blankly for a moment.

"Do you—do you love me?"

"I don't know," he said. "Maybe."

"You don't know?" The laughter bubbled up in me. But I felt like crying, too.

"Anyway," he said, before I could say anything more, "does it really matter? Does it make a difference?" I remember now the way his lips set, stubbornly.

"It matters to me," I said. Again—it was an echo of that night. He had not answered it then, I remembered.

He didn't answer it now, either. "I told you," he said, looking away from me, "I don't know."

"It doesn't change what I feel," I told him. "It won't make any difference."

"I know," he said. And then uneasily, "Well, will you want more than this?"

"Will you?" I asked.

"Yes, I will. Of course, I will." He stopped, looked at me as though he were trying to gauge what I could take, how much —take without buckling, I suppose. "But there won't be any more," he said. "There never will be any more."

I said nothing.

"We must accept that now," he said, his voice soft. "Now, Sara."

But still I said nothing. Then I nodded, and suddenly felt very tired, worn out by this war of mine—the war that went on inside me.

Then the war outside intruded. The siren went off again. It pierced the air. I sat absolutely still. He got up, caught my hand, pulled me up; we went into the house together.

He said he wanted to listen to the radio. There were code words being broadcast, the words summoning different army units. But as he turned away, I put my arms around him. I pressed my body against his back, and my face into the damp nape of his neck. The sharp smell of him exploded in my skull. My palms lay on the clean, flat, hard muscle of his chest.

"Hold me please," I whispered. "Just hold me." I felt his heart quicken. He turned, his pale eyes narrowing. I was afraid, for one terrible moment, that he would push me away.

Instead, his hands slid slowly down my back, very gently at first, and found my buttocks, and he stroked me there very gently. And then, convulsively, he pulled me close, pulled me up against him, so that I came to the sweet, hot, hard center of his body.

It was very simple for me. Yes. I mumbled something that seemed wordless, something animal, something that meant yes. *Yes.*

"Is this all you want after all?" he asked. "This?" And held me against him again, against the root of his body. His mouth spread into a soft, sensuous smile—almost a cruel smile. A satyr's smile. He seemed to be enjoying my fever, my fear, my hunger. My yes.

"No," I said. "No."

But he didn't hear that. Or didn't want to. "This?" His laugh delighted now, deep in his throat. "Yes, this is what you want, after all."

I wanted to say something else. That I loved him. That this was only part of it, that there was more. There had to be more. But I didn't say it. I thought no, don't cry, don't ever cry. It was part of the bargain, I knew, not crying.

"Hold me," I said, "just hold me."

He was still holding me, in the same way. His eyes glittered. He was waiting.

"Yes, this," I said.

"Now?" He seemed to be laughing at me again.

I nodded.

The sunlight quivered around him. A halo of light. He pushed me back onto the cot and lay beside me. Then he touched me. He put his hand on my naked flesh, then gently between my thighs—he pushed them apart. My willing, aching, open thighs. And then he came into me. I remember the exact moment, the feel of his flesh locking into mine, the way my body curved around him, held him, held him inside me, the way my knees pressed to his sides.

"Lie still," he said. "Yes, like that. Still. Just like that. You're lovely, you're lovely inside. Did you know that?" He whispered it in my ear. "I want to stay here, like this. Inside you. I'll come if you move, I'll finish."

But I could not stop trembling. I was flesh and blood and nerves. He was agony and joy. My love. The way he filled me. His eyes were like the wide blue sky. He *was* the sky, the whole beautiful sky, everything. And all of that he placed inside me.

I was glass, then. I shattered—like the window might shatter, on impact. When he came into me, I came apart beneath him. A million glittering shards of glass. Then, again and again, like that, I was made whole again, and I came apart again. He went deep and deeper. A burst of white hot light; I was falling.

He raised himself a little. He put his palms on either side of my wet face. He smiled. He kissed me. I held the sweet syrup of his mouth in mine. I felt him tremble then, too. I pressed my damp face into the rank wet of his armpit. Wanting the odor of his flesh on my body, the salt of his skin on my lips, the taste of him forever in my mouth, on my tongue. He smiled an almost absent smile, his arms still around me.

"I love you," I said.

"No," he said, "I give you pleasure." He smiled at me sleepily. "But that's easy—it's very easy."

"No, joy." I said and rose on one elbow to look down at him. His eyes were closed now. "That's infinitely better." But I don't think he heard me. He put his arm around me and pulled me down. We slept.

Later, I lay there watching him. I put my hand on his chest, just to touch it. I traced his ribs through the lean brown flesh. I put my mouth on his throat. I felt him shiver. He was awake again.

"Do you love me?" I asked, though I knew I shouldn't ask it.

He didn't answer. His eyes darkened, he put one hand up and his fingertips rested on my lips; he was shushing me, crooning it now, sshh . , . and then he rose and pushed me back against the pillow.

He started gently. He stroked my body, then put his hand between my thighs. I gasped. He touched me there, and then he came into me again. Harder this time, with more violence, his thrust a punishing joy. As though such a question could always be destroyed with such savage possession. But the question would not be destroyed.

It was not again as it was that first time. Never again like that. It has always been beautiful and more, much more than I deserve. I've always wanted to be more beautiful for him. And to give him more. I've wanted him to ask more of me. I never say that. When we make love, he fills me, I am not empty. But it was never again like that first time. Maybe that's all you have a right to. One time like that.

32

THAT NIGHT WE STOOD ON THE FRONT LAWN IN THE GRASS, Gideon and I, and stared up at the sky. There were no streetlights, the houses were all dark, and beneath the trees the shadows were dense and black. A metal ornament in one of the gardens gleamed in the starlight. My sandaled feet were wet and cold; Gideon's feet, too, I suspect, but we didn't move.

We looked at the sky over Jordan. Near the horizon, it was strangely bright, a wash of light, flickering now and then. And because it seemed so close, we thought we could hear the war—a low rumble now and then in the distance. I still wonder if we really did.

Josh had driven me home, had coffee, and left. The car's headlights were painted to narrow slits for blackout driving, and Avigal called when he got home. That was at dusk. She'd been waiting for him, she said. She'd returned the day before from Jerusalem, long before the shooting started. Her mother was not with her, however, she had remained in Jerusalem, had insisted on it. Ridiculous woman, Paulette said when she heard that,

266

stupid. Gideon then tried to reach Yudit, but he couldn't get through to her flat now.

Paulette stood on the terrace and watched us in the grass. At one point she asked what we saw there, anyway. A few minutes later, she said that if the planes came after all, they'd be upon us before we knew it, we'd have no time to do anything but fling ourselves headlong into the wet grass. And contract pneumonia. I almost laughed, but I don't think Gideon thought it funny. He turned and went to sit with Paulette on the terrace. I remember now how much I longed for a cigarette. I stood in the grass and longed for it, knew I should not smoke in the house, and could not smoke out there on the lawn or on the terrace. If I lit a cigarette, it would be seen for miles.

In Tel Aviv that night, we heard later, there'd been some shelling and more sirens, and people hurried down, twice or three times, into the shelters or stood jammed together in windowless hallways until the all-clear sounded. Here, though, people stayed home or, if they were not yet bored by the anticlimactic nature of the frequent air raid alerts, made their weary way into the trenches. A few—our neighbors on either side among them—took their children to the American School; there, they camped that night, and two or three other nights, in the large concrete bomb shelter. The children of the diplomats had already gone, the diplomats' wives had gone as well, and even, I imagine, some of the diplomats. In any case, the shelter was empty, except for those who lived near the school and felt an urgent need of concrete.

Actually, the shelters turned out to have no immediate function. Gideon's assumption had been correct. In a series of raids in the very early morning hours of the 6th of June, the Israeli air force had destroyed most of the enemy planes while they were still on the airfields. The airfields in the Sinai, in Jordan, Syria, and Iraq. Pilots dropped their bombs, swung round to come home, refueled, were re-equipped with bombs, and set off again. Efficient, that army. A matter of priorities, Gideon said.

So efficient, in fact, that the war soon began to seem almost unreal—less real, certainly, than the three weeks of anxiety that had preceded it. Heard of, but not actually heard. Mapped extensively, photographed, but not actually seen.

There was some shelling, of course: Jerusalem, Tel Aviv, some of the border settlements. At the beginning, in Natanya, on the coast, a curious woman standing on her balcony was killed. A lone Iraqi plane got through and did that—but that may have been just a rumor, that it was an Iraqi plane. As everything began to seem a rumor: an unexplained, unexplainable, ultimately unbelievable series of conquests, which finally we had to believe but still could not explain. Silence, and then the victories listed. Rumor. Until the names on the casualty lists were published. Until we counted our dead and our wounded.

An old childhood friend of Avigal's was dead—a young man who had been living abroad and returned to fight in this war. Arieh Berendt was dead. He left a widow and four children. The engineer, Baruch's friend—the man who liked Wagner and respected German technology and believed. . . . Well, what does that matter, what he believed? He was dead, too. Baruch's brother lost a leg in the Sinai.

Months later, in the fall, on a trip to Nablus on the West Bank, as we drove through the parched landscape of the enemy, I saw for the first time the burnt-out steel of war. I noted the way the yellow dust rose and fell and filmed the dull metal. The tanks were like huge, broken and dried carapaces, the soft animal flesh that had once been inside now gone. That's all I actually saw of the war.

But that's history now, isn't it? Everyone knows what happened. On the 8th of June, Nasser capitulated. But the war did not come to an end until all of Sinai as far as the Suez Canal was in the hands of the Israelis, along with the West Bank of Jordan—including Jerusalem, of course—and the Golan Heights. That took less than a week. There were no trumpets, though, no drums, no confetti, no parades. If there was elation, it was because we'd faced annihilation and had somehow escaped; if jubilation, because it had come so close—far closer than even we could imagine.

What it meant, everyone said, was that the Arabs would now

have to recognize the State of Israel. The shooting was over, that argument ran; if they wanted their land back—and surely they did—they'd have to recognize and deal with the conquerors. That followed. It was obvious, wasn't it?

As it turned out, it was obvious only to us. . . .

33

I THOUGHT GIDEON WOULD BE AMUSED BY MY NEWS. MY job. Not what he would have wanted, but it was work. And perhaps he'd mellowed. Perhaps he'd even find it funny. I wanted to call him anyway and tell him, but there was no answer at the beach house. I called again, and this time I let the phone ring ten or twelve times before I hung up. After that I called the house on the grounds of the institute. Perhaps he had had to go there for some reason, and Paulette had gone with him. But there was no answer there either. I tried to call Josh then, but he was not at his desk. Finally, I was put through to the department secretary, who told me that Josh had been called into the army and that she didn't think he'd be back before the end of the next week, or later. As for Gideon, he wasn't in that day, which was a Friday. He might be back in his office on Sunday or Monday. Technically, he was still on vacation. But I could try next week, she said. He might be in.

When I hung up, I stood at the café counter for several minutes without moving, until the waitress came up beside me and plunked her huge battered metal tray down on the formica.

The rattle of glasses startled me. I asked how much I owed for the call, paid and left.

I was feeling a little let down now, and uneasy, for no good reason. Just, I told myself, because I hadn't known about Josh and the army. When I'd spoken to him three days before, he'd said nothing. It was unexpected, that call-up. Not that this army service was dangerous or anything like that—not anymore. It meant only policing the cease-fire lines or acting the soldier in an army of occupation. He would not relish that much, I thought, but he was in a special unit; he'd surely have other, more pleasant duties. I thought about that first. Then I thought about Gideon. I wondered if I ought to take a bus out to the beach house. I rejected that. No one was there—it would be depressing. Finally, I went to the supermarket to do my marketing.

It was very crowded. I had to wait on various lines for varying lengths of time. That didn't matter, of course, for I had nothing better to do. When I finally got back to the flat, though, I was very hungry. I ate a sandwich and drank some cold coffee.

It was very hot that day, I remember. Just keeping cool and clean took time. I showered twice—once when I came in from the street, once before I left the house again.

I tried to call the beach house again, of course. Then the institute. But it was past two now, and that café would close soon and the secretary at the physics department, who may have heard something meanwhile—but what?—would have gone home by now. I ordered an iced coffee at the café, sat outside in the shade of the awning, and drank it. Tried the beach house once more, and then, for the first time, Avigal's apartment. No answer there either; she might be at her mother's place in Jerusalem. And then the institute and Gideon's house once more, but still there was no answer.

And no answer the next morning. Since it was Saturday, I had to walk over to Dizengoff because the café on Arlozoroff was closed. I called the beach house again, then the house on the institute grounds, then Avigal's apartment. By that time I'd remembered Avigal's mother's maiden name—she used that now—and I called information and got the number in Jerusalem.

I called—or I tried to call—but something was wrong with the line, or the phone. There was no ring at the other end of the line.

I called the operator, who informed me that she couldn't check it now, I don't remember why. But it wasn't ringing, I said. Oh, well, she said, maybe it *was* out of order. I hung up, angry. Or frantic. Something.

I tried in the afternoon again. All three numbers. No, four. This time, it was Avigal's number which seemed to be out of order. The operator confirmed that. I asked when it would be fixed, that phone.

"*Mi yode'ah?*" she said. As though that would cover all the many problems of which she was ignorant. Nobody knew, obviously, why should she? I said, well, would it be fixed soon? "Our men are all occupied now," she concluded in English—I suppose she recognized the accent—then disconnected me.

I tried Jerusalem again that afternoon, and that evening. Yudit's apartment. The first time I tried the number, the busy signal interrupted the dialing. Then, when I could get through to the city, Yudit's line was busy. A few minutes later, I called again, and this time it rang and rang and rang, but no one answered. Or I supposed it rang at the other end, I couldn't be certain. It was evening then. I smoked a cigarette, had some coffee, sat at a café table on Dizengoff and stared at the passers-by.

Afterward, I went back to my apartment, sat on my balcony and smoked another cigarette, then took a shower and got into bed. I tried to read, but couldn't concentrate. I got up and went out to sit on the balcony. Then, I got dressed again and went down to the café on Arlozoroff.

It was open by now, since it was after the Sabbath. I tried calling again. It was past ten. I sat at the counter, my shoulders hunched against the noise behind me, the laughter, the talk. The café was full. The tables in the little enclosed garden were all occupied. The lady with the concentration camp number was behind the counter making coffee, slicing cake, scooping up ice cream. There was the clink of china, glasses, spoons, and ice cubes and the hiss of the espresso machine, through which, I was certain, I could hear nothing; but I dialed anyway, again and again. And waited, counting the rings at the other end. Other *ends*. Still no answer. No answer anywhere.

When I got back to the flat it was almost midnight, but still too hot to sleep. I went out on the balcony and sat there in the dark. The night was heavy, breathless, but still alive with light and sound. Two streets over, the crowds still streamed down Dizengoff. Across the narrow space between this apartment house and the next, my neighbors were playing some card game on their neon-lit terrace, oblivious of me. Around the corner of the same house and one flight down, I think, a party was in progress. That apartment was wide-open to the night, its lights streaming into the trees; Dixieland jazz, exuberant young voices and laughter escaped into the night. Somewhere, a phone rang and was answered.

If I had a telephone, I thought, I'd know where Josh was because he would have called. I would know he was all right. I'd know where Gideon and Paulette were, and Avigal. I might even be with them. They would have called me. By then, of course, I'd worked out where they might be. I'd decided they were wandering around in the Old City, the dark alleys of the walled city of Jerusalem, in the Arab bazaar, or sitting in the back room of some shop that Gideon had frequented in the old days. Gideon would be talking now with the merchant. Yes, that's where they were now, surely. Sipping strong black Arab coffee from little cups, in the back room of some antique or jewelry shop in the *shuk*. Gideon, Paulette. Avigal, too, maybe. Maybe even Josh. I placed them all there; that's where they all were.

The phone rang again somewhere, and it was answered: the same phone, or another.

The next day was a Sunday, a business day. I'd have to go to work. The new job. But after work I'd also go to the main post office on Allenby and order a telephone. I decided that was absolutely essential. It didn't matter how much it would cost. I would even get Gideon to invoke his *proteksia*—if he could— so I would not have to wait the usual year or two.

I lit another cigarette and smoked it. I thought of Gideon laughing with his old friend in the antique shop. Or was it a jewelry shop? I imagined him talking about the past. Then that, too, slipped from my mind. Like the phone.

I remembered, instead, the day I'd seen him last. It was Monday. His lips had been dry when he'd kissed my cheek but there had been a sheen of perspiration on his brow. We were all hot, all of us perspiring. Paulette's face was damp. She'd looked exhausted by the heat, washed out, imperfectly dried. She was unusually quiet that day. She sat and watched, but said very little, her dark eyes resting on him most of the time. All of the time.

"Not to discourage you," Gideon had said as he lifted the newspaper from the other chair on the terrace and started to fold it, "not to discourage you too much, it gets no easier. The average human body—even the healthy human body—does not adapt well to this climate." He made a weary gesture at the sun, said something about the *sharav* (merely a heat wave, it turned out, but a heat wave that always seemed endless). He spoke now about the headaches of the past, and the headache of the present, which did not seem to go away, which lingered. Maybe was growing worse. No surcease now. He began to talk about the differences between *sharav* and *khamsin*.

"There's no difference I can see," Paulette said. And did we want something cold to drink?

Gideon grimaced; Paulette thought iced tea was the answer to everything, he said, even an Israeli summer.

"Well, do you want some?" she asked him. He nodded. After she went inside, we just sat there, Gideon and I. We did not talk for a while.

I thought, in fact, that he'd fallen asleep in the heat. But when Paulette came out again, and I reached for the iced tea gratefully, held the chilled glass against the side of my neck, he said, "Does it bother you much?"

I said yes, it did—a little.

"It'll get worse," he said, seriously, "not better. The first summer is actually the easiest. The only way to stand up to it after that is to spend a summer in the Alps now and then, or in London. Then the next two years are bearable—just."

I said I'd planned on the Alps for the summer after this.

He began talking about how expensive it was, but I reminded him again about my wealth. I wanted to make him laugh, but he was being serious that day. He said he'd forgotten that—about the money. "I'm glad. You'll need it. I can't leave you very much. None of you."

Paulette looked stricken, then determined. She began gathering up the papers now, those that had slid to the stone floor of the terrace. She was folding them more carefully than he had done, giving all that her attention, but at one point in this process she said to him, in a low voice, "You are really talking such nonsense."

Gideon ignored that. I said, "Well, there's always Jerusalem. It's cold at night."

He said that it wasn't the same, not at all.

"It's the weather," Paulette said firmly. "I get depressed, too, in this weather."

And Gideon, who must have realized how miserable she was at that moment, held out his hand to her. When she took it, he pulled her over to sit on the fragile arm of his chair. She rocked a little; his arm went around her plump waist, and he held her.

He had not finished, however. "In any case," he said, "if the weather doesn't depress you, the newspapers will."

He tapped the one newspaper still in his lap. "All we're concerned with here, it seems, is what the rest of the world is saying about us. A national mania. We're in a popularity contest. So—*what* are they saying about us? Do they love us? Or admire us? Or fear us?" He laughed, but not with good humor.

"Well," I said, "it seemed to be admiration for a while."

"No doubt," he said. "For a while, yes, we had the world's admiration. As it is now, it's the Arabs who have the pity. We, of course, are the aggressive, war-loving Jews. Somehow, for some strange reason, no longer pacifist, no longer timid nor law-abiding—not law-abiding on an international scale. We had the world's admiration for a while, all right, but even when it looked as though we'd go under, we didn't have their sympathy. The only time we have their sympathy is when we are marching docilely to the gas ovens. And even then, it's qualified. It seems to depend on how many of us have been gassed. It has to be six million exactly. And whether we were docile enough." He seemed exhausted at the end of this.

I started to protest, but I don't know why, even now. It was what I felt, too, that day. It was what I felt whenever I read a foreign newspaper.

"Well," Gideon said, "it doesn't matter anyway. In some sense, everyone marches to the ovens. . . ."

Then he patted Paulette on the hip. She rose promptly. He rose, too. He said he was tired. That headache. He was going to lie down for a while. He went into the house, leaving Paulette and me on the terrace. We did not look at each other. We sat there mute, unwilling—or maybe unable—to speak of what was most in our minds.

How long ago was that truncated afternoon? Only days ago. I left late—well past five. Gideon was still asleep. We didn't wake him. But I telephoned the next day, at the beach house. I asked how he was. He said he was fine—except, of course, for the headache. There was a moment of silence. I asked if he'd gone to a doctor. "For a headache?" he'd demanded and laughed.

Then, quite unexpectedly, he said, "But you—you sound happy."

"Do I?" I asked.

"Yes." And, "Are you?"

"Happier," I said, in my cautious way. Because I did not want to attract the attention of the jealous gods.

"Yes," he said, "be happy." And that was the way that conversation ended. I'd not phoned him in the middle of the week. On Tuesday, Josh came. On Wednesday, I went for the interview at the art gallery. There were other applicants for the job, I was told, but I should call again on Friday.

When it was Friday, I called. I had news for Gideon then. I thought—no, I knew—he would be amused at this—my new job, in the art gallery at the Hilton. He'd laugh. I longed to hear his laugh. And Josh's laugh, too. I'd tried to call them both, but there'd been no answer. Not Friday . . . not today, Saturday.

276

My neighbors across the alley switched off the light on their terrace and, a moment later, lowered the blinds of their bedroom window.

A baby began to cry somewhere.

The music from someone's party ceased abruptly.

I lit another cigarette and sat there on the balcony smoking it. I wondered if I ought to go down to the café and try once more to phone the beach house.

Then I turned my head. Josh stood in the doorway to the balcony. He said, "Why is your door open?"

I remember rising and going to him, putting my arms around him. I remember his arms around me, and the way we stood there in the darkness, holding on to each other.

I said I'd been trying to reach him. I'd tried Friday at the institute, and finally, the secretary had said he'd been called up. Indeed, he was wearing his old, scruffy uniform. Had they let him go already? He just nodded. I said I'd tried to phone Gideon, too, to tell him about the job I'd found: not that he'd be too pleased with it, but I couldn't—could I?—live my life in the faint hope of pleasing Gideon.

I don't remember now what Josh said to this. Nothing, perhaps, to this either.

I began to talk about the job. I remember thinking how silent he was; still, I went on and on. About the job itself, about my hours, about my duties, and the salary. After a while I stopped talking; I recognized the frenzy that made me talk on and on like that. The frenzy, or the fear—I can't be sure now which. Beneath my words, in any case, was the knowledge that he was going to say something, something I didn't want to hear. Which I had to hear. I held it off as long as I could, then I stopped. Josh put his hands around my face, his palms cupping my ears, as though he would shield me from this, from the sound of this. But what *this* was, I didn't know. Or yes, I knew. I think I knew already.

"Do you think Gideon will mind?" I said. "About the job, I mean. It's not very productive, but we can't all be productive, can we? Will he mind?"

"No," he said gently, "I'm sure he wouldn't have minded."

The tense was not lost on me. I stared at him. I felt dizzy for a moment, but I didn't cry, not then. He caught hold of me, held me. Then he told me about it.

On Wednesday afternoon, when the headache was very bad, Gideon had gone into the bedroom to lie down. He'd fallen asleep, as Paulette had hoped he would. She'd decided to let him sleep. He seemed, she would say later, to need such a lot of sleep.

When Josh had been summoned by the army, he'd telephoned Gideon first. That was on Wednesday in the afternoon. He'd called the beach house, and Paulette had answered; she'd said Gideon was resting and she didn't want to disturb him. She'd give him Josh's message when he woke. She'd said Josh must take care of himself. She'd spent the rest of the afternoon sewing and, at suppertime, decided she'd let Gideon sleep on. He'd looked so rested then, she said. She thought sleep would cure the headaches.

On Thursday morning, she realized he wasn't going to wake at all. Frantically, she tried to reach Avigal in Jerusalem, but the line wasn't working for a while. And Josh—but Josh was in the army then. She was alone. She'd called the doctor, who had sent an ambulance at once. She went to the hospital with Gideon in the ambulance. She sat there beside him in the hospital. She hardly moved away from his bed.

He'd never wakened, but she was there. They told her that he probably would not waken again, but she didn't move.

On Friday morning, from the hospital office, Paulette finally got hold of Avigal. She sent her a telegram. Avigal came at once. She was there when Gideon died, sometime in the early hours of Saturday morning. They were both there, Paulette and Avigal. But not Josh, not I. Afterward, Avigal had called the army; the army had finally gotten hold of Josh. And Avigal had sent him to my place, to tell me.

He said that Gideon had slid very easily into death. That was something to be thankful for, anyway. As he'd slid into the coma three days before, and before that, into sleep. As each night, he'd slid into sleep. In contrast to that other time, fifty-six years before, when he'd been pushed, been thrust into life, had come into it screaming, as we all did, and lived it—a little differently from the rest of us, maybe—but lived it. Lived it.

The theory, Josh went on, was that the original tumor—which had in the course of treatment shrunk so dramatically—must have metastasized, gone to the brain, taken root on its surface, grown outward, over the whole of that good brain. Like a net, the cancer cells had covered it, then pulled tight, very tight. Even if it had been detected, they'd said, even if Gideon had gone to the doctor's at the first sign of those headaches, they could have done nothing; it would have been inoperable. Those headaches that Gideon had ascribed to the heat, to the *sharav*, to the *khamsin*, to the Israeli summer—before those headaches grew unbearable, he had escaped from them into death. But, of course, they wouldn't know for sure, the doctors said, not until the post mortem was completed.

I think I began to cry then, because only then did I fully believe it. Josh put his hand on the back of my head, on the knot of hair, and pulled me to him, my face burning and wet, into the warm, fragrant flesh of his throat, into the open collar of his shirt. So he would not have to see the working of grief in my face, maybe, or the working of pain, or of rage. So that he could somehow, in some way that would help, stifle my grief. He said, "It's all right, Sara. It's all right."

"He knew," I told him. "He knew he was dying."

"Maybe," Josh said. "Or maybe he was just very tired. The funeral is tomorrow. I'll drive you, we'll go together."

I came awake in the warm darkness. The clock said 4 A.M. I did not move at once. My naked body curved close inside the curve of his, so close that the beat of his heart seemed to be mine, too, and where our bodies touched, almost everywhere, my skin was moist with my perspiration and his, too. His breath brushed soft, in slow rhythm against the nape of my neck. I wanted to turn toward him now and hold him and take him into me.

But he slept, and I knew how my own body ached for sleep, as well as for the solace of his. I got up in the darkness and

279

crossed the room. I groped for his cigarettes where I knew they lay, on the sideboard, with his wallet, his coins. I moved softly so I would not wake him. I did not want to wake him now.

"Sara?" His voice startled me.

I was at the window, standing in the bars of pale light that came in between the slats of the blinds. Starlight or distant streetlight, or maybe the beginning of day.

"Yes?"

"Shall I put on the light?"

"No."

I knew he could see me from where he was, from where his head rested on the pillow, could see my nakedness outlined in the bars of light. I wanted him to see me, and, inexplicably, I wanted him to want me so that I could refuse him. I wanted to refuse him as much as I wanted him. I felt I could do that, that I must do that. That I did not need him, after all. Just as I'd once, long ago, shown Gideon how little I had needed him.

"Come on back to bed," he said.

"Where is Avigal tonight?" I asked.

He had not expected that, but he answered promptly enough. "With her mother. I took her there before I came here. Paulette," he added, "is alone. She wanted to be alone."

"What will you tell Avigal?" I asked. "Tomorrow."

"That I stayed with you," he said. His voice was low and very controlled, but there was anger in it.

"Just that?"

"Yes, just that. She won't ask anything else."

"Why?"

"Because she knows about us. She knows, I think. . . ."

I folded my arms across my chest. "Well, after all, what is there to know?" I said. "A roll in the hay. That's a polite way to put it. A good lay—*am* I a good lay?" I blew out a stream of smoke; it rose sinuously in the bars of light. I heard the bed creak under his weight. "Or maybe you'd call it something more —more precise?"

He was beside me now, and had caught hold of my arm and twisted me around. His shoulders were silvery in the faint light. "Stop it."

280

I said, "Look, this is ridiculous. I don't blame you. Really, I don't. I asked for it. For that. In fact, you didn't want me. Remember? I knew that. I forced myself on you."

"Oh, yes," he said, "you raped me." There was no hint of amusement in that icy voice.

I could hardly breathe now. So hot. And then he put both his hands to the sides of my neck and held me so, in a vise.

"What do you want?" he demanded.

"Nothing. Nothing. I don't know."

"A declaration of love? Is that what you want?" He was shaking me in fury. I thought he might kill me like that, holding me like that, but I didn't care.

I said no. I said no several times, until the sound of "no" grated in my teeth like sand. "You don't have to love me," I said. "And you can leave anytime. I'm eminently leavable. Even people who love me leave me."

I thought he was going to thrust me away then, as his hold on my neck slackened. I put my arms around him, but he was aloof and rigid in my embrace. I grew fearful—and then, my thoughts incoherent. I couldn't think anymore, but the rage at least had died.

I felt his arm on my back.

"Don't leave me," I said. "Please don't leave me."

"No," he said, "I won't."

I pressed my face into his throat. My lips moved on his skin, against the warm beating pulse of his throat. "I couldn't bear it if you left me—"

"I won't."

And so he stroked away my grief and battled with my rage, and then he led me back to bed. I opened my body to receive his. He possessed me, and I, in turn, possessed him and held him prisoner with my knees.

34

AVIGAL CAME LAST WEEK AND BROUGHT THE BABY. SHE
gave Naomi into my willing arms and went ahead of me, onto
the terrace, and sat down, pulling her skirt up a little, white
cotton and ruffled, extending her long slim brown legs into the
lone patch of full sunlight there. She watched me holding her
baby, fondling her baby.

She always seems faintly amused by that. She looks at me as
I press my face into the baby's creased, powdered neck, watches
me as I breathe in the slightly sour smell that clings to all
babies. . . . When I smile at her, she returns the smile, and
then, perhaps, she stretches her arms gratefully and yawns and
says how tired she is, how heavy the baby is getting.

She did that last week, and then she lit a cigarette and observed, "You're very physical, Sara—do you know that?"

"It runs in the family," I said. She laughed.

When Avigal comes here now, she often brings the baby with
her, lets me hold Naomi while we talk. A lot of the time, I suppose, we talk about my life, which is really not very interesting,
for I cannot communicate much to her. Or to anyone. Or we

talk about hers, about what she calls her "flirts," which is Israeli for flirtations, but that word suggests the flutter of eyelashes, an arch laugh, the swing of a hip. . . . No, they are not that, not that at all. They are direct and basic confrontations, what they are the world over. Why should they be any different here? We are not an ascetic people.

We speak of Avigal's "flirts," and sometimes she speaks of Josh. She is always the one who brings him up. And I listen and I think: she knows. Then, I *know* she does. Yet the very next moment, she may say something that suggests she is, after all, ignorant of us, of what he and I are to each other. No, let me amend that: of what he is to me, of what he is in my life, that he is my life.

I don't know. Those afternoons often bewilder me. I grow confused, but still I'm pleased when she comes to visit. I feel close to her. We are sisters, after all, and closer perhaps than most sisters. And rivals, too, as most sisters are, in a sense. But I know, of course, that Avigal has given me what I have—that is, she would have given it to me if she had had it to give. I know that. I do not imagine that I could have wrested it from her. She would have relinquished it. I remind myself of that. I also know it is not a gift outright. It never has been.

I held the baby and said that Naomi looked like Josh. She does. The baby has Josh's smile, the lips that are not full but still sensual, sharply modeled. Her eyes are like his—that lovely glassy blue like liquid crystal—but fringed with Avigal's dark lashes.

"I don't know," Avigal said, her eyes narrowing a little as she peered at the baby. "Most of the time I think she looks like *Abba*. And you know something? Like you, too, a little."

I felt a surge of pleasure at this, but I'm not sure why, exactly. Anyway, I said, those were Josh's eyes.

But Avigal wasn't listening anymore. She'd turned away. She made some comment, completely unconnected, about this new apartment of mine. She'd twisted around and stared out at the sea, at that little patch of sea glittering in the late afternoon sunlight—the bit you can glimpse from my balcony, on either side of which the hotels loom up. She turned to face me once more, and then to look beyond me, into the shadowy living room behind me. She said the sofa looked comfortable enough. I knew what she meant. She meant for Josh, for when he stayed over. I knew she meant that, because the very next moment she darted me a quick, sharp, distinctly malicious smile. You are not fooling me, the smile said.

I licked my lips and waited, but she'd lost interest in that already. She was talking about the sea now, saying that the sea was what she'd miss most in Jerusalem. Once more I said she could still get a flat in Tel Aviv—why not?—but I didn't sound enthusiastic about this, nor persuasive. I never do. And she did not reply. Instead, she said inconsequently, "No, everyone is happy this way."

I said nothing. Again I waited. I'd decided long ago that I'd answer truthfully if she ever asked about us, about Josh and me. If she confronted me, I would not lie. I told Josh that. It did not upset him. In fact, he'd laughed. If she asks, I'd said. "She never will," he'd said.

She never did.

She did not now, either, though I waited, breathless. It was at times like this, when she said things like this. . . . But, in the end, that was all she said.

I rose abruptly and handed the baby over to her, and went into the kitchen to get us both something cold to drink. When I came back, I took the baby again, and Avigal, staring at us, said suddenly, "You ought to have a baby, Sara."

I said that would not be so terribly bright, that I was unmarried now and likely to remain so. I didn't expect to get married again, I said.

She shrugged impatiently. "So what? You have someone, don't you?"

Just like that. We'd talked about it once before. Just like that. She'd asked that same question with what seemed the same simple curiosity. And I had nodded. "You could say that," I'd said.

"Well, then," she said now, "why not? I mean, the baby would not be a bastard, or anything like that. Not here. You'd have to be married to someone else for the baby to be that. Not the man—*you*. It's the *Halakah*. You know that, don't you?"

I said I did. Yes, I knew that. And I laughed. I wanted her to think that I considered the whole idea ridiculous. I did not tell her how much I longed for a child, for his child. Or how, when I held him in my arms, I willed his seed to take root in me, how I dared not move so that the sweet liquids of his body not escape, how often I'd lain with my face pressed into his damp shoulder, my whole body aching for his child, nor how I had exulted when, once, I thought I had conceived, and then when I began to bleed one morning . . . but I never told him. Nor her. I told her none of that.

"It's too late," I said. "And maybe I can't. I don't know."

"Lucky you," she murmured. And then, a fraction of a second later, "Me—I'm pregnant again."

She smiled as she spoke. A slow gentle smile, not triumphant. It longed to comfort me, that smile, to assure me that the earth would not crack open, that it would not shift, that what lurched so painfully in my chest would grow calm again.

When I could speak, I said, "Are you happy? You look happy."

"Well, Josh is happy, anyway."

"If it's a boy," I said, "we—you, you can name him Gideon." I held the baby closer. I put my face against her neck again, against her silky dark hair. I said I hoped the baby would look like Josh.

"He will," Avigal said briskly.

Then I realized what she thought I had meant. "No, what I meant is that it's nice—if it's a boy—if he looks like his father."

Avigal shrugged. "I suppose so. Anyway, no fear. I'm always careful. I married Josh because I knew that when I wanted children I would want his. That's why. That's really why."

She stood up and walked to the edge of the long balcony, where she turned, leaned back, hands out, braced on the railing —as Gideon had once done, in my old flat—and now she faced me.

"You know," she said, her voice thoughtful, "*Abba* could

285

never understand that. He thought Josh was too private a person. Those were the words he used—'too private.' He couldn't see why I wanted to marry him, a man like that. Afterward, though, I think he saw why."

"Why?" I knew I should not ask it, that this was not the sort of conversation I should be having, not with Avigal. Still, I asked it.

She didn't think it strange. "I don't know if I can explain it," she said. She made an elaborate gesture of defeat. "Very complex."

"Of course," I said. I lifted my glass and sipped at the iced coffee. I kept my eyes averted now, willing her silently to stop. But it was too late.

"I knew," she said gravely, "I knew marrying him would be for good. I mean, he's not like us, Sara, you and me. We— we're like *Abba*, I guess. We stay only as long as we want to. Only as long as there is something."

I did not speak.

"Go on," she said, her voice rising in challenge, "go on, admit that, Sara. We don't find it easy to cut it—I don't mean that—but we do it, don't we? I mean, you'd end it, wouldn't you, if you got bored—wouldn't you? If you got bored with—" She paused, then went on. "We, both of us, do that. I do it. But not with Josh, of course. I mean, I'm *married* to him, and that's that. For good. Till death do us part. That's the way he is. That's what I wanted, needed."

I didn't reply to this either.

"A person like me," she said, "I know what I'm like." She laughed deep in her throat. "But so does he. Anyway, I don't think he ever cared for me like that—you know, in that exclusive way."

My lips had gone quite dry now, and my throat. I thought again, helplessly, that I ought not to be listening to this. Or, perhaps, this was exactly what I should be listening to. I smoothed the baby's hair back—she was playing with the gold chain around my neck, pulling at it.

"I don't mean he doesn't care for me," Avigal said. "Of course, he does. In his own way."

286

"Of course."

"It just never bothered him—not really."

"Are you sure?" I asked.

She nodded. "Yes," she said firmly, "I'm sure. It never bothered him. Even before you came."

For a moment, there was utter silence. Even the baby made not a sound. Everything seemed to cease, even our breathing. Avigal looked at me, a sudden, stricken look in her eyes. I licked at my lips.

"What have I to do with it?" I asked, my face expressionless.

The baby began to whimper, and I realized I was holding her too tightly.

Avigal got up and came toward me. She took Naomi from me and, for a moment, just stood there above me, holding her.

"Nothing," she said.

I tried to think of something else to say, but my mind was blank now, numb with relief, perhaps.

And Avigal took up the conversation again as though nothing had happened, just where she had left off. "No, Josh doesn't care much—but *Abba* did."

"Yes," I said. "He minded about Arieh, didn't he?"

"Who?"

"Arieh. Arieh Berendt." I remembered then that Arieh had been killed in the war, burned to death in his tank at Ashmura, near the Syrian frontier. When the news had come, it had come with news of other deaths, and grief had been for all of them. I had not thought then to examine Avigal for signs of a special grief.

"What are you talking about?" Avigal asked.

"Arieh."

"I never had anything with Arieh," she said. "What made you think I did?"

"I saw you together," I said.

Avigal sat down with the baby now. She said, "Where?"

"I thought I saw you. . . ."

"You couldn't have. Or maybe at *Abba*'s house? Is that what you mean? That's the only place we ever met." She seemed amused. She was laughing. But I could not have been mistaken.

Maybe she wants that for herself, I thought. Maybe that's something she doesn't want to share with me. As was her right. But that derisive laugh, that seemed genuine enough. And the gesture of disbelief.

Well, that is the usual tenor of our conversation. Confusion. Bewilderment. Sometimes, a strange cold wind . . . then the calm—for we always end it that way, with calm.

We ended up that day speaking of Paulette, and then of me, of how much more Jewish I might feel after the ritual immersion, and the test, after I'd passed. She always laughed about that decision of mine; she said it had not made Paulette feel any more Jewish. All that had been done for Gideon. And now that she was back in France, she certainly didn't think of herself as a Jewess—or did I think she did?

"But, in any case," she said in a comforting tone, "you're not Paulette. She came to it with no connection at all."

"And I?"

"You? *Abba* is your connection, isn't he?" She rose with Naomi in her arms. Then she looked down at the baby, tilted her chin, and she said, "Yes, you're right, Sara. Those are Josh's eyes, aren't they? His eyes, all right."

When Josh telephoned, I told him that I knew about the baby.

For a moment, he did not speak.

Then I said, "Are you happy?"

"That's all I ever hear Americans talk about," he snapped. "What sane man could be 'happy'? What is there to be happy about?" It was the usual rant.

"Are you?"

"Yes, of course, I'm happy. Are you?"

I did not reply to that. I began to speak about something else, but that was in my mind—that, the new baby. Fear, the usual fear, clawed at me. Then, at the end of our little conversation, when I thought we'd not speak of it again, he said, "This changes nothing. You know that. I mean, it depends on you. If you want me to come, I'll see you on Sunday night. I've a meeting in Tel Aviv on Monday morning, so I can get away on Sunday evening. . . ."

And when I could not answer, he said, "Sara?"

I said, "Yes." I closed my eyes and imagined him at the telephone, sitting at his desk, the way his elbow must rest on the desk, the way he extended his legs, and the one hand deep in the trouser pocket, jingling the coins.

I knew then that I could not understand him, that I never had, might never, never would. That I could not understand that tortured look that came into his eyes sometimes, when I lay in his arms and told him how much I loved him; that I could not understand the way his fingers moved so gently over my face, and then across my lips, to stop my speaking of it. Nor the way he gathered me up so close and held me when we made love; or thrust me away sometimes when I wanted him most, and then just sat there looking at me, hopelessly, silently. I would never understand it, not ever; not the laughter, nor the inexplicable sadness, nor the sometimes obsessive desire for my flesh, nor the rejection of it.

I remember once saying to him that I was his Paulette. "Gideon told me once that she always wanted him. Always."

He said, "And you?"

"Yes. Yes."

"Do you?"

"Yes. . . ."

"Now?"

I remember that I touched his face. I bent over him and kissed his mouth, and his eyes slitted in that blue, blue sensuous smile. I asked, "Are you tormenting me?"

"Of course."

"Will you always torment me?"

"Of course. Always."

It was as close to a declaration of love as I would ever get. And I remembered that as he said my name once more. "Sara? Are you still there?"

I said, "Yes, I am. Always."

289

There was silence.

"I'll see you Sunday, then?" I asked.

"Yes, Sunday."

"I love you," I whispered. "Do you know that?"

"I know."

"Yes," I said, "of course, you do."

SALLY ROSENBLUTH teaches English at the Israel
Institute of Technology in Haifa, Israel. Born in
Providence, Rhode Island, raised in New York City,
graduated from Brooklyn College and the University
of Windsor, Ontario, she has lived in Israel, off and on,
since 1964. She has also spent a year in Rome. This is
her first novel.

Temple Israel
Minneapolis, Minnesota

IN HONOR OF
THE 10TH WEDDING ANNIVERSARY OF
MR. & MRS. JON GORDON
FROM
ROSIE & ANDY GELLMAN